THE NEXT LIFE

LISE GOLD

Edited by Claire Jarrett

Cover design by Lise Gold Books

New beginnings are often disguised as painful endings.

— LAO TZU

REINA - MONDAY

This house has been like an empty shell since I moved in permanently. I'm constantly aware of my own breathing and register every footstep I take on the hardwood floors. The weight of my soul thuds heavily, reminding me I'm the only person left in this big, modern mansion. All the work, all the love I poured into it. The open-plan kitchen fitted out with the latest appliances. The glass staircase that spirals so beautifully around its own spine-like axis. The spacious terrace with the long, narrow pool overlooking the ocean. The interior designer I hired to make every detail just perfect, so my life would be perfect. So *our* life would be perfect. And then she stole my husband. Nothing about this is right, and I realize that each time I look around, staring at this endless perfection. All it does is remind me of everything that's broken. Everything I've lost.

Villa Reina, named after me, used to be our summer home, the place where we spent quality family time on week-ends and during the holidays. It was a place of happiness and fun, and wanting to hold onto memories of those halcyon days, I insisted on keeping it after the divorce. I don't know what I was thinking; perhaps it would have been better to stay in New York, where I had more friends all-year round. Apart from my friend Sasha, no one but my daughter has visited over winter and the space that used to be filled with laughter, music and lively debate is now a hibernating carcass, still, as if waiting for something that will never return.

I open the kitchen cupboard, grab a mug and put it under the state-of-the-art coffee maker. The thought of barista-standard coffee at home seemed like a good idea at the time but now the sound of the grinding beans is killing me, and I wince. *Too much wine last night.* Everything here is polished to perfection, and when I see I've left a fingerprint on the stain-less-steel grinder, I wipe it off with the silk sleeve of my equally spotless robe. Nola, my housekeeper is nothing but efficient and although I could easily take care of the cleaning myself now, I like having her around. She works for my ex-husband too, and we gossip about him. Out of the friends I've made here in the Hamptons over the course of twelve summers, Nola is one of the few who has always been on my side.

In Aubrey, our interior designer—or 'Bree' as she likes to be known—my husband found a younger, blonder, and pret-tier version of me; fresh-faced and trim, with supermodel legs and a smile to die for. She also happens to be successful and super creative, and with Sandeep being a celebrated architect, they found a lot in common. He moved straight out of our house into the blonde bombshell's dreamy, bohemian palace down the road. I can't blame our mutual friends for preferring to spend time with the happy couple. It's certainly bound to be more fun than hanging out with a depressed woman who doesn't know who she is anymore. I'm no longer Sandeep's wife, and I'm no longer Reina, the always cheery crowd-pleaser and wife.

My daughter Nicole moved here with me until she started at NYU last fall and ever since, I've been painfully aware of her absence. I suppose every mother has to go through this, and I'm no different. She still comes home on weekends, and that's when the house comes back to life, and that's when I feel a tiny sparkle of happiness, see a glimpse of my old self again. When our joint voices ring through the corridors, and her music blasts from her room. When I smell bacon frying in the morning. Her meaty cooking used to make me nauseous but now it makes me happy and excited for the day ahead. I luxuriate in her company when she's here.

Nicole is my everything. She's witty, intelligent and very pretty, with her long dark hair, sharp brows, big, brown eyes and full, plump lips. She's not tall but has this enormous presence—her confidence and friendly demeanor dazzling everyone when she walks into a room. I used to be like that, and some people say she looks like me, but I don't quite see it. With Sandeep being Indian and myself of Lebanese descent, she's just a beautiful concoction of cultures, blessed with the best of both worlds.

Our son, Eddie, is amazing too, but he's more of a daddy's boy. Sandeep and I were young when we had him, and the father-and-son relationship has morphed into a friendship. They hang out and play golf together and now that Sandeep isn't here anymore, I don't see that much of Eddie. Anyway, he's gone backpacking with his girlfriend, and I don't expect him back anytime soon. He's somewhere in Goa at the moment, kite surfing and sleeping in hammocks on the beach while he looks for items to sell on his website. He runs an online business that allows him to travel, have fun and still make an impressive living. I keep track of his social media posts and send him messages every day to see what he's up to, but it's only once a week that I get a reply back, and it's never much more than *'All good. Miss you, Mom.'* He doesn't really miss me; I know that, and that's fine. But Nicole does miss me, I think. Or maybe she just feels sorry for me. No job, no purpose… *Poor Mom.*

She'd be right to think that, because I have no purpose. Not since I don't have a family to take care of. I'm not a homemaker anymore, and my life has become nothing more than a string of predictable events and a lot of waiting. I wait for my cleaner, hoping she's in a chatty mood, I wait for my daughter to come home on the weekends, and I wait for the day to be over. Nicole left last night, and I have to wait for another five long days before I see her and feel whole again.

Mondays are the hardest. Don't get me wrong; I don't sit around and do nothing all day; I just feel flat. I go to yoga at eleven am, and after that, I usually grab a green juice with Sasha. Sasha is the wife of a real estate mogul, and they practically live next door. We used to be very close, but now we're in a weird space. We don't socialize like we used to; it was always the four of us. Our Thursday cookouts in our backyard have been cancelled, but our Saturday morning tennis games at their estate are still on track, only it's not me making up the doubles anymore. My ex-husband brings his new flame nowadays, and I know it puts Sasha in a difficult position.

Crossing the open living area with coffee in hand, I grab my phone, open the sliding doors onto the terrace and sit down in my usual chair by the pool. Our poolside is a slick space; a spacious slate terrace with white designer furniture. It's early May and soon, New Yorkers will start flooding the Hamptons, and the traffic will make it difficult for Nicole to drive down every weekend. Perhaps I'll plan a couple of trips to New York instead, so I open a booking website and scroll through available hotels. As much as I'm looking forward to summer and having more people around, it will also be the first summer I've spent on my own, the first summer I'll be attending parties and events solo, and I feel the need to get out of here for a while, to get as far away as I can from that toxic, happy home down the road, where I suspect they're currently fucking each other's brains out before starting their day—no doubt one that will be filled with inspirational projects and interesting meetings.

"Good morning, Mrs. Kumar."

I startle and look up to find a woman in a white tank top and denim shorts standing by the pool with a toolbox in hand. "Hi. Who are you?" Shading my eyes from the sun, I narrow them as I study her. "And how did you get in here?"

The woman holds up a key fob that opens our gates and simultaneously taps the logo on her red baseball cap. "Barry broke his arm; he won't be coming in anytime soon, so Pool Masters sent me instead. I'm Belle."

"Oh. Is Barry going to be okay?" I ask. Truth be told, I don't know Barry very well, and I actually thought his name was Larry. Although he's been servicing the pool three times a week, he's not much of a talker. When he first started, I offered him coffee and refreshments, but he always declined, so, eventually, I gave up.

"Yeah, he'll be fine. Just had a nasty fall." The woman's eyes shift from me to the pool, then to the wooden hatch that breaks up the poolside tiles and leads into the underground machine room. "He told me where everything is, so no need to get up," she adds when I'm about to.

"Okay. Well, let me know if you need anything." I give her a smile. "Oh, and Belle?"

"Yes?" She bends down, opens up the hatch and straightens herself again, turning to me.

"It's Miss Amari. I'm not a Kumar anymore."

"Oh, sorry about that." The way she says it sounds like she's referring to my divorce rather than her using the wrong name. "I'll change it in the system."

"Thank you, I appreciate that. Can I get you a coffee?" I ask, for some reason not wanting the conversation to end. "Or something cold instead?"

Belle shakes her head and smiles back. "I'm okay for now. The pool looks in shape, so I'm sure I won't be long."

Watching Belle descend into the machine room, I note she doesn't look like a 'Belle'. Belle sounds Southern, and everything about her screams New York; her accent and her appearance. But Belle is also a very feminine name, and this woman is… a little rough around the edges, perhaps? She's lean and muscular, and her hair is short and choppy. I don't usually stereotype, but the way she moves and talks makes me think she might be gay. Women like her used to give me a pleasant physical reaction in college, and I suppose I still feel somewhat of an attraction to her type. I just haven't been around women like her since I met Sandeep.

A message from Sasha lights up on my phone, pulling me out of my thoughts. *'Hey hun, do you mind picking me up on the way to yoga? The housekeeper borrowed my car.'*

'Sure. I'll see you in half an hour', I reply, then get up and grab a bottle of cold water from the fridge and make another coffee, just in case Belle wants one later.

"Belle?" I yell, glancing down the steep concrete stairs that I've actually never seen before.

"Yeah?" She squints against the bright sunlight as she looks up at me.

"I have to go soon, so I'll put this here for you in case you want it, okay?" I place the beverages on the edge of the pool, then quickly close my robe when I realize Belle is staring at my cleavage as I'm bending over her.

"Sure." Belle quickly averts her gaze and looks into my eyes instead but this too, is making me nervous for some reason. Her eyes are intense, her expression curious as if she's sizing me up. "Thank you very much, Miss Amari. Have a good day, I'll be back on Wednesday."

BELLE - MONDAY

The first house I'm visiting today is absolutely stunning and so is the woman who lives here. She puts down a coffee and a water for me, chats for a moment, then turns to leave but not before I catch another glimpse of her cleavage. Once again, I try very hard not to stare. She's so pretty; long, dark hair, flint like eyes and perfectly arched brows. She's petite with a child-like, almost shy smile, but there's also a certain sadness to her. I've seen it before many times. The Hamptons is often the last-chance saloon, a place where couples buy a house with the idea of spending more quality time together in order to save their marriage but more often than not, they fail to repair what's broken.

I know she lives here permanently. My records tell me this pool is one of the few that's been serviced over winter. Normally we shock the water by adding unstabilized chlorine, then a winterizing product to keep the pool free of algae before the winter cover goes on but instead, it's been heated twice. It must have been lonely here in the cold months. Very few people who own a second home in Southampton come here between October and March and the rental prices are so extortionate that no one considers renting in winter as it's simply not worth it. However, the beach is beautiful and quiet when it's cold, so maybe she likes that.

As I check the temperature of the water, which is supposed to be an exact twenty degrees Celsius in this particular pool, I see Miss Amari has changed into figure-hugging sportswear and she's talking to what I assume is her housekeeper on the terrace. Yoga perhaps? Women are all into yoga around here, always striving to look their best. If that was her aim, she's certainly succeeded. The black knee-length tights and tank top show off her curves and amazing breasts that may or may not be real. She's toned and when she stretches, I catch a glimpse of her honey-colored midriff. *Eyes on the pool, Belle,* I remind myself.

My job is fascinating in many ways. I get to see a glimpse of lives very different to mine, a sneak peek into another world. Miss Amari's world is rich, polished and designed to perfection, but my guess is that she lives here alone and spends her days wondering what she could have done differently to stop her husband from straying, beating herself up about something that isn't her fault. I wouldn't trade my life with hers for the world. Her kitchen is the size of my whole apartment and even though she drives a reasonably understated car, her Mercedes hybrid still costs more than Pool Masters pays me in a year.

Just as I close the hatch to the machine room my phone rings, and I grab my coffee and take the call while I walk to the end of the yard. Through the wrought iron gate in the secure fence, I see a stilt bridge that stretches over the dunes, down to the beach. It's a stunning location; the house is so close to the ocean that I can hear the gentle pulsing of the waves. "Hey, Jules." I smile, happy to hear from my friend. She's also the booking manager for an

9

agency I work for part-time and she's calling from her work number.

"Hey, babe. A booking just came in for tonight. I know it's a little last-minute. Are you available?"

"Yes, no problem. Where am I going?"

"West End Road, Mrs. Ashworth. She asked if you could come earlier as she wants to have dinner with you first. She's offering seven-hundred dollars extra."

"Sorry, I can't do that," I say. "I want to put Suki to bed before I leave. The usual time is fine for me, though." It's totally ridiculous that someone is willing to pay seven-hundred dollars just to have dinner with me, and as tempting as it may be, I have to draw the line somewhere, especially with a four-year-old. Besides, my clients tend to get carried away if we spend too much time outside the bedroom, confusing reality with a fantasy they've paid a lot of money for. Mrs. Ashworth is one of those clients and I don't want her to get the wrong idea about us.

"Okay, I'll let her know you'll be there at eight-thirty."

"Great." I glance at the house and lower my voice, but Miss Amari has disappeared from my line of sight. "Any special requests?"

Juliette is silent for a moment, possibly scrolling through her notes. "No. Just bring your extension." She chuckles. "Same as always."

"Okay." I give a conspiratorial laugh and roll my eyes skyward. "I'll be ready for pick-up at eight." Mrs. Ashworth has a dirty mind, but her vocabulary is sparkling clean, and she's even managed to come up with a word that makes a strap-on sound innocent.

"Perfect, have fun. And on a personal note, I'll see you on the weekend," Juliette chimes before she hangs up.

Sliding my phone back into my pocket, I take another moment to enjoy the view before I head to my next job. The beach looks inviting today, with the ocean lying peacefully behind the sand that sparkles in the golden sunlight. It's a priceless view, one that undoubtedly looks even more spectacular from the top floor of the house. A man is strolling along the shore, throwing a ball for his dog. The Labrador enthusiastically tears into the white foam to catch it, then comes running back, its ears flapping as it shakes out its coat right in front of the owner, making the man laugh out loud. I smile as I watch them and think of Suki, who's been begging me to get her a dog for months. We don't have the space in our small apartment, and I can't expect her sitter to be responsible for both a child and a dog when I'm at work, so I've told her she'll have to wait a couple of years.

Behind me, I hear gates open, the rattling sound pulling me out of my thoughts. Turning to grab my toolbox, I watch Miss Amari get in her car and drive off.

"*A*re you okay, honey?" Sasha looks at me intently. It must be the dark circles under my eyes that make her worry; I've had trouble sleeping lately.

I'm about to mumble my usual 'I'm fine', but something about the way she asks makes me want to open up. "Not great, to be honest with you," I say, a little uncomfortable as I haven't had a serious conversation in months. Sasha and I don't talk like we used to, that intimacy has gone. The nights when the four of us—her, me, Sandeep and her husband Igor —used to get tipsy on cocktails followed by deep conversations around the firepit have been replaced by yoga and green juice, and this crammed hipsteresque coffee and juice bar is not a place one would naturally open up. "I just feel flat and…" I pause and shrug, poking a straw through the lid of my cup before I drink from my kale juice. "I just feel really fucking purposeless and I don't know what to do with myself. I thought it would get better eventually, but it's only getting worse."

"Hmm… I'm so sorry to hear that." Sasha stares at me while she slurps from her own carrot-apple-ginger concoction. "Isn't it nice to have the house to yourself though? Your own little paradise where you decide what happens?"

"No, I don't like being there alone. It feels hollow." I arch a brow at her, a little irritated that she seems surprised by my confession. "What did you expect? That I'd be ecstatic that my husband left me out of the blue?"

"Of course not. I just thought…" Sasha clears her throat. "Well, it's been almost a year since you split up, and I thought you'd appreciate your freedom eventually. That you'd enjoy your new life once you'd gotten used to being on your own, you know?"

"You're right," I say, reminding myself that I'm essentially very lucky. "I shouldn't complain. I have enough money to live comfortably, I have a beautiful home, two wonderful children, my health…"

Sasha pushes my hand down as I raise it. "I didn't mean it like that. You have every right to be hurt, sad and depressed; you wouldn't be human if you weren't. But you can do anything you want now, Reina. Anything. And you're doing nothing." She's silent for a moment, chewing on her straw. "Honestly, sometimes I envy you."

"How can you say that?" I pause and return her stare. "I thought you were happy."

Sasha shrugs and reluctantly shakes her head from side to side. "I am… We are, but it's not what it was when we first met and we're long past the phase of being in love. Igor and I are more like a well-oiled machine, I suppose. We work seamlessly but our marriage has become mechanical." She sits back, then lets out a long sigh. "Have you never dreamed of starting over? Even when you were with Sandeep?"

"No. My current situation is my worst nightmare. I'd never leave my family."

"I know that. But have you never fantasized about being with someone else?"

"That's not the same thing," I say resolutely. This is not where I expected our conversation to go. Frankly, I don't know what I expected. A little pity, maybe? Some reassuring words, her telling me everything will be fine? But instead, she seems jealous of my freedom.

"But you have?" Sasha presses on.

"Everyone fantasizes, but that doesn't mean I wanted out, or that I'd act on it. It doesn't mean I wanted my heart shattered and our family broken apart. Sandeep made his fantasy a reality, I didn't. That's the difference."

Sasha nods and gazes out of the window, following a jogger who's passing by. He's a good ten years younger than us. Handsome with a great body. "Can you keep a secret?" she asks.

"Of course."

"It could ruin my life if what I'm about to tell you gets out," she continues, turning back to me with a warning stare to let me know she's never been more serious.

"I promise I won't tell a soul." I'm relieved she feels secure enough to confide in me. It means our close friendship has survived the past year, and that she still needs me in her life even if she hangs out with Sandeep's new girlfriend way more than me nowadays.

"I cheated on Igor," she says, her big, blue eyes widening as if she immediately regrets her confession.

"You didn't..." Leaning in, I continue in a whisper. "Are you serious?"

"Yeah." Sasha leans in too and lowers her voice. "Lately I've been wondering what it would be like to sleep with someone else after twenty years with the same man. To be honest, I've thought of little else." She pauses. "And so I did."

"Okay." I try not to sound too shocked because I want her to feel comfortable talking to me. Sasha, my friend, a loving mother and loyal wife has cheated on her rich, handsome, likeable and successful husband. "How did it happen? Did you just meet someone you felt attracted to?"

"No, I hired someone I was attracted to." She glances at the door, making sure no one from our yoga class has entered the premises.

"What do you mean?"

"Come on, Reina. You know exactly what I mean." Sasha pulls a business card out of her purse that says 'Hamptons' Escorts' and hands it to me. "I found this in the restroom at a beach bar. As soon as I got home, I checked out their website and last week, when Igor was away for work and the kids were with friends in New York, I booked a sexy, young man to give me the night of my life."

"Noo…" My jaw falls wide open.

"Uh-huh. Ben was twenty-nine, tall, blond and ripped, and he cost me twenty-five hundred dollars plus travel expenses. It was so worth it." She licks her lips and gives me a wicked smile. "He came to our house and I was super nervous, but he was amazing at putting me at ease. We had a drink together, he gave me a massage and after that, we had hours of amazing, animalistic sex like I've never experienced before."

"Fuck… So, it was good?"

Sasha chuckles and plays with a lock of her bleach blonde hair. "Yes, it was out of this world good. It was so good that I can't stop thinking about it. The upside is that I won't have to worry about him calling me, and I don't feel guilty because there are no feelings involved. I don't know Ben's real name, I'm not in love with him, he's not in love with me and so my marriage will survive this weird phase I'm going through. In fact, it might even make my marriage stronger because I won't look for distraction elsewhere and it's made me appreciate what I have a whole lot more, if that makes sense."

To me, it makes no sense at all, but I don't say that.

Finishing my juice, I contemplate what she's just told me. "Are you planning on doing it again?"

"I might, if another opportunity arises. It's kind of addictive." Sasha crosses her arms in front of her and purses her enhanced lips. She's the typical Hamptons mom. Always dressed to look her best, her nails and hair pristine. "Look, I was eighteen when I met Igor— one year older than you were when you met Sandeep—and Ben's only the third man I've had sex with."

"Sandeep's the *only* man I've ever slept with," I say, putting down my cup that is as empty as my life. "The only one." It's a sad fact to admit but also true.

Sasha gasps. "God, I thought I was a saint. How have we never had this conversation?" She whistles through her teeth. "Was it even good with him?"

"What? The sex?" I pause for a moment to think about that. "It was okay, I suppose. I have nothing to compare it to. But sex was never that important to me. Mostly, it was about love and connection and trust."

About to reply, Sasha opens her mouth, but a message comes in on her phone and she groans in frustration. "Damn it. Igor wants me to pick up his dry-cleaning. Our house-keeper had an emergency—that's why she borrowed my car —and I thought it could wait, but he needs his favorite white shirt for a meeting this afternoon or he won't survive the day."

"Can't he pick it up himself?"

"Apparently not." Sasha rolls her eyes. "Do you mind if we stop off there on the way back?"

"No, that's fine. I'm ready to go if you are." I slide the card back to her, but she shakes her head.

"You keep it; I should have gotten rid of it, but I felt this strange urge to keep it as a reminder. Have a look at their website; it might inspire you." She slings her purse over her shoulder and gets up. "This conversation isn't over, though, I have so much to tell you. Want to talk over a glass of wine later in the week?"

"Yeah, absolutely," I say, my answer a little more eager than I meant it to be. Relieved that Sasha and I seem to be back to where we were before my life fell apart, I grab my purse and my yoga mat. It's the first time since my divorce that I actually feel as if I've had a meaningful conversation, and I can't wait for us to continue what we started. "How about tomorrow?"

"Can't. We've got a dinner party. But I can do Thursday."

"Thursday works for me." I don't even need to check my diary; it's been close to empty lately. Aside from the fact that the summer season hasn't started yet, singles are generally not invited to lunches or dinners. Parties, sure. They want us to make up the numbers. But sit-down events where people actually talk to each other seem to be reserved for couples only.

"Great." Sasha lingers for a beat, then steps forward to give me a hug. "I miss you, Reina."

"I miss you too," I say, swallowing down the lump in my throat. I contemplate throwing the business card into the trash can by the door as we walk out but change my mind and slip it into my gym bag instead. It's not for me, but I'm still curious...

"*M*ommy!"

"Hey, sweetness." I kneel down and embrace Suki when she throws herself into my arms. She's always happy when I come home, and my heart floods with love every waking minute she's with me. Inhaling deeply against her hair, I squeeze her tight and kiss her forehead. "Have you been good?"

"As good as gold," Jackie, her sitter, says. "So, you're heading out later?"

"Yes, but not for a while. Are you sure you're okay to stay on? It was all a little last-minute."

Jackie smiles. "No problem, hun. Want me to cook some food for us?"

"Not a chance, I'll do it," I say, aware that Jackie is in her late sixties and has been on her feet all afternoon. "Why don't you go and relax or take a nap? Suki can help me make dinner."

"Yes!" Suki grabs her stool and pushes it toward the kitchen countertop. She loves to help out, and even if that means I have to spend ages cleaning up after her, it's worth seeing the smile on her face.

"Thank you, Suki." I turn on the kettle to make Jackie a cup of tea and usher her toward the couch.

"Hey, I may be old but I'm not out of juice," she protests, but I can see that she's tired. Jackie used to live next door when we were kids and she looked after us several days a week. She's always been like a mother to me and now I couldn't be more grateful that she's minding Suki. She drops her off and picks her up from preschool three days a week, she stays on in the evenings when I have escort jobs and we usually have dinner together before I head out again. At the weekends, Suki is all mine, though, so we get to spend more quality time together than most kids with working parents.

"Please. Just take a nap." I hand her a fleece blanket. "How about stir-fried rice?"

"If anyone needs a nap it's you," she jokes, and shoots me a mischievous grin. Jackie knows what I'm up to tonight, and she's okay with it. I've always been comfortable telling her everything and so I told her about my side gig, when I first started. *'As long as you enjoy it and they treat you with respect, I'm not going to judge,'* she said with a blush on her cheeks, then added: *'But please, don't ever tell your father.'*

Jackie and my father have a strange relationship. They're best friends, but it never turned into anything more than that, even though sometimes they seem like a married couple. When Jackie moved to Sag Harbor a few years back she suggested she could help look after Suki. She never had a family of her own, perhaps because she was always waiting for my conflicted and indecisive father to ask her out. He never did, but Suki is like a grandchild to her, and life has been a lot easier since she moved two blocks down the road. Jackie's family to me and when the time comes, I'll look after her in return. That's just what we do. We all look after each other and make the best of a very complex situation with a painful history.

"I don't want rice," Suki yells from the open kitchen.

"Okay. Then what do you feel like?" I ask her. "Pasta?"

She thinks about that for a moment, then nods. "Yes, pasta. With broccoli."

"Sure," I say. "With broccoli sauce and parmesan. That's a great idea." Thankfully she likes vegetables. According to Jackie, I was the opposite when I was younger, but I seem to have lost my sweet tooth. I hand Suki a head of broccoli and a bowl, and she eagerly starts tearing off the florets. Of course, half of them end up on the floor, so I grab a strainer too, to wash them later. "Did you have a nice day with Aunt Jackie?"

"Yes," she says in a whisper while concentrating on her task. Her bottom lip juts out in the most adorable way while her little fingers fiddle with a floret that's too large for her liking.

"And how about school? What did you do this morning?"

"We learned about baby animals."

"Oh yeah? What kind of baby animals?"

Suki stops what she's doing for a beat and turns to me with a serious frown. "Chicklings and lammies. They're born in spring and they're small and then they grow big."

"That's right." I smile back at her. "Did you know that Grandpa has lambs now? They were born last week. We can go see them tomorrow if you want."

At this, Suki's face lights up. "Yes!" She throws her hands in the air, dropping another floret in the process. "Can we go now?"

"No, honey, not now. We'll go tomorrow. You have to have your dinner and sleep first and then you can wake me up, okay?"

Suki sulks for a beat, contemplating whether to throw a

tantrum or not. She's been a bit unpredictable lately, but I've been assured that's totally normal behavior for a four-year-old. "Okay," she finally says, then turns her attention back to the broccoli. "Can I touch the lammies?"

"Yes, if you're gentle, you can touch them. They're still babies and you're a big girl, so you have to be very careful with them."

"I'm four!" Suki holds up three fingers, then looks at her hand and adds a fourth.

The random statement makes me laugh and I hold up four fingers too. Yes, you are. And soon you'll be..."

"Five!" Suki now holds up six fingers, and she grins from ear to ear, knowing she's cheating.

I pick her up and kiss her chubby cheek and she screeches with joy. From the couch in the living room, I hear Jackie laughing and as always when I feel overwhelmed with love, I take a moment to appreciate how lucky I am.

*B*ack at the house, I check the poolside to see if Belle is still there but of course, she's long gone. It's weird that I feel a little disappointed that our conversation was so short-lived, so I ignore the strange flutter in my core and try to think about something else. She only came in to service my pool, and I shouldn't be so interested in her.

"Are you looking for something?" I turn to find Nola behind me.

"No, I'm not." Heat rises to my cheeks and I feel caught out, even though I'm on my own property and I've done nothing wrong. "Sorry I didn't have much time to chat this morning. Did you have a nice weekend?"

"It was good," she says. "I worked Saturday morning... for him who shall not be mentioned, but otherwise I just relaxed with my family."

"Great. How are the kids?" I refrain from asking about Sandeep and Bree today. It's getting old, and I'm aware that I've started to come across like some desperate ex-wife who can't let go. Besides, I don't want Nola to feel like she has to pick sides; she worked for Bree before I hired her.

Nola gives me a small smile, as if she's aware that questions are burning on my tongue. "They're unhelpful and difficult mostly," she jokes. "Jack stayed in bed the whole day yesterday and Filipa came home drunk in the early hours after clubbing on Saturday night, but at least they didn't get themselves in any serious trouble. Not as far as I know anyway."

I laugh and let go of my gym bag when she takes it from me. "They're just teenagers. Don't worry; it will pass."

"If you say so." Nola props the bag under her arm. "There was some serious drama with Sandeep and Bree on Saturday, though," she adds, narrowing her eyes at me.

"Oh, really?" I arch a brow, drawing the words out slowly.

"Yes." Nola's expression turns serious, and she takes my hand. "Promise this will remain a secret between you and me?"

"Of course." I mean it; I love Nola and I'd never betray her trust or put her job in jeopardy. However, it's also peculiar that she's the second person to confide in me today.

"Okay." Nola bites her lip, clearly bursting to get it out. "This might upset you..."

"Please, just say it." I raise myself onto the kitchen counter because I have a feeling I'd better be sitting down for what's about to come. "Have they split up?"

"No, it's worse than that. Bree is pregnant," she says dramatically.

"Pregnant?"

"Yes, she's pregnant. And Sandeep is not happy because he's always told her he doesn't want any more kids." She points to her ear. "I never eavesdrop, but at the same time, I hear everything, whether I want to or not. I'm invisible in most households."

"Fuck..." I take a moment to let the information sink in. My ex-husband got his younger girlfriend pregnant. Nola's eyes meet mine, and she looks sorry for me. She always told me this was just a phase, that Sandeep and I would get back together. "I assume she's keeping the baby?"

"Yes. She was toward the end of her first trimester by the time she told him and even if she wasn't, she's wanted to be a mother for as long as I've worked for her."

"Wow. Okay. And Sandeep wasn't initially onboard?"

"No. But he'll come around. He has no choice."

"So, they're having a baby…"

"Yes." Nola grimaces, fearful she's upset me. "Are you okay?"

"Yeah, I think so. I just didn't see this coming." I let out the breath I've been holding and rub my face.

"I don't think anyone did." Nola lowers her voice. "Apart from Bree. She hasn't been taking her pill. I clean the bedroom and the same strip has been sitting on her night-stand for the past six months."

"Jesus." My voice goes up a notch. "So she planned this…"

"I believe so." Nola shrugs. "Anyway, I didn't mean to upset you, I just thought you should know."

I try to analyze how I feel about this and truthfully, it's a slap in the face. The love of my life is starting over, doing the exact thing I thought he'd never do with anyone else; starting a family. Family is everything to me and my only consolation when Sandeep left me, was that he would only ever have one family, and I would always be part of that unit. It was something sacred between us that we'd created. Now, he's going to have another one, like it's no different from buying a new car or a house, planned or not. "Thank you, I appreciate you telling me. My lips are sealed."

Nola nods, then goes to work unpacking my bag. She throws the towel, my yoga pants and tank top on the floor on top of a pile of dirty dishcloths and pulls out my water bottle to empty. "I saw there was a new pool lady in this morning," she says, changing the subject.

"Yes. Belle. She seems nice." I quickly take the bag back from her, so she won't find the business card in the side compartment.

"Oh." Nola sounds surprised that I know her name and I don't blame her. I've probably referred to Barry as Larry on a couple of occasions and I can't for the life of me remember what the gardeners are called as the agency rotates different ones. "She dropped by before she left. She said everything was fine and she's going to replace the sand in the filter on Friday. Apparently, it's been a while."

"Yes, it has." Truthfully, I have no idea when the sand was last replaced, just like I have no idea about anything household related. God help me, I barely know where the washer is. "Did she say it was going to be a big job? I don't remember how long it took last spring."

"She didn't say, but it will take a couple of hours, probably." Nola looks up. "Why? Is Friday not convenient? I can call them and ask her to come another day, or—"

"No, it's fine," I interrupt her. "Just curious, that's all." Gesturing toward the staircase, I say: "Well, I'm going to take a bath. I'll be back down in a while if you want to have a coffee with me."

I TAKE off my clothes and run myself a hot bath. The master bathroom is stripped bare of clutter and is completely white. Two egg-shaped sinks with long mirrors and two deep, walk-in rain showers take up the corners of the square space, and a huge, oval-shaped tub is placed under the window facing the pool. In the middle is a divider with clothing hooks and marble dressing benches to both sides. I thought long and hard about how to make it a stylish and functional family bathroom, but now it feels more like a fancy dressing room in a private members gym—sterile and lacking in warmth—rather than the cool beach vibe I was going for. Sandeep was the mastermind behind our impressive house. He designed this mid-century inspired villa overlooking the Atlantic. But I was the homemaker, and I took that role very seriously. Obviously, I wasn't nearly as good with interior design as his new flame who made our living room look stunning, but I did my best. I was a good mother, a good wife, I excelled at entertaining but that wasn't good enough for him and he's moved on in the most dramatic of ways. Maybe it's time for me to move on too. I'd convinced myself I had, but this news hurts and has dug up painful memories.

As I let myself sink back against the cushioned headrest, I close my eyes and replay my conversation with Sasha. I can hardly believe she envies me for my situation. Should I really be grateful for the opportunity to start over? And if so, where the fuck do I start? Is hiring an escort not a little seedy? Isn't it wrong? Could I? I don't think so. What would I say if my children ever found out? I've had fantasies about sex with other partners, sure. In fact, I've had many, but never about paid sex, and this scenario seems extreme. If I could have anything, what would it be? Belle's smile flashes before me and I shake it off with a groan.

Before I met Sandeep, before I got pregnant and had a shotgun wedding, before I was a mother, I was a different person with a different lifestyle. I was a college student living in a nice apartment in Manhattan—courtesy of my wealthy parents who moved back to Beirut when I was seventeen. They thought my chances of succeeding as a woman would be better in the US, so they left me with a dual nationality and a housekeeper who no doubt reported back on my every move, but she was kind and caring, and I didn't mind being on my own. I flourished then; I was inspired to make a successful career for myself, to have a full life. Photography was my passion, and my dream was to study photography at Yale. The applications were ready and perfected long before I could submit them; they were neatly tucked away in my desk drawer, waiting for the day I graduated high school. I partied a lot, had crushes on both men and women, but I never acted on those crushes, and I never fell into the vicious circle of alcohol and drugs. I made good choices. If a 'Belle' had shown interest in me back then, I probably would have turned her down because of my upbringing. Because I was taught that it was wrong. This was only twenty-two years ago, but it feels like a lifetime.

And then Sandeep asked me out one day. He was a smart, charismatic and handsome architecture student, and I couldn't find a reason to say no, so I said yes. One date led to another and then, boom. Ten weeks later I was pregnant. It was a shock to both of us as we'd used contraception. Our parents pushed us into marriage, so we tied the knot before Eddie was born and even now, knowing we were way too young for such a serious life, I don't regret anything. Having Eddie, and five years later Nicole, truly made me feel whole as a person.

My parents bought us a lovely townhouse in Brooklyn, I became a stay-at-home mom and when Sandeep got his masters and started working, we were a fairly wealthy family. Once he'd made a name for himself and started his own company, we became what most people would consider to be 'rich'.

And now, here I am, only thirty-nine and I have no purpose. Already, I feel like I've lived a whole life, yet nothing is left of it. We sold our house in New York and the Hamptons house was put in my name after the divorce. My father left me a lot of money when he passed away five years ago, so if I'm sensible, I won't have to worry about my finances ever again. But I need something to focus on, something that defines me as a person. Something to pour my heart and soul into the way I did when I was bringing up our family. Something to keep my mind from wandering back to my broken marriage and the happy couple expecting a baby. Because without it, who am I?

BELLE - MONDAY

"*B*, come in." Mrs. Ashworth, the woman I've been visiting every other week for a year or so opens the door wider and gestures to the atrocious pink, velvet couch. By now, I've learned quite a bit about her. I know that she's married and in her fifties with two children. I know she has a hissy cat called Mr. Handsome, and I know she runs a successful business that has something to do with rental cars. She's bisexual, a little kinky and she loves shopping, red wine and mint chocolate chip ice cream. I also know her husband is on a business trip; he always is when she books me, and apparently, he turns a blind eye to whatever happens when he's away. God knows what he's up to himself; that's probably how they justify their infidelity to each other. Maybe this keeps them together, maybe it's driving them apart. Either way, it's not my problem to worry about.

"You look great," I say, casting an eye over her skimpy, purple dress. Too much bleach in her hair and too enhanced in the looks department, she's not really my type but it doesn't matter. I love sex and I love women and making them come hard has always given me a kick. With my lucrative side hustle, I can do that whenever I want without having to subject myself to the complex and frustrating world of dating and relationships and that's worked a treat for me so far. "Very hot."

"You charmer," she coos, and trots to the kitchen to open a bottle of wine. Cindy Ashworth—she prefers me to call her Mrs. Ashworth—likes our routine, which starts with a glass of Châteauneuf-du-Pape and a bit of flirting before we have a bath together. Then she takes me to her bedroom where I'm in charge. I tie her up, tease her relentlessly, and then I fuck her with a strap-on until she's too tired to carry on. She's asked me to stay over many times, willing to pay me simply to hold her in her sleep, but I've never taken her up on that offer. Jackie expects me home just after midnight and even if she was available all night, I want to be home when Suki wakes up.

I take the glass of red from Mrs. Ashworth and drape my other hand over the couch's backrest so she can nestle herself in the crook of my arm. "How are you today?"

"Oh, you know…" She rubs her temple. "Really busy and stressed. The shareholders are on my case and Mr. Handsome had to go to the vet for his booster and then I couldn't find his vaccination card and…" She stops herself, pats my thigh and squeezes it. "Anyway, I just had to see you. I need to release some tension." Batting her fake lashes at me, her eyes lower to my lips. "You always have this amazing way of relaxing me and making me forget about everything."

"I'm glad I can be of help." And just because I know she wants to hear it, I add: "I've been looking forward to having my way with you."

"Mmm…" Mrs. Ashworth chuckles, and then Mr. Handsome jumps between us and hisses at me. "Did you hear that, Mr. Handsome? B's going to make me feel good," she says, ignoring the fact that her cat's practically threatening to kill me. If someone were to sketch a caricature of Mrs. Ashworth, she would be a tall woman with big lips, high cheekbones, enormous boobs and an aggressive hairless cat permanently attached to her lap.

"I think he's jealous," I say, and cautiously hold out a finger for him to sniff. I love animals, but this one's always had it out for me, and when he hisses again, I quickly retract my hand.

"Nonsense. He's a sweetie pie," she says, stroking his head. "And so are you." She gestures to the bag I've placed next to the couch. "What goodies have you brought with you today?"

"If I told you that, it would ruin the surprise now, wouldn't it?"

"Mmm..." she says again, excitement visible in her gaze. "You know I like surprises." Her top lip is twice the size of her bottom lip, and she has the tendency to jut it out. The line of filler feels hard when I kiss her but it's not unpleasant, just different. Most female escorts don't kiss, but I shook off that rule on my first night. Throughout my life, I've kissed way more women than I see now on a regular basis, and if I kept everything sterile and clinical, my clients might as well use a vibrator. They want to feel a woman, the weight of a body draped over them. They want warmth and affection and admiration. They want someone who will treat them the way they deserve to be treated, and I can do that better than anyone else. I perk them up when they're down, and I give them something to look forward to. By the time I leave, they all have a smile on their face and that makes me happy in return.

I run my tongue over her lips and she moans softly. We kiss, deep, hard, wild. It doesn't make me feel much other than satisfaction when I hear her sounds of pleasure, and it doesn't turn me on but still, it's not unpleasant. My hand slides into the neckline of her dress to caress her breasts.

31

Pinching her nipple, I smile against her lips when she moans loudly and shifts on the couch. I know she likes it, so I pinch harder until a guttural groan escapes her.

"Bad, bad girl," I whisper, bringing my mouth to her ear. "You're making too much noise. What if your husband comes home and hears us?" This is exactly what she wants me to say, and I can already feel her chest rising and falling rapidly against my hand.

"I'm sorry, I'll be quiet," she says. Soon, she'll do it again, though, just so I'll have a reason to punish her.

"Is your jacuzzi warm?" I gesture to the sliding back doors. We normally go to her en suite bathroom but the look in her eyes tells me she likes that I'm suggesting something different tonight.

"Uh-huh," she says through heavy breaths.

"Good. Because I've brought some new waterproof toys." I move back, so I can look her in the eyes. "But you'll have to be really quiet or the neighbors might hear you. Can you do that?"

Mrs. Ashworth nods eagerly and I get up and grab my bag to take it outside. It's a beautiful night, so why not enjoy it? The sky is streaked red when we reach the jacuzzi on the back patio, and a few lonely clouds drift dark against the crimson. Mrs. Ashworth doesn't have a sea view, but she does have a huge backyard with a pristine lawn that stretches far and wide behind the pool. Palm trees and tropical plants rise from every corner and there's a stylish bar next to the jacuzzi that could hold at least ten people. With a bunch of beautifully dressed people scattered around, it could easily pass for a scene from a Slim Aarons photograph, but tonight it's just her and me and the silence of an uninspiring, wealthy neighborhood. Opening my bag, I mentally prepare myself to give her the best night so far. I always strive to be the best.

REINA - TUESDAY

*T*he escort website looks high-end. It's not seedy in any way, and there are not even references to sex on the first page. No red, no pink, just white and gray tones. Underneath the drop-down menu is a pretty black and white picture of a man and a woman dining in a fancy restaurant. At first glance, they look like an ordinary couple, but upon closer inspection, the woman is wearing hold-ups and the man has his hand on her knee under the table.

The tabs 'our ladies' and 'our gentlemen' at the top of the page direct me to the escorts and instinctively, I find myself drawn to the list of female escorts. There's a filter for 'men only', 'bisexual' and 'women only', and I click on the latter. Only five women appear in this section and I'm not surprised. I suspect very few female clients book a female escort around here, and I feel a sting of unease—a sense that something is wrong with me—even for just looking. Anyone I know apart from Sasha would consider me a creep for checking out escorts online, and I make a mental note to delete my search history in case Nicole borrows my laptop over the weekend.

It doesn't sit quite right that I was drawn almost instantly to the female section, yet anticipation still flares inside me when I scroll through the profiles of the women who are available for F/F sex. 'Angel', the first one, looks too good to be true. With a perfect figure, long, blonde hair and big, blue eyes, she also looks super straight. The second and third women, 'Red' and 'Tatiana', are gothic looking and specialize in S&M. This scares me a little, so I skip past them. With their black hair and dark makeup, posing with whips and floggers, they look too intimidating to even consider. Not that I'm actually going to do this, of course…. *Am I?*

"No," I mumble out loud, then take a sip of my white wine. I've had more than I should already, but the news about Bree being pregnant has upset me, and I need the wine to numb my thoughts. Simultaneously, the wine drove me to pull the business card Sasha gave me from my gym bag and now I'm sitting in Sandeep's old office behind my laptop. I locked the door, which is ridiculous as I'm the only one here. It feels kind of dirty and somewhat depraved, but I remind myself that this is just an idea, a fantasy that's brewing. Being on this website is the naughtiest thing I've ever done, and it feels like a significant moment in time; the point where I take my boring, safe existence back into my own hands and decide I'm allowed to do whatever the fuck I want to. I don't need Sandeep; he's hurt me, he's moved on, and I have to let him go and stop dwelling on the past. I don't belong to him anymore and he doesn't belong to me. I certainly don't need him between the sheets; it was never that great anyway and perhaps now it's my time to discover what I'm about because Sasha was right; I could do anything at this point in my life and yet I'm doing nothing.

I scroll further down and my breath catches at seeing the fourth lesbian escort on the page. I don't register exactly what it is at first that draws my attention to her face. Something just feels oddly familiar, and then it comes crashing down on me.

"Belle," I mutter under my breath and take another long drink of my wine, then refill the glass. She's seriously cute, with her dimples and cheeky smile. Her big, brown eyes that beckon me to click on her stare playfully into the lens. What is she doing working for an escort service? She already has a job, and doesn't seem like the type at all, but then we only exchanged a couple of sentences. Nobody knows what dark secrets people hide behind closed doors. She's registered under the name, 'B', and unlike the others, she looks happy rather than seductive. That makes her more approachable somehow yet at the same time, there's also something extremely sexual about her. "Fuck." I have to admit, I find her immensely attractive. Scrolling through her three profile pictures, I study each of them at length, taking in every detail of her. Again, unlike the others who are dressed in expensive lingerie, Belle's wearing jeans and a slinky, gray jersey T-shirt. *'Trust me; I look good naked'*, it says underneath and I chuckle, partially because I've seen her in real life and have no doubt that she looks amazing naked, and partially because it's a little cocky, and that amuses me.

'I will make you feel like no man or woman ever has.' Another bold statement, but I believe her. Heat spreads between my thighs when I imagine her mouth on my neck, her body draped over mine, her hands roaming over my naked flesh... It's been a long time since I've felt aroused, and it's a pleasant surprise.

Going back to her main profile picture—the close-up—I stare at her charming, youthful face for minutes on end while I finish my wine. She's not that much younger than me—thirty-three, her profile informs me—but she's got this vibrancy about her that draws me in and makes me want her like nothing else. Of course, I refrain from clicking on the 'book' button, but I do look at her availability. Three nights a week, 8:30 pm to12 pm. Twenty-seven-hundred dollars. *'A drink, a shower and then, whatever makes you scream.'*

For that price, she'd better be good. Immediately, I feel ashamed for even thinking that, because how can you put a price on a human body? Besides, even if I wanted to, I could never book her. It would be highly awkward seeing her the next day when she comes in to service my pool after a night servicing my body and I don't even know if I'd be into sex with a woman. The cool, composed, Lebanese woman in me makes me jump up in utter shock at my own thoughts. *What the fuck am I doing?*

Abruptly, I close the laptop, prop it under my arm and venture downstairs. It's dark and stormy outside, but the beach is calling me. I haven't been down there since last summer, worried I'd bump into Sandeep and Bree out on a romantic walk. But they won't be out in this weather, and I feel an urge to walk for miles, to conquer the strong gusts of wind blowing against the reinforced windows that run along the entire length of the house. I need to clear my head, to think, to come up with a plan that will give me some direction in life. But most of all, I need to ban Belle from my mind before the idea of having sex with her takes over every inch of my imagination.

BELLE - WEDNESDAY

"*M*ommy, I want to see the lammies."

"Honey, not today, okay? I promise we'll stop by Grandpa's farm again on the weekend." I run my hand through Suki's dark hair and plant a kiss on her cheek.

"But why can't we go now?" Suki asks.

"Because I have to work. Jackie is coming. You love Jackie, don't you?"

Suki shrugs and puts on her sulking face, jutting out her lower lip. "Yes, but Jackie won't take me to see the lammies and I want to see the lammies."

I hold my breath for three counts and smile at her. I love Suki more than life itself, but she's entered this stubborn phase, where each question is answered with another question and she has obsessions that last for months on end. The latest one involves Grandpa's lambs that I took her to see yesterday. Suki sat in his field in a white dress, looking like a little angel while the lambs hopped around her. She absolutely adored them, and so she wants to go back again and again and again. It's all she can talk about. "We'll go see them on Saturday. Just three more sleeps."

"Why do I have to sleep? I don't like to sleep."

When the doorbell rings, I let out a sigh of relief and let Jackie in. "Hey, Jackie. Brace yourself, she's on a roll today."

"What's new?" Jackie chuckles and picks up Suki to cuddle her. "Nothing I can't handle. I'll take her to the playground. What time will you be back?"

"I might be a little later than normal today; we'll have to clean up after last night's storm. Do you mind?"

Jackie shakes her head and shoots me a smile. "Not at all. I'm all yours."

"I can't thank you enough. I've been doing so much overtime lately that I was going to take the afternoon off to meet up with my new accountant, but it looks like I'll be busy clearing leaves all day. Is five okay?"

"No problem. How is it going with the accountant?"

"Okay, I think. Nearly done, and I'm seeing a wholesaler to put in my first order next week."

"How exciting!" Jackie puts Suki on her hip and looks at her. "Mommy's going to start a booming business, did you know that? She's going to be the party queen of *the Hamptons*. Do you know what a party queen is?" We both laugh when Suki shakes her head with a goofy grin. "Mommy is going to make lots of people very happy with fun stuff for the pool."

"Pool?" Suki repeats and looks up at me. "You work in a pool." I don't think she's actually been in one before, we always go to the beach. Unlike most people in the Hamptons, we don't have a pool or even a yard and have to make do with the balcony. My father and Jackie don't have a pool either and neither does my friend Juliette. All my clients do, but they live in a different world. Not a happier or better one per se, just a different one, and I truly hope that growing up on a wealthy peninsula won't affect Suki in the sense that she feels she's been deprived, because she's a lucky kid who is showered with love and attention.

"That's right. It's a hole in the ground filled with water," I say, then add: "But it's a bit boring. There's no sand so the beach is much more fun."

"Oh." Suki grabs a piece of honey-soaked pancake and stuffs it into her mouth, seemingly happy with my explanation. She does love the beach and luckily, we live nearby.

I steal a piece of pancake from her, grab my purse and squeeze her shoulder. "I have to go, honey. Will you be good?"

"Of course, she's always good," Jackie says, ruffling a hand through Suki's hair. "So, how about the playground? Does that sound like a plan?"

As I blow Jackie a kiss and head for the front door, Suki's yells: "I want to see the lammies!"

Driving off in my Pool Masters van, I'm surprised to feel a subtle tingle of nerves when my company app tells me who my first customer is. I'd forgotten Miss Amari was on the schedule today and it's a pleasant surprise because I liked her. She was kind and polite. *And hot,* I think to myself, then quickly shake off the thought as I'm not supposed to have the hots for my clients.

It's very green this time of year and the rising sun casts a beautiful light over the road ahead of me. The route from Sag Harbor to Southampton consists of long, straight roads that are lined by pristine lawns, tennis courts, manicured hedges, mature specimen trees and hydrangeas. The houses here are typical of the Hamptons, with their white trims, wooden shingles, weatherboards, pitched roofs and dormer windows that make for picturesque homes. Cyclists slow down the traffic but no one's in a rush here. Few are going to work, apart from real estate brokers who are so easy to identify it amuses me. One stops next to me in front of a traffic light. Tall and handsome, check. Convertible, check. Navy suit, check. Big watch, check. Designer shades, check. When the lights turn to green he speeds off, only to abruptly stop at the next set of lights again.

New York has way more charm than the Hamptons in my opinion, but it's our home and it's a safe place for Suki to grow up. We like living in Sag Harbor and we love the ocean. Being so close to the beach is priceless when growing up; I vividly remember long happy days playing in the sand and swimming in the ocean with my sister, who would have loved the quiet strip of beach in front of Miss Amari's house if she were still alive today. As always, a stab of sadness hits me when I think of her, but I've become very good at pushing it away, only allowing the pain to flow freely when I'm alone with my memories.

I pass *Duck Walk Vineyard* and take the road toward *Little Plains Beach*. Driving down *Little Plains Road*, I catch a glimpse of the clear, shallow water behind the beach. Compared to other houses along this road, Miss Amari's house is relatively modest. It doesn't have tennis courts or an endless driveway but that doesn't mean it's small. With direct access to the beach and views over the Atlantic, I'm sure it's worth at least twelve million, if not more. The narrow strip of private dunes gives the property a sense of serene seclusion, and so do the tall trees and natural hedges to both sides of the wrought iron gates.

When I walk around the house into the backyard, Miss Amari is standing on the patio like she's been waiting for me. And damn, does she look drop dead gorgeous. I've always thought attraction is something that grows over time, but the lingering tug is potent and very real. It's been a while since I've felt physically attracted to someone; I'm so used to having willing bodies around me due to my escort job that I've forgotten what it feels like. *Stop it, Belle. Don't even think about it.*

"Good morning, Miss Amari."

"Belle…" Although I'd expected her and she's right on time, I'm still completely thrown at seeing her. Does my hair look okay? My outfit? I got changed three times this morning after waxing and grooming for hours and I still don't feel the light-yellow bikini and sheer, white kaftan are good enough. I've tried my hardest to look like I haven't made an effort at all, like I'm just lounging by the pool after waking up like this. In reality, my hair's been styled, I've painted my nails, I put on some makeup—just enough for it to look natural—and I'm on my third coffee because I've been up for so long. The attempt to ban her from my thoughts last night failed, and instead, I dug out my vibrator that hadn't been used for a decade and literally waited for it to charge while I stared at her pictures online. Now that she's here, I have no idea what to do with myself. "How are you?" I ask, my voice high-pitched while I force an awkward smile.

"I'm great. It's a beautiful day, right?" Belle smiles back at me from across the pool. "How about you?"

"I'm good, thanks. Just finishing off some stuff before I head into town." That's a lie, but I don't want her to think I have no plans, so I've carefully orchestrated my setup and placed my laptop under the big, white parasol at the end of the long dining table.

"I won't keep you, then," Belle says.

"No, I didn't mean it like that." I cringe at the words that leave my mouth at an almost desperate speed and volume. "Would you like a coffee? I'm going to make one for myself."

"Sure, why not? Thank you." Belle inspects the pool and picks up the big net she's brought along. Last night's storm has blown leaves into the pool, and to my utter delight, she starts walking up and down the length of it to scoop them out. Her legs are tanned, her shorts showing off her toned thighs. Her biceps flex as she drags the net along. It's not an easy job; I've done it myself a couple of times, and it took a lot of strength. *She must be strong...*

"Cappuccino?"

"Yes please, no sugar."

I watch her from the kitchen as I pretend to re-fill my own cup and make her a coffee, taking my time so I can indulge in her. It wasn't like this on Monday. I wasn't so consumed with her until I found out she was an escort, and until I knew for sure that she was into women. Am I into women now? That's a very interesting question as I'm clearly into Belle.

"Here you go." My gaze drops to her hands as she takes the cup. My first thought is that they're surprisingly delicate for someone who does manual labor, but then I remind myself this isn't her only job and that she must take very good care of them.

"Thank you." Belle takes a careful sip and when I clumsily linger, drinking my lukewarm coffee, she turns toward the beach. "You have an amazing view. I service a lot of pools along this strip, but I haven't seen anything quite so exquisite as this."

"Yeah, it's pretty special. The morning light is beautiful when it hits the dunes."

"Do you go to the beach a lot?" she asks.

"I went for a walk last night, actually, in the storm. It was nice."

She nods and when her eyes meet mine, I feel arousal stirring. "I sat on my balcony out myself, walking back from a job after work. I love stormy weather."

"Oh… Do you work at night, too?" I ask, although I have a pretty good idea of what she's been up to.

"Sometimes." Belle puts her cup on the bench along the front of the small pool house that contains a bar and a pool table and picks up the net again. "I work when I can. I have a young daughter, so I plan my schedule around the sitter. Luckily, Pool Masters are pretty flexible."

"You have a daughter?" Nothing could have baffled me more, but I manage to keep my surprise to myself.

"Yeah, she's four. Do you have kids?"

"I do, but they're a lot older and they've moved out. My son is twenty-two. He's traveling with his girlfriend at the moment and my daughter is seventeen. She started her first year at NYU."

"Oh." Belle looks puzzled. "You don't look nearly old enough to have kids of that age."

I chuckle nervously at the compliment, playing with a lock of my hair. "I was young when I had them. I'd just turned eighteen when Eddie was born."

"Wow. And now you're…" Belle pauses. "Divorced? Do you mind me asking? I just assumed, since you changed your name."

"Yes, I'm divorced," I say. "My ex-husband moved a couple of blocks down the road to live with our interior designer."

"Fuck…" There's a hint of disgust in Belle's tone, and she winces. "Sorry to hear that."

"It's okay," I say. "Time for me now, I suppose. I just need to figure out what's next." There's an awkward silence, and I realize I've shared way more than I should have with someone who's only come over to take care of the pool. This, really, is the moment I should leave her to do her job. "Well, I'd better get back to what I was doing. Let me know if you want anything else."

"I appreciate that, but I'm good." Belle points to the big bottle of water next to her toolbox. "The pool will look sparkling in an hour if you want to swim. I'm adding some chemicals; they just need to settle before you can go in."

"No problem, I'll wait." I shoot her a smile and make my way back around the pool and into the kitchen. Inside, I lean back against the fridge and clutch a hand to my chest. My hands are shaking, and I feel breathless and funny inside. I've never felt like this around anyone. Not when Sandeep and I first met, not on our first date, not even when I first slept with him. *Fuck. I really do have a thing for Belle.*

BELLE - THURSDAY

Suki runs up to her grandfather and he picks her up and spins her around. "It's good to see you, kiddo. Back so soon, huh?"

"The lammies," I explain, and we exchange a humorous look. "I said we'd come on the weekend, but she couldn't wait, and I had the afternoon off." It's the first year that Suki's taken a keen interest in animals, although 'interest' is probably an understatement. She's obsessed with her animal farm children's books and loves to watch nature documentaries with me.

"Aha. You liked them, did you?" My father walks through the farmhouse and opens the kitchen door that leads into the backyard. It's not really a farm. Not in the traditional sense, but he has a barn with quite a few chickens and sheep and sells eggs, sheep's yoghurt and cheese at the local farmers market in East Hampton to support his meagre pension. This is where I grew up; a small farm in East Hampton. It's one of the few left after many farmers sold off their land due to the rising value. Farms were bulldozed and turned into villas and hotels, fields that held crops are now manicured yards surrounding stately mansions. The once serene views are obstructed by gates and hedges, but that's life, all part of the growing economy, I suppose.

While my father takes Suki to see the lambs, I turn on the kettle to make us a coffee and smile at the framed picture of my sister, Suki's mother. It's set up like a shrine on the windowsill, with candles burning on either side. They're always lit; my father keeps them going day and night. Even after three years, it hurts just as much to look at her but when I'm here, I let the grief wash over me, rather than fight it. Suki is the greatest comfort my father and I could wish for. She looks like her mother. I look like her mother too, and so Suki looks like me. People assume she's mine and I don't make a habit of telling people she's not. Because really, she is. The same blood runs through our veins. I'm the closest family she has, and I've adopted her. She calls me 'Mom' and loves me like a mother. I love her like a daughter too, more than anyone could ever imagine.

Suki kind of knows I'm not her real mother. When she was old enough to ask who the woman in the picture was, I answered honestly, but she's too young to really understand. Sometimes I find her staring at it quizzically, and in those moments, I'd give anything to know what's going through her mind.

Through the window, I watch Suki and my father open the small barn to let the lambs out. I laugh when I hear her scream in excitement and pick up the two mugs to join them.

"Here." I hand one to my father and perch next to him on the crumbled low wall that surrounds the yard. "It could do with some upkeep here. I can mow the lawn today, and maybe order some bricks to fix this wall?"

"Thank you, honey. But I'll keep the grass long for a while, the sheep like it. And the wall..." He shrugs. "I don't mind that it's a little rugged."

I nod, and we sip our coffee in silence while Suki runs around to stroke the lambs. My father likes everything to stay the same, and that includes scratches in the wallpaper and dents and rips in the furniture. Nothing ever changes; he won't allow it. But as he's not getting any younger and terrified of it being demolished if he sells it, he's decided he wants me to have it. "I'm sorry but I can't take over the farm," I finally say, starting the conversation I've been putting off for months. "I've thought about it like you asked me, and I really can't do it."

"I know you don't have the time and money for the upkeep, sweetheart. I should have never brought it up." My father glances at the house. "It's just hard to imagine it won't stay in the family. So many beautiful memories of your mother and your sister lie between those walls and if I move, I'm worried they'll fade."

"I'll make sure you won't forget." I rub his shoulder and pull him against me. "Look, Dad, I know it won't be easy for you to move, but it's for the best. You're waiting for your hip replacement and even if you fully recover from that, it's just becoming too much for you to maintain."

"Yeah." He lets out a long sigh of frustration. "Suki loves it here, though, and this farm has been in the family for generations. What if she'd want to live here one day?"

"Dad," I try carefully again, "I work long days, I'm saving up for Suki's future, I'll be starting my own business soon and I can't afford staff to take care of the animals on top of my sitter. How about we just get someone over to value it? I'm not saying you should sell it now, but it will give you something to think about."

"You're right, I'll keep it in mind." His eyes light up when one of the lambs starts skipping around Suki, making her shriek in pleasure. She tries to get up, but the lamb jumps up at her, making her tumble over while the other three curiously come closer to see what mischief their brave sister is up to. Suki doesn't mind. In fact, she loves it, and reaches out to stroke it. "How's work?"

"It's busy. I've got some extra hours in because one of our employees is recovering from an accident, and I'm also doing two nights this week." My dad thinks I'm hired to do emergency services for last-minute rentals at night. He would never understand if I told him what I really do.

"You can always bring her over here, you know." His bemused eyes follow Suki, who has now given up on trying to stand upright and is crawling behind the lambs on all fours.

"It's fine, I've already asked Jackie. She's dropping by later by the way. I thought I could cook dinner for the four of us?"

"That would be nice." My father smiles. "Suki and I can get some eggs from the barn and there are at least a dozen ripe tomatoes around the front."

"Don't get up. I'll get them later." I try to stop him, but he's already up, walking toward the cobbled path that leads around the side of the house. When he thinks I'm not watching him, I can see that he's limping.

"So, did you look at the website?" Sasha whispers. We're sitting at a bar in Southampton village, both sipping a perfect martini. Sasha is dressed in a skin-tight blue knee-length dress and I'm wearing jeans and a black, silk top; I look seriously underdressed next to her.

"I did," I say, glancing down at my heels that are resting on the frame of the stool. I pulled my favorite pair out of the back of my shoe closet for tonight, dusted them off and even felt a sparkle of excitement when I put them on after months of wearing flats.

"And? Did you see 'my Ben'?" she asks, making quote marks in the air. "What did you think of him?"

"Oh, *your* Ben," I tease. I can't possibly tell her that I've skipped the men altogether, so I shoot her a wink and say: "Yeah, he's quite something. I can see how that was one hell of a night."

"Right?" Sasha grins. "Oh, Reina, I'm so glad I can talk to you about this. Keeping it to myself was killing me. I won't make a habit of it, though. I've been thinking and..." She pauses. "Well, it was just one of those things I had to get out of my system, and even though I want to, I'm not going to do it again."

"Do you regret it?"

Sasha takes a moment to think about that, then shakes her head. "No. It was foolish and reckless to put my marriage at risk like that, but I don't regret it. That night will give me something to fantasize about for many years to come."

"Good. And I agree, it's probably smart not to do it again. If Igor found out, you might lose him and it's not worth it. But I'm glad you told me and I'm here for you whenever you want to talk." I pat her hand. "This is nice, Sash. Just you and me." I wave a finger between us and our cocktails.

"Yeah. It's been weird since your divorce. With Igor and Sandeep being friends, and I'm so sorry if I—"

"Hey, don't apologize," I interrupt her. "It's fine. I know you're in a difficult position."

Sasha nods. "Thank you for understanding. Maybe we could make Thursday our night, whenever we're both free? You and me, a couple of drinks, just to catch up? Because I need more girl time and if I'm being honest, Bree is a bit of a bore."

"I'd really like that," I say, delighted that Bree is not on the top of her friends list.

Sasha finishes her cocktail, orders two more, then turns back to me. "Anyway, we're here to talk about you. Were you not tempted by the escorts? Or have you thought about signing up for one of those dating apps?"

"Escorts are not for me and I think it's too early for dating apps."

"Nonsense. It's never a good time to do scary things, so now is as good a time as any," Sasha protests, waving her phone at me. "Did you not see anyone who made you wet on there?"

"Me? You mean on the website?" My cheeks flush at her

cocktail-induced question and I'm grateful for the dim lights in here. "I ehm…" I bite my lip, unsure how much to share, but Sasha has shared her biggest secret with me, and I want to entrust her with mine in return.

Her eyes widen when I remain silent, and she points a finger at me. "You naughty woman! You booked someone, didn't you?"

"No, I didn't, actually," I say hastily. "I swear, I didn't. But this really weird thing happened."

"What?" Sasha leans in, hanging on my every word now. "Tell me."

"Well, the pool service company sent a replacement for Barry."

"You mean Larry? The guy with the funny haircut?"

I chuckle and shake my head. "Turns out his name is Barry. Anyway, they sent this woman, Belle, and there was something about her that made me think of her in a way I haven't thought of anyone in years and years."

Sasha frowns. "I don't understand. In what way?"

"In a sexual way," I say, deciding to just tell it like it is. "I found her attractive." I hold up a hand when Sasha opens her mouth, undoubtedly about to attack me with a string of questions. "Wait, just let me finish before we discuss this. So, I went to yoga, leaving Belle to do whatever it is she does, and that's when you gave me the business card. And when I checked out the website the following night, she was on there." I lower my voice to a whisper. "My pool lady is an escort. She works for them. Women only."

Sasha stares at me with her mouth agape. "Wait, let me get this straight. Your new pool service lady works for Hamptons' Escorts… Okay, that's a weird coincidence, but what really baffles me is what you told me before that." She tilts her head and regards me. "I didn't know you were interested in women."

I chuckle uncomfortably and shift on my stool. "I've had crushes on girls when I was younger, but I never went there."

"And now it's something you might want to try?"

"Maybe." I shrug. "I can't stop thinking about her. She's awoken something in me, and now I'm confused and I have no idea what to do with myself. To be honest with you, there's not much I *can* do."

"You could hire her. Wouldn't that be the obvious next step?"

"No, I can't," I say resolutely. "She comes in to service the pool three times a week. It would be weird because we'd see each other."

"But you want to?" Sasha navigates to the website on her phone and scrolls through the list of lesbian escorts. "Which one?"

"'B," I say, pointing to Belle's picture. Again, the sight of her makes my breath catch and I move away from the phone as it's too much to handle in company.

"Oh my God..." Sasha narrows her eyes as she studies Belle and I hold my breath, awaiting her judgement. "You devil," she finally says. "She's kind of sexy. Even though women are not my cup of tea, I totally get what you see in her." She's way more understanding than I expected.

"There's more," I continue. "She told me she has a four-year-old daughter."

"Really? Hmm…" Sasha slips her phone back into her purse, pushes the next martini my way and attacks her own. She's drinking like a fish tonight; I'm not even halfway down my second and she's already on her fourth. "Do you think she has a partner? A wife, or a husband?"

"I don't know. I can't imagine her with a man, and it seems unlikely that's she's in any relationship with her line of work."

"Why don't you just ask her?"

"Yeah. I might do that." I sigh deeply, blowing out my cheeks while I absently stir the olive around in my drink. "I can't stop thinking about her and it's really stressful." I'm aware I'm telling Sasha more than I planned, but it feels good to share, and I feel less alone with all these strange emotions that have been haunting me for days. "I stopped thinking about women that way when I met Sandeep, but since Monday it's all been flooding back, hitting me like a ton of bricks and I'm all over the place."

Sasha throws her head back and laughs. "You know what? I would have never imagined you with a woman but seeing you now, listening to you talk, it's like you're a different person and I get it. I promise, I get it. I was a different person with Ben too."

"Or maybe this is just who I am," I say, not sure of anything anymore.

BELLE - THURSDAY

"*D*id you have fun with your old man?"

"Yeah, it was nice. Jackie came too. I don't understand why those two don't just get the awkward part over with and start dating already." Juliette and I are sitting on my balcony, watching the world go by. Below the street is riddled with people heading for the bars and restaurants and The Oyster Bar underneath my apartment has a long queue of patrons waiting for a table. It's nice up here, with the sound of laughter and music in the background, and the smell of food from the restaurants.

Juliette laughs and refills her mug with tea from the pot between us. "Still best friends?"

"Yep. Still besties. And she does his laundry every week. I mean, it's blatantly obvious they like each other, and she sees his dirty underwear on a regular basis, so what the hell are they waiting for? It's been thirty years since my mother died."

"She was your mother's best friend," Juliette says. "Even after thirty years, I can see how that doesn't sit well with either of them."

"But it would be good for him to have a companion. I'm

worried about him. He's walking with a limp and the farm is becoming too much for him. He's so stubborn, though. He won't hear of moving anytime soon." I glance at my tea, not feeling it anymore. "Hey, do you want something stronger? I have a nice Scotch. You and Cameron can stay over if you want."

Juliette chuckles and rolls her eyes at me. "Here we go again. Sure, why not? It's almost bedtime for him and I'm enjoying this." She gets up and points to the convenience store across the road. "You pour that Scotch and I'll go get him a toothbrush."

"CHEERS." I clink my glass against Juliette's and take a sip, savoring the golden liquid that warms my throat. It's been a while since they've stayed over. Nowadays, life gets in the way and we rarely have a strong drink together anymore. "To the wildest thing I've done in weeks."

Juliette lets out a roaring laugh. "Same here, hun. Five years ago we were both total party animals and look at us now. A glass of Scotch on a Thursday night is as bad-ass as it gets." She downs the whiskey and leans back with a delighted sigh. "Life isn't so bad, though. My mother is retiring soon, so she'll be able to look after Cameron more, which means I can start dating."

"Ooh… you're ready to date" I ask in a teasing tone. Juliette's boyfriend left her not long after Cameron was born and like me, she's been struggling with being a single, working mom over the years.

"Yeah. I'm ready. All in all, I'm in a good place. I have my life in order, I can pay my bills, Cameron is doing well and I just got my car fixed." She winks. "It's the little things, right?"

"Absolutely." I refill our glasses and sink back in my chair too, propping my feet onto the balcony railing. "And where are you planning to meet the lucky guy?"

"Oh, I don't know." Juliette brushes her auburn hair behind her ears. "Online, in bars, at the beach, maybe?" She narrows her eyes at me. "What about you?"

"Me?" I laugh. "I can't date while I'm escorting. It would be crazy. No woman would be okay with that."

"True. But you won't be doing that for much longer, right?"

"No. I was thinking maybe three more months, just to save up a little more before I start working for myself."

Juliette nods. "So, once you stop doing what you're doing, you can start dating too. We could double-date." She shoots me a cheeky grin and adds, "It's not like you're going to steal my men."

"Gross, no." I look over my shoulder and glance into the living room to make sure Suki and Cameron haven't snuck out of her bedroom. "But dating with a kid is difficult, don't you think?"

"I don't know. I'm yet to find out." Juliette purses her lips. "I guess it would have to be someone who loves kids and someone who's responsible... And good-looking, of course," she adds, then shakes her head with a groan. "Okay, I'm basically fucked."

"I'm sorry, I didn't mean do discourage you. I love that you want to get out there and meet people again."

"No, you're right," Juliette says. "The only single guys here are real estate agents and all they want is a bit of fun between the sheets."

"That's not true. Dave from the convenience store is single," I say, and we both burst out in raucous laughter.

"Thanks for the suggestion, but I prefer someone under the age of seventy." She tilts her head and regards me. "Have you not met someone you've felt attracted to? In all the time you've been back from New York?"

"No," I say resolutely, then hesitate for a moment. Sipping my whiskey, I think of Miss Amari.

"What?" Juliette nudges me. "Come on, tell me. I know you're holding back."

"It's nothing. Just a woman whose pool I started servicing this week. I felt attraction for the first time in years but it's pointless. She's straight and rich and I don't even know her; it's purely physical and entirely one-sided."

"How can you be so sure it's only one-sided?"

"Because I just told you, she's straight." I roll my eyes at Juliette. "And even if she wasn't, she's way out of my league." Still, as the night grows darker and the alcohol relaxes me, I allow myself to picture her before me and indulge in the flutter that spreads through my core. Pointless or not, it's nice to feel that good old tug of desire again.

REINA - FRIDAY

I seem to be going from bad to worse. I felt bewildered this morning, when I woke up in a pool of my own sweat at four am, the throbbing between my thighs so intense that I had to use my vibrator for the third time this week. I genuinely thought of hiring an escort then, as I lay awake, staring at the ceiling after three orgasms. Not Belle, of course, but someone else, just to get this sexual energy out of my system. But no matter how many times I scrolled through the list of appealing ladies, I didn't feel like sleeping with one of them apart from her.

My body is hypersensitive, and I'm constantly lost in my own thoughts while my mind spins, trying to make sense of what is happening to me. I, Reina Amari, am attracted to women. At least one in particular.

It's just a crush, I keep telling myself, but if this is a 'crush', it's the first time I've had one, and that thought scares me even more. I'm unfamiliar with this feeling of constant restlessness, of infatuation, admiration, arousal. Belle has consumed me, and she doesn't even know it. If she did, I bet she'd be seriously freaked out. *Sad, lonely rich divorcée, lusting after the pool technician.*

When I came downstairs and saw my reflection in the living room mirror, I knew I looked like I was trying too hard. Dressed in a beautiful yellow summer dress, high heels and my hair styled to perfection, it was too late to change into something more casual. Belle was already in the backyard and had spotted me through the glass façade. She greeted me with a wave, and I waved back, way too eagerly.

My eyes are sternly fixed on the coffee maker as I wait for the cappuccino to fill the cups, and I tell myself to calm the fuck down. This means nothing to Belle; I'm just the first in a long string of clients during her day and I need to keep that in mind. Just before she's about to head into the machine room, I slip outside with her coffee and a plate filled with chocolate chip cookies.

"Hey there, Miss Amari." Belle shoots me a grateful smile when I put her coffee and cookies down. "You're spoiling me. You really don't need to do that, you know."

"Of course I do," I say, averting my gaze and pretending to look at a ship in the distance. Her closeness is too much, too intense, and it's getting worse each time I see her. She's wearing a navy tank top and denim shorts today and when she pulls her cap further over her forehead her top hikes up, giving me a view of her toned belly. "It's morning. Everyone needs coffee in the morning."

Belle laughs, and the sound of it sends butterflies to my core. "Well, I appreciate it." She glances at my legs for a split second, and if I'm not mistaken, she casts her eyes over my cleavage too. "You look beautiful, by the way. Special plans for today?"

Heat rises to my cheeks at the compliment and suddenly I have trouble balancing on my heels. "Just going to get some groceries later. My daughter's coming home for the weekend."

"Nice. I bet you miss her."

"I do, but I'm also very proud of her." Searching for something to keep the conversation going, I gesture to the wheelbarrow containing three big bags of sand she's brought. "Nola told me you'll be replacing the sand in the filter?"

"Yes, we usually do it at the start of the season. It's quite a big job, so it might take a couple of hours."

"No problem," I say, delighted with the news. "I'll be around until midday."

BY THE TIME Belle has finished, I've moved inside with my laptop as I was worried I'd be staring too much if I stayed by the pool. The stool closest to the sliding doors at the kitchen island is my favorite spot, and it's where I normally spend my mornings when it rains. I probably look like I'm doing all kinds of important things but in truth, I'm ordering lingerie online. My underwear drawer is filled with old, washed out bras and panties, and even my nicest sets are dated. It doesn't matter if no one will see it; it's time I treated myself to something that will make me feel sensual.

I gasp when Belle suddenly walks in and click away the Agent Provocateur website.

"Sorry, Miss Amari. I didn't mean to startle you." Belle hands me a tablet with a stylus attached to it. "I just need you to sign this before I go. It's the check for the sand, we'll charge it to your account."

"Oh." I blank out for a moment, as if I can't remember my own name. She's standing really close, and I can smell her delicious, tanned skin. She smells of sunshine and coconut lotion, mixed with a hint of sweat that drives me wild. "You can call me Reina," I hear myself say.

"Reina, like this house? Pretty name. It means queen, right?"

"That's correct. How do you know?"

"I speak a little Spanish. Are you Spanish?"

"Lebanese. My parents are from Beirut, Lebanon."

Belle looks me over, her eyes burning into my flesh. "So that's where you got your exotic looks from. Do you speak Arabic?"

The 'exotic' comment makes my pulse race. She's been nothing but professional so far, but if I'm not mistaken, there's a hint of flirtation in her voice. I'm probably just imagining it, but still, I can't shake off the feeling that there's a certain energy between us. "Not really. I grew up in New York, mostly."

"Nice. I lived in New York for a couple of years. It was great, but I'm happy to be back here. The ocean, the salty air and the..." Belle's voice trails away and her smile drops as she looks down at something on the kitchen counter.

I freeze when I see it's the Hamptons' Escorts business card. I left it there and completely forgot about it. *Fuck. Fuck. Fuck.* "I found it in my ex-husband's office," I'm quick to say, as it would be awkward not to mention it. Simultaneously, I know I sound nervous and caught out.

Belle stares from me to the card and back, clearly not buying my excuse. I wouldn't believe me either; I'm aware of how I look right now, my eyes wide with panic and my cheeks bright pink. Then her expression softens, and she smiles knowingly and nods. "Sure." It's possible that she doesn't know I know about her secret life. She probably thinks I've been checking out the men. "But even if it *was* yours," she continues, "it's nothing to be ashamed of. It's just a service like any other service."

"So you know this company?" I ask, handing her back the tablet.

Again, Belle looks at me, with intense interest this time. "I think you know I do, Reina." Just the sound of my name coming from her lips makes me twitch, and when I remain silent, too stunned to think of anything to say, she shoots me a wink and turns on her heel. "Well, it was a pleasure. Have a lovely weekend with your daughter and I'll see you next week."

BELLE - FRIDAY

*L*ate in the afternoon, when I arrive at the toy wholesalers after work, I'm still beating myself up about my behavior this morning. I shouldn't have flirted with her, but I did. I guess I was so thrown at seeing the Hamptons' Escorts business card on her kitchen island that I didn't think anything through. Maybe she didn't even see me on the website. Maybe she was checking out the men. Maybe the card really was her ex-husband's, but her reaction was extreme, and today I noticed her looking at me in a certain way. *With interest.*

"Can I help you?"

"Yes, please." Despite my anxious mood, I manage a smile. I've been looking forward to this moment for a long time and I need to put the conversation out of my mind. "I'd like to see your pool toys."

"Sure. I'm Randy, happy to be of assistance. Anything specific you're looking for?" The sales manager glances at my stained top and ripped shorts. He probably thinks I'm a gardener sent out to get toys for her bosses' kids.

"Just show me everything you've got. I need a huge selection."

Randy's eyes light up at this and he walks ahead to an aisle filled with inflatables. "We have just about anything from kids' inflatables to floating bars and there's lots of crazy stuff toward the back."

"Great." I glance over the enormous selection. "Let's start with the small things. The pink, sprinkled doughnuts look like they would be perfect for a bachelorette party. Are they good quality? I need toys that will last."

"They're good," he says. "And they're the biggest ones of their kind on the market. They have an inner seat and a cup holder. Wait, let me pull one down for you." He grabs a long stick and lifts one of the doughnuts on display off the hook. "Fifty-nine dollars. That includes a repair kit for small punctures."

I run my hand over the thick rubber. "Looks good. I'll have fifteen, please. Ten pink and five of the mixed ones."

Randy looks surprised but doesn't comment as he types it into his iPad. "I'm not sure if we have that many in stock. It would take about two weeks to get them here."

"That's fine, I'm not in a hurry; I still need to sign my storage lease. How about the floating bars?"

"This is our biggest and most spectacular floating bar," he says eagerly, pointing to a ten-seater with a round table in the middle. "It's four-hundred-and-seventy-nine dollars. Ten cup holders, a dip in the middle to place a wine cooler and comfortable backrests. It's hanging too high for me to get it down here, but if you give me an hour, I can arrange that."

"No need, I'll have two of those please. I've already checked out the reviews online." I point to the smaller floating bar that holds six. "And two of those." My excitement grows as we browse the aisles. This is it; I'm really doing it. It's taking my mind off Reina and that's a good thing. At the same time, I'm a little afraid that I'm pouring my savings into something that won't work.

"May I ask what you're planning on doing with all this stuff?" he asks.

"I'm starting a rental business. Party props."

"Great idea." The way Randy looks at me makes me think he's wondering why he hasn't thought of this himself. "Lots of parties in the Hamptons. Have you approached any party and wedding planners yet?"

"Yeah, I have. The season hasn't started yet but some of them have already come back to me with enquiries, so I thought I'd better get the stock in before I give them a quote."

"Good for you." Randy opens a picture on his iPad and shows it to me. "This might interest you. We don't have it in stock, but we can order it for you."

"Wow." I eye the twenty-five-foot-high climbing wall that is attached to the edge of the show pool. "I've never seen that before."

"Glad I'm able to show you something new," he says with a grin. "It's safe for adults—provided you can swim of course —as you can only fall into the water, and it's fantastic for those who want something active. I've only sold one of these, ever, but they're popular in the Emirates for some reason. Perhaps they have bigger pools there."

"There are plenty of big pools here too. How much?"

"Twenty-seven hundred dollars."

"Okay." I look at the rest of the pictures while mentally scrolling through my budget and try to analyze who would want to rent something like this. Admittedly, I can't think of anyone who wouldn't want to have a go at it because it looks fun. Having a unique product people can't get else-where is a bonus, so I nod and hand him back the iPad. "I'll take it."

As I say it, Randy pumps his fist, then laughs at himself,

rolling his eyes. "I swear, I don't even work on commission, but I love toys and you're my dream customer."

I laugh too and give him a hearty slap on his shoulder. "So you know how everything works, and how to set it up properly?"

"Oh, yes. It's my job to know how everything works."

I cast my eye over him and note that he looks quite buff underneath the oversized baby-blue company polo shirt he's wearing. "Looking for a side job by any chance?"

"Are you serious?" Randy frowns. "Doing what?"

"Just setting things up, really. Making sure it's all safe and solid. I can't offer you a contract of course, and I'm aware it's highly inappropriate to discuss this at your workplace, so maybe we could talk over a beer instead..." I glance around to make sure no one's listening in but we're all alone. "I need someone to help me on a freelance basis until my company gets off the ground, so if you have some spare time outside your job, I'd be happy to give you the hours on a trial basis, if you're interested."

"I most certainly would." Randy beams. "I could do with the extra money; my wife and I are expecting a baby and I only work here four days a week."

"Okay. Then let's meet up to discuss it." Randy is seriously keen. I haven't thought this through, but it seemed like a no-brainer, just like it was a no-brainer for me to start this business after seeing how the other half lives and how they struggle to get rid of all the things they buy, just for a party. I can't even count the times someone's asked me if I'd like an inflatable unicorn, a waterproof beer pong set or a beach volleyball net. Just like my clients' cleaners and gardeners, I can't accept any of those; I don't have a pool and I don't have the storage. At least not yet. They buy things because it fits the theme of their party. Money is not the issue; the issue is getting rid of the stuff cluttering their backyards. Most people here are environmentally conscious, they don't want to be seen throwing things away, so hiring would be the perfect solution. As far as party planners are concerned, I can only assume they'd be delighted with the opportunity to hire everything they need from one place, saving them a lot of time, stress and effort.

"I'm in. Are you local?" Randy asks.

"Sort of. I'm in Sag Harbor."

"Perfect. I'm in East Hampton, we can meet up somewhere in the middle." He beckons me to follow him, now bouncing like a kid in a candy store. "And now that I know the kind of stuff you're after, I have so much more to show you."

"Awesome." I follow him and chuckle at his enthusiasm. Randy was exactly what I needed to get my drive back.

"*N*icole!" I give my daughter a long hug and pull her inside. "How was the drive?"

"Long and slow," Nicole answers with a groan, then rolls her shoulders. "I'm hungry. What's for dinner?" She heads straight for the fridge, grabs a carton of orange juice and takes a long drink from it.

"I was a little distracted today, so I've ordered Chinese. It won't be long." I don't comment on the fact that she's not using a glass. I'm so happy she's here that I can forgive her less than ladylike manners. "How was your week?"

"Busy. I'm starting fieldwork next week, so I've been trying to get ahead with studying for my exams." Nicole puts the orange juice back, wipes her mouth with the sleeve of her hoody and looks me over as if suddenly only then, noticing me. "Oh, wow. You look super nice, Mom. Your hair… it's so lovely and straight."

"Thank you." I blush and pull my hair behind my ears.

"And your heels and your dress…" She walks over to me and fingers the linen silk blend of my yellow summer dress. "Is this new?"

"No, I've just never worn it."

"Oh. Are you going out tonight?"

"Of course not, you're here," I exclaim. "Just thought I should take care of myself a little better, that's all."

Nicole's mouth stretches into a wide smile. "Good for you. I'm happy to see you're doing better. Have you spoken to Dad?"

"No. I have no reason to talk to your father anymore. Have you?"

"No." Nicole averts her gaze, and I know she's lying. Sandeep's probably told her that Bree is pregnant and asked her to keep it quiet until he's ready to tell me himself. He must be dreading the moment, but now that I'm over the initial shock, I know I'll be able to stay calm and friendly. Perhaps the realization of finding myself attracted to a woman after twenty-two years of marriage to a man has overshadowed everything else that's going on in my life.

"You should go visit him while you're here. He'd like that," I say. "You still haven't been to their house yet."

"Nah." Nicole grimaces. "I don't mind going out for lunch with him, but I'm not jumping to see him and Bree together. Maybe a coffee somewhere on Sunday, we'll see." The gate buzzes, and Nicole gratefully embraces the opportunity to end the conversation. Grabbing some change for the delivery man from the bowl on the kitchen counter, she sprints out the door and toward the gates. "Foooooood!" she yells, making me laugh. She comes back with a big bag full of all her favorite dishes I've ordered, and as she opens it, the smell of chow mien, deep-fried seaweed, Sichuan eggplant, crispy Peking duck with greens, pancakes and plum sauce, wonton soup and steamed vermicelli rolls fill the kitchen. It's way too much for two people, but I know she likes leftovers for breakfast, so I've gone a little overboard. "Yum, I'm starving," she says, opening the boxes.

I take plates, chopsticks, glasses and a bottle of white wine outside to the dining table and Nicole brings the food that she's attacking on the way. Normally, I sit at the head of the table, but this week I've been sitting on the side as it gave me an unobstructed view of Belle. Without thinking, I pull out that same chair and take a seat. Nicole shoots me a fleeting look of confusion but doesn't comment. "Are you still enjoying New York?" I ask as I pour the wine.

"Yeah, I am. You always ask me that." She plates some eggplant and passes me the box.

"I'm your mother. It's important to me that you're enjoying your life. What are you doing this semester? Is it interesting?"

"I suppose. I'll be able to give you an answer to that question in a couple of months; it's still too early to know." Nicole purses her lips and chews her cheek. "What did you want to do when you were younger?"

The 'younger' comment stings. "Hey, I'm still young," I say, playfully kicking her foot under the table. "I doubt many of your fellow students have a mother who's still in her thirties."

"Only just." Nicole rolls her eyes and laughs. "I'm sorry, just kidding. You know what I mean."

I take a sip of my wine and glance over the dishes on the table. I'm not hungry; I haven't been able to eat all day, totally thrown by the incident with Belle, but I plate up anyway. Even if it's just the two of us, it's still family time, and I'm going to eat, appetite or not. "Well, I suppose I wanted to be a photographer."

"Really?" Nicole's puzzled look tells me she can't quite believe I have an artistic bone in my body. "I knew you liked photography; you bought all the art in here, but I didn't know you wanted to work in the field. Were you good?"

"I considered myself to be better than average. Not sure

how good I'd be now; I haven't had much practice other than using my phone to take pictures in the past decade."

"Do you have any cool pictures lying around somewhere? Where's your camera?"

"I think I have some upstairs in a box in the study. My camera is there too, I think, but it's very old, just like me," I add, arching a brow at her. "I'm sure there are much better ones on the market now."

"Sorry, Mom, I didn't mean to be ageist." Nicole blows me a kiss. "Don't you feel like taking up photography again? Now that you have more time on your hands?"

"Maybe." I'm hesitant as I'd honestly not considered it, but she's right; I do have way too much time on my hands and it's actually not a bad idea.

"Excellent," Nicole says, taking my vague reply as a yes. "Why don't we get you a new camera this weekend? We could buy one online, or go into town? Yes, let's go into town. Lunch and shopping, just the two of us."

"Okay. Lunch and shopping it is," I say, happy at the prospect of spending a day in the village with my daughter. As I entertain the idea of having a camera in my hands after so many years, I feel an itch to see the world through a lens again, to capture the essence of everything I love.

"I just want you to find yourself again, Mom. Like you want me to enjoy life, I want you to be happy too."

There's a silence between us while I ponder her statement. It seems like an awfully mature thing for her to say and I'm a little taken aback by it. Has it really been that obvious to her that I've been going through a bad time? I've tried my hardest to hide it, being the best version of myself on the weekends when she's here. "I know, honey, but I am happy. I'm feeling so much better already."

"Yes, I've noticed that. There's something different about you. Not just your appearance, there's something else."

Again, Nicole studies me, as if she's waiting for a confession. Is she waiting for me to tell her I've been on a date or met a man in the grocery store, or online? Waiting to find out why I'm suddenly prancing around on stiletto heels again and taking care of myself like never before? There's nothing to report, of course. At least nothing I'm willing to share, so I simply smile.

"It's just time to move on," I say, focusing on my food. Yes, I feel different today, but I also feel terrified and confused because even with Nicole here, all I can seem to think of is Belle.

"I'm glad you said that. Because I wanted to talk to you about something." Nicole pauses. "There's this party at a friend's house in Brooklyn at the end of the month, and I kind of want to go. It's on a Saturday but the traffic will be horrible coming here, and—"

"Of course, honey. Stay in New York and enjoy yourself," I interrupt her. "You don't need my permission. I want you to come home because you want to be here, not because you're worried about me being alone."

"But I can't help but worry about you." Nicole shrugs. "And just to clarify; I love coming here. I love the ocean, and I love you. This is my home and *you're* my home. I just don't want you to be lonely."

My eyes sting with the sentiment, and I swallow down the lump in my throat. "I promise you I'm not lonely, okay?" I look at her intently. "You're an adult and you're growing into your own person, so stay in New York whenever you want, you hear me? Whenever you want. And when you come home, there will always be Chinese takeout waiting for you." Reaching out over the table, I squeeze her hand. "As long as you call me and let me know you're okay, I'll be fine."

BELLE - SATURDAY

"*I* don't want to go to the bank. I want to see the lammies." Suki protests as I'm getting us ready to leave.

I finish brushing her hair and start braiding the left side of her hair. "We have to go to the bank, sweetie. Mommy needs to open a business account."

"Why?"

"Because I'm starting my own company and I need to pay for lots of stuff that I've ordered."

Suki turns and frowns in the cutest way. "Why?"

I laugh, and secure the elastic in her braid, then start on the other side. "So that we can have a nice life, you and me. So that we can get a bigger house eventually, and so you can study and be whatever you want to be. Don't you want that?" Hearing myself talk, I can hardly believe I'm the same person I was three years ago. Working behind the bar in New York nightclubs, sleeping my way around town and living in a shared apartment with three friends, I lived for the moment and never planned further than a day ahead. Now, I have a child to take care of, a mortgage to pay, I'm about to start my

73

own business and life couldn't be better. My sister gave me something meaningful before she passed away. She gave me the gift of devotion, responsibility and love, and although I still miss her every day, having Suki in my life makes me feel strong and positive.

"Study?"

"Yeah. It's when you go to a big-girl school and they teach you how to do a job." I think of Reina telling me about her daughter. They must be close if her daughter still comes home on weekends, and I can only hope that Suki will do the same when she's that age. I've been analyzing our brief exchange over and over and I'm sure Reina knows I work for Hamptons' Escorts. If she knows, that also means she was browsing the lesbian escorts… "What do you want to be when you're older?" I ask in an attempt to distract myself from Reina. "You don't need to decide now, of course, and you can change your mind whenever you want. And if you don't know, that's fine too."

"I want to be a princess," Suki says, matter-of-factly.

"A princess? That's not a job." It amuses me how girlie she is, considering I'm the opposite. She clearly takes after her mother. Linda used to dress up like a princess when we were younger and I liked to be the prince, never getting it quite right wearing my father's checked shirts.

Suki tilts her head back to look up at me. "I want to be a princess with a job."

I chuckle. "Okay. What job?"

"The same as you." She grins. "I want to swim in pools."

"I don't swim in pools, honey. I clean them. But if that's what you want to do then you can."

"Yes. I want to come to work with you." Suki slaps her little hand on her thigh. "And I want to swim too and I want to be a princess."

"Maybe I could teach you how to swim. That would be a

good start, wouldn't it?" I doubt she'll have the same dreams in three years' time, but it's kind of cute that she wants to be like me right now.

"But I *can* swim."

"Yes, you can swim. You swim really well, but I mean without your armbands." I tap her shoulders twice, my cue that her hair is done, and she turns around with a frown.

"With nothing?"

"Yeah, just with your arms and your legs. It might take some practice, but you'll get there. We'll go to the community pool. It will be easier than in the sea and Juliette and Cameron might want to come too."

Suki mulls over my proposal which must seem outrageous to a four-year-old. Swimming without armbands. Crazy. "Okay. Can we go now?"

"No, Suki. The pool is closed now," I say, wincing at my little white lie. "We're going to the bank, and then we're going to get groceries." I shake my head at her and smile. At least I've managed to distract her from 'the lammies.'

NO ONE ever said this was easy. After our visit to the bank, I'm juggling a stroller full of groceries and Suki is pulling me along the pavement. She considers herself too old for the stroller now, but it's the only way I can multitask. I use it to transport stuff whenever she's with me, so I can hold her hand at the same time. Today it's filled with frozen peas, wilting spinach and melting ice cream among other items but that doesn't mean we'll get back to the freezer any faster.

From the corner of my eye something catches my attention and I stop abruptly to glance across the road. "Wait, Suki," I say, narrowing my eyes to make sure I'm not imagining things.

"Mommy, you're holding me too tight."

"Oh, sorry, honey." I realize I'm squeezing Suki's hand as I see Reina coming out of the funny little tech shop on the corner of our street and loosen my grip. She's with a girl who I assume is her daughter; she bares a remarkable resemblance to Reina. Younger of course, a little curvier and dressed way more casually, but their big eyes, long dark hair and full lips are the same. The girl lifts a Polaroid camera, but Reina seems reluctant—or perhaps shy—to be in the picture. Suddenly she looks up, as if she can feel my eyes on her, and I wave from across the street and hear myself calling her name. "Come on, let's go say hi to mommy's friend. We'll just be a minute."

I feel nervous as I lift Suki up and cross the road, and from the look on Reina's face, I think she's nervous too. My heart is pounding but it's too late to turn back, so I raise my chin and give her a wide smile.

REINA - SATURDAY

*P*erusing the store filled with everything photography related, I'm overwhelmed by their selection. We've ventured out to Sag Harbor, as the only specialist shop on the peninsula is here. It's a sweet fishing village with a very local crowd and a bohemian vibe. I've never been in this part of the Hamptons; most of my friends live in the villages and hamlets in and around Southampton and Easthampton, tucked away behind private hedges in their big villas. It's nice to get out of my neighborhood, and it's made me realize how small my world really is.

"How about this one?" Nicole picks up a huge camera. The lens alone is bigger than her two hands gripping the body as she points it at me.

"That one's for filming long-distance," I say with a chuckle. "I don't need a sniper camera. A simple, semi-professional digital or hybrid with good focus will do. Glancing over the shelves, my attention naturally gravitates toward a Nikon D6, as all my previous cameras have been by the same brand. Picking it up, I rub my thumb over the rough surface and admire the lens. The camera's an unusual shape; square instead of rectangular, but it feels robust and comfortable in my hands.

"What are you planning on shooting?" the sales assistant who has been listening in, asks me.

"I'm not sure yet. The beach, the ocean, wildlife, people maybe?" I told him I didn't need help, but now that I'm faced with so much choice, I kind of do. "What do you think?"

"I think that DSLR is a great choice. It's pricey, but one of the best we have. You know about cameras?"

"I used to, but that was a long time ago," I say, folding my hands around it and lifting it up to peer through the lens. Its vision is crystal clear, way better than my old camera and that doesn't surprise me. Technology must have come a long way since I was in my teens and early twenties.

"It's got a silent setting for wildlife photography, an incredibly accurate auto-focus system and the quality is top-notch. It's also weatherproof and suitable for all environments, day or night," the sales assistant continues. "I'd say it veers more toward professional and it's often purchased by journalists or sports photographers, but it's easy to use and designed to capture moments, rather than scenes."

Securing the neoprene lined band around my neck, I note that its weight is pleasant. Not too heavy for long walks, and not too light. There's nothing worse than a flimsy camera; I want to know that it's there. "I like it."

"You have good taste."

"I do," I joke. I bet he's already sized us up to work out if I can afford it. Although Nicole's wearing torn jeans and an unbranded gray T-shirt, I'm sure the Givenchy Antigona bag I bought her for her seventeenth birthday has not gone unnoticed and neither has my Bottega Veneta purse. I'm not one to splash out on things; one nice purse is all I need, and I've had this one for years. But with that in mind, I'm also aware that I haven't treated myself to something special in a long time, and I really, really want this camera.

"I can throw in an additional five-year guarantee and a Polaroid camera for the young lady," he says, hoping Nicole will persuade me. "And I'll include two vintage color film packs and one sepia film pack."

Of course Nicole is excited. It's the perfect suggestion for someone of her age. "Yes, Mom! I'd love one of those." She gives me her best doe eyes and I laugh as I don't need persuading; I've already made up my mind.

"Okay. I'll take it."

Nicole eagerly takes the box containing the Polaroid camera from the sales assistant and starts loading in the sepia film while I pay, discuss the basic settings of my new camera and sign the paperwork for the guarantee. If I'd known something as simple as a cheap Polaroid camera would make Nicole so happy, I'd have bought her one long ago.

"Smile!" she says, about to snap a picture of me while we exit the store.

"Oh, please don't. I don't like having my picture taken." In a reflex, I lift a hand in front of my face and turn away slightly.

"Come on, Mom. This is a big moment. You finally have a good camera again."

Shaking my head with a chuckle, I give in and hold up the shopping bag while I smile at her awkwardly. Spotting something, or rather *someone* familiar in my peripheral vision, my cheery expression quickly shifts to one of shock. It's Belle, and she's standing on the opposite side of the road, watching our back-and-forth banter. Her hand is holding that of a little girl, who I assume must be her daughter, and she's got a stroller filled with grocery bags in the other.

"Hey, Reina!" She waves at me, lifts the child onto her hip and to my surprise, she crosses the road. My heart beats wildly as she comes closer, so violently I'm barely able to greet her back.

"Hey, Belle," I manage. My voice doesn't sound like my own when I'm face to face with her. She looks so different without her red cap and shorts. Instead, she's dressed in washed-out jeans and a navy T-shirt. A white linen shirt is draped over her shoulders, and her hair is casually slicked back. She's so incredibly attractive that I find myself staring. Today, she doesn't look like Belle the pool girl, but she does look like 'B' the escort. *Just like her profile picture.*

"And you must be Nicole." I'm impressed Belle remembers her name, and I can see Nicole's puzzled. She knows all my friends and Belle is certainly a little different than them in the looks department.

"I am." Nicole shakes her hand and smiles at the little girl. "Hey there, cutie. What's your name?"

"Suki," the girl mumbles, while she sucks on her thumb.

"That's a pretty name. How old are you?" Nicole asks. I realize I should be asking these questions, but I'm too stunned to hold a conversation.

"Suki is four," Belle says when Suki doesn't answer. "And she's getting too heavy to carry." She puts her down and takes a hold of her hand.

"Aren't you a pretty girl?" I finally say. Suki giggles and half hides behind Belle's leg.

"She's so cute. I love kids." Nicole smiles at Belle. "How do you know my mother?"

"I service her pool," Belle says. "I work for Pool Masters."

"Oh." Nicole glances at me, probably wondering why I've lost my tongue. "What happened to Larry?"

"Barry." Belle chuckles. "He broke his arm; I'm just filling in for him." She looks from Nicole to me and back. "What are you guys doing in Sag Harbor?"

"Mom just bought a new camera." Nicole points to my

bag. She told me she used to be quite a good photographer back in the day, so I wanted to see for myself."

"Is that so?" Belle arches a brow at me. "If I were you, I'd start with that beautiful view of yours."

"Yes, I think I will." Finally, I work up the courage to lock my eyes with Belle's and the effect that simple action causes is astonishing. I hadn't expected to see her here. It's out of context and it's confusing, making me break out in a cold sweat. My core is fluttering, my pulse racing, and I wish I could check myself in a mirror to see if I look presentable. "And what are you doing here?" I stammer.

"Me? Oh, we live here." Belle points to the first restaurant in a row of many. "Right over there, above The Oyster Bar."

"How lovely," I say, glancing up at the two-storey building with a wide balcony that overlooks the street. I don't know where I expected her to live. I thought about it, and even tried to find her on social media but to no avail. Frankly, I couldn't picture her living anywhere since pool maintenance and escorting are such contradicting worlds, but now that I see her here, it makes sense. "Right in the middle of all the action."

Belle laughs. "Not sure there's much action in Sag Harbor, but we like it, don't we, Suki?" She turns the stroller in the direction of The Oyster Bar. "Well, it was nice to see you. We'd better get the ice cream into the freezer."

"Yes, it was nice to see you too." I blow a kiss at Suki. "And you." Lingering on the spot, I ponder over where to go next. We can't stay here in front of the store, but I don't want to go in the same direction as Belle either. That would be weird after we've just said goodbye. *Oh God, I'm overthinking things.* "How about we drive to Southampton Village instead and have lunch at that shrimp place you like?" I ask Nicole, then start heading back to the car without waiting for an answer.

"But I thought you wanted to stay in Sag Harbor," Nicole

says, following me. "You said the shops and restaurants looked nice and that you wanted to have a look around."

"I know I said that, but I'm really hungry, so we might as well go somewhere we know the food is great." Turning to her, I give her an apologetic shrug. "If you don't mind, of course. You're not into shopping anyway, right?" I feel a need to get out of here because I have no idea how to behave after seeing Belle. It was too much, too overwhelming. Neither her nor Nicole have any idea about how I feel, and I'll make sure they never find out.

"I don't mind," Nicole shrugs. "But…" she pauses while we put our bags in the car and get in. "But what I don't understand is why you were you being so weird with that woman."

"I wasn't. She's just the woman who services our pool."

"Exactly. So why were you quiet and all fidgety? It was like she made you nervous or something. Has she done anything to make you feel uncomfortable?"

"No. God, no." I look skyward and attempt a laugh. "I honestly don't know what you're talking about." Desperate to change the conversation, I point to the Polaroid picture she took of me. "How do I look?"

BELLE - SUNDAY

Sunday is my favorite day of the week. Juliette and I decided to drive to Montauk with Suki and Cameron to get lobster rolls at 'Rolls', a little shack along the main road, just because we had a craving for them. It's a popular spot and we've come early to make sure we could grab a shaded table on their terrace. Families and millennials are crowded around their blue picnic tables under rickety bamboo canopies. As it's one of the few places where the rich and famous weekend crowd mingle with the locals, Juliette loves to come celebrity spotting here. Although she's always denied it, she's a bit of a wannabe at heart, which is sort of endearing in a weird way. She reads all the gossip magazines, keeps up with scandal and intrigue surrounding the Hamptons' socialites and occasionally tries to drag me to the latest hotspots.

Juliette closes her eyes and moans as she bites into her roll. She's got three in front of her, and I'll be surprised if she manages to finish them. "Mmm, I've missed this. So, so good. Why are they closed over winter? It's just not fair."

"So, so good," Cameron says, closing his eyes and mimicking his mother.

I laugh, noting he has it spot on, including the dramatic eye-roll at the end. "Are you guys excited to go to the pool later?"

Cameron nods. "I can already swim," he says, stuffing a fry into his mouth.

"Me too," Suki chimes in. "I can swim in the deepest of the deep." She's beyond pumped and is telling Cameron all about it, throwing in an assortment of imaginary scenes involving sharks, mermaids and a princess who cleans pools. More and more ketchup ends up on her cheek as she's talking and eating at the same time, to the amusement of people around us.

"Here we go, guys. Three lobster rolls, fries and a Coke." A woman puts down a tray with food and joins the couple who are laughing about Suki's spectacularly incoherent story. I smile at the woman and try to keep a straight face when I see it's Mrs. Ashworth. She stares at me for a moment, blinking as if she's processing the situation, perhaps doing an internal risk analysis. The people she's with are much younger; I suspect the boy might be her son as he looks like her. It's not the first time this has happened to me, so I turn back to my food and grab my phone, pretending to reply to a message. Bumping into a client seemed like a big deal the first time it happened but by now I've worked out that playing it cool is a simple way to avoid unnecessary stress. I don't want her to panic. She's married and obviously doesn't want anyone to know about her escapades. As soon as she sees that I'm chilled, she will be too, and everything will be fine.

Mrs. Ashworth turns to our table, equally amused by Suki. To my surprise, she doesn't ignore me, and she doesn't urge her companions to leave. "Is this your daughter?" she asks instead. "She's adorable."

"Yeah," I say, a little uncomfortable. I don't like clients knowing anything private about me, but I can't ignore them, pick up Suki and walk off either, so I put an arm around her and pretend to be amused. "She's got a lot to say today; she's not normally that talkative."

"She seems very bright for her age. She must get that from her mother." Mrs. Ashworth is giving me the eye, turning sideways so that the couple opposite her can't see what she's doing. So far, I've managed to keep my private life separate from my escort work, but this is getting too close to home and the look she's giving me is making me feel highly uncomfortable, especially with Suki here.

"She's clever all right." I give them a polite smile and turn to Juliette. "How about we finish this on the beach?"

"What? That makes no sense. We came early because..." Juliette falls silent when she finally takes her attention off her food for a moment and looks up to see Mrs. Ashworth staring at me. I'm not sure if Juliette remembers who she is, she must cross-check many clients a week, but a subtle flinch tells me that she does. I'm grateful when she starts packing up Cameron's food, despite his protests.

"Do you live by the beach?" Mrs. Ashworth asks Suki. "If you're such a good swimmer?"

"No. I live in Sag Harbor. Number forty-nine Main Street," Suki says matter-of-factly, then starts rattling off the information I taught her to memorize in case she ever got lost. "My mommy is Belle Rodgers and her number is—"

"Okay, that's enough, Suki," I interrupt her. "Only if you can't find me, remember?"

The couple laughs, but Mrs. Ashworth seems fascinated. "Sag Harbor is nice," she says. "We went there for dinner yesterday." She gestures to her companions. "My kids are visiting for the weekend."

"How lovely. Well, you've certainly got the weather on your side." I try to sound casual as I close the cardboard containers and pile them up.

"Do you all live there together?" Mrs. Ashworth asks Suki.

"Mom, that's a bit intrusive, don't you think?" Her daughter shoots her a puzzled look, clearly confused as to why her mother is so interested in our lives.

"Yes, we do," Juliette lies with a smile, rescuing me by pretending to be my partner.

I note that Mrs. Ashworth is now following Juliette with her eyes. "Excuse us. We promised our kids we'd eat on the beach. Have a lovely day."

"But you said we were going to the pool," Cameron protests through the mouthful he's still chewing as Juliette pulls him along toward the car. "I don't want to go to the beach. I want to go to the pool."

"Yes, we're going to the pool, don't worry." Juliette whispers, strapping them both in while I start the engine.

"I'm so sorry about that." I glance in the rearview mirror as I drive off, half expecting Mrs. Ashworth to be following us like some delusional maniac. "I'll stop somewhere nice where we can sit down for a picnic."

"Don't worry. It's not your fault, that woman is—" She turns on the music loudly so Suki and Cameron can't hear her in the back. "She's creepy as fuck, even seemed a bit obsessed."

"Tell me about it. She wasn't like that when I last saw her. I mean, she certainly didn't ask me any personal questions."

"God, you just never know, do you?" Juliette shrugs. "I can only check if they don't have a record and if they are who they say they are. I can't check for lunacy unfortunately. But

I'll put a red-flag in the booking system, so she won't be able to book you again."

"That's probably for the best." Letting out a sigh of relief, I pull into the nearest beachside road where a sign tells me there are picnic tables. "Let's just forget about it and enjoy our lunch. I'm sure it will be fine."

This Monday morning couldn't have been more different from last week. I'm still on edge, but for other reasons entirely. It's not Nicole's absence that's gotten me jittery, but rather the anticipation of seeing Belle this morning. I'm dressed in leggings and a crop top as I'm going to yoga later and feeling a little self-conscious at the amount of skin on display, but I'm sure most of Belle's clients walk around in skimpy bikinis while she's working. I doubt any of them look at her the way I do, though. Or do they? What if Mrs. Roberts from next-door is into female escorts? What if someone from my yoga class has slept with her?

It's only been a week since I first saw Belle, but it feels so much longer. When something consumes your mind twenty-four seven, time seems to slow down and I can't stop thinking about Friday, and about our encounter on Saturday. I think she's worked out that I know she works for Hamptons' Escorts, I'm sure of that. Not that she gave anything away when we saw her in Sag Harbor; she was nothing but friendly and relaxed. I've replayed our conversation in front of the photography store—which was highly awkward from my side—over and over in my mind, wishing I'd said something different. Wishing I had come across as a grounded, carefree woman with a flirty edge—but not flirty enough for her to know how much I desire her—when in reality all I did was come across as a clumsy idiot.

The wind and the ocean block out the noise from the front of the house, and I can't hear the gates open, so when she appears again, it's like a welcome surprise and I feel my face light up at the sight of her. *I'm such a looser.* I try to wipe the smirk off my face as I stand there, looking like a one-woman welcome committee. *Almost forty and obsessed with the pool girl. It's pathetic. Utterly pathetic.* "Hi, Belle."

"Good morning, Reina." Belle gives me a wave and takes a moment to admire the view before she turns back to me. "Not a cloud on the horizon."

"Yes," I say, cursing myself for being once again, lost for words. Like an addict, I'm waiting for my next hit of her and she doesn't disappoint. My body fills with heat and adrenaline floods my veins. It's delicious and worrying at the same time. "I was just admiring the blue sky. Coffee?"

Belle looks at the machine room, then lingers for a moment before she shrugs and walks around the pool toward the terrace. "Sure. I'd love one."

Her coffee is already waiting, and it's still warm when I lift the cup from underneath the machine.

"Have you tried out your new camera yet?" she asks, taking a sip.

"Yes. I went for a walk this morning; figured out all the settings. It's amazing. So much better than my previous one."

"Good." She smiles. "Can I see some of your shots?"

"Oh…" Biting my lip, I glance inside at the camera on the living room table. "I'm not sure how good they are. I'm not a professional, but you're welcome to have a look…" I fetch it and switch it to 'view' mode, then hand it to her.

"I know nothing about photography, but these are beautiful," she says, flicking through the photographs I took during sunrise this morning. Inching closer, she points out a close-up of a seagull with a fish in its bill. The upcoming sun is framing its head like a halo, and in the right-hand corner, an incoming wave is splashing against a rock. "And this one's incredible."

"Thank you. I was happy with that one too." I can feel Belle's breath misting over my neck when she speaks, and her body is almost touching mine as we scroll through the pictures together.

"You're very talented, Reina." When she turns to me to hand the camera back, our eyes lock, and I find myself unable to move, and unable to look away. There's no way she'll miss the longing in my gaze, but I can't help myself. "Are you okay?" she whispers after a long silence. There's something different about our interaction today. It's more intimate, like we're sharing an unspoken secret.

"Uh-huh," I say, swallowing hard as I put the camera on the terrace table.

Belle nods, never taking her eyes off mine, and with that look, she's crossed the line of professionalism. This is not a conversation between employer and employee. "You seem nervous around me." Her long lashes flutter as she lowers her gaze to my lips. "Are you?"

"I am."

"And is that a bad thing?" she asks when I don't elaborate.

"Depends."

"You're not making this easy for me, with your one syllable answers." She chuckles and brings her hand to my hair, brushing a dark lock behind my ear.

"Sorry…" I can barely hold myself up. My legs feel like

jelly and my heart is beating so fast that I'm sure she can hear it. This can only go one of two ways; either she walks away, or she kisses me right now, because the way she's looking at me, she might as well. "It's difficult for me to explain. It makes no sense, but…" I shake my head, because I just can't say it. "Never mind."

Belle's expression changes in the most magical way. Her eyes darken, and a flirty smile plays around her mouth, causing her dimples to deepen. It makes me weak and wet and all mushy inside. "You know I work for Hamptons' Escorts, right?"

There's a long silence between us. Whether it's real attraction, or whether she's just fishing for a new client, I have no idea, but right now, I don't care. "Yes, I saw you on the website."

"And you were browsing the female escorts?" Her tone is strangely soft and reassuring.

"Yes. I didn't expect to see you on there."

Belle chuckles. "I can imagine that came as a surprise; I don't make a habit of telling people." She continues to stare at my mouth, and I feel wetness pool between my thighs. I wish she would grab my face and kiss me senseless, but she doesn't. "If you're interested, Reina, if there's some part of you that I can help you explore, then my schedule's free tomorrow night."

I take in a quick breath and inch back a little, because this feels more real than I ever intended it to be. Now that my secret is out, it scares me more than anything, yet I'm unable to tear my eyes away from her lips. "Oh…" Leaning against the patio table, my hand is grasping the tabletop so hard my knuckle turns white, and she covers it with her own.

"I'm sorry. I've overstepped." She doesn't look one bit sorry as she says it.

"No, it's fine." Panic takes over and again, I have no idea

what to say or how to behave, so I take a step toward the door and stare up at her, hoping I don't look terrified. "I have to go," I hear myself say, and turn to grab my bag. "Yoga."

BELLE - MONDAY

Okay, I've said it. I've planted the suggestion in her mind. Reina wanted me; I could see it in her eyes, and I wonder if she sensed the same desire in mine. She disappeared so fast I barely saw her leave, her tires screeching as she drove off. Last week, she didn't leave until ten am, so I know she's early and has too much time on her hands to think. I imagine her sitting in the car in front of the yoga studio, wondering what the fuck just happened. Flushed, taking long, deep breaths in the driver's seat, her eyes closed and her head tilted back, exposing her delicate, elegant neck. A rush of arousal courses through me and I imagine running my tongue over it. I didn't mean to make her feel uncomfortable, but she'll come around and I'm confident she won't file a complaint against me.

My flirting was reckless, but I don't regret it. Although I desperately wanted to kiss her and I believe she may have welcomed my mouth, I couldn't. Not only because it would have been highly inappropriate considering I'm here to work but also because it would have sent out the message that I'm seriously into her. Yes, I find myself drawn to her, but she can never know that. This way, if she books me, I get to sleep with a woman I'm attracted to and Reina gets to explore her sexuality and feel very, very satisfied afterward.

My clients feel good after a visit from me, not because I'm so amazing at what I do, but because they crave physical contact and attention, and because deep down, they've always been curious about women. I've been doing this work for three years and I've yet to come across an 'out' lesbian client. Most of them are straight, or so they claim, and it's liberating for them to let go without having to worry about their family finding out, or their friends judging them. They don't have to stress about being a good lover in an unknown territory either. They can simply lie back and enjoy the ride. Reina is no different and if she takes the plunge, I know I can make her feel amazing. And if she changes her mind and decides women are not her thing, well, then at least I've helped her figure that part out.

It was a lucky coincidence that my Tuesday night became available. Worried that Mrs. Ashworth was getting too invested after our run in during lunch, Juliette cancelled her standing booking. I'm not comfortable with her talking to Suki and knowing where I live, and I don't want to see her again. Certain clients have gone a step too far over the years, following me around or declaring their eternal love, and that's the point where I call it a day. I'm not on social media and they don't know my real name but people with money have a way of figuring out what I don't want them to know. There is no love between an escort and a client; it's all in their heads. It's a fantasy that would never work in real life, but some fail to acknowledge that. I simply don't see how a transaction and feelings can go hand in hand, they're two entirely different concepts. Love is not for sale, ever, and love can only develop when the circumstances are realistic. Everything else is just a jumble of false emotions and desire.

When the front door slams and the housekeeper walks in, I realize I've been daydreaming, still standing next to the terrace table where Reina left me with my coffee in hand.

"Good morning. It's Belle, right?" She says, leaning against the back door. "I'm Nola."

"Yes, good morning, Nola. How are you?"

"I'm good, thank you. Is Miss Amari not in?" She glances over her shoulder around the open living space, then out at the yard.

"She went to yoga," I say, and down my coffee. "She just left."

"Oh." Nola frowns as she checks her watch, then walks back into the kitchen. "Do you want another coffee?" she asks, turning on the machine.

"No thank you, I'd better get back to work." I don't think Nola hears me as the sound of grinding beans echoes through the kitchen.

"How is Barry?" she yells over the noise.

"I'm not sure," I say honestly. "I don't know him very well, but they've scheduled me in for six weeks, so I suppose that's when they expect him to be back at work."

"Okay, I hope he recovers." Just as I'm about to turn back to the pool, Nola brings two coffees over. "Anyway, if I'll be seeing you on a regular basis, we might as well get to know each other, right?" She hands me a cup. "I'm here three to four days a week, just half days. Miss Amari doesn't make much mess on her own, so I work for other people too."

"Rei—" I stop myself there. "Miss Amari seems like a nice person to work for."

Nola shoots me a puzzled look, aware that I was about to use her first name. She stares at me for a beat, then continues without enquiring further. "Yes, she's very kind. I promise you won't have any trouble working here. Where do you live?"

"Sag Harbor. I have an apartment on Main Street."

Nola whistles through her teeth. "That's pricey. How can you afford that?"

I'm not surprised she asks me this. We're both staff on basic pay, no different to each other and Sag Harbor is pricey indeed. Truth is, if it wasn't for my escort job, we would have still lived with my father. "It's only small. I make it work."

"Hmm…" She pauses and regards me again. "I live in Holbrook, close to the airport. In a basement apartment with my husband and two kids," she adds. "Troublemakers, all of them including my husband. Are you married?"

"No, but I have a young daughter."

"Oh…" Nola sits down and props her feet up. "Tell me about her." She clearly has no intention of doing any work quite yet. Glancing at my watch, then at the spotless pool, I decide that I can spare another five minutes, so I sit down with her and enjoy the morning sun.

"*D*o it," Sascha whispers. "Do it, do it, do it."

"Shh…" I utter, fighting to keep my backward position in the King Pigeon pose. After having Eddie, I took up yoga and although I don't religiously practice every day, I do just fine in the advanced class. "Not here."

"Come on, you have to. She practically dared you to, you can't back out now." I regret updating Sasha before class as she's so excited for me that she can't stop talking about it.

"Sasha, I said not here," I hiss.

"Silence, please. Come on, ladies. Just five more minutes and then you can talk all you want." Our instructor walks between the struggling bodies and starts counting down from ten. "That's good. Now slowly come out of your position, shift onto your hands and knees and get down into Child's Pose."

I let out a long sigh of relief when I finally bend forward, relieving my muscles from the strain. Stretching my arms out in front of me, I bring my head between my knees and concentrate on my breathing. *In, hold, out, hold. In, hold, out, hold.* My shoulders feel lighter already. I should really attend more than one class a week, especially when I'm so tense.

"Okay, now sit up, slowly move your legs in front of you and lie down on your back." Our instructor is still standing next to us, making sure we won't interrupt his class again.

We do as he says, and I close my eyes. Normally, I drift right into a blissful state of nothingness, but I can't seem to do that today. Sasha has always envied me for being able to meditate. She told me all she thinks about during this part of the class is our Argentinian instructor on top of her, minus his tight pants. I must be the only woman in class who hasn't got a thing for him, and I think I know why now. My mind drifts to Belle and her lips, to her eyes staring into mine with that curious and indeed—Sasha wasn't wrong—daring glimmer. *If you're interested, Reina, if there's some part of you that I can help you explore, then my schedule's free tomorrow night...*

"Hey, wake up." Sasha pokes me and I shoot up.

"Oh, sorry." I blink, disappointed to be ripped out of my daydream.

"You've never dozed off in class." She holds out a hand to help me up and I grab my bag and follow her outside to our cars.

"I didn't doze off. Want to get a juice?"

A mischievous smile plays around Sasha's lips. "I don't think we'll have time for that." She points to my purse. "Give me your phone."

"Why?"

"Just give me your phone."

Lacking the energy to argue with her, I unlock it and hand it over. "What are you doing?" I look over her shoulder and see that she's on the Hamptons' Escorts site, scrolling down Belle's page to the 'book' button. "Hey, stop it!"

"Back off, I'm helping you," she simply states, pulling away when I try to snatch my phone out of her hands. "You know you want to, and Belle's not awkward about it as she practically told you to book her."

"But I don't know if I'm ready yet. I don't think I am."

"You'll never be ready, so you might as well rip off the Band-Aid and do it." Sasha shamelessly takes out a couple of cards from the leather slots in my phone cover and holds up one of my credit cards. "Is this one okay to use?"

I open my mouth to protest but I'm out of excuses. I can always cancel, I think to myself, and that's probably what I'll do when I get home. "Yeah, that one's fine," I say with a resigned sigh.

"Great." Sasha looks giddy as she enters my card details and waits for the confirmation page to appear. "All booked, subject to a criminal check..." She then takes my driver's license, snaps a picture of it and uploads it. "They'll confirm in two hours. Tomorrow night, eight-thirty to midnight. Belle will make all your fantasies come true," she quotes the page in a teasing tone.

"Fuck," I mutter. "This is the most terrifying thing I've ever done. What if she doesn't like me? What if she's repulsed by me?"

Sasha laughs. "She won't be repulsed. From what you told me, there might even be some mutual attraction and besides, it's her job. This is for your pleasure and yours only."

"It doesn't feel right to pay for sex," I say.

"Trust me; you'll change your mind about that soon enough."

I sit down on the brick wall behind my car and let it all sink in. *Belle is booked for tomorrow night. A person, a woman, booked for sex. I'm going to have sex with Belle. I'm going to have sex with a woman for the first time in my life. For hours, I'm going to have everything I fantasized about in the past week. Or maybe I won't. Maybe I'll realize it was just some silly infatuation, and that in hindsight, I'm not attracted to women at all. Maybe I'll disap-*

point her. Maybe she'll laugh at me. At that, I burst into tears, and no matter how hard I try, I can't stop crying.

"Hey, come here." Sasha must be shocked as she's never seen me like this. She takes me into her arms and squeezes me tight. "I'm so sorry, that was out of order, I shouldn't have pressured you. Do you want me to cancel it?"

Shaking my head, I sniff and wipe my nose. "No, it's not you. Well, it is you," I say with an uncomfortable chuckle. "But you did what I'd never dare to do, so thank you for that. But…" My breaths become quicker again, and I force back another outburst. "I just feel so insecure."

To my surprise, Sasha's eyes well up too. She squeezes my shoulders before she lets go and lifts my chin to meet her eyes. "Reina, you are so amazing. Do you even realize that most of the men in our circles would kill to be with you? Not that you care, of course," she adds with a hint of humor. "I get why I've never seen you flirt with another man now. It all makes sense, you just preferred women and you didn't even know it. But believe me, you are a very attractive woman."

"Right." I sniff again and clear my throat. "You're biased because you're my friend, but I appreciate the pep talk."

"Bullshit." Sasha pulls me up, takes me by my shoulders and turns me toward the car window so I can see my reflection. "Look at yourself, Reina. You're a beautiful, exotic woman in the prime of your life. You don't need to worry about money, you're single, your kids have moved out and this is your time to shine, to pursue your dreams and figure out what inspires you. So go figure it out. Take a good look at your life and ask yourself what it is that you want. You have the world at your feet and its time you explored your options. We both know there's one thing you crave so start with that and by tomorrow, you'll be able to tick that one off your list."

I nod and take a deep breath. "Okay. It's just so…" I pause. "So soon."

"Anything new and scary always feels like it's too soon. But we have…" Sasha checks her gold watch. "At least six hours to shop for lingerie and something snazzy to wear before I have to be back home, and we can stop off for a pedicure and a wax on the way to the mall." She winks. "Preparation is the best medicine for nerves."

"*H*ey babe, guess what? You have a brand-new client tomorrow." Juliette is ringing just as I'm driving home from my last job of the day.

"Oh... It's been a while since I've had a first," I say. "But I suppose the summer season is starting." Approaching a traffic light, I slow down and groan at the line of cars in front of me. The roads are getting busier by the day and soon it will take me double the time to get anywhere. "Where am I going? Hotel? Home?"

"Southampton, private home. Reina Amari. I ran a check, she's all clean." Juliette sighs when I don't reply. "What's the matter? Not feeling it? I can email her and cancel."

Opening the window, I suck in fresh air. Even after our forward exchange this morning I didn't expect Reina to book me so soon—if not at all—and it comes as both a pleasant surprise and a terrifying shock to my system. *Reina Amari.* The car in front of me is coming to a halt again. So many traffic lights. "No, don't cancel her," I finally say in a strangled voice. It's like I'm back in my old life in New York, looking forward to a night with a woman I'm seriously into, and I forgot what it felt like. The butterflies, the anticipation, only this time it's much, much stronger and I feel nervous as hell.

"Okay. What's up? Do you know her?"

"Yeah." The tightness in my core is killing me and I squeeze my thighs together as I drive down the main road at a snail's pace. "Remember that woman I told you about? The one whose pool I service?"

Juliette gasps. "Don't tell me it's her. Is it her?"

"Yeah. It's Reina. I can't believe she's booked me."

"Did you tell her about Hamptons' Escorts?"

"No, it was just a crazy coincidence. She saw me on the website and recognized me." I pause. "Jules, this has never happened to me before. Being booked by someone who knows who I am."

"Well, you did say you had the hots for her," Juliette says.

"Yes, I'm insanely attracted to her." I clear my throat and try to sound less on edge than I am right now, because sleeping with Reina Amari is pressure personified. "So, eight-thirty? Any requests?"

"No, nothing in the notes."

"I'm not surprised. I don't think she knows what she wants, and she may not even go ahead with it. As far as I'm aware, she's never been with a woman." I bet I'm just as on edge as Reina is right now, but Juliette doesn't need to know that. "Don't be surprised if she cancels."

"Well, you know the deal. No refunds ten hours before booking."

"I know, but I doubt the money would be an issue to her."

"Hmm... You like her, she likes you. Go figure." Juliette chuckles. "She'd make a perfect sugar mama."

"Hey, that's not funny, you know I'm not like that." Blowing out my cheeks, I release a deep sigh. "Sorry, I didn't mean to snap. I'm just worried that... What if she's not into me?"

"You mean what if she's not into lesbian sex? Are you kidding me? You never say stuff like that." Juliette is laughing out loud now. "Where did my ultra-confident friend Belle go? You used to brag you could convert any woman to your team."

"Yeah, well, I'm a different person now," I say. "Besides, I haven't slept with someone I've actually been into for years. It's a little daunting."

"You'll be fine, it's like riding a bike" she assures me, still in an amused tone. "And if Reina decides that she's not into women after all, then that won't be on you. It will simply confirm her preference of gender. And then that will put an end to it."

"Right." I drape my arm over the edge of the window and take a deep breath. This morning when I was face to face with Reina and longing to kiss her, everything seemed so simple. It was like my one-track mind from three years ago, from before Suki, had taken over and I'd lost all ability to think straight and weight out the consequences of my actions. What was I thinking? That it would be a good idea for her to hire me for sex just because I wanted her? That after that, everything would go back to normal and that I'd show up to service her pool and we'd have a coffee together as if nothing had happened? "I just haven't thought this through. If I'm being honest, I did encourage her, and I shouldn't have done that."

"Don't worry," Juliette says, once more trying to put me at ease. "You're making too big of a deal out of this. It's a transaction for a service and Reina's no different from your previous clients other than that you find her smoking hot. And I don't see how that can be a bad thing." When I don't reply, she says: "Belle? Are you there?"

A car horn beeps behind me and I realize I'm standing still in front of a green light. "Yes, I'm here." I clear my throat and pull myself together as I move away. "You're right. I'm making a big deal out of this and it's not. I'll make sure Reina Amari has the best time tomorrow."

"That's the spirit. Listen, I'll send a cold bottle of champagne along with your driver. Courtesy of Hamptons' Escorts for our new client. I've got another call here, so I've got to go. Good luck tomorrow, okay?"

After Juliette hangs up, I continue my drive in a state of mild anxiety. But then I remember that I have to pay three months upfront for the storage unit I've just signed the lease for. *Just a little longer.* And in the months I have left, I might as well have some fun along the way.

*B*y the time the intercom alerts me someone's at the gate I'm so nervous that I contemplate ignoring it. I've paid, so it wouldn't be a crime to make Belle head back into the night. In fact, I imagine she'd be delighted with the easiest twenty-seven hundred dollars ever made, plus it will save us both the awkwardness next time we see each other. The repetitive sound of the buzzer puts me on edge and although the black Honda Accord I see on my screen is discreet and doesn't carry a logo, I'm still imagining my neighbors talking about it as it pulls up on my drive. What had I expected? That she'd let herself in using her Pool Masters fob and suddenly appear in my living room wearing only a pair of dungarees and her red cap?

I wait, leaning back against the fridge door, hoping she'll get the hint when I pretend not to be home. But the gate buzzes again and again, and anxious to make it stop, I walk over to the device on the wall to open the gates anyway. Not raised to ignore people, the least I can do is offer her a drink and explain that this was all a big mistake. That I'm really not the kind of woman who would pay for physical pleasure and that I just got carried away, confused while going through a difficult time in my life.

When I open the front door and watch her get out of the car, I see that she's dressed not much differently to when I saw her in Sag Harbor, apart from her face that is disguised behind large Aviator sunglasses. Although her white linen shirt and blue jeans don't make her stand out, she looks sexier than ever, like she was born to wear them.

"Hi, Reina. I was afraid you might not let me in," she says in a husky voice, removing her shades to take me in.

"Would that have been so bad?" I open the door further and she waves at the driver, then brushes past me.

"Yes. I think it would have been a shame for the both of us. You look gorgeous by the way." Belle points to my new, soft pink satin robe. After trying on numerous dresses—none of which I felt comfortable in—Sasha came up with the idea of getting this instead. She assured me that it was the perfect garment as it's elegant and comes off easily but now I just feel like a fraud, like I'm playing some twisted game, that I'm trying to appear hard to get. I can't go through with this and I don't know how to tell her.

"Thank you." I instinctively close my robe a little further and step back. "I've ehm... I've actually changed my mind. I can't do this and I'm sorry you came all the way out here. Please stay for a drink, though, I don't want it to be awkward." Her car turns on my driveway and heads back toward the gates. "Maybe you should wave him back? Ask him to wait?"

"It's fine. He's never far." Belle puts a hand on my shoulder. "And I totally understand if you've changed your mind." She smiles at me and holds up a bottle of champagne. "But since you mentioned that drink, we might as well have this. Shall I open it? It's cold."

"Okay. Thank you." I gesture to the couch. "Please sit down. Unless you prefer to be outside?"

"Yeah, let's go outside. It's a lovely evening." Belle crosses the room to the back terrace and opens the bottle on her way. Instead of heading for the dining table, she chooses the two-seater couch by the pool and sits back with her legs stretched out in front of her and her ankles crossed, her chest pushed out as if she's ready to take on the world. She's behaving differently tonight, more assertive. Maybe she's playing a role, maybe this is the real her, but my reaction is the same either way. Arousal floods my system as I grab two champagne flutes from the kitchen cupboard. She looks so good, so fresh, so self-assured and she seems totally unfazed by this unusual situation. Yesterday, there were boundaries in place, but tonight, she has an air of command about her that is incredibly sexy. I really wish I could do this; God knows I want her, but I'm too terrified.

Belle fills the glasses, then taps the space next to her. "Come sit here," she says, looking me over once more. Her smoldering eyes set me on fire and her gaze leaves a trail of flames all over my body. I know exactly what she's doing, but I sit down anyway. I'm sure this isn't the first time a woman has freaked out after booking an escort and Belle's clearly trying to put me at ease so I might change my mind. I wonder why, though. What would she get out of it?

She hands me my glass and we clink before taking a sip. The way she licks away a drop from her lips, slowly, deliberately is an act of seduction—one I'm sure she's performed many times before. *Is she enjoying this?*

"Don't be nervous," she says, placing a hand on my thigh. "We're just having a drink and if you want me to leave after, I'll go. We don't have to do anything."

"I know." So many questions tumble through my head, and I take a moment to get my thoughts in order. It's hard to think with her hand there, sending a delicious ache between my thighs. "How long have you been doing this?" I finally ask after a long silence.

"Three years." Belle smiles. "And you're probably wondering *why* I'm doing this…"

I shake my head. "I don't want to overstep. That's your private business and I'm sure you don't normally discuss things like that with your clients."

"True. But my clients generally don't know who I am. They don't even know my real name, but you do. So, I'm happy to tell you why I do this, if you tell me why you booked me. That's a fair exchange, don't you think?" Belle takes another sip of her champagne and continues when I don't answer. "Like most, I started escorting for money. I was a bit of a wild child, three years ago, living with friends in New York and going out every night, when Suki suddenly became a part of my life."

"But I thought Suki was four," I say. "Did you adopt her?"

"Something like that. But that's a story for another time." A hint of sadness crosses Belle's features. "I moved back to the Hamptons and needed to give her a home, a stable environment, and escorting seemed like a quick and fairly pleasant way to provide the means to an end." She shrugs, and as quick as it came, the glimmer of sadness is gone. "I like sex, you see. Sex with women, and so far, I haven't regretted doing what I do. A friend of mine suggested it; she's a booker for Hamptons' Escorts and I had a reputation with women back then, so she figured I'd be good at it. It was only meant to be for a year, this side job, until I got us an apartment and saved up enough money for emergencies. But here I am, three years later. We've moved, I've had my life— our life—in order for a while, but escorting is easy and fun and so I keep putting off quitting. I'll give it up soon, though. I don't want Suki to know and it's only a matter of time before someone in our circles—and with that I mean the moms from preschool—find out. But another couple of months won't hurt."

"So you enjoy this…" I say, sounding surprised. "With all your clients?"

"Most of them." Belle smiles. "So far, at least. Every woman is beautiful in her own way, and I like to make them feel good." She moves her arm to the backrest of the couch and plays with a lock of my hair.

"Hmm…" My eyes flutter closed for a beat and I shudder, the sensation so overwhelming that I have to remind myself to breathe. *In, out. In, out. It's just my hair.* The champagne is going to my head as I haven't been able to eat all day.

"Your turn, Reina," Belle says softly. "When I saw that business card, I knew it was yours, and not your ex-husband's. I hope I wasn't out of line."

"No, it's fine. But how did you know it was mine?"

"You were nervous around me. And that meant you'd been checking out the women."

"It must have surprised you," I say. "I'm not the type."

"Not really. Most of my clients are actually married to men and would consider themselves to be straight."

"Really?" Mentally scrolling through my list of female friends and acquaintances, I wonder if anyone I know has slept with Belle.

"Yeah. So why you?" she asks.

"A friend recommended me to the company; she'd booked a male escort through them," I say. "I only looked because…" My voice trails away and I pause. "I don't really know why I looked, I was curious I suppose, and I found myself going straight to the female section. And then I saw you…" I stop myself again; I can't tell her I have this ridiculous crush on her.

"And your curiosity turned into interest," Belle concludes.

"It appears so."

"Have you been with a woman before?" Belle trails a finger down the length of my neck and rests her hand on my shoulder.

"No," I say in a breathless voice, staring down at her hand as if it's about to pull me into the vortex of all my fears and desires combined. A warm glow spreads between my legs and I feel something I've never felt before. It's an intense sensation, a need for her to touch me there so strong that I almost drop my glass. With a trembling hand, I put it on the table and have no idea what to do with myself. Leaning back again is daunting, so I stay perched on the edge of the couch.

"Do you mind if I touch you?" Belle asks, shifting closer and facing me. "Be honest."

"No, I don't mind. I like it." I wish I had the ability to say something witty, or at least something more articulate, but words fail me. When she brushes my cheek and looks into my eyes, I know I want this more than anything in the world.

"Good." Belle's lips pull into a small, flirty smile as she leans in, agonizingly slow, bringing her mouth to mine. Her hand moves to the back of my neck and she caresses me with her thumb. "Can I kiss you?" she asks.

I hesitate for long moments, then nod, and the moment her soft lips brush mine, I become liquid. It's like every part of me melts until there's not a single solid cell left in my body. Even my thoughts feel like hot lava, slowly rolling over rock, demolishing the old and creating a new, yet unknown landscape. Somewhere in the back of my mind, vague thoughts linger. Soft... So soft... More...

Belle's luscious lips part, and she pulls me tighter against her. In a sexy, languid pace she explores my mouth, taking her time before her tongue meets mine. I moan and allow myself to sink into the kiss, to let her have me. It's indulgent, exciting, arousing and so many things I can't even name. I read somewhere that escorts don't kiss their clients, and I forgot to ask Sasha about it, so I wasn't prepared for this. Not for the kiss, and not for what it would do to me. Not for how it would turn me liquid.

For one blissful moment, I also forget that I've paid for this and when I remember, I immediately push the thought away again and run my fingers through her silky, dark hair. Right now, I just want to pretend. She tastes of mint and champagne; a strange but delicious combination I'll cherish in my memories forever. Everything about this kiss will stay with me; I'll make sure I never forget. The scent of fresh citrus on her body, the sensual touch of her hand slipping into my robe, stroking my shoulder blade, her lips, more persistent now as she tilts her head and deepens the kiss. I moan again, louder this time and the sound of this newfound pleasure—my own sound—is alien to me. Belle moans too, so quietly that I can barely hear it. Is it real? Or is this just what she does? I push that question away too, as I don't want anything to ruin the moment.

When she pulls away and trails a thumb over my cheek, I shiver and meet her eyes. She looks aroused, but maybe that's just my wishful thinking.

"Did you like that?" she asks.

I don't need to answer; I know my expression says it all, but I stammer a reply anyway. "That... That was amazing."

Belle bites her bottom lip and leans in again. "You're a very, very good kisser, Reina." This time, she's less careful in her approach, kissing me like she's taking what *she* wants, and it sends me into a frenzy of sensory overload. All I want is more, and Belle gives it to me. Pushing me back into the couch cushions, she shifts so her upper body covers mine. Her warmth and weight feel like water after crossing a desert, and I drink her in greedily. There's no going back now; I couldn't even if I tried.

My nerves have subsided, pushed away by a desire so deep I could drown in it. I don't need to prove myself to her; she just wants to make me feel good, and so I relax into her caress and decide to trust her entirely.

Kissing her way down my neck, Belle sucks and bites at my flesh and with every tiny sting, I twitch and moan. She shifts and wedges her hand into my robe, tracing the curve of my breasts over my new bra. I gasp when she skims my nipples that have never felt so sensitive before. My body is ready for this. *I'm* ready for this.

"How about you show me your bedroom," Belle says when she tears herself away from my neck. Her gaze lowers to my mouth, as if she's genuinely dying to kiss me again.

"Are you sure?" I whisper, then chuckle when I realize how ridiculous that question is.

"Yeah." Belle shoots me an amused look. "But only if you are."

BELLE - TUESDAY

Reina's robe falls open, revealing a glimpse of her body underneath the satin fabric. My reaction is intense; a hunger, a profound need to make her come so hard she'll book me again and again and again because it's the only way I'll ever have her. That kiss slayed me and she has no idea that I need this as much as she does.

Nerves flare through my core as I follow her up the ultra-modern, floating staircase, watching her hips sway before me. It's strange as I've only felt this nervous twice: the first time I had sex, and before my first job as an escort. I know she has a thing for me; no one reacts to me like she does. Sure, I'm confident and I know what I'm doing, but this longing is something I haven't witnessed with any of my clients, nor any of my previous girlfriends before. It's the longing of a woman who has repressed her sexuality her whole adult life. That side of her is begging to be discovered and I'm the lucky person who gets to feed her appetite and fulfill her desires. And I want her. I genuinely want her. Tonight is not a job; it's a privilege, an honor. Nothing could have prepared me for how it would feel to have my lips on hers.

Reina's hand is trembling as she opens her bedroom door. It's a beautiful modern space, just like the rest of the house. In other circumstances, I'd comment on the spectacular view, the floor to ceiling windows or her enormous wooden bed with its hand-carved headboard, but tonight, my attention is undivided. The last slivers of sun cast a warm glow through the room, and the tall palm tree blowing in the wind outside creates a theatrical shadow over the high, white walls, occasionally brushing dark shapes over her angelic face.

"Can I take this off?" I ask, inching my thumbs under the lapel of her robe.

Reina takes a deep breath before she pulls at the tie, causing the robe to fall open. "I've had two kids," she says, practically apologizing for her body that is absolutely stunning beyond belief. Her full, real breasts are like a breath of fresh air compared to the enhanced and lifted ones that are practically the norm in the Hamptons, and her skin has the color of honey. My guess is she hasn't been told how gorgeous she is often enough, and it saddens me that she's insecure.

"You are so incredibly beautiful," I whisper, and I mean it from the bottom of my heart. The champagne-colored lingerie set frames her figure like a work of art, hugging and emphasizing her subtle curves. When I slide off her robe, Reina smiles shyly and crosses her arms in front of her chest, but I take her hands and kiss them.

"I think you should lie down," I say, pointing to the bed. While she lowers herself against the abundance of stunning cushions in the middle of the bed, I start unbuttoning my shirt and let it fall to the floor.

Reina glances at my small breasts in the white Calvin Klein sports bra, then shifts her attention to my fingers now undoing my jeans. She looks intrigued, curious and as I slide them down, revealing matching white briefs, she licks her lips and intense sexual need flashes in her eyes. Standing there for long moments, I give her time to take me in. She's never been with a woman, so I need to take this slow, let her get used to seeing my body.

"Fuck..." she mutters, and that surprises me as Reina doesn't seem like the type of woman to use such profanities.

I shoot her a flirty smile and get on the bed, then position myself on my hands and knees over her, my mouth lingering just above hers. "Just tell me if you want me to stop, okay?"

She nods and lifts her head slightly, her eyes begging me to kiss her. Kissing Reina is confusing because it makes me lose control. It's arousing, all-consuming and organic, like a free-flowing river. She pulls me in and I moan as we swallow each other whole. Her arms are around me and her nails scrape over my back as I turn to her neck and trail soft kisses down to her collarbone and her breasts, following the edge of her bra. At this point I'd normally ask my clients what they want, but I doubt Reina has any idea. She's enjoying this, though; the way she moves, lifting her chest to meet my mouth is a mesmerizing sight. I slide my hands under her arched back to unhook her bra and meet her eyes to make sure she's comfortable with me taking it off.

To my surprise, Reina swiftly removes it herself and throws it across the room like she's been dying to get it off. The sight of her beautiful breasts makes me salivate and I stare at her nipples that rise and fall rapidly with her quick breaths.

Fuck. I want her so badly. Just a gentle brush of my hand draws a loud moan from her mouth, and when I fold my lips around one of her perfect, hard, pink pebbles, she cries out and bucks her hips. So turned on that I have trouble holding back, I force myself to wait a moment before I move to her other nipple. Her reaction is astonishing and comes from deep, deep within.

"Oh my God," she mumbles, pulling me harder against her. I twirl my tongue around it, then tug gently, using my teeth while I watch her. An eruption of pure joy has settled over her features and she's a beautiful mess, her eyes closed as she moves her head from side to side.

Continuing to kiss my way down her ribcage, I caress her belly and stop just below her navel before moving back up. I want to make her wait, to make her first time last. Her lashes flutter, the hairs on her arms rise and her heart is pounding rapidly when I run my hand back up over her breasts, using my other to steady myself above her. Her nipples are rock hard, her cheeks rosy and her breaths pass her lips in an irregular blend of quick intakes and long exhalations.

"Are you okay?" I ask, more out of courtesy than concern because there's no way she's uncomfortable. Splaying my fingers wide, I caress her and knowing where I'm heading, she's hardly able to answer.

"Uh-huh." Reina's voice goes up a notch, telling me I've hit one of her erogenous zones, just above her hipbone. I'm always observant; it's my job. I aim to get to know my clients' bodies first, explore their reactions to everything I do. Stroking her there again, she moans loudly, and I move down, sink my face against her soft skin and drag my tongue over the spot. "Yes..."

Reina shifts impatiently, and when I tug at her panties, she lifts her hips so I can pull them down. "Please," she mumbles.

My breath hitches at seeing the thin strip of hair between her thighs, at her glistening sex when she spreads her legs a little. I can feel her heat radiating against my chest and long to run my tongue through her wetness and taste her. God, I want to taste her, but I can't because this is a job. Not without protection. I'm afraid to break our organic interaction by walking over to my bag and ripping open the packaging of dental dams, so I slide back up and cover her body with mine.

We both sigh at the contact and fall into a longing kiss, our limbs tangled and our hips thrusting into one another like we're long-lost lovers. My thigh between her legs, my hands in her hair, her leg wrapped around my hips and her fingers squeezing my behind, pulling me tightly against her. Our desperately needy body language is so far removed from the cold reality of an escort and her client and although in theory this makes no sense, it's wonderfully simple and abundantly clear. I want her and she wants me and right now, we need each other in a way that is entirely tangible and physical.

Sliding my hand between her legs, I run a finger through her hot folds, and she lets out a strangled cry and throws her head back.

"I want you," she whispers against my lips. Those three words wash away my restraint and all I want is to make her explode. Her whole body is shaking when I enter her with two fingers, and I kiss her again, moaning as I feel her wetness coating my fingers. Our mouths are locked, our bodies one, and I fuck her slowly and deeply, moving into her as if in a trance. It's beautiful to hear her pleasure, to feel her need, to know that I'm giving her something special that she's never had before. Reina opens up like a flower and sucks me into her deepest depths until I'm lost in her and she's lost in me. I feel her clench when I curl my fingers and lift my head to look at her. She arches her back, her muscles tensing while she holds her breath, her eyes widening at me in surprise. And then, she comes crashing down with a strangled cry and clasps her hand over mine, holding me inside her while she rides out her climax. Her eyes shut tight and her brows furrow, and she bites her bottom lip so hard I'm afraid she'll make it bleed. It's a painfully beautiful moment and not wanting it to end, I draw it out for as long as I can. Stroking her hair with my other hand, I remove dark strands from her clammy forehead. She looks spent and content and sad at the same time and when a tear rolls down her cheek, I brush it away.

"Are you okay?" I'm worried when she doesn't answer right away, her gaze absent as if she's totally lost in thought. But then she smiles and places a hand on my cheek.

"Yeah. I'm just..." Reina pauses, searching for words. "I had no idea," she finally says. "All these years, and I had no idea."

All I can do is smile back because now is not the time for conversation. She needs time to reflect and gather her thoughts. It can't be easy when you find out that you're attracted to women at the age of thirty-nine, especially with a whole life behind you. I kiss her forehead and roll off her, and she nestles herself into the crook of my arm like she belongs there. Holding her tight, I stroke her hair while we lie there in silence, wishing the night would never end.

REINA - TUESDAY

Sandeep never touched me with such understanding. I couldn't even touch myself the way she does. Belle mapped out my body, studied it in detail like it was the only thing that mattered to her, and then she made me explode until I had nothing left to give. Lying in the crook of her arm, draped half on top of her, I wonder if she's like this with all her clients because this is nothing like I imagined an escort experience to be. Perhaps it's different with two women, or maybe she has her own ways. All I know for sure is that my life will never be the same again.

"Do you always keep your underwear on?" I ask, trailing a finger over the elastic of her sports bra.

"Sometimes. I didn't want to overwhelm you." Belle shoots me a wicked smile before she takes it off. "But I think you can handle it now."

Staring at her small, perky breasts I'm not actually sure I *can* handle it, and immediately arousal shoots through me again. I never expected to be so turned on by another woman's breasts, but I realize then that there's nothing more bewitching than her naked form. I'm overcome by an urge to possess her, to explore her body like she explored mine. "Can I touch you?" I ask, so softly I can barely hear myself.

Belle takes my hand and brings it to her breasts, then slides it over the delicate dips and curves. When my fingertips brush her nipples, she closes her eyes and moans softly, and her hand takes a tighter hold of mine. I kiss her because I want her to moan into my mouth, to pour all her pleasure inside of me. "You feel so soft," I say, taking over when she lets go of my hand and starts caressing my back and my behind. I'm like a virgin; clumsy, uncertain, curious but determined. Not determined to get it over with but determined to make this good for her too. My mouth is drawn to her neck and I kiss my way down to her collarbone while I breathe in her lovely scent. Her skin is warm against my lips, her nipples hypersensitive when I run my tongue over them. Smiling at her quick intakes of breath, I know I'm doing something right.

I drag my hand over the smooth skin of her belly but stop when I feel her muscles tense. Does this mean she likes it, or does it mean she doesn't? I don't have a fraction of her confidence, but I do have a deep desire to make her feel good so I'm willing to take my chances. She's in charge and if she's uncomfortable, she'll tell me.

Finally finding the courage to move farther down, I slide my fingertips under the elastic of her boxers and Belle doesn't stop me. She shivers, and when I find her wet, hot flesh, she lets out a soft moan. Her heat stirs my own arousal even more and I feel my hand tremble as I explore her.

Belle's hips shoot up when I drag my fingers back up and repeat the movement, hopeful I'm doing the right thing. It shouldn't be any different from touching myself, but it feels so new to me that I'm second-guessing everything I do. Her breaths quicken, though, and soon, she's moaning louder and spreading her legs apart. Moving over her delicious body, I kiss her, and she laces her fingers through my hair and kisses me back. This touches me to my core. It's knowing that she wants me that makes me ache to give her everything and more. I watch her eyes flutter closed as I stroke her, and without warning, she suddenly tenses up, lets out a long, deep moan and starts shaking underneath me. She's climaxing and all I can do is pull my face away from hers to stare at the mesmerizing sight while I continue to stroke her. With her eyes shut tight, her lips parted, her head tilted back and her whole body trembling she looks like a fallen angel, feeding off our sins.

My face breaks into a huge smile and when she opens her eyes again and sees my smug expression, she chuckles.

"I'm sorry, that wasn't supposed to happen," she mumbles, then covers her face with her hands as if she's mortified. "Oh, God."

"Why?"

"Because you're paying me for *your* pleasure, not mine."

"Are you saying you just had an orgasm?" I ask, drawing out my words in a teasing tone. "I thought you were pretending." The latter is a lie, because what I just witnessed felt very, very real.

Belle laughs. "I wasn't pretending. I'd be ridiculous if I did that."

"Hmm…" I try to wipe the grin off my face but it seems permanent. "So, is it against the rules?"

"Kind of. It's against my rules." She turns on her side to face me and pulls me in. "I don't usually let clients touch me intimately."

"Why not?"

"You sound like Suki," she jokes. "So many questions…"

"I'm sorry." When she nuzzles my cheek, I close my eyes and lean into her touch. It feels comforting and warm, and it makes me want to fall asleep in her arms.

"Don't be." Belle kisses me softly on my lips. "I only do things I know will be pleasant for me, like pleasing others. It's the best way of keeping myself out of uncomfortable situations, otherwise I couldn't do this job. I should have discussed the ground rules with you, but you were so nervous, so I thought it best not to overcomplicate things and just let everything happen naturally."

"I understand. Thank you for making me feel so comfortable." I run my hand over the curve of her hip, marveling at her body. "Why *did* you let me touch you?"

Belle gives me a small smile. "Because I wanted you to." When I roll off her, she turns on her side, props herself onto her elbow and regards me. "You look like you're enjoying this."

"I am. Would you mind if I booked you again?" Dusk is falling, reminding me that time is passing and I wish I could suspend time.

"Of course not, I'd like that very much." Stroking my hair tenderly, Belle seems to ponder over something. "You know, if you did a test, we could have a lot more fun next time."

"A test?" I frown. "You mean an STD test?" For a split second, I almost feel offended as I've only slept with one man in my life. But then I remind myself that this is her job, that she doesn't know me and that I'm no different to any of the other women she sleeps with. And then I remind myself that Sandeep had an affair and that Bree must have had a whole string of lovers before him.

"Yeah. So I can use my tongue on you in a way that will blow your mind," she says, licking her lips. "Trust me, it will be worth it."

Her words make me squirm and now all I can do is stare at her mouth and imagine it between my legs. *Her tongue. Fuck.*

"Think about it," Belle says. "But for now…" She shifts on

top of me and pushes her hips into mine. "For now, we still have time and I want you to lie back and relax."

~

GLORIOUS HOURS PASS and I wish I could function properly, but steamy flashbacks keep overtaking my mind. I'm forgetful, distracted, even totally absent, and when Nola raises her voice and calls my name I'm aware that I haven't taken in a single word of what she just said to me.

"Sorry, what was that?"

"I asked if you're planning on celebrating your birthday," Nola says. "It's in two months, and not to put any pressure on you, but you know how hard it is to arrange something last-minute in the Hamptons, so if you want my help, it would be good to know sooner rather than later."

"Oh right, my birthday." My stomach flips at the thought of turning forty. "I haven't thought about it, to be honest with you. Maybe I'll just skip it altogether this year."

"But you skipped it last year too," Nola says. "I mean, I totally understand that— Sandeep had only just moved out— but don't you think it would be nice to celebrate your fortieth? You seem so much happier now." She pauses. "Although you're also very, very distracted."

"Yeah, I am, sorry. I'll have a think about my birthday." I step out of the tub and put on a fluffy, white robe, then wrap my hair in a towel. Nola's seen me naked countless times and I'm so comfortable in her presence that I don't even think twice about the fact that she's standing right next to me, hanging up fresh towels.

"No pressure, we'll make it work if you decide to go ahead with it," she says with a smile. "By the way, I hope I'm not overstepping here, but have you met someone?"

"What?" My face flushes and for a moment I wonder if Nola is psychic.

"A man," she clarifies. "Not that it's any of my business."

"A man?" I laugh and walk to my dressing table in the bedroom. "No, I haven't. Why do you ask?"

"You just…" Nola chuckles as she places the last towel on the shelf, then follows me. "You're acting like a woman in love. You're all over the place, you're up late and you have this glow about you."

"I am not in love!" I exclaim and laugh along with her. The real reason I'm up late is because I have no idea how to behave around Belle, who is currently in the backyard. I want to see her and talk to her, I really do. But I also need time to process what happened last night. When I woke up, our night felt like a dream, like it had never happened, but then I caught a waft of her scent on my pillow and reality came crashing down on me. I slept with a woman and I liked it. No. I loved it. And now what? Nola makes my bed, and that's probably why she's speculating. The sheets were pretty sweaty and messy, and my bedsheets are never messy. "I swear, there's no man." This is all true, so I don't even have to lie. A crush? Sure. A little obsessed? Yes. But I'm not in love and certainly not with a man.

"Just teasing you." Nola picks up the empty laundry basket. "But if you want to talk, I'm here, okay?"

"Thank you," I mumble, more to myself as she's already disappeared down the stairs. Appraising myself in the mirror, I note that I'm fine seeing the subtle crow's feet around my eyes. Belle made me feel beautiful and that energy still lingers. She gave me the impression that she truly wanted me and that for a couple of hours, I was all that mattered. It's amazing what feeling desired can do to someone, and whether it was real or not, I cherish the aftereffect.

Still, I'm not looking forward to turning forty. Several

women have told me their forties were great. That it was a time when they started feeling more secure in themselves and stopped caring so much about what others thought of them. 'Fuck being young,' a woman in my yoga class said. 'I'd never want to go back in time.' But me? I feel like I'm stumbling right into puberty and I don't even know who I am anymore. Most of all, though, I'm suddenly terrified of what others will think of me.

I put on moisturizer and scroll through my phone while I wait for my skin to hydrate. A message from Sasha, asking me if I still want to have drinks tomorrow, a charity ball invitation for July and an enquiry from my mother regarding a birthday present are awaiting my reply but instead, I navigate to my doctor's practice and book an appointment for an STD test. *So I can use my tongue on you in a way that will blow your mind.* Her words have been on repeat in the back of my mind since I woke up, and I just can't let it go. Not even twenty-four hours after Belle's first visit and I'm already fantasizing about splashing out on her again, my body raging with longing.

Outside, I hear Nola's voice, and then Belle's. Her voice draws me like a magnetic force and without thinking, I get up and slide open the balcony doors. There she is, looking as fresh-faced, cute and sexy as ever. Denim shorts, a navy T-shirt, her red cap and that smile that makes me weak in all limbs. I stare at her hands, remembering how they felt exploring my body. I stare at her mouth and can still feel her lips against mine. And then Nola looks up, and Belle looks up and our eyes meet in a loaded exchange. I'm nailed to the ground and remind myself that I'm supposed to greet her—that that would be the normal thing to do—so I take a deep breath and smile.

BELLE - WEDNESDAY

*H*er perfume still lingered on my skin when I came home, and I didn't want to wash it off. And now I'm back here in a different capacity, mixing chemicals for a pool that's barely used and only really needs servicing every ten days. Perhaps I should tell her she's wasting money —someone should have a long time ago—but if I did, I wouldn't see much of her in the precious time I have until Barry is back from sick leave.

Reina hasn't come out, and I wonder if she's hiding from me somewhere in that big house. I wouldn't blame her; it's not like we share a personal relationship, and maybe she's mortified, now that it's hit her what she's done. If this was it, then I will cherish the memory and stay out of her way as much as I can. But one thing I'm certain of: she will cherish the memory too, no matter what she tells herself.

I did something very out of character last night. When I was in bed, exhausted, yet wide awake with adrenaline, I looked her up. There wasn't much to find on Reina as her social media profiles were set to private, but then I found Nicole and there was an endless stream of information and photographs that taught me more about her mother. I initially thought her ex-husband was the one with the money, but it seems that Reina's even wealthier than him. There were holiday snaps of them visiting her mother in their family palace in Beirut. Their house on Stuyvesant Street in East Village, New York, where she lived with her husband and kids until they got divorced must have been worth a fortune and she has some very powerful friends. She was rather a socialite there, perhaps she still is. After all, I have no idea what she gets up to at night. Through Nicole's channels, I found pictures of Reina and her husband at the Met Gala, and of her and Nicole on some billionaire's yacht.

As I started forming a picture of her life, I realized how much is at stake for her. Her family in Beirut, her place in society… If anyone found out she'd hired a female escort, the scandal would follow her for years to come and the consequences may be devastating. Reina is not a woman who could easily come out, and I feel for her because last night it was clear that she's very much into women.

Nola, the friendly but terribly nosey housekeeper, waves at me from the terrace and shouts that she's making me a coffee. I'm surprised there's no full-time staff here. Most people I work for have a live-in housekeeper and a full-time gardener, but here, everything is outsourced. The only constant is Nola. She told me Reina is very flexible and that she can work this job around her other households, that Reina's kids are polite and tidy and that it's the easiest job she's ever had.

"Thank you," I say when she comes over with a cappuccino and a slice of cake. "Honestly, you shouldn't. I'm only here for a little while today; there's not much to do."

"But you need to try it," she says, sipping her own coffee. "I made it myself. It's Polish."

"Wow. You're a baker?" I take a bite and moan in delight. "It's delicious."

"I try," she says cheerfully, then turns to look up at the bedroom balcony where Reina has appeared. She's dressed in a white robe, her hair is wrapped in a towel and she looks like a Greek goddess. The hint of cleavage is tantalizing and as I stare up at her I feel my lips pull into a wide smile. *My queen.* For long moments, Reina looks as if she's seen a ghost, but then she finally smiles back at me, turning the nervous tightness in my core to a delightful flutter. It's not a polite smile; she seems genuinely happy to see me. "Hi, Belle," she shouts enthusiastically.

"Good morning, Reina." An awkward moment follows in which we stand there and linger; me looking up at her, and her looking down at me. She's too far away to have a conversation and even if we could, what would we say to each other with Nola here?

Reina backs away, clearly thinking the same. She gives me a wave and casts me one last glance over her shoulder before she retreats to her bedroom, where I imagine she'll strip off her robe. *God, I want her so much.*

"You call her Reina…" Nola shoots me a puzzled look.

"She asked me to," I say with a shrug.

"Hmm… she keeps telling me that too, but I just can't get used to it." Nola takes a sip of her coffee and glances up at the balcony again. The sliding doors are closed but she still lowers her voice. "She's in a funny mood today."

"Oh?" I'm thinking Nola is crossing a line here, but I pretend I'm all ears. After all, I'm just the pool technician, and staff do tend to gossip among each other. "What do you mean?"

"Her bed," Nola whispers. "It didn't look the way it normally does in the mornings. She's also got new lingerie, I just put it in the wash. And the way she's acting..." She pauses for effect. "I'm almost certain she had a man over."

Biting my lip to force back a grin, I remain silent. *If only she knew.*

"I'm sorry, I shouldn't have said that," Nola continues, waving a hand. "I'm gossiping again."

Yes, you are. I cast her a bemused look and squeeze her shoulder. "It's okay, I won't tell anyone."

"Please don't. I'm just so happy for her that she's finally moving on and letting go of that ex-husband of hers." She smiles. "I think Miss Amari's in love."

I can't tell Nola my own theory; that Reina's acting bewildered because she's confused about her sexuality after a night with me, so I hand her my empty cup and grab the net I've brought. "If she is, then good for her." I start dragging the net through the water, letting Nola know I'm here to work. "Thank you so much for the coffee and the cake. It was delicious."

REINA - THURSDAY

The next evening Sasha and I are dining at Hush, a club in East Village. Their roof terrace is filled with a mixture of locals and East Coast millennials who have escaped their parents' homes for the night. We must be at least ten years older than the average crowd here, and I'm glad I dressed casual in jeans and an off-the-shoulder white top as Sasha looks completely out of place in her long, baby pink satin dress. Not that she cares; Sasha likes to flaunt her curves and thrives on being the center of attention. After a stint on a reality TV show—it was short-lived as she got sick of the cameras following her around—she's still regularly photographed on the society pages and is somewhat of a celebrity around here.

"Will you stop flirting with everyone?" I say incredulously when she smiles at another man passing our table. "What's up with you?" She's already made eyes at the DJ *and* our waiter, who are both in their early twenties.

"Hey, I'm just looking. Nothing wrong with that," she retorts, flicking her blonde hair over her shoulder. "I'm sure Igor looks now and then."

"I'm sure he does, but you're full-on tonight."

"Just a bit of fun," Sasha says with a happy shrug. "I'm so glad to be out with you again and able to talk about saucy stuff without men around. Why was it always the four of us before?" She takes a sip of her white wine and helps herself to a piece of haloumi from the sharing platter between us. Her mood is bouncy and it's infectious.

"Yeah, why was that?" I smile and clink my glass against hers. "I prefer this too."

"So, tell me honestly." Sasha leans in closer. "Was it really as good as you said it was?"

"Yes." I shoot her a smirk and shift in my chair at the familiar flutter of butterflies. "It was mind-blowing." I lean in too and continue in a whisper. "I booked an appointment with my doctor for an STD test, so we don't have to be careful next time. It was her idea."

Sasha's eyes widen. "Next time?"

"Uh-huh." I narrow my eyes at her. "But if you tell anyone, I will kill you."

"Of course," she says, as if that's a given. Her expression turns serious then, and she regards me for long moments. "So, what are you going to do?"

"What do you mean?"

"I mean, you like to have sex with women. From what you told me, you prefer women to men, at least one woman in particular. So, are you gay? And if you are, what are you going to do?"

"I don't know." The question is one I've asked myself over and over today. "I don't have to decide now, do I?"

"No, but it's something to think about. Not that it matters if you're gay or straight," she hastily adds. "But if you're sure, you might want to talk to your kids at some point, so they're not totally taken by surprise when mommy suddenly starts dating a woman."

"But… I can't imagine myself dating a woman," I say.

"Can you imagine yourself dating a man?"

"No. I suppose that seems unlikely too now." I groan and bury my face in my hands. "Oh God, Sasha, what am I going to do?"

"Chill out. This can be our secret for as long as you want. But I think you're panicking and turning this into a way bigger deal than it is. Lots of people are gay."

"Like who?" I ask. "In our circles I mean."

"Our circles could do with a little diversity; I think it would be welcomed. Besides, this is the Hamptons. It's not like you're living with your mother in Beirut."

Sasha's words flood me with dread. "Please don't remind me of my mother. She wouldn't survive if she knew."

"She doesn't have to know, ever. How often do you see her?"

"Only about twice a year, and I usually visit her. She says her cats get upset if she leaves her home for longer than a couple of nights." I roll my eyes. "Her twelve cats. Even though they have their own housekeepers who tend to their every need."

"Her big, fluffy Persian cats. I've seen them, I follow them on Instagram." Sasha laughs. "Ruby is my favorite. The white one with the grumpy face."

"They all have grumpy faces," I say, laughing along. "She just had personalized four-poster mini-beds made for all of them. It's totally ridiculous."

"Well, there you go, saved by the cats. It's not like she's going to show up unannounced. And your uncle, that mega rich guy, isn't he gay? You said he has a male companion who follows him everywhere and I saw those pictures of you and him on his yacht; he does look a little camp."

"Yes, I'm pretty sure he's gay, but he'd never openly admit to that."

"But everyone suspects he is, right? And he never married?"

"No. He's still single at fifty. I think my family knows; it's just not mentioned." I sigh and take a long drink. "Enough about me. I don't want to think about any of this, it's making me anxious."

Sasha smiles at me and refills my glass. "Of course. Let's just dish some dirt."

"I've got some juicy gossip for you," I say, oddly relieved that my ex-husband has given me something to take my mind off Belle for a moment. "Guess who's having a baby?"

BELLE - FRIDAY

*R*eina is looking sleepy when she ventures outside in the thin silk robe that she wore for me on Tuesday evening. "Hey," she says with a shy smile, and hands me a coffee. "Please ignore my rough appearance, I had a late night."

"Another late night?" I joke. "Don't worry, you look beautiful as always." As the words leave my lips, I realize it's probably too much, but I don't care. She truly does look beautiful and oddly vulnerable with her messy hair and face free of makeup. And then I imagine waking up next to her, seeing that sleepy face first thing, and feeling her body heat against mine.

"Thank you." She smiles shyly. "I'm having my coffee on the beach. Would you like to join me? Unless you're busy? I don't want to keep you from your work."

"I think you know your pool is getting more attention than it needs," I say with a chuckle, and follow her to the gate. "I was actually going to suggest you bring the service visits down to once a week unless you have guests coming."

"I did wonder about that since the kids aren't here, but I

didn't want to put anyone out of work." Reina types in a code to open the gate and we cross the stilt bridge that runs over the dunes toward the beach. She's barefoot, her toenails painted a light pink. Het feet are flawless, just like her elegant hands and I can't stop looking at them.

"That's very sweet of you but I can assure you that we have more than enough work."

"Okay, well in that case, I'll think about it," she says, heading down the steps. The beach lies quietly before us as we sit down on the bottom step of the bridge. It feels intimate to be here with her, like we've just crossed a line by venturing off the premises. "How are you?" It's a simple question, but she makes it sound loaded, as if my wellbeing is genuinely important to her.

"I'm good," I say casually, trying to contain the tug of longing in my lower abdomen. "How are you after the other night?"

Reina absently looks out over the ocean, clutching her mug in both hands. "I've been all over the place to be honest with you. It's... It's a lot to process." She pauses and finally turns to meet my eyes. "But it was incredible, and I want to do it again." There's a long, loaded silence and then she says: "I've booked that test."

"Oh..." I lick my lips and glance down at her mouth, wanting to kiss her so badly now that I can barely contain myself. I want to tell her that she doesn't have to book me, that I'm at her mercy and that she can have me whenever she wants. Right here, right now, whenever, wherever. But I can't say that because this is not a relationship, and it never will be. It's an arrangement and I have to protect myself. "I look forward to next time."

"Do you really?" Reina studies me and I can see that just like me, she's confused by this strange intimacy between us.

Yes, Reina. I think you're amazing and I can't stop thinking about you. I want you, I crave you. I swallow hard. "Yeah, I do. You're special." We're getting dangerously close to the point of falling into a kiss, so I lean back, prop my elbows on the step behind me and change the subject. "Is Nicole coming home this weekend?"

Something crosses over Reina's face. It's subtle but it doesn't go unnoticed, and I regret changing the course of our conversation. "No. I'm going to see her in New York," she says, painting on a smile.

"Nice. When was the last time you were there?"

"Last year, when I signed my divorce papers." Reina shrugs. "I've been avoiding New York and even hired someone to move and store my things after we sold the house, so I wouldn't have to go back there. I just couldn't bring myself to face mutual friends or visit places Sandeep and I used to go together. But I'm ready now. In fact, I'm looking forward to it." A loved-up couple strolls along the beach and we follow them with our eyes. They can't be older than twenty-five and stop to kiss every few steps, leaving a regularly interrupted pattern of footsteps in the sand.

"Do you miss the city?"

"Sometimes." Reina shrugs. "But my life there was with my family. If I moved back, it wouldn't be the same. I have friends in New York, and I've missed them over winter but most of them have a place in the Hamptons, so they'll be back soon and anyone else can always come and stay with me as I've got plenty of space. What did you do in New York?" she asks.

"I went there to study, initially. Although I always did pretty well in school, I dropped out of university, too distracted with the big city lifestyle to focus on what was important. So, I ended up working in bars and clubs and loved the attention I was getting from women. Pleasing them became a game to me and I think that's where it all started."

"What did you study?"

"Finance."

"Finance?" Reina looks puzzled. "I'm aware that I don't know you very well, but I have trouble picturing you working in that field."

"Yeah, me too. I don't know what I was thinking." I say with a chuckle. "I think I just wanted to prove myself initially and I actually didn't tell my father about dropping out until a year later. He was just so proud of me for being the smart one in the family and I didn't have the heart to tell him it wasn't for me. But eventually I had to, and he took it better than I'd expected."

"Are you close to him?" she asks.

"Yeah. My mom died when my sister and I were very young, and he's been a great parent. Jackie, our neighbor helped out a lot back then. She still helps out with Suki so she's part of the family too."

"I'm sorry about your mom. Can I ask what happened?"

"Breast cancer. I was three, so I don't really remember her." I pause, thinking this conversation is taking a very personal turn.

"Still, it must have been horrible for you," Reina says. "And your sister? How old was she when your mom died?" She waves a hand and shakes her head, rolling her eyes skyward as if cursing herself. "I'm sorry, never mind. I didn't mean to interrogate you."

"It's okay." I put a hand on her knee, then retract it when we both stare down at it. Everything we say or do now seems so loaded and I just don't know how to behave around her anymore. "My sister, Linda, was two years older than me, but she died too," I finally say. Unsure why I'm telling her all of this but somehow really wanting to, I cast her a smile to let her know I'm okay talking about it. "She was Suki's mother."

"Oh, God." Reina runs a hand over my cheek, and I lean

into her touch, cherishing the contact. "You…" I think she's about to say: 'you poor thing', but she stops herself. "And you adopted Suki?"

"Yes. Suki's father was not in the picture and when she got sick—my sister had breast cancer too—she made arrangements for me to be Suki's legal adoptive parent in case she wouldn't make it through." Reina looks like she's about to cry, so I take her hand in mine and kiss it. She scoots closer then and puts an arm around me and we sit there for minutes in silence, listening to the waves and the seagulls that are circling above us.

"You're brave," she finally says. "I admire your strength."

"I'm not brave. I had no choice other than to get on with it, but I love Suki and we have a pretty good life now. She's happy and that's all that matters."

"And you? Are you happy?" Again, the question seems loaded, and I need a moment to think about it as I've actually never asked myself if I am.

"Yeah," I say. "I enjoy seeing Suki smile, growing up, making friends, learning things… I enjoy living here and going to the beach on weekends. My dreams are different now, more tangible, I suppose. It's not about living my life to its fullest or eternal passion. It's about stability and inner peace." Turning to Reina, I decide it's my time to interrogate her. "And you? Are you happy?"

Reina chuckles and shakes her head as if she's got no idea. "I think I'm happy. Happier than I was a while ago anyway. But I might be the opposite to you now. I quite like the idea of living my life to its fullest and chasing eternal passion or whatever it is you called it. I've never done that before."

"Then you've made a great start," I say. "Exploring your sexuality is only the beginning, so enjoy the ride and don't feel ashamed. Everything you crave right now is natural. You may have buried it, but it's always been there and, in the end, you are who you are."

Reina nods. "Thank you. I'll keep that in mind."

Finishing my coffee, I get up and take her hand to help her up. Reina holds onto me for way longer than necessary, and as we linger on the steps the pull is so strong that I eventually let go so I won't crush her against me. "I have to go to my next client."

"Of course. Sorry to keep you here. I didn't mean to get so personal." Reina's face flushes as we cross the bridge.

"Don't apologize, this was nice. I enjoy talking to you."

"Me too." She stalls by the gate and smiles. "So, I'll see you next week?"

"Yeah. I'll see you Monday. Have fun in New York."

REINA - SATURDAY

"It's so weird to have you here, Mom," Nicole says as we walk through our old neighborhood. It's the first time I've been here since I left the house in distress after stumbling upon a saucy email from Bree addressed to my husband. After that, I only came up for a meeting with our divorce lawyer. Nicole thought it might be 'cathartic' for me to visit Stuyvesant Street and its surrounding areas again; that's how she put it anyway. And so here we are, aimlessly strolling around after a long lunch in Manhattan. It felt daunting at first, but now all that is left is a strong sense of disassociation, like this is a different world and I'm not a part of it anymore.

"It's weird for me too," I say. Nicole still comes to the neighborhood to visit friends and since she only spent a couple of months with me in the Hamptons before she moved to NYU campus, not much has changed for her. "But I think I like being an outsider. It's nice to enjoy the city without tons of plans."

"Good." Nicole removes her hoodie and ties it around her waist. The days are getting warmer and soon New York will be unbearably hot and clammy. "Let's have a drink some-where, I need shade."

Our old street is one of the few diagonal streets in New York, crossing East 9th Street between Second and Third Avenues, and Sandeep and I chose this neighborhood because of my love for historic buildings. We pass St. Mark's Church in-the-Bowery, one of the many reminders of New York's Dutch past, and an understated Federal-style home with red bricks laid in Flemish bond, the oldest in the East Village. Around the corner is my favorite Japanese take-out and a little farther the bar where I regularly met up with friends. A new bar has opened next to it, and my attention spikes when I see a rainbow flag over the door and 'ladies only weekend' scribbled on the whiteboard outside. I'm not sure why I feel the need to go in there; it's not like I want to check out women. Belle is the only woman on my mind and even though it will never go anywhere, the thought of flirting with someone else is unthinkable. Perhaps I just want to be around others like me, so I won't feel quite so different, or maybe I'm curious about the kind of places Belle used to hang out. "Let's check this one out," I say without thinking. "It says they have a courtyard."

Nicole looks at the flag, then shoots me an amused look. "Okay, whatever you want, mama bear." She probably thinks I'm oblivious and that it will be funny to see the look on my face once I realize we're in a lesbian hangout.

Inside, it is nothing special. In fact, it looks rather dated for a newly opened bar, but the bartender is super friendly, and the music upbeat. I order a Coke for Nicole and a gin and tonic for myself and no one gives me strange looks or asks questions. Only a couple of tables are taken but when we pass through the back door with our drinks, there is a courtyard filled with women, talking and laughing around the colorful tables. A huge tree hung with rainbow lanterns shades the space and the sun poking through the crown leaves a beautiful pattern on every surface. Although it's lovely and cheerful, I immediately regret coming here because it's also very busy and I feel overwhelmed by the energy.

"You can have this one, we're just leaving," a butch looking woman says to Nicole as she and her friend get up. She shoots Nicole a wink, but Nicole doesn't seem fazed.

"Thanks, that's very kind of you," she answers with a warm smile that turns into a cheeky grin when I sit down opposite her. "You're looking a little flushed, Mom. Are you okay?"

"Yeah. I'm fine." I swallow hard and make sure I keep my eyes on Nicole only. "Was that woman flirting with you?"

Nicole chuckles. "I think so, but I don't mind." She leans in and lowers her voice. "You didn't know this was a gay bar, did you?"

"No," I lie. "Did you?"

"Yeah. I've been here a couple of times with a friend. A friend-friend," she quickly adds.

"Oh." I smile. "You don't have to reassure me. I wouldn't mind if you dated women."

"Really? Are you sure about that?"

"Of course. I just want you to be happy." Nicole looks surprised and I don't blame her. A year ago, my reaction would have been quite different, I suppose. I wanted the world for her; a degree, a job, a nice home, a husband, a family. I still do, of course, but I see now that not everything is as simple and black and white as I always assumed.

"How did you suddenly become so open-minded?"

"I'm no different than before," I lie again. "We've just never had this conversation." I stir my drink and finally gather the courage to glance around. So many gay women. Most of them are sitting in groups, some look like they're on a date. One woman curiously glances my way. She's probably wondering what I'm doing here; everyone looks a lot more casual and individual than me, and dressed for Manhattan, I look way too dramatic in my maxi-dress and big shades. Turning back to Nicole, I ignore her continuous stare. "Have you ever dated a girl?"

"Mom!" Nicole feigns astonishment. "Are we really going to talk about this?"

"I just want to know what goes on in your life," I say honestly. "We never talk about your love life."

"Right." Nicole downs half of her drink and raises a brow at me. "Okay, if you really want to know…" She pauses. "I did date a girl once and it wasn't for me. I mean, it was fun while it lasted, but I prefer boys. And yes, I met someone but it's still very new; we've only seen each other a couple of times."

"Oh." I smile, delighted that she's opening up to me. Nicole's always kept her cards close to her chest, like me I suppose. I've never been much of a talker, but something has changed. "So you've been dating?"

Nicole laughs. "We're not living in the eighties, it doesn't work like that anymore," she says, making me feel ancient. "Boys don't show up at a girl's door with flowers to take her out for dinner. We just hang out with mutual friends and I've been to his place twice. He has his own apartment."

The apartment comment worries me, but I try not to let it show. "He's not much older than you, is he? What's his name? What is he studying?"

"He's twenty-three. His name is Tyrell and he's a rapper." Nicole shoots me a daring look, awaiting my criticism. She knows exactly what I'm thinking. *A rapper. No steady job or income, no future. Not good enough for my daughter.* I force myself to try and see things from her perspective and refrain from falling into an interrogation. My parents were furious when I told them I was pregnant with Sandeep's baby. He didn't come from a wealthy family like me, and it led to a lot of friction, with Sandeep feeling like he was never good enough. I suppose that gave him the drive to prove them wrong and to become hugely successful, but still, it was very difficult, and I never want Nicole to be in that position.

"Okay. As long as you're happy, honey. If it works out, I'd love to meet him."

Nicole's eyes widen. "You're not going to lecture me?"

"No." I purse my lips and shake my head, then change my mind when I picture Nicole with a baby bump. "Actually, I will lecture you but only for a moment. You see, having you and Eddie was the best thing that ever happened to me and I wouldn't change anything for the world. But I never got a degree and I want that for you. It's difficult when one day you find yourself in a situation where you have to start over, and you have no idea what to do with your life. So please, when the time comes, use protection, okay? And only have sex when you're ready."

Now it's Nicole's time to blush and she lets out a strangled laugh. "I'm not a virgin anymore. And yes, I do use protection, so don't worry." She reaches for my hand over the table and squeezes it. "Don't be shocked, Mom. I'm almost eighteen. And I know you probably think everyone talks to their mothers before they have sex for the first time, but in reality, that's not the case. None of my friends do, it just happens when it happens. Besides, you had your own problems last year and I didn't want to stress you out even more."

"Honey, I don't ever want you to feel like you can't talk to me. Please know that I'm always here for you, no matter what goes on in my life." She's right; I am shocked to hear that she's had sex, but I was pregnant at seventeen so it would be hypocritical of me to disapprove. She's a grown-up now, much wiser than I was at that age. "But I'm glad you told me, and I meant what I said about Tyrell. I'd love to meet him."

"Thank you," Nicole says.

"For what?"

"For not judging me." She sits back, visibly relaxing. "It's hard to grasp that I'm sitting in a gay bar with my Stepford mother telling her I'm dating a rapper and talking about sex."

"Hey, I'm not a Stepford mother!" I exclaim.

"Maybe not anymore, but let's face it, you were before." Nicole humorously narrows her eyes at me. "Come on, Mom. You spent most of your time worrying about what to wear to events, what to serve at dinner parties and who to invite."

"Hmm…" I laugh because she does have a point. "I did do that, didn't I?" Two women start kissing at the table next to us. Although I'm not a fan of PDA, it's rather sensual to watch and I feel myself staring at them, totally intrigued. The way their lips touch, and the way their hands move through each other's hair… It's arousing. *Do Belle and I look like that when we kiss?* "Well, from now on, things are going to change," I say, tearing my eyes away from them.

BELLE - SUNDAY

"Mommy, can we go to the pool again?"

"We're going to the beach later, honey. Cameron will be there too." I take a tighter hold of Suki's hand as we cross the road to the Harborside Café. "I just need a coffee and a moment with my Sunday newspaper. You can play on the iPad if you want, and I brought a coloring book too." Glancing over my shoulder, I can't shake the uncomfortable feeling that someone is watching us, but I don't see anyone I know.

Grateful there's a shaded table free at the end of the terrace by the water, I let the breeze cool my skin and order a cappuccino for myself and a lemonade for Suki. Boats and modest yachts are sailing into the marina, the day trippers still early enough to secure a mooring spot. I like watching people and seeing the excitement on their faces when they arrive here for the first time as it really is a pretty town and I'm proud of where I live. Suki is taking her crayons out of my bag and seems quite happy to keep herself busy for a while, so I settle into my newspaper and enjoy some downtime.

"Fancy seeing you two here," someone says when I'm engrossed in an article. Immediately recognizing the voice, I freeze and look up to find Mrs. Ashworth standing next to our table.

"Hi, Mrs. Ashworth," I say hesitantly, glancing at Suki who is concentrating on a jungle illustration in her book. And just out of politeness, I add: "How are you?"

"I'm great, thank you." Mrs. Ashworth runs a hand through her bleach-blonde hair and bats her lashes at me. "But please call me Cindy, we've become acquainted well enough to drop the formalities," she adds with a wink. To my utter shock, she takes a seat at our table. "I got a call to say you were unavailable and I must say, I was very disappointed."

Again, I nervously check on Suki, who is now smiling up at Mrs. Ashworth, recognizing her. "Hi," she says.

"Hey there, sweetie. What are you coloring there?"

"An elephant." Suki lifts the coloring book to show her. "I made him blue," she adds with a cheeky chuckle.

"That's very creative. What are you and your mommy up to tod—"

"Okay, Cindy," I try carefully, cutting her off. "It's nice to see you but I'm just here relaxing with my daughter. If I upset you in any way, I'd appreciated if we could talk in private at a mutually convenient time."

Cindy actually looks pleased with this and leans in closer to me. "That's not a problem. How about we have dinner tonight?"

"No, I didn't mean dinner," I say, doing my best to stay polite. I'm pretty sure she's followed us here and if she's delusional in any way, I don't want to push her over the edge. Glancing around, I note that there's a quiet spot in the corner of the terrace and gesture there, figuring it's probably best to get it over with so she won't get any ideas of us going out on a date. "Suki, stay here where I can see you for five minutes, okay? I'm just going to talk to Cindy for a moment, I'll be right back."

Suki frowns but doesn't protest and turns back to her crayons. Ms. Ashworth sighs as she gets up, then follows me to the empty table.

"Why are you being so distant with me?" she whispers. "What have I done?"

"You haven't done anything, Cindy. But I keep my job and private life strictly separate, and I don't want to socialize with clients outside the visits. That's my daughter over there. Don't you understand it's highly uncomfortable for me if you start asking her personal questions and follow us around?"

"I didn't follow you," she says, raising her voice in defense.

"Come on, I know you did. You don't even live around here."

Mrs. Ashworth looks hurt, but I make no effort to console her. If I do, it might only make it worse. "I'm filing for divorce," she says, swallowing hard. "So I'll be a single woman soon. We can see each other as much as we want, and you can move in with me if that's something you might like to consider."

Staring at her in utter shock, I shake my head. "Please don't do that. Don't leave your husband unless you're in an unhappy marriage. We're not in a relationship. You hired me as an escort. That's something else entirely." I try to keep my sentences short in the hope my words will get through to her.

"But…" She attempts to grab my hand, but I slide them both into my pockets. "But I can take care of you. Both of you."

At a loss for what to say now as she's clearly not taking no for an answer, I resort to the only thing I can think of. Lying. "I'm in a relationship, Cindy. With the woman you saw me with in Montauk. I asked the team to cancel your booking because you were getting too personal with me. I'm in love with her and we're serious."

"So it was true…" Her lip trembles ever so slightly and she leans in. "What's her name?"

"That's private," I say, somewhat relieved to see her delusion shatter and at the same time worried of what she might do now.

"Tell me her name," she hisses. "You betrayed me."

"Cindy," I say in a calm voice. "I did not betray you. You and I are not in a relationship." It's hard to believe the calm and collected woman I've visited in her beautiful home is a total nutcase but she's clearly highly unstable and possibly dangerous. "I'd like you to stay away from me and my daughter, okay?" When she doesn't answer, I add: "Is that clear?"

Cindy remains silent, her fists balled in front of her. For a beat I'm worried she might punch me, but she finally gets up and walks away. My heart is racing and I feel sick at the thought of her getting divorced because of me. As I head back to the table, I plaster on a smile, making sure Suki doesn't notice how upset I am.

REINA - SUNDAY

"This was fun. Really, it was," Nicole says as if she's surprised that she hasn't been bored around me. I zip closed my weekend bag and give her a long hug.

"Yeah. I'd love to do this again. And don't worry about not coming over next weekend, just enjoy the party, okay?" Nicole stayed in my room last night after a late dinner, and we watched movies in bed just like we used to when she was younger. This morning, we hit the hotel gym together and after that, we had a sauna before attacking the breakfast buffet. I could have stayed with friends, but I didn't let anyone know I was coming. It's not that I didn't want to see them, I just wanted to have Nicole to myself and wasn't sure if I was ready to face anyone but her in the current state that I'm in.

"Come over any time." Nicole squeezes my arm. "By the way, are you celebrating your birthday?"

I shake my head. "I don't think so, honey. I'd love to have dinner with you, though, if you're around?"

Nicole frowns. "But you're turning forty, Mom. It's a big one."

"I wish everyone would stop reminding me of that," I say with a chuckle. "I just don't feel like organizing anything, okay? It's not that I don't have time, I just don't feel like calling all these people I've been avoiding for so long. It's become a thing, I suppose and besides, you know I don't like being the center of attention."

"Oh, God. You really have been way too isolated," Nicole says. "Why don't you leave it with me? Seriously, I'd love to organize a party for you. Nothing big, I promise. Just your closest friends. They know what you've been through and trust me, they don't blame you for not returning their calls, they'll just be really happy to see you again."

"I'm sorry, but I'd rather just spend it with you..."

"Okay, it's your birthday." Nicole sighs and shoots me a smile. "Then at least let me organize something special, just with the two of us. A surprise."

"Sure. That sounds nice." I'm not into my own birthdays, I've never been comfortable with them. I used to love organizing dinners and cocktail parties but that was different as they were never about me. For my thirtieth, Sandeep took me and the kids to the Maldives because I refused a party, and we had a wonderful time there. We stayed in this beautiful cabin with a glass floor built over the ocean and I didn't have to worry about getting dressed or feeding the kids. No pressure, no stress and no family apart from our own sweet little bubble. That was the last time we had a real holiday together. We've visited my family in Beirut regularly, and we've had many long weekends in the Hamptons, but there was never time to get away from obligations. Sandeep was busy with work, I planned my life around the New York social scene and the kids grew up and preferred to hang out with their friends. They were all just excuses, though, because really, we stopped making time to put our marriage and family first.

Looking back, I don't think we were as happy as we could have been as there was always something missing. That something, I've come to realize, is passion. The glue that keeps couples together for a lifetime, the oil that makes the marriage machine run smoothly in the intimacy department, the magic elixir that enables relationships to work, even when times are tough. There was a lot of love, but the passion was never there. And sometimes, even love isn't enough.

I don't think I had a clue what passion was before I met Belle. But now, it's like it runs through my veins. Only sadly, she's an escort, who I'm paying to make me feel good. It's one-sided and there's no love involved, and therefore, it's not real. Still, after being deprived of passion my whole life, I crave it like I've never craved anything before.

With a sigh, I grab my phone and fall back on the bed. I still have half an hour left before check-out, so I scroll through my emails and find the results from my STD tests that I had done before I drove here on Friday. Although I'm not surprised that they're all negative, I still feel a flicker of relief. If Sandeep strayed once, he may have done it before and that's been bugging me.

Without my daughter here to distract me, my thoughts are consumed with Belle once more. A frisson of excitement runs through my body as I navigate to Hamptons' Escorts and see that she's available on Tuesday. It still feels wrong to pay for sex but having slept with her once, she's become like a drug to me and if this is the only way, I'll take what I can get. No one will ever know. As I enter my card details and press the 'book' button, I wonder if she'll get a notification. Will she be excited? *Don't be silly*, I tell myself. I'm just a client like any other client. Whether she enjoyed it or not, it's her job and I need to keep reminding myself that I mean nothing to her.

I've thought about her being with other women, and I hate that I feel jealous. Jealousy is a new—but not particularly pleasant—emotion to me, and it's messing with my head. Even when I found out Sandeep had been cheating on me, I didn't feel the way I do now. I was angry and hurt, sure, devastated even, but not jealous. The thought of him and Bree in bed together didn't cause this almost unbearable heavy knot in my stomach like when I imagine Belle with someone else and that makes no sense at all. I want to know if she has favorite clients, if she thinks about them outside her appointments. I want to know if she fantasizes about them, if she fantasizes about me.

When the confirmation message comes in, I let out a sigh of relief and then immediately, nerves take over. It's exhausting to be so emotional all the time, yet I've never felt more alive than I do now.

BELLE - MONDAY

*I*t's hard being here, refraining from physical contact while all I can think of is her upcoming booking tomorrow. Reina is struggling too; I can tell by the way she looks at me like she wants to rip my clothes off. Our morning talks have become somewhat of a comfortable habit, but today, I can almost taste the tension in the air.

We're sitting on the bottom step of the bridge again, both with a coffee in hand. Reina is wearing yoga clothes; a black strappy crop top, black leggings and sneakers, and her camera is hanging around her neck. At least I've done my job today, so I don't have to feel like I'm taking advantage. With my next appointment not until eleven, I accepted her invitation to come down here with her.

"The light is beautiful this morning," she says, looking out over the ocean.

"It is." I smile and do my best not to stare at her breasts in the tight yoga top. No one gets my libido raging like Reina does. "How was your weekend in New York?"

"It was really nice, actually," she says. "Just Nicole and me.

She stayed with me in my hotel room." She hesitates. "We went for a drink in a gay bar."

Her statement almost makes me choke on my coffee, and I turn to her with a frown. "Really? Did you talk to her about—"

"No, of course not. I didn't tell her about you, if that's what you mean," she quickly says. "We just happened to pass this place and I wanted to go in."

"And?"

"And nothing. I felt a little awkward at first, but everyone seemed very nice and..." she pauses. "Well, it was interesting, seeing women together."

"But you grew up in New York. Surely you must have been exposed to lesbian couples on many occasions."

"Yes, but I never really took much notice, if you know what I mean. I never paid much attention to what was going on around me." She shrugs. "I'm just trying to figure out this sudden change in me."

"I think you know what's going on with you."

Reina wets her lips as she looks at me and, God, I want to kiss her. "Yes," she says. "I think I do." The electricity between us crackles during the long silence that follows and then she says: "My test results came back. I'm clean." She blushes profusely as she holds up her phone, showing me the page.

I'm all too aware that I'm dangerously close to doing something stupid. "That's good," I finally say. "I have tests done on a regular basis, so you won't have to worry about me either." Another silence follows. "So, I'll be seeing you tomorrow... I'm looking forward to it."

"Yeah. Me too." Her voice is breathy as she continues to stare at me. Suddenly, as if it's too much, she snaps out of her trance and turns her attention back to the ocean. "How was your weekend?"

"It was very nice. I took Suki to the beach with a friend

and her son, and we saw my father," I say, leaving out the awkward situation with Mrs. Ashworth. "I'm starting my own business, so I've also been busy with that."

Reina's widening eyes tell me she's surprised to hear this. "Oh? What kind of business?"

"I'm starting a prop rental for pool parties. Anything you can think of, I have it. Furniture, lighting, decorations, pool toys…"

"That sounds like fun. And let me guess; is Suki testing all the pool toys?"

"No, the beach is too rough for expensive inflatables, and we don't know anyone with a pool, so I haven't shown her anything yet."

"Oh. Of course." Reina says this as if she's only just now come to realize that not everyone in the Hamptons has a pool. "You can always bring her here if you want to use my pool or have easy access to the beach. I know how difficult it is to find a parking spot by the beach in summer, and I have a huge drive and there's no one here but me."

"Thank you, that's very sweet, but I don't think it would be a good idea."

"Why not? I have all this space and the perfect facilities, and no one is enjoying it."

I study Reina and see that she's serious. Of course, Suki would love to come here, but I'm already in over my head and I don't want to draw my daughter into the mess I'm knowingly creating by falling for a client. "I'm afraid it would blur the boundaries," I say carefully. "I can't bring Suki to a client's house."

"I'm sorry, I didn't think about that." Reina shoots me a regretful look. "You're right. I understand." She looks down at her coffee and frowns. "Can I ask you something?"

"Sure."

"Why do you work for Pool Masters? If you make so much more money with the escort work?"

"Two reasons," I say. "Firstly, I want Suki to see me going to work every morning, doing a normal job like all other parents. I also want my father to know I have a job; he doesn't know about my escort job. And secondly, I simply need the job at Pool Masters for our medical insurance."

"Right. I can see how escort work wouldn't necessarily provide that." Reina shoots me a knowing smile. Medical insurance is obviously not something she's ever worried about. "It must be strange to live a double life."

"Not really," I shrug. "I see escorting as a performance, an act. And since it's only two or three nights a week, and less if I don't feel like it, it's just something I enjoy doing. With some nights more enjoyable than others," I add, needing her to know that she's special.

"Do you have favorite clients?" she asks. If I'm not mistaken, I'm sensing some jealousy, so I smile and lock my eyes with hers.

"Only one."

Clearly busted but pleased by my answer nevertheless, Reina blushes profusely, then narrows her eyes as a man approaches. He's barefoot, dressed in khaki shorts and a white T-shirt and he's walking in a brisk pace, until he spots us. He stops, lingers, then turns around and starts walking back.

"Do you know him?" I ask, relieved this is giving me a way out of a difficult conversation.

"Yes, it's Sandeep, my ex-husband," she says, staring at him pensively. "He was probably on his way here and didn't expect me to have company."

"Oh. Should I go?"

"No. Please don't." She takes my hand when I'm about to

get up. "I already know what he wants to talk about anyway. Him and his new girlfriend are having a baby."

"Jesus, Reina. That must be difficult." I squeeze her hand.

"It's..." She shrugs. "It's okay, actually. I've known for a few weeks, so I'm over the shock, but he doesn't know I know. It must be bothering him; he's not one to go for a walk on a Monday morning. He's a total workaholic."

I nod. "Is his office in the Hamptons?"

"No, he works from home. He used to have an office in New York, but now that he designs for the rich and famous, he only takes on really big jobs and keeps it simple with a team of freelancers who also work from home. He travels a lot, though."

"So he's a big name in his field?" I already know he is; I looked Sandeep up too but it would freak her out if she knew that. He designed one of the most high-tech office buildings in the world, situated in Dubai and he's won lots of prizes for his work.

"Yeah. He's very talented. And he's always had this drive to prove himself because I was... well... I was wealthy when we met, and he wasn't. Anyway, he soon managed to turn that around."

"Do you still have feelings for him?"

"No. He's the father of my children, so there will always be something there. But it's not like this."

"Like this?"

Reina shakes her head, heat rising to her cheeks again. "I mean, what I feel for him is not sexual and I don't think it's ever been. That's what I was trying to say," she hastily explains. She watches Sandeep fade into a white speck in the distance and I'm trying to grasp how anyone could ever leave the beautiful, kind and sexy Reina. Perhaps he always felt that she was never into him that way but if I had her, if she was really mine, then I'd never, ever let her go.

REINA - MONDAY

"*J*uice?" Sasha asks, opening the door to the juice bar next to the yoga studio without waiting for an answer.

"I think I might need something stronger," I joke.

"Why? Trouble in paradise with that Belle of yours?"

"Shh… not so loud." I scan the menu, then order my usual, and Sasha does the same. We've become predictable, the pair of us, but at least we now allow ourselves to let our hair down over cocktails once a week. "I'm seeing her tomorrow," I whisper as we walk to the bar by the window, snapping up the last two available seats. "Seeing her as in—"

"I know what you mean," Sasha interrupts me with a chuckle. "But that's a good thing, right?"

"Yeah. It is. I'm so nervous, though."

"But you've already been through it once. Surely it gets easier when you know what to expect?"

I consider that, then shake my head and give myself a stern talking to. "No, trust me; it does not get easier. If anything, it's getting fucking complicated." I sip my juice and hesitate. "Promise me you won't laugh?"

"Never." Sasha crosses her heart, her expression innocent like a little lamb.

"I think I'm infatuated with her," I say, lowering my voice. "Seriously, Sash, there might be something wrong with me. I'll grab any excuse to talk to her when she's over servicing the pool and I've told her really private things about myself. And I can't even look her in the eyes properly because it's just too much. She makes me feel unhinged just by being near."

Sasha props her elbow on the bar, cupping her cheek as she turns to me. "Okay, that is a little funny, but I promised not to laugh so I won't." She quirks a brow as she looks me over in amusement. "I don't think you're obsessed, Reina. I know it's only early days but I think you're in love with her. Have you considered that?"

"I'm not in love with her. I can't be," I say defensively but deep down, I know she might be right. I've never been in love before so how could I possibly know what it feels like? "I'm paying her to sleep with me. That doesn't feel very romantic."

"I know. That doesn't mean you can't fall for her. She obviously has a way with the ladies. Super charming and all."

"That's the problem. I don't know if she's like this with everyone or just with me. I know we have chemistry, I'm sure of that. But maybe she's just one of those people who has chemistry with everyone. She's very sexual."

Sasha nods and thinks about that. "Well, there's only one way to find out. You need to ask her out on a date."

"No way." I gasp. "I can't ask her out. If she turns me down, I'd be embarrassed and if she says yes, then I'd be going on an official date with a woman."

"And?"

"And, I don't think I could do that. In public, I mean. I

have kids and a position in society. I'm not even sure myself if I'm—"

"That's why you need to date a woman. To know for sure." Sasha shrugs. "You're single and your kids are practically adults. What are you so afraid of?"

"Everything!" I exclaim. "I'm afraid of everything, don't you get that? My feelings, the fact that she sleeps with other women... and I haven't even thought about what happens if we go further down the line. She has a kid, what if we did date and it didn't work out? And if it did work out, what would my friends say? My mother?"

"As for your mother, we've already discussed that. She's far away and you have your own life. As for your friends, I'm your friend and I'm cool. And if they're not cool, they're not real friends, simple as that. We're not in the Middle Ages. Or in Wyoming," she jokes.

"Easy for you to say. You're not the one falling in love with an escort." There. I've admitted it. I'm halfway to falling madly in love with Belle.

Sasha's amused expression drops, and she puts a hand on my thigh. "Honey, whatever happens, happens. Do you feel like you can talk to her?"

"Yes."

"Good. Then talk to her and just tell her how you feel. That's the only way to get a perspective on your situation." Sasha hesitates for a moment before she continues. "I just need to warn you about something, and you have to promise me not to get upset, okay?"

"Okay... what is it?" A feeling of unease creeps over me because I have an idea of what's coming.

"Well, she's an escort and you're a very wealthy woman. That's all I want to say, really. Just remember that if you're going to explore your relationship with her."

"Are you trying to say Belle's just after my money? She's not like that."

"No, I'm not. But just keep that in mind. After all, you don't really know her."

For a second, I want to shout at Sasha. I want to tell her that she's not cool, that she's reacting just like anyone else would and that it's not helpful. I want to argue that I *do* know Belle, because I feel like I do. Even without knowing all the facts of her life it's like I really see her, and I think she sees me too. But Sasha's never met Belle and all she knows are the facts that I've given her. She just wants to protect me and because of that, I can't blame her. "Sure," I say, letting out a long sigh. "I'll keep it in mind."

BELLE - TUESDAY

I should have thought this through, but that's the problem with attraction, isn't it? The pull of attraction makes you go right against every reason. This won't end well; I know that, yet I'm still here, pushing away the alarm bells in the back of my mind. When there's genuine chemistry, it feels wrong to get paid for what I do but what's the alternative? I'm no match for someone like Reina.

My driver stops in front of the house and as soon as I step out of the car, it starts pouring down with rain. I rush to the front door and it opens wide, revealing the elegant and breathtakingly beautiful woman I've been fantasizing about all day. It's a shock to my system to see her again even though I was here yesterday. She's wearing her satin robe and her perfectly smooth curves and hard nipples are visible through the fragile fabric. Reina has no idea what she does to me.

"Come in." She walks me to the kitchen, where she grabs a dishtowel and starts drying my hair. The way she presses her body into mine while she runs it over my face sends a surge of longing through me. "You're wet."

"I am. Are you?" I ask with a flirty smile.

Reina returns my smile. "Very." Her voice is breathy and her eyes filled with need as they lower to my lips. As if on cue, we fall into a passionate kiss, our tongues colliding in a frenzy of lust, our mouths locked tight and hard. The towel falls to the floor, my hands are in her hair and hers are under my shirt. There's no talking this time, no drink to settle the nerves and no gentle exploring. The in control and composed woman I normally am when I visit clients is gone too and I'm absorbed by her.

Pushing her against the kitchen island, I brush her hair away and devour her neck, breathing in her scent. She has such a delicate neck, soft and shapely, and the vein at the base is throbbing frantically against my lips. Her heart is pounding hard; I can feel it drumming against my chest as I press my body into hers.

Reina tilts her head to the side and moans while she clutches onto me like a life raft. The sweet little breathy sounds of her pleasure make me shiver as I slide her robe from her shoulder to kiss it.

"Let's go upstairs," I mumble against her skin while I cup her breast. "I've been dying to taste you."

"ARE YOU COMFORTABLE?" Reina's at my mercy and she loves it. Besides the intense heat in her eyes, uncertainty, anticipation and a hint of fear seep through her gaze as I finish securing her wrists to the bedframe.

"Yes," she says softly, her hands tugging at the silk restraints. She's wearing a white lingerie set that despite its sexy cut, looks strangely innocent and almost virginal on her. Her V-cut lace bra is hanging off one shoulder, baring a rock-hard nipple, and her white Brazilian panties are drenched with her arousal.

This was my idea, but she didn't think twice when I suggested it. Our chemistry is too intense, our interaction too organic and I can't let her touch me again because it really messed with my head the first time. Making myself even more vulnerable to someone who is paying me is not an option, yet I've never found myself so conflicted. Yes, I enjoyed it very much—too much—but I also have to keep in mind that Reina just transferred twenty-seven hundred dollars to Hamptons' Escorts, of which two thousand will be in my account tomorrow morning. *She's paying me. This isn't real.* It's my mantra for tonight and I'm mentally repeating it over and over, reminding myself of what I am to her. Someone who brings her a sense of excitement. Someone who is helping her explore who she is. Someone she's physically attracted to. Someone who will always be her dirty secret. And someone who will be replaced by a partner as soon as she feels better about herself and starts dating again. This is what I am, and I'd better own it or she'll be the biggest mistake I ever made.

I straddle her and watch her for a while, pulling, twisting underneath me, contemplating using the word that will free her within less than ten seconds until she finally gives up and acquiesces. Reina stops resisting. She trusts me.

"That's a good girl," I say, drawing a nervous chuckle from her lips. "Stay still and enjoy the ride. I promise I won't hurt you." I know Reina is not the kind of person who likes to be spanked, my instincts are strong with her. She relaxes a little at my words, but her chest is still heaving fast, the exposed nipple calling for my mouth. Wearing only my boxers, I grind myself into her center and smile when she moans. Her eyes shift between my face and my breasts while she bites her lower lip. She likes my breasts.

"You have no idea how much I want to taste you." I bend forward to kiss her slow and deep until she's a moaning, jerking puddle of wetness. Oral sex is not done in my line of work. Not without protection, but she's been tested and besides, I've already promised to use my tongue on her and to blow her mind, so I've crossed every boundary there is to cross. After fantasizing about this non-stop for the past week, I yearn to have my mouth between her thighs. Her chest shoots up when I twirl my tongue around her nipple and softly nip and bite. Another long moan, and then she holds her breath as I move farther down. The spot above her hipbone gets extra attention; I love how it makes her wiggle in pleasure and her restraints are only heightening her arousal. My hands slide up her thighs, pushing them apart and she groans and spreads her legs farther, inviting my mouth to the most secret part of her. She smells sweet and the thin strip of hair tickles my lips as I kiss it so softly, barely touching. My hot breath blowing over her sex is enough to make her cry out.

"Jesus, Belle..."

I look up at her for a moment and she meets my eyes, her gaze dark and loaded with anticipation. I love it when she says my name and soon, she'll be screaming it out. Again, I blow, and wait, and the waiting is driving her mad.

"Please," she begs in a strangled voice. "Please. I can't take this anymore."

I simply stare at her in silence and then after long moments and without warning, I lean in and trace the full length of her sex with the tip of my tongue. The unrestrained and drawn-out cry that escapes her is paired with the sinful jerking of her hips against my mouth and I moan too, drinking in her intoxicating juices. She tastes divine, just like I knew she would, and I press down harder and repeat the action, this time lingering on her clit. When I suck it into my mouth, she lets out another loud cry and I know she's already close. Sliding two fingers inside her, I twirl my tongue around her clit. I can feel her racing pulse everywhere and she's swollen and ready to explode.

"Oh my God…" Reina tenses up and elevates off the bed, the combined delight of my fingers and my tongue tipping her over the edge. I close my eyes as her walls contract hard and fast. "Belle! Fuck!"

It's thrilling, wonderous and so very raw. Her legs wrap around my neck as she lets go, lifting her hips to chase my tongue. I linger in the moment, drawing it out while I listen to her beautiful cries. In this moment, Reina is mine, and just for now, part of this is real. I don't want to let her go.

"Will you untie me?" I ask when I'm finally able to speak again.

"Of course." Belle pulls at the ties and I'm free in seconds. She takes my hands, laces her fingers through mine and settles herself on top of me to kiss me. "Are you okay?"

"Yes." I smile at her and take her face in my hands. "I'm still shaking."

"I can feel it." Belle shifts between my thighs, her hipbone resting on my throbbing center. "You're amazing, Reina," she says, brushing a lock of hair away from my face. "Seriously amazing."

Our eyes lock and it feels so intimate that confusion strikes me again. "You're the one who's amazing," I say, and lift my head to kiss her again. "I want to taste you too." When Belle's breath hitches and uncertainty flashes across her features, I regret saying it. "I'm sorry, forget it. I know you don't normally allow that, I just got carried away."

"Don't be sorry." Belle looks at me, really looks at me and I'm certain that the arousal in her eyes is not an act. I've turned her on by voicing my desires and now her reaction is turning me on too. She clearly wants it, so why is she resisting me? "Fuck it," she finally mumbles, then takes off her boxers. "Are you sure?"

"Yes." My breath catches when I see her completely naked, and longing surges through me at the thought of going down on her.

She rolls off me, allowing me to shift on top of her, and I move down and run my hands over her thighs, staring at her glistening sex. My body is raging with an intense carnal need to have my mouth on her. It's daunting and beautiful at the same time, her throbbing flesh pulling me in. "Are you sure?" I whisper as I lean forward, still watching her fight an internal battle.

Belle doesn't answer. She hesitates for long moments before she reaches for the back of my head and laces her fingers through my hair. Bringing me closer, I can hear her heady breathing as I kiss the soft, neat triangle of hair. My lips are barely touching her, but her hips jerk violently and she mutters a curse. She's so sensitive, so aroused, and when I run my tongue over her, our combined moans fill the room.

Belle is delicious. Women are delicious, and God, I could do this all night, every night. She tastes unique like nothing I've ever tasted, but she's my new favorite flavor. Doing this to her feels surreal, and I lick her harder. Basking in her moans that make me want her even more, I circle my tongue around her clit and mimic what she did to me. What she did to make me explode. It doesn't take long before she's bucking her hips against my mouth, fisting my hair in her hands and when I move lower and dart my tongue inside her because I feel an inexplicable need to do so, she suddenly holds very still before she lets go. I can feel her orgasm in every cell of her body. Her legs are shaking, her hands trembling as they tighten, pulling me closer, and she stifles a scream, resulting in a guttural cry that ends in a quiet moan. I stay there for a while, not wanting to stop until she's entirely still and spent and as her body loosens her hands relax and she lets go of my hair. Sliding up to meet her mouth, we kiss, tasting each other, weaving our limbs into a tangled web, pulling each other in as tightly as we can.

"It's been a long time since someone did that to me," she says in a husky voice. "That was incredible."

"Well, I certainly enjoyed it." I trail a finger over her waist and her hip, marveling at her beautiful curves. Going down on a woman is a tantalizing new sensation; an experience I could get used to.

She can barely speak through her ragged breathing as she continues. "But this is…" she hesitates. "This isn't right."

"How can it not be?" I ask. "It felt pretty damn perfect to me."

"I'LL GET YOU A REFUND. I can't let you pay for this," Belle says, slipping into her navy tank top before layering up with her denim shirt. She's been quiet for the past half hour and I can sense she's upset.

"What do you mean? I don't understand…" I wish she could stay but even if she didn't have to get home to Suki, she looks like she's very keen to leave all of a sudden and it hurts me.

"Come on, Reina. You know this isn't right."

Meeting her eyes, I shoot her a questioning look. "Why? Because it's so good? Because we have chemistry? You know we have chemistry, right? I could swear there's something between us. Or is it because I like you too much?" I don't think 'like' is quite the right way to phrase how I feel but I'm afraid to overwhelm her with my feelings.

"Yes. All of it," she says with a sigh, as if she hates to admit it. "And because I like you too."

She likes me too. So I wasn't imagining it. A feeling of euphoria washes over me at her words and we both stare at each other. "You like me," I repeat.

"Yes. More than like," she admits. "But I have to protect myself. I can't fall for clients."

"Then why don't we do this differently? We could meet up in a normal capacity. A date, maybe?" I blush, hardly believing I just said that. Sasha's suggestion seemed ridiculous yesterday but now that she's told me we can't do this again, I'm desperate to hold onto her in any way I can. "Or you could come here on the weekend? Nicole is staying in New York and Nola won't be here. I'll cook for you and we can talk."

"I can't do that." Belle puts on her socks and her sneakers and scans the room for anything she's forgotten.

"Why? Because you don't do dates?"

"No." She pauses, glancing at the door as if looking for an escape route, then changes her mind and sits on the edge of the bed. "Look, you and I can never date, don't you understand that?" she asks, taking my hand. "My clients fall for me all the time because I'm the first person to pay them physical attention at a point in their lives when they need it most. They have a fantasy, I make that fantasy come true and they get carried away for a while. But in the end, I'm not what they want. They want a wealthy man who can take care of them, not an escort with a kid." She shrugs. "Believe me, I'm not what you want, Reina. This is just a storm in the still waters of your life. It will pass."

"You don't know what I want."

"Oh, really? Because let's say we started dating, would you ever take me to parties as your girlfriend? Would you introduce me to your family? Would you be willing to accept my daughter? Because that's what a relationship is. It's not just me showing up on the doorstep of your multimillion-dollar mansion when it suits you."

"Hey, that's not fair," I say, raising my voice.

Belle sighs. "I'm sorry, you're right. I shouldn't have said that but please try and see this from my perspective. We come from different worlds, you and I. We make no sense together."

"Is this about money?"

"Yes and no," Belle says. "Reina, we both know you're fabulously wealthy and have powerful friends. Don't think I haven't seen those pictures on the shelf above your fireplace. I'm a single mom who services your pool and my best friend is my booker from the escort agency. How do you think our lives could ever come together? What on earth would your friends and family think of me? Even if I quit my escort job, wouldn't you be worried they would find out about my past? And what if this is just a phase to you? I have Suki to think of; I can't just date anyone, let alone a straight woman who's so out of my league I can't even begin to describe it."

"I don't care what anyone thinks of me." As I say it, I know that may not be entirely true, and I also know she has good reason to say all those things. Could I really come out to my family? How would I feel if we were seen out and about in public together, holding hands, or kissing? Until now, she's been my biggest secret and I could deal with that because I was sure no one would find out. Sensing my inner conflict, Belle simply nods and squeezes my hand, her expression sad but resolute.

"No, Reina. We can't date, it will never work. But for what it's worth, this has meant more to me than you'll ever know." She gets up and walks out of my room, leaving me in bed feeling more conflicted than ever. I want to run after her and tell her nothing matters because no one's made me feel the way she does. I want to beg her to give me another chance but knowing what's at stake for her and knowing deep down that this is something I have to think through very carefully, I do nothing. When I hear the front door close, a sense of overwhelming sadness takes over. Glancing at the bed, I miss her already so I get out, put on my robe and head downstairs to pour myself a glass of wine.

It's still raining and fat droplets trickle down my face as I head for the beach barefoot with my wine in hand. I need the weather to wash away my confusion as I let Belle's final words sink in. I didn't imagine it. Everything I felt was real and she felt it too. It's a small comfort, but it doesn't make me feel any better. Lightning flashes overhead, a bold pattern of blinding forks pulsing through the sky. Waves crash wildly against the shore, the power of the ocean reflecting my inner turmoil. Maybe Belle is right, maybe this is for the best. Storms are beautiful, unpredictable and delightfully dangerous, evoking wonderment and excitement. But they can also be destructive.

BELLE - TUESDAY

"*H*oney, are you okay?" Jackie looks worried when she sees me.

"Yeah. I think so." I fall back on the couch and let out a long sigh, then realize that I'm not okay at all. "My client... she's..." My voice trails off and I swallow hard, looking down at my hands resting in my lap.

"Was she rude to you?" Jackie straightens her back, her protective instincts kicking in. "I swear, I will kill her if she did anything to hurt you or—"

"No, it's nothing like that," I interrupt her and shoot her a reassuring smile. "I have feelings for her, Jackie. I'm totally head over heels and I didn't know what to do so I told her I couldn't see her anymore."

"Oh..." Jackie stares at me for a moment, then heads for the fridge, opens two bottles of beer and hands me one. Sensing I need to talk, she sits next to me and puts an arm around me. "This was bound to happen at some point, sweetheart. You can't just have sex and expect to never develop any feelings at all."

"No, I normally have no problem detaching myself," I say.

"But it was different with Reina. There was just this instant attraction and even though she only booked me twice, it just got too intimate for me to handle."

Jackie nods and runs a hand over my cheek. "Maybe it's time that you stop doing this sooner rather than later. There's no need to carry on for another couple of months just for the sake of the money. It's not worth it if it upsets you like this."

"Yeah." I don't have the energy to argue against that and anyway, I know she's right. I've had no joy from my jobs in the past two weeks. All I thought of was Reina, she's completely taken over my mind.

"What about her? How does she feel about you?"

"She said she wanted to go on a date." I hold up a hand when Jackie's about to say something. "Stop, Jackie. She was married to a man for most of her life and she's very rich. I was foolish letting myself get carried away like this. It's likely that it's just a phase to her and eventually she'll end up with a man."

"Right. Of course." Jackie gives me a sympathetic smile. "But she can't be all that straight if she's sleeping with you…" She chuckles, lightening the mood a little.

"That's true. But it's too complicated for me." I shrug. "I think I upset her, and I should probably apologize for that. I feel bad about how I left."

"Were you rude?"

"No. I just told her the truth. That she and I could never work because we're too different and that I have to think of Suki with every decision I make."

Jackie carefully chooses her words in the silence that follows. "You've been incredibly selfless, Belle. And I'm so, so proud of you for doing so well and for being such a great mother to Suki. Believe me; I saw you struggle in the beginning, and sometimes it was incredibly difficult not to step in.

I didn't because I knew it was important for you to do right by your sister, and that you needed to own that sense of responsibility." She pauses and pulls me in. "But having a child doesn't mean you can't seek out your own happiness and allow yourself to make mistakes. It's okay to make mistakes so don't rule out a chance of love just because you think it won't work out. No one is perfect and Suki doesn't expect you to be."

Jackie's eyes are so kind and warm that I almost burst into tears. Almost, because I haven't cried in years and I'm not going to start now. "I just don't want to bring someone into Suki's life who won't stick around. She's lost too much already."

Jackie shakes her head, disagreeing with me. "Honey, you haven't even been on a date. Suki doesn't need to meet her unless it gets serious." She pauses. "Besides, I think most of all, she just wants to see you happy."

I hear her words, but they don't click into place. "Trust me, this will bring me nothing but heartache." Taking a long drink of my beer, I stare up at the ceiling and try to erase Reina's face from my mind. "Another client has been following me around," I say, feeling a need to confess everything that's been bugging me lately. "She showed up at the Harborside Café when I was there with Suki and she basically suggested she'd get a divorce so we could live happily ever after."

Jackie gasps. "No…"

"Yeah. I had to have her blocked from the system."

"Are you going to call the police?"

"I can't. She hasn't done anything wrong. Not really." I sigh. "I think that was the last I'll ever see of her, though. I lied, told her I was in a relationship, and she was pretty upset when she left. But my point is that some women think I'm the one just because I'm their first woman. Because I've made an impact on their life and made them reconsider what they want, but it doesn't work that way."

"I see. And you think this woman, Reina... You think she's getting carried away too?"

"It's possible, I have no way of knowing. I should probably apologize to her, then keep my distance." Picking at the label on my bottle, I'm thinking out loud. "I don't know why I'm being so emotional, maybe because it's Linda's anniversary tomorrow."

"Maybe. I've been a little out of sorts myself," Jackie admits. "See how you feel after tomorrow."

"Yeah. Want me to pick you up so we can drive to the cemetery together?"

"That would be great."

I finish my beer and get up. "Thanks for the talk, Jackie." I turn as I'm about to go into Suki's bedroom to check on her. "I hope you know how much I appreciate you."

"I do know, honey." Jackie gets up, walks over to me and gives me a hug.

"What's that for?" I ask, hugging her back tightly and cherishing the comfort, however small. It's been a long time since I felt this way, but it's also been a while since I let someone in, and I know Reina's going to be hard to let go of.

"Because you need one. I'm here for you, okay?" She steps back and smiles at me, her kind eyes telling me everything will be fine with time. "I'm here."

REINA - WEDNESDAY

*B*elle hasn't been in this morning. At first, I was worried it might be because of me, but the man who came in her place assured me that she wasn't sick, and that she'd planned this day off weeks in advance. I miss having her around, and in an attempt to stop myself from thinking of her, I've come down to the beach with my camera. Sitting cross-legged on a towel in the shade of the parasol I brought with me, I zoom in on something splashing in the ocean ahead of me. *It's a seal.* I haven't seen one since I bought my camera and I kick off my sandals and wade in, trying to get closer as I focus on the spot where I saw it disappearing under the surface. My heart skips a beat when it pops its little head up again and looks right at me, and I feel a surge of excitement when I manage to capture it just perfectly. It doesn't seem scared, just curious, and even swims toward me until my phone rings in the pocket of my shorts, scaring him off.

Groaning in frustration, I fish it out, then groan once again when I read the name on the screen. "Hi, Mom," I say, putting on a cheery tone.

"Hello, Reina. I haven't spoken to you in a while, so I thought I'd give you a ring."

"Yes, it's been a while." I wade back out and lower myself into the sand, allowing gentle waves to wash over my toes. My shorts are getting wet but as long as my camera stays dry I don't care.

"Where are you? It's so noisy."

"I'm at the beach and I was just taking a photograph of a seal." Looking out over the surface, I'm disappointed to see it swim away. "But it's gone now, so never mind."

"Are you back into photography again?" she asks.

"Yes, I bought a new camera and I've been practicing. I'm really having fun with it."

"You were always artistic." My mother coos something silly and incoherent, which means one of her cats has just climbed onto her lap. "So, how are you? How are you and Sandeep? Is he back home yet?"

Already regretting picking up, I let out a long sigh and shake my head. "We're divorced, Mom. He's not coming back."

"Nonsense. Every marriage has its ups and downs." She clears her throat before continuing the standard speech I've heard too many times to count. "It's never the fairy tale portrayed in movies, but a strong marriage can—"

"Can overcome anything," I say, finishing her sentence. "Yeah well, it's not going to happen and you need to accept that it's over. I've accepted it a long time ago." There's a silence at the end of the line and I'm hoping she'll finally let it go. When I filed for divorce, my mother was the biggest challenge in the emotional process. I had no problem telling the kids and my friends, but I waited three months to tell my mother, putting if off because I knew it would turn into a never-ending discussion and total denial. It seems that even though she has been thousands of miles away for over twenty years, she still manages to dominate my life from across the pond.

"But you could talk to him, make amends. Whatever has happened—"

"What happened was that he had an affair. He's now quite happily living with his new girlfriend." I leave out the part where they're having a baby as my mother would likely be straight on the phone to him and I don't want that. Separation is semi-acceptable, divorce is not, but having a child with someone else falls into a whole different league. "Anyway, even if he wanted to come back, I'm not interested."

"Why not?" she asks incredulously. "Surely for the sake of the kids you'd want to try and repair this."

"The kids are fine and I'm fine. Let it go."

"They're not fine. I saw pictures of Eddie and Maddie on Instagram and they're sleeping in shacks and hammocks. Clearly your separation has taken a toll on him already."

"Divorce, Mom, not separation," I correct her. "And Eddie is thoroughly enjoying himself. He's backpacking and it's by choice, not because he's homeless, he'll always have a home here with me. Now, let's talk about something else or I promise I'll hang up."

"Very well." A dramatic sigh follows, and then she says: "Your Uncle Achmed was here yesterday. I had him and his friend over for dinner. They're a strange pair, those two. Very close friends, even though they couldn't be more different."

That's because they're a couple. "How nice. How were they?"

"Oh, they were just getting ready to attend a summer ball somewhere in Switzerland. He's very cosmopolitan, Achmed. They brought me some very special dates from Dubai, they were delicious. I'll ask him to send you a box." She produces some more squeaky noises, and I can actually hear purring. "My babies are fine too. Ruby is just asking for her lunch and

181

she's had an upset stomach for the past two days so I can't talk for very long."

Then why did you call me? "Okay, Mom. I'll let you go. Is Ruby going to be okay?"

"Yes, I believe so. I had a vet over here yesterday and he told me three days of steamed chicken breast would do the trick. I've been terribly stressed, especially since I've brought a new baby into the household, so there's a bit of tension here while they're all getting used to each other."

"Another one?"

"Yes. Her name is Reina, I named her after you. She's the prettiest Persian I've ever had. A long, snow-white coat and bright blue eyes."

Weirdly, this is probably the nicest thing my mother has ever said to me, and I find myself smiling. "That's sweet. Take good care of them and I'll book a flight to come over and see you soon."

"Thank you, honey. And please do bring Sandeep and the kids over. It's been almost two years since we were all together."

BELLE - WEDNESDAY

*P*erhaps I should have told Reina I wouldn't be coming in today, but I wasn't thinking clearly when I took off in a rush last night. The anniversary of Linda's death is always a difficult day for me and knowing that this might be the first year that Suki can understand the truth, only makes it harder.

Heading for her grave with big bunches of white lilies, my father, Jackie, Suki and I cross the cemetery in silence. We never speak much on this day; we're just here to remember her, all in our own way. Past the bent willow that arches over a network of narrow paths, her white headstone shimmers in the sunlight. It's strange to think Linda's been reduced to this, a piece of white marble with her name on it. The quiet spot in the back of the cemetery is beautiful, though, with wildflowers now scattered throughout the grass. She's lying next to my mother, who has a similar headstone, and both their graves are tidy, the red roses my father put there are still blooming. He visits several times a week, even in winter, but I only come once a year as I'd rather remember Linda the way she was; always positive, sweet, caring and good-natured. It's not fair that she was taken from us so soon, but after grief counselling and turning all my attention to Suki, I've accepted her death, and now I can be here without bursting into floods of tears.

Still, it's difficult and as if she knows I'm struggling, my usually talkative Suki silently tightens her grip on my hand and looks up at me as we come to a halt by her mother's grave. My father places the extra vase he's brought next to the other one on the stone plateau, slides the flowers in and adds water from a Coke bottle. Then he takes the basket with daisies—my mother's favorite—from Jackie and places them on her grave. He's always made sure my mother has fresh flowers; he used to bring us here every week when Linda and I were young, and now he's doing the same for Linda. Knowing how I've felt, I can't imagine the pain he's been through, but he still smiles his way through life. What strength that must take, and I admire him for it. Unlike my father, I never went to church and although I wasn't completely onboard with the 'angels' part of the inscription he ordered for the headstone, I like it now.

Linda Rodgers
Singing with the angels
Beloved daughter, sister and mother
Your voice will always ring through our hearts

"LINDA," Dad murmurs. "We're here." Then he takes a deep breath and looks up at the sky. "Honey, I hope you're taking good care of her."

"Linda," Suki repeats quietly.

"Linda was your first mom," I say, pointing to the picture

that's placed in front of her headstone. It shows Linda with a beaming smile at a festival in Nashville. She's wearing a bohemian white dress and she's got flowers in her hair. It was where she became pregnant following a one-night stand with a handsome stranger after performing as a backing singer for a big act. "She was also my sister and a very good singer."

"Can I have a sister?" Suki brightens the mood a little with her random question, and we all chuckle.

"I don't think that will happen, honey. But you can have as many friends as you want. Sometimes friends are just as valuable as family." I pick her up, lift her onto my hip and kiss her cheek.

"Is Linda in heaven?"

"Yes, she is. She's with Grandma. We all miss them very much, but we'll see them again one day, a long time from now." I'm not sure why I'm telling her this as I don't believe in heaven, but it seems like the right thing to say to a four-year-old.

"How many sleeps until we see them?" Suki asks.

Jackie smiles at her and shakes her head. "For you, many, many sleeps. Too many to count, so don't worry your little head about it."

Seeing Suki's puzzled expression, a lump forms in my throat. At least she won't ever feel the stabbing pain of loss since she doesn't remember her mother. I don't remember mine either and it's much easier that way. Over the years I've formed my own idea of who she was, combining photographs I've seen and stories my father and Jackie told me into a mental collage of a sweet, beautiful, smart, loving and inspiring woman. Of course, no one is as perfect as I picture her, but I like my imaginary mother and it worked for me growing up.

"Four years," Jackie says. "How time flies." She sighs

deeply and puts an arm around my father who is getting teary.

"Are you sad, Grandpa?" Suki asks.

"Sometimes, sweetheart. Sometimes I'm sad because I miss the people I loved very much." He leans in and strokes her cheek. "But you know what? You make everything better. And so do your mom and Jackie."

Suki grins and reaches out for him and I place her in his arms. "Better," she says, pushing a finger against his nose. She looks so much like Linda when she laughs and deep down, I hope my sister is somehow aware that she's here with us, that she's turned into a sweet, brave girl with an amazing future ahead of her. I hope she knows that I've grown up and calmed down and would do anything to protect Suki, and that the three people here love her more than anything in the world. It's true. She does make everything better.

REINA - FRIDAY

uzzing open the gates, a tight knot forms in my stomach. Waiting for Belle has had me worried all day and I had no idea what time she'd be here. 'Can I come over tonight?' she asked me after servicing my pool this morning. It can only mean one thing: she doesn't want me as her client anymore, not in any capacity. She had an apprentice with her and neither of us knew how to behave with the young man around, so we ignored each other mostly.

It's clear that she's busy arranging her replacement so she won't have to come back and I don't blame her. I'm paying her to look after the pool, and I've been paying her for sex. There's something very wrong about that and I won't deny that it's been bugging me all along. I don't want her to think of me as some spoilt rich woman who thinks she can get anything she wants as long as she throws enough money at it.

When I open the door, I curse the anxiety twisting in my stomach. I know it's stupid to fall in love with an escort. It's foolish and reckless and naïve, and still, it doesn't stop me from wanting her all the time, from dreaming of having some sort of relationship with her. My need to be with her is so strong that I'd take anything at this point. Anything.

"Hi," I say, letting her in. "I expected you earlier. Are you not seeing someone tonight?"

"No, I cancelled."

"Oh." I head to the fridge and pour two glasses of wine. She looks serious and if she wants to talk, I need one.

"No thank you," she says when I offer her a glass. "I drove."

I nod, suspecting she wants to get this over with quickly. "I know what you're going to tell me."

"Do you?" When Belle steps toward me, I suppress a moan at her closeness.

"Yeah. I won't book you again." I say simply, pretending this isn't hurting me. Kissing her is all I can think of but I refrain. "No hard feelings, I promise."

"Thank you, that's probably for the best. I ehm... I wanted to say I'm sorry if I've hurt you or upset you." Her voice is low and croaky, and a little emotional, if I'm not mistaken.

"Don't worry about me, I'm fine." The brave smile I put on is only half-hearted. "And I'm sorry if I got too close." We linger in silence, ignoring the roaring charge between us. I look at her, she looks at me, and I can almost feel her internal struggle. I'm waiting for her to turn around and leave but instead, Belle reaches out to trace my cheek, her shifting expression shocking me. It's not the look of regret or pity. I've seen that look before, in bed.

"What are you doing?" I whisper when she leans in, backing me up against the kitchen counter. I feel her abdomen against mine, her breasts against my chest.

"I have no idea." Belle sounds as confused as I am, yet there's no doubt we both want the same thing. Her lips brush mine, and without hesitation, I curl my fingers around her neck, pull her closer against me and kiss her hard. I've missed her, and when she wraps her arms around me and kisses me back hungrily, I know she's missed me too. Knowing she wants this, knowing she craves me makes kissing her even more heavenly and instinctively, I reach for the hem of her tank top and lift it. She doesn't ask me if I'm okay, she doesn't go slow and it drives me wild when she tears off her top, then pulls up my dress before lifting me onto the counter. This is not about me anymore. This is about her and me. About us, together.

Belle spreads my legs and steps between them and carnal desire oozes between us while we make out in the kitchen like it's the first time. In a way, it is. It's the first *real* time. I feel her nails scrape over my shoulder blades underneath my dress that is hiked up to my midriff now, and I slip my hands into the back of her jeans to squeeze her behind.

"I want you, Reina," she mumbles against my mouth, and moves her hand between my legs.

Her words heighten my arousal; it's incredible to feel wanted like this. I know she can feel how wet I am as she rubs her fingers over my panties, making me moan loudly. Again, her touch isn't careful or considered but hard and urgent, and I want her to fuck me like never before. She doesn't even bother taking off my panties and wedges two fingers under the edge, finding my drenched center.

"Fuck! Yes!" I cry out, throwing my head back when she enters me with two fingers. Belle fucks me hard and fast, then adds a third finger, and my body can barely keep up with all the delicious sensations that hit me one after another. I love how she lifts her gaze to stare into my eyes with a look that says she's really, really enjoying this too. This is raw and sexy and impulsive and everything that I'm not, at least not until today. I feel an enormous climax building and cling onto her while she draws it out of me faster than I thought physically possible.

"Mmm…" Belle moans when she feels my contractions, and she curls her fingers, making me cry out so loudly that my voice echoes through the house.

I cup her face to kiss her, needing all of her at once and give into the waves of pleasure that wash over me again and again. I'm still basking in aftershocks, gasping in delight every few seconds, when the front door suddenly swings open with force.

"Mom! Are you okay?"

Somewhere in the back of my mind, I register the voice is Nicole's, and I also note she sounds panicky. And then *I* panic, because I'm sitting on the kitchen counter and Belle is between my legs and her fingers are inside me. And my daughter, who wasn't supposed to be here this weekend, has just barged in. *My daughter.*

Belle is clearly more prepared than I am because in a matter of seconds, she's pulled out of me, yanked my dress down and put on her top. Now, she's staring at Nicole, wide-eyed with her hands deep in the back pockets of her jeans as if she's trying to hide them from the world.

"Nicole… this is not…" I stop myself there as this is clearly exactly what it looks like and there's no point claiming otherwise.

Nicole drops her weekend bag and stands nailed to the ground, silently looking from me to Belle. I see a hint of recognition in her eyes before she glances at the pool and back to us again. Raising a hand to her mouth, she takes a step back through the open door.

"Nicole, please wait. Let me explain…" I know what she's thinking. Mommy's gone mad. Mommy's messing around with the staff. Mommy's having a mid-life crisis. Mommy's not who I thought she was. And then I see her eyes are red-rimmed and I'm worried about her more than I'm worried about this situation.

Nicole doesn't answer but bolts quickly out the door.

"Wait!" I jump off the counter and run after her, but she's already in her car and reversing in our driveway, opening the gates with her remote.

uck. Why? I wasn't meant to do that. My knuckles turn white from clasping the steering wheel so hard my hands hurt. *Fuck.* Now I've messed up her life completely. Reina's expression as her daughter walked in on us will never leave my mind, and neither will Nicole's gasp of disgust and utter shock. I knew there was a risk we wouldn't be able to keep our hands off each other, but I hadn't anticipated this.

Now she'll have to explain something to her daughter that she probably doesn't even understand herself. She'll have to explain why she was having sex with the pool woman on the kitchen counter and with that, there will be many, many questions she hasn't even had the time to reflect on.

"Fuck!" I curse, this time out loud, and slow down so my driving at least is less reckless than my behavior. What I did was selfish and stupid. I cancelled my client tonight because I couldn't imagine sleeping with anyone but her, and then I showed up at her house and acted like some horny teenager. And then her daughter walked in. Her daughter of all people.

I didn't go there with the intention of doing what I did. I

wanted to apologize, talk to her so there wouldn't be any awkwardness between us. But then I saw her and all my restraint evaporated. No woman has ever made me behave out of character and make me loose myself like this. I have to get Reina out of my mind and the only way to do that, is to cut all ties. I instruct my phone to call the Pool Masters office, and impatiently wait for someone to pick up. Luckily, it's Sam who I've known for years.

"Hey, Sam, it's Belle here."

"Hey there. You okay?"

"Yeah. I was wondering if you could do me a favor. It's about the morning shifts I've taken over from Barry."

"Okay, what can I do for you?"

"Well, I know I said I was happy to do it, but the sitter told me the long days are too much for her. Do you think you could find someone else?"

"Oh." Sam pauses and I can hear tapping noises. "Let me have a look… Okay, we have options here. I can make some calls, but I can't promise anything. It should be okay, though; I'll get back to you."

"Thanks, Sam. You're a lifesaver. I'll talk to you later," I say, putting on a cheery voice. After hanging up, I call Hamptons' Escorts and I'm greeted by Juliette, who sounds a little stressed.

"Hey, hun. It's Friday night and I'm really busy. Do you mind calling back later?"

"This will only take a minute," I say, getting straight to the point. "Will you take me off the system, please?"

"For tonight? I already took you off this afternoon when you asked me to," she answers impatiently.

"No, I mean, could you take me off entirely?"

"What?" She hesitates. "You mean you're not going to see out your three months?"

"No. I'm done." A sting of unease hits me when I realize

I'm giving up my main source of income, but I simply can't keep doing this. First Mrs. Ashworth, and now this. It's becoming too much, too complicated, aside from the fact that I feel like I'm cheating on someone I'm not even in a relationship with and never will be. I'm angry with myself for letting it come this far, for doing the one thing I always promised myself I wouldn't: falling for a client.

"Babe, are you okay?" Juliette's voice softens.

"I'm fine, just get back to your calls, we can talk later."

"No way. My bestie just quit out of the blue and I want to know why."

Frustration takes over and I slam my hand on the steering wheel. "Because I messed up, okay? I went to Reina's house and I fucked her in the kitchen and her daughter walked in on us. You should have seen the look on her face." I pause and shake my head. "I can't do this anymore, Jules. I'm getting invested, and it feels too emotional now."

"Oh, babe." She sighs. "Are you sure?"

"Yes. Everything has changed; I had a good thing going but I know I won't enjoy the work anymore. I'm going to focus on setting up my new company for a while. I need a break." *I need to get over Reina.* "Please cancel all my standing appointments too. I'm sorry if that gives you any trouble."

"No, no, I'll deal with it right away." She clears her throat. "It's going to be okay, babe. Just breathe. Can we meet up tomorrow?"

"Yeah. I'll pick you up for the market. Same time as usual," I say, and try to breathe steadily before I hang up.

Oh God, I've done it. I've taken the leap. My life now lays dauntingly uncertain ahead of me and I have no idea if my business will take off or not. Having something to fall back on was easy. Too easy maybe. But still, it was what I needed with Suki. It's time to focus and network now and forget about women altogether. If I stay busy enough, I'll be able to stop thinking about her and she'll forget about me too. Maybe this was the push I needed. It's better this way.

REINA - FRIDAY

he house is even more charming close-up than the glimpse I caught through the hedge when I stopped here once to see what my ex-husband and his new flame were up to. The front yard—an English style yard as Bree first described it to me when she was designing our living room interior—is filled with wildflowers, birdfeeders, cute fountains and rose bushes. Everything looks like it's spontaneously sprouted out of the ground, yet I know she's planned every blade of grass to the tee, just like she planned to steal my husband while pretending to be my friend. I don't even care about that anymore. I don't care that he's left me for her, and I don't care that she's pregnant and that they'll probably live happily ever after in this bohemian paradise. All I care about is Nicole and that she's okay.

Seeing her car in the driveway sends a rush of relief through me. At least she didn't drive back to New York in her current state, but the fact that she's here must mean that she's terribly upset as she's refused to visit Bree's house until now. Sandeep and Nicole occasionally meet up for lunch in Southampton, but other than that, they're not nearly as close as they used to be. This is the first time since he moved in that I'm actually grateful he lives close by.

The bungalow-style villa is painted in a hideously trendy shade of mint, the front door two shades darker, just like the window frames. It opens before I have a chance to ring the bell, and when Sandeep appears, I take a step back, shocked to see him up-close after a year of deliberately avoiding each other. I can tell he's uncomfortable too and the twitch in his eyebrow would have amused me if I wasn't here because of what just happened.

"Reina. Hi."

"Hi." I hold up Nicole's bag. "She forgot her stuff."

Sandeep nods. "Did you two have a fight or something? She's crying in the guest bedroom and she won't tell me what's wrong."

"No…" I realize that I'm not prepared for this conversation at all, and I can't possibly tell him what actually happened. "So you don't know either," I say, hoping I sound convincing enough for him to let me off the hook. She might tell him, she might not, but for now, I prefer to keep my cards close to my chest.

Sandeep doesn't look convinced, but he doesn't pry either. I suppose he feels guilty enough toward me as it is and doesn't want to rub me up the wrong way. "No, I don't."

"Can I see her?" I glance over his shoulder into the hallway, suspecting Bree is lurking in the background, listening in on our conversation.

"She told me to leave her alone, but I can ask." Sandeep takes the bag, gestures for me to stay in the doorway and heads to the left down the corridor, giving me a peak into the living room. I catch a glimpse of an Indian rug and a designer couch filled with matching cushions. I imagine them sitting there together, but it doesn't hurt. Bree's shoes and coats are in the hallway, but I see none of Sandeep's, and this amuses me. When he designed our house, he went out of his way to figure out clever storage so we wouldn't need a hallway. He hates them and thinks they're mundane, which I've always disagreed with. I mean, who doesn't need a place to put shoes and coats with a long mirror to check how you look before you leave the house? I even considered having one built after our divorce, just to annoy him.

"Sorry." Sandeep appears again. "She doesn't want to talk to you right now." He gives me an awkward smile. "I'm sure she'll come around, whatever it is."

"Yes, I hope so." I manage to return his smile. "Were you on your way to see me on the beach the other day? I saw you in the distance."

He briefly glances over his shoulder. "Yes, but it can wait. You had company, so I turned back."

"Just a friend," I say, praying Nicole won't sell me out.

"A new friend? I couldn't see his face; he was too far away."

"Her name is Belle." I chuckle, realizing her short hair must have given him the wrong impression from afar.

"Oh." Sandeep awkwardly clears his throat. "Anyway, how are you?" His brow twitches again as he asks the question, no doubt dreading the answer. He's probably bracing himself for something like 'How the fuck do you think I am?', but I smile dutifully back at him.

"Not bad." I don't mention that I've just had the most thrilling fuck in my life, even though it ended on a highly painful note. "You?"

"Same," he says, and shrugs. "We're good."

There's a silence, and I wait for him to tell me about the baby, but he doesn't. Perhaps he's worried I'll cause a scene here. "Well, I'd better go then. Will you please ask Nicole to call me? I know she's not a kid anymore but I'm worried. She looked like she'd been crying before she arrived."

"Of course. I'll ask her to call you," Sandeep promises. "And I'll try to talk to her."

"Thank you. How's Bree by the way?" I ask as I step away.

Sandeep frowns, as if he can't quite believe the kind of conversation we're having. I'm not sure what he'd expected but it probably wasn't this civilized—albeit artificial—and I'm sure it throws him. "She's good," he says, then pauses again. "She's..."

"She's what?"

"No, I just meant she's been fine. Work, life..." His voice trails away and then the opportunity has passed. He's not going to tell me now, but I know he will when he's ready.

"Right, that's good." I fiddle with my keys and walk back to my car. "I'll wait to hear from Nicole."

"Okay." After an awkward exchange of polite smiles, Sandeep steps outside and casts another quick, shifty look over his shoulder, then joins me by the car. I open my window, giving him the chance to speak. "Reina..."

"Yes?" I lock my eyes with his and the anger I was convinced would overtake me once I saw him again still hasn't shown its evil self.

"I just wanted to say that..." He leans forward and rests his elbow on the top of the car. "I just wanted to say that I'm sorry. For what I did to you."

I sit with his apology for a while as it's the first time he's actually said this to my face, and I want to give him an honest reply. "Are you happy?" I ask.

"Yes. I think so."

"Then I'm happy for you," I assure him. "Take care."

"How do you feel?" Juliette asks. "Now that you've taken the leap. I didn't think you'd quit before your business was properly off the ground. I thought we had agreed three months."

"Scared," I say honestly, letting go of Suki's hand. My father who is tending to his stall at the Sag Harbor farmers market, spreads his arms and lifts her up. Cameron follows and immediately sits down in one of the two children's-sized folding chairs my father has ready for them. Suki and Cameron look forward to their trips to the farmers market, partly because they get some pocket money for 'helping' him, and partly because sitting behind their toy till makes them feel terribly grown-up and important. My father waves at me, letting me know he'll keep an eye on them while Juliette and I get some groceries and go for a coffee. "Escorting was my safety blanket, an easy way to make money, and I've never been very entrepreneurial, so I guess all I can do is work hard and hope for the best."

Over winter, the farmers market in Sag Harbor belongs to the villagers. It's a social place where we reflect, catch up on the week and sample the produce before we buy it. Now that most of the seasonal crowd has returned, it's too busy for small talk. My father barely produces enough goods to keep up with the summer demand, and he's usually sold out before midday. Expanding the farm is not an option at his age and anyway, making artisanal cheese and yoghurt has always just been a hobby to him.

"You can still have your job back, if you change your mind. The boss was gutted that you left us." Juliette smiles at my father and calls: "Thank you, Frank!"

"No problem, I couldn't do this without them." He shoots us a wink and turns back to Suki and Cameron, taking his time to get them settled before turning to one of the many customers queuing.

"Thanks, Jules, but I won't change my mind," I say. "I want to be someone Suki can be proud of. She's almost five and understands more than I realize sometimes." I shrug. "Don't get me wrong; I was never ashamed of my job, but it's certainly not the life I want for her, so I should set her the right example." I stop off at one of the stalls to buy a seeded baguette, and Juliette buys a gluten free loaf. "Besides, after Reina, I just can't do it anymore. I need some time to forget about her."

"I understand and I'm sorry if I didn't take you seriously. I had no idea how deep this went." She lowers her voice. "But I'll miss our laughs about your clients."

"Yeah, me too." I chuckle. "No more spanking Mrs. Palmer with random kitchen paraphernalia, pretending she's my naughty sous-chef."

Juliette laughs too. "I sent Red over as your replacement yesterday, but Mrs. P wasn't happy and offered double to get you back. You must be good."

"To be honest with you, I was starting to run out of ideas

and her kitchen was a total mess after each session. I feel sorry for her cleaner."

"I guess you've taken food porn to a whole new level." Juliette looks over her shoulder to check no one is listening in. "So, what exactly happened yesterday? You were all over the place on the phone, I think I might have missed something."

"It's all a bit of a blur," I say, the gloomy feeling in my core spreading. "I went over to Reina's house to talk, after leaving in a hurry on Wednesday. I wanted to end things in a decent way because I love spending time with her, and I suppose we were on our way to becoming new friends. But then I saw her and this insatiable hunger took over. Reina kissed me first I think but as I said, it's all a blur. And then one thing led to another faster than I could fathom and Nicole, her daughter, walked in on me fucking her mother on the kitchen counter. She was really upset and drove off. I think that just about sums everything up." I pause, remembering the mortified look in Reina's eyes. "I messed up big time."

"Hey, it takes two," Juliette says. "You're both adults, you didn't do anything wrong."

"I may have ruined Reina's relationship with her daughter. Everything about that is wrong."

"Will you see her again?"

"No, I can't go back to that house, there's a good chance her kids will be there over summer. I've asked Pool Masters to swap my shifts with someone else, so that's the end of it." I let out a long sigh. "I should have never allowed myself to get close to her."

"You can't fight the real deal," Juliette says. "It's rare."

"It's unrealistic. That's what it is, end of discussion." I walk over to the coffee stand and order three cappuccinos, one in a take-out cup for my father, and we sit down at a picnic table.

"Sure, boss." Juliette rolls her eyes.

"Hey, I'm not your boss. At least not yet," I say, changing the subject.

"What do you mean?"

"I have my first event coming up soon, through a party planner I signed up with a while back. It's a sweet sixteen with about forty teenagers at a house in East Hampton. I was wondering if you could help me out, if you want to make some extra cash?"

"You have your first job? That's great."

"Yeah. And I need this first one to go really well so that I can get more gigs out of it. Imagine all the parents who will be there with children around the same age. It's the perfect self-marketing job." I manage a smile, not quite feeling the excitement I should. The booking came through last week, but my mind has been so occupied with Reina that I hadn't thought about it much. It's time to focus, though; I've invested too much in this to let anything slip. "So, are you in?"

"Absolutely. What do you need me to do?" she asks.

"Just help me out, make sure the proposal for the planner is perfect. I need to send it to her as soon as possible."

"Of course I'll help you. This is so cool, Belle." Juliette beams. "I don't want your money, though; you know the way to my heart. Just cook me a meal and pour me a large glass of wine."

REINA - SUNDAY

The beach is deserted when I saunter toward the shore on Sunday morning. The sand is cool against my bare feet, and the scent of last night's rainfall hangs thick in the air. A layer of mist dances over the ocean, featherlight and translucent. Raising my camera, I take a couple of pictures of the mesmerizing view in the morning light. It has a blue, almost eerie tone to it, and it feels incredibly lonely at this time of day.

Spotting a crab, I lay down to get a good close-up of it, then continue to wade with the water up to my ankles. I've missed this; just me and my camera. The sand is smooth all the way up to the first enormous sleeping villas along this stretch, still void of footprints. Soon, adults, children and dogs will venture out to enjoy another morning in their home away from home and it's nice that the Hamptons are coming to life again.

When I realize I've almost reached Sandeep and Bree's house—the point where I normally turn and walk back—I see a figure in the distance, sitting on the beach, facing the ocean. It's Nicole. Zooming in on her, my heart breaks when

I see her expression, and I refrain from taking a picture. She looks so sad. She still hasn't called me, but she sent me a message telling me she's okay and although I've respected her plea to leave her alone for now, I feel an urge to approach her. I can't help it; ignoring her would go against my motherly instinct.

"Mom?" Nicole looks up at me and frowns.

"I swear I didn't know you were here," I say, holding up a hand. "I was just walking and taking some pictures and—"

"It's okay. I know you wouldn't do that." Nicole turns my way, hugging her knees. "How's the new camera?"

"It's great, I love it." When I see no anger in her eyes, I point to the sand. "Can I sit with you?"

Nicole hesitates for a moment, then says, "Okay."

I sit down cross-legged, put the cover over my lens and stare out over the ocean, waiting for her to speak first.

"Are you gay?" she asks after a long silence.

"I'm not sure, honey, but I think so. Would you mind if I was?"

"No..." Nicole fiddles with the hem of her T-shirt. "But... you've been with dad all your life. Were you even happy with him?"

"Of course I was happy. Your father and you and your brother were my whole life. I've loved being a wife and a mother. I still love being a mother, and always will." I pause. "But now that everything has changed and I'm starting to accept that, I feel an urge to explore who I am, to be not only a mother, but my own person, if that makes sense. And what I'm currently going through is a part of that." All I can do is be honest with her now and I hope my answer makes sense.

She nods. "Were you ever with a woman before dad?"

"No. I've had mild crushes on women when I was younger, but I've only ever been with your dad. Sexually, I mean."

Nicole grimaces, as if the words 'dad' and 'sexually' are too much for her to handle in one sentence. Another long silence goes by before she asks: "Are you in love with the pool lady?"

"We're not serious, and her name is Belle," I say, immediately regretting my defensive tone.

"I know, I just had to say it." Nicole lets out a sarcastic chuckle. "It's just so cliché, it's almost funny. I mean, I thought dad was a cliché, but you've trumped his midlife crisis by miles."

I can't help but laugh too because when she puts it like that, I can see what this looks like. "It's not a midlife crisis, and I don't think your dad is going through one either."

"Are you sure about that? He told me last night he's been thinking about buying a Ferrari. Bree is against it because—" Nicole stops herself then.

"Because she wants a big family car?" I say, unable to resist.

Nicole's eyes widen. "You know?"

"Yes, I know Bree's pregnant. Your father hasn't told me yet. Perhaps he's still working up the courage."

"Does it upset you that they're having a baby?"

"I was a shaken when I first found out," I admit. "But I think I can be happy for them. What about you?"

"I don't know. I guess I'll have to get used to the idea." When Nicole scoots closer and rests her head on my shoulder, I fight back tears of happiness. My girl is back again, and everything will be okay.

"I imagine this is hard for you. Moving to campus, your parents being away from New York, your father starting a new life and me..." I let my voice trail off because I don't really know what it is I'm doing. Instead, I put an arm around her and pull her against me.

"No harder than for you," she says. "Are you going to tell

dad about the pool lady? Sorry, I mean Belle," she corrects herself.

"No, I wasn't planning on it. It's none of his business and as I said, it's nothing. It's not serious whatsoever." As the words leave my mouth, I know that's not true. Our paid encounters aside, I know what happened between Belle and I was real. The mutual attraction part, at least. "But if you feel the need to talk about it with him, then it wouldn't be fair of me to ask you to keep it to yourself."

"I won't tell him. He kept his affair secret for months, he doesn't deserve to know anything about your life." Nicole gives me a small smile. "Besides, Dad and I never talk about real stuff anyway. He just asks about my exams and boyfriends and that kind of stuff."

"And? How is the boyfriend?" I ask.

"Tyrell and I had a fight. He keeps cancelling on me whenever he gets a last-minute gig." Nicole's shrugs. "It's his job, so I do understand but it just made me feel rejected. That's why I came here on Friday. I was upset and I just wanted to be home."

"I'm sorry to hear that, honey. And then you found me like that." I bury my face in my hands, cringing as a series of flashbacks of my daughter walking in on me and Belle loom large in my mind. I hope to God that she never finds out Belle's an escort.

"I thought you were being attacked," Nicole says. "You were screaming." When I groan, she laughs and puts an arm around me in return. "Oh well, at least you were enjoying it." She takes the camera from around my neck and turns it on. "Can I see the pictures you've taken?"

"Of course." All tension from the past few days seeps away from me like the outgoing tide, and I finally allow myself to smile.

BELLE - MONDAY

*W*ith Barry's shifts diverted to someone else, my Monday morning lies ahead of me. I try not to think of the fact that Reina will find out I've stopped working for her and instead, I open the list of local party organizers I've been meaning to call. Out of the thirty-eight names, I've only approached three so far, of which one has agreed to work with me after confirming my proposal. Until I looked into it, I had no idea there were so many but then again, the Hamptons is a playground where just about anything is celebrated.

Suki is at preschool and I'm rarely here without her, so the silence feels strange when I'm sitting at the balcony table with my laptop and a coffee. Most of my orders have arrived and I spent yesterday in my storage container, organizing everything. It's a little crammed but it will do for the coming year and if I need to, I can always upgrade. Just as I'm about to type in the first number, my phone rings, and it's Jackie.

"Hey honey," she says. "I was just checking to see how you were doing."

"I'm okay," I say, ignoring the tight knot in my stomach. I

haven't told Jackie what happened with Reina. "I'm about to call those party organizers and try my luck."

"That's great. Actually, I have someone here who will interest you; I'm sitting with a friend from book club. She's a stylist, or a stager, I think is what they call it, for a big real estate company, and she's telling me all about her super interesting job and how she makes places look pretty for sale. They throw these spectacular viewing parties over one or two nights and invite potential buyers over."

"That does sounds interesting." Mentally I'm already doing the math, imagining the most spectacular pool sides in the Hamptons, decorated by me. Why had I not thought of this myself? These parties are thrown regularly whenever big properties come up for sale.

"I thought so too." Jackie pauses. "Listen, we're sitting at the Harborside Café, if you want to join us? Rose would love to meet you."

"Absolutely, I'd love to meet her too." I glance down at my outfit, then check my watch. "Just give me fifteen minutes, I need to get changed." I swiftly clear the balcony table and swap my T-shirt for a blue shirt. Opportunities like this one don't come up often, and I thank my lucky stars that I have Jackie in my life.

"I LIKE THIS," Rose says, flicking through the brochure I brought. "I like it very much." When she smiles at me, she doesn't strike me as the typical stager. Older, and not as polished as most people in real estate, she has a certain quirkiness to her, an authentic essence of creativity perhaps. "Now let's get down to business before we start the small talk. I prefer to do it the other way around, it's much more pleasant," she says leaning in. "I'm willing to give you all my outdoor business against a twenty-five percent discount."

"Twenty-five is a lot," I retort, ignoring Jackie who is kicking me under the table. I don't want to seem too keen; especially if this might become a long-term contract, I need to keep my cool.

"Not if you take the ease of the job into account. The houses are often not occupied so you can set up whenever you want and if there's one thing you won't get, it's bad reviews or complaints because it's not personal. In fact, most of it is pretty straightforward. On top of all that, we always pay on time—unlike a lot of estate agents, we don't wait until after a property gets sold—and we have regular work." Rose tilts her head. "So, what do you say?"

Rose is very convincing, and because I have a good feeling about her, I smile and shake her hand. "Why not? Let's try it, I'm grateful for the opportunity." She's nothing like Jackie's other friends I've met over the years; she's way more on the ball and she seems like one of those people who always gets what she wants.

Jackie is beaming and holds up her cappuccino. "Excellent. I knew you would be a good match. I just knew it."

"I'm looking forward to doing business with you."

"So am I," Rose says. "Jackie has told me so much about you."

Observing the rather sweet, smiley exchange between Jackie and Rose, I'm confused as to why they seem so close, despite the book club connection. "How long have you known each other?" I ask, pointing a finger between them.

"Four years." Jackie beams. "Since our mutual friend Jeanette started the book club."

"Yes. We have fun there, don't we?" Rose says, nudging her. "Everyone else is so serious, but Jackie says it like it is and she always makes me laugh."

Considering I've never heard of Rose, I wonder why Jackie's kept their friendship so quiet, but I don't pry any further as I have a feeling there's a lot that Jackie's not telling me. "Yes, Jackie's funny," I agree with her, then add: "Would you like to hear some stories?"

"Oh my God, yes please!"

Just like I thought. This is not your average friendship; Rose is way too keen to know more about Jackie from my point of view.

"Please don't," Jackie begs with a chuckle. "Only Belle knows the worst of me."

"I wouldn't say it's the worst," I say in a teasing tone. "In my opinion, it's the best." Rose leans in and she's hanging on my every word now. Her all-business demeanor is gone, replaced by fascination.

"Tell me more," she says, leaning into Jackie.

REINA - MONDAY

"Where's Belle?" I ask when a man from Pool Masters arrives on Monday morning. I was already waiting for her with a coffee, so I hand it to him instead.

"Good morning to you too, and thank you very much for the coffee," the blond, beefy hunk jokes before giving me a wide smile. "Sorry, I didn't mean to be cheeky. I'm Ralph and Belle won't be coming here anymore."

"Oh. Do you know why?"

"Nope." He shrugs. "We're a big company and I don't know her very well. Maybe she swapped shifts."

"Okay." I try to calm myself as this man will no doubt think I'm acting strange. "Well, that's a shame. She was really good and very nice. But I'm sure you are too," I add, returning his smile. "Anyway, I'll be inside. Let me know if you need anything."

Back in the kitchen, I steady myself against the kitchen counter and stare at the spot where I was perched only days ago. Was that a pity fuck after all? Some weird way of saying goodbye? It didn't feel that way, but then again, it wouldn't be the first time I've been wrong about someone. I was wrong about my own husband, for God's sake. Was it Nicole walking in on us? Or was it just too much for her?

Belle's absence stings, and I know it's not fair but the man now throwing chlorine tablets into my pool annoys me, simply because he's not her. I was up at four am, unable to sleep because I thought I was going to see her. I hoped we could continue what we started on Friday as I've longed to make her scream like she did to me. I've longed to kiss her and to hold her again, to look at her. But that's not going to happen now. A sense of desperation and abandonment creeps up on me and the feeling almost chokes me. The urge to see her face is too strong to resist, so I open my laptop and navigate to the Hamptons' Escorts website but my stomach drops when I see she's disappeared from the system.

"What the fuck?" I mutter, cursing when I refresh the page to no avail. I search on her name again and as expected, the message 'not found' comes up. My frustration is replaced by worry then. What if something happened to her? I take my phone from my robe pocket. The robe I bought with her in mind. The robe covering my saucy lingerie meant for her eyes only. I don't have her number, so I dial the escort agency and ask the booker if Belle's available next week just to check if she's okay.

"Belle no longer works for us," she says in a chirpy tone. "But we have lots of other amazing women in our portfolio. Would you like me to talk you through them?"

"No," I say, appalled that this booker is talking about women like she's simply selling goods. It makes me sick, even though I myself am one of the very people who have participated in the scheme of putting a price tag on women's bodies. I'm disgusted by myself, like that time I ordered a down duvet and boasted to my friends about how lovely and warm it was, and then Nicole showed me a video of how the chickens are kept in the factories. That's how I feel right now, only way, way worse. "Is she okay?"

"Yes, I can assure you she's totally fine, it happens sometimes. Our escorts move on to other career opportunities. I'm not in a position to disclose any personal information about her, though. But how about our new girl, Leila? Have you had a look at—"

I hang up before she finishes her sentence and sink to the kitchen floor. Resting my head against the cupboard, I look up at the ceiling in despair. I must ban her from my thoughts. She clearly doesn't want anything more to do with me, so I need to stop trying. *Don't cry*, I tell myself. *Don't cry, it's just a stupid, stupid crush.*

"Miss Amari? What are you doing on the floor?"

"Oh, hey, Nola. I'm just…" I sigh. "I don't know what I'm doing."

Nola kneels in front of me and places her warm hand on my cheek. I haven't seen much of my own mother over the years, and I think Nola knows that as she's naturally taken to fussing over me since I moved here permanently. It's sweet, but right now it doesn't help as her kind smile only chokes me up more. "You look so sad."

"It's nothing."

Nola gets up, sensing I don't want to talk. She glances at the pool before she puts her purse on the counter and checks her phone. She's always on the phone and I don't mind that. Her kids who are in their twenties now, her sisters, her husband and God knows who else ring her non-stop, all day long, but her silly ringtone of some Polish party song always makes me laugh. "Where's Belle? Is she not here today?"

At that, I start crying and mutter a curse at myself for doing so. I tell myself to get a grip. There's no real drama, no death. No one in my family is in trouble or sick, yet Belle vanishing from my life seems to overrule everything else. "I don't know where she is," I say through sniffs. "But I don't think she'll be back."

Nola looks puzzled and kneels down again. "I don't understand," she says, pulling me into a hug. "Why are you so sad about that?"

I don't answer and Nola doesn't pry. "Let me make you a cup of tea. Or would you prefer a coffee? I brought some marble cake I made on the weekend; the chocolate one you like."

"I'd love a tea." I get up making sure to keep my robe closed tight so she won't see a glimpse of my lingerie as I don't want her to make that connection to Belle. Not that she would; I don't think anyone could imagine me sleeping with a woman unless they actually walked in on me like Nicole did. "But let me make it. Do you want one?" Wiping my tears, I manage to compose myself and turn on the kettle.

"I think it would be good for you to get out of the house a bit more," she says carefully, grabbing two mugs. "I volunteer at the special needs summer camp on Tuesdays. They're just starting their first week of the season." she pauses. "You're welcome to come along, if you'd like."

"Oh…" I stare at her as I pour water into the mugs, welcoming the change in topic. "I didn't know you volunteered. You have so much on your plate already, working full-time and taking care of your family."

"I enjoy it," Nola says with a sweet smile. "Going there always puts me in a good mood and I've missed it over winter. We play games, in and out of the pool, we do crafts, we take day trips to the beach and sing and play music. That kind of stuff."

"That sounds nice," I say carefully, not wanting to commit but not entirely against the idea either. Distraction would most certainly do me good. The kind of distraction that does not involve parties or alcohol.

"It is. I can introduce you to the team and see how you feel? You'll need a CRB check but I assume that won't be a problem?" She shakes her head when I'm silently taking in her idea. "I'm sorry, I'm getting carried away. It was just an idea, and I don't want you to feel pressured in any way."

"No, no, not at all. I think you're right; I probably do need to get out of the house more. In New York I actually had a life. I was on the board of the City Parks Committee, I worked for Sandeep part-time, I was on the school committee and the rest of my time was filled with social obligations. It's been quiet here and I actually wouldn't mind doing something different." I swallow hard, suppressing another outburst. "Do I have to commit?"

"Absolutely not. As a long-standing volunteer, I can recommend people, but if it's not for you, then that's totally fine and no one will mind. They have enough volunteers in principle, but any extra help is always welcome."

Taking a couple of deep breaths, I nod. "Okay, I'd like that."

"Great." Nola seems both pleased and surprised as she pulls me into a hug. "Just come along and see what you think. No strings."

BELLE - MONDAY

"So, what's the theme of the party?" Juliette asks. "We need a starting point for your proposal."

I scroll through the notes the party organizer sent me. "There is no theme as far as I'm aware."

"No theme?"

"No. Theresa's arranging invitations, food, drinks and a DJ and she's turned to me for the props. She just wants to see what I'd recommend for a sweet sixteenth."

"Okay, well no theme is unusual in the Hamptons," she says. "Focus on Insta-life, then you'll be safe. Your proposal needs lots of props that will look great in pictures. Don't forget this generation's mindset; if it's not recorded, it never happened. If you're sixteen, everything must be eternalized and filtered."

"That's pathetic."

"Yes, it is but that's Gen Z for you." She points to the pink flamingos on my screen. "Definitely offer those. And you need to go with a color scheme, for sure. It will look great in pictures. My hunch is pink."

"Pink? Isn't that a little cliché for a sweet sixteenth?

"No, pink is all the rage nowadays, so just go with it. Pink water, pink lights, pink flamingos, pink table coverings and the LED fountain with pink light. It's perfect." She scrolls through the rest of my inventory on my laptop and points to a picture. "Throw in the pink plastic cups. If Theresa is smart and jumps onto your wagon, she'll find some sparkly pink straws and pink cake or whatever it is they're eating."

"Okay." I add screenshots of everything she's pointed out onto a page and smile at how good it all looks together. "Thanks, babe. I wouldn't know what to do without you."

"It's not as hard as it seems. Most people don't know what they want until they try it. Just like with escorts," she teases.

I turn at Suki's voice behind me. "Mommy, can we have an ice cream?"

"Sure, sweetie." I point to the freezer. "But only one each, you hear me?" Before she runs off, I pull her in to kiss her chubby cheek and tickle her until she screeches and wiggles in my grip. She's been so happy with me being home every night that I don't regret quitting Hamptons' Escorts for a minute.

"What else?" Juliette asks.

"Nothing, that's it."

"That simple?" Juliette looks at me incredulously.

"Yeah. It's a rental service, really straightforward."

"Gosh." Juliette glances at her own notepad, jots down the rental prices, then adds them all up. "Almost three-thousand dollars." She whistles through her teeth.

"Minus six-hundred in labor," I say. "And don't forget this is the very first event. I need regular bookings after this."

"Have faith." Juliette turns her attention to the living room, where Suki and Cameron are munching on ice cream in front of the TV. "They're awfully well-behaved tonight. What are they watching in there?"

"Don't worry, it's parental controlled," I mumble, making

notes. We laugh when we hear dogs barking, and then Suki and Cameron are laughing out loud. "Some kind of dog movie?"

"Yeah, it's *Beverly Hills Chihuahua*," Juliette says, leaning back and sticking her head inside. "Must have been Cameron's idea, he loves that movie and he knows how to work the remote. He's been begging me for a dog ever since the first time he saw it."

"Oh boy, God help me." I follow her gaze and see Suki looks mesmerized. She's got the widest grin on her face and her free hand is balled into a fist shooting up each time there's a moment of tension. My heart melts and I have to refrain from walking over there to pick her up for another cuddle. "I hope she won't start asking for a dog again."

"Trust me, she will." Juliette puts her pen down and scoots the notebook in my direction. "So, now that your weeknights are freed up, how about we ask Jackie to mind the kids and go out together?" When I remain silent, she tilts her head and shoots me a mischievous look. "Come on, Belle. It's been forever."

I hesitate, then laugh at her pleading expression. "Sure, why not? But I'm not doing an all-nighter, I'm past that stage. Bars are good enough for me."

"How about a club opening?" she suggests, grabbing her phone from her bag to show me an invitation. "Shaker Room is opening its rooftop terrace for the season in two weeks' time and it's invite only, so it won't be too busy. Civilized, super casual and if we're lucky there will be lots of singles. I can book a booth if you're in."

Studying the invite that doesn't look too wild, I shrug. "That looks good to me. How come you get invited to stuff like this?"

"Through work. The idea is that I network," she says, rolling her eyes. "But really, it makes no difference. If people want to hire an escort, they'll seek it out and find that we're the only service provider on the peninsula. If the idea has never crossed their mind, then they're not suddenly going to book someone just because I gave them a business card. So really, there's no point in networking when it comes to this, but as long as my boss keeps forwarding the invites, I'm happy to occasionally take him up on the offer. So, you're in?"

"Yeah, I'm in," I say, thinking a night out will be a nice distraction. "It has been too long and we're way too young to be so boring. I'll ask Jackie if she's available."

REINA - TUESDAY

The main clubhouse—a basic, one storey L-shaped building painted in rainbow colors—is surrounded by a nice big yard full of picnic tables. There's a fenced-off pool, a playground, a pond with stepping stones, koi carp and waterlilies, an outdoor gym, and the beach is only a short walk from here. As we follow the path from the parking lot, Nola and I are welcomed by an older black woman in a yellow Camp Rubin T-shirt.

"Nola!" she yells, throwing herself onto my housekeeper. There's hugging and kissing and comments about them looking great and about how long it's been.

"This is my friend Reina," Nola says, and I feel a surge of warmth, not only at the 'friend' comment, but also because she's finally using my first name. "She's just here to see what we volunteers do."

"Yes, I have you on my list, thank you so much for coming along. I'm Dawn, and I'm the director of staff and volunteers."

"It's lovely to meet you. This is an amazing setup you've got here," I say, genuinely impressed.

"Yes, it's fabulous, isn't it? The Rubin family who live further down, own the charity, and they built the camp on their land. They have a daughter with Down syndrome, so they're personally invested."

"Bob and Marla Rubin?" I ask, only then making the connection to my acquaintances.

"Yes." Dawn looks surprised. "Do you know them?"

"As a matter of fact, I've been to a couple of their fundraising dinners." I'm ashamed to realize that I didn't know until now what exactly they were fundraising for, other than that it had something to do with disability. After paying a whopping two-thousand dollars for a table, I just showed up in my pretty dress and socialized, our conversations centered around anything but the actual cause. I suppose I felt like I'd done my bit and didn't have to worry about the details.

"Well in that case, thank you very much for your support," Dawn says with a beaming smile, then beckons us to follow her. "We have kids here with learning and emotional needs as well as physical and mental disabilities." She points to the three yellow buildings next to the clubhouse. "Our seven counsellors live on site with their assigned kids, and we have five students, an art therapist and three nurses who work here full-time over the summer. And our loyal volunteers of course, such as Nola, who has been helping out since we started Camp Rubin back in 2014." Dawn rubs Nola's shoulder, then pulls her in. "Our first group of the season—twenty-two mentally disabled kids aged between ten and sixteen—should be here in an hour, so we're just setting up coffee for the parents who are dropping them off, and there will be snacks and lemonade for the kids. I'll be doing a welcome speech and also an overview of the activity schedule. It might be nice for you to sit in, so you'll know what to expect."

"That sounds good." I smile, noting that I feel totally at ease with this warm-hearted woman, and that I'm actually looking forward to the day ahead.

Dawn glances at her clipboard. "Your CRB check hasn't come through yet I see, but you can help in the kitchen if you'd like to get stuck in today."

"Sure, I'd love to. What do you want me to do?" Dawn opens the door for us and we step into a big hall. Along the sidewall is a stage with rows of chairs placed in front. The walls are covered in pictures and artworks and there's a playpen and a corner filled with stuffed animals. There are long rows of dining tables and at the far end is the kitchen with a healthy snack display and big tea and coffee earns on the buffet counter. It looks cheerful, like a primary school, and the other volunteers and staff members all smile and greet us when they pass.

"If you don't mind, you could both help in the kitchen, refilling the coffee and tea urns when they run out." She turns to Nola. "Why don't you take Reina there and show her where everything is? We have fifty minutes before this hall will be filled with people."

THE WELCOME SPEECH is chaotic but fun, with the kids unable to curb their enthusiasm and parents animatedly discussing how happy they are. The loudest are the ones who have been here before. They know what to expect and are reconnecting with old friends and hugging the volunteers and workers. Others are shy, standing in a corner or latching onto their parents who try their best to put them at ease.

For the parents, it's an opportunity to get a breather, I've been told. From the care and stress that having a disabled child can bring. For the kids, this is a place where they can have fun and feel as if they're a part of a community. Most parents here could not afford to take their kids on holiday as special care is expensive, and the Rubin charity makes it possible for the children to get away and enjoy swimming, sports and lots of fun activities.

Nola is sitting next to me with a girl on her lap. She's actually almost the same size as her, but Nola has her arms wrapped around her waist, gently swaying her from side to side while we listen to the speech. The girl ran up to her as soon as she arrived and hasn't left her side, and I love seeing this side to Nola.

The main message of the welcome talk is kindness, caring and sharing, and Dawn also talks about how powerful the impact of music is. Some kids never speak to people, but they will sing along to songs around the campfire all night long, or even get on stage during karaoke night, she says, then thanks everyone and gives the cue for one of the volunteers to put on a song which some recognize and start singing along to. I find myself getting sucked into the happy energy and when a boy to the other side of me takes my hand, I almost choke up and start singing along too.

BELLE - THURSDAY (TWO WEEKS LATER)

"*I* love this place," Juliette says, glancing around the rooftop terrace. It's decorated in typical Hamptons style, with bright and whitewashed furniture, blue accents and pineapple palms that give off a beachy vibe. "Lots of hot guys. We should come here more often."

"Sure. I love hot guys," I joke, clinking my beer bottle against her martini glass. I'm more the type to have a beer in my local and 'Shaker Room' is a little contrived for me, but the music isn't too loud, the drinks are cold and the vibe is good, so I'm not complaining. It's nice to be out and do something for myself, other than just working and being a mom, and it's clear Juliette feels the same as she's in an extremely bouncy mood tonight.

"I'm serious, Belle. We live in the Hamptons, so don't you think it's time we start living the Hamptons life a little?" She shifts her attention to a group of women, all dressed up to the nines. "The blonde is cute. What do you think?"

I follow her gaze, completely uninterested in any of the women here. Back in New York, before my sister's death and before I adopted Suki, I would have had at least one of them in bed by the end of the night. But that was another life. "Nah. Not for me."

"Why not?" Juliette frowns. "Straight women never stopped you from having fun before. Remember all those nights out on our summer breaks? You were killing it in the ladies' department, and I know you did the same in New York; I kept up with your social media."

"Were you spying on me?" I ask with a chuckle.

"Not spying, just curious." Juliette shrugs. "Envious is a better word, I suppose. I always wanted to live in Brooklyn but unlike you, I never got away so when you moved there, I was a little obsessed with your life."

"Well, it was fun, but it was also very empty. Trust me, you haven't missed out on anything." I glance at the group of women again and shake my head. "I'm just not feeling it anymore, Jules, but I'm fine here if you want to go talk to someone. Or I could be your wingwoman?"

"Hmm…" Juliette glances at my jeans and white linen shirt, then at her own little black dress and stiletto heels. "If you go with me, they'll just assume that I'm your girlfriend. Everyone thinks we're a couple anyway, it's so annoying." She laughs. "Sometimes I wish you'd just wear a dress so we wouldn't have this problem."

I arch a brow at her and shoot her an amused look. "Really? Is that what people think?"

"Yeah. One of the moms at preschool referred to you as my 'partner' in a conversation, and when I said we were just friends, she told me all parents assumed we were together."

"Jesus, no wonder you never get asked out on a date. That's just…" My voice trails away as I catch a waft of a familiar perfume. I'm not sure what it is, but it stirs me to my very core. Looking up, I glance around, and my breath catches when I see Reina walking up to the table next to us.

She's wearing a backless black dress that makes me ache for her and she's holding hands with a tall, blonde woman.

"Oh my," Juliette says, following my gaze. "That's Igor Stravinski's wife. You know, the real estate mogul. She's in the tabloids sometimes."

I don't know who Igor Stravinski is and I don't care because Reina, my Reina, has just taken a seat and she picks up the drinks menu and starts talking to the waiter. Suddenly, as if she knows I'm watching her, she glances around, and her eyes meet mine. Her lips are still parted, stalled in the middle of a conversation. Her companion notices what's going on and looks my way too, then asks her something, but she doesn't acknowledge the question. At a loss for what to say or do, I simply smile at her, because that's how I feel. My whole body has become one big smile and at the same time, I'm trembling with nerves. She might ignore me, she might come over and throw a drink in my face. After all, I deserve that for disappearing.

"Who is that?" Juliette whispers.

"It's Reina," I say, never taking my eyes off her. A warm, gooey glow spreads through me when she returns my smile, shyly at first, then wider. It's so strange seeing her outside her house, like an escaped horse roaming around freely. I know that's silly, of course. She probably goes out all the time, but I was never able to imagine what it would be like to meet her elsewhere.

"Really?" Juliette narrows her eyes and studies her. "Oh yeah, I recognize her now." She waves at them before I have a chance to grab her wrist and Reina's friend waves back at Juliette, then takes Reina's hand and pulls her up.

Resisting at first, Reina looks like she wants to escape, but she gives in eventually and follows her friend to our table.

"Hi," her friend says. "I'm Sasha and this is Reina, but I believe you two already know each other." She holds out her hand and I get up to shake it. "Belle," I say, only taking my eyes off Reina for a split second. Then she turns to Juliette, who looks a little starstruck. "Are you two together?"

"Gross, no!" Juliette exclaims. "Will everyone stop saying that? I'll never find a decent man if everyone keeps assuming I'm with her." She laughs and shakes Sasha's hand. "I'm Juliette. Belle's friend. It's very nice to meet you, and it's lovely to meet you too, Reina."

Apart from greeting Juliette, Reina still hasn't said a word and Juliette and Sasha exchange semi-nervous looks.

"Can we join you?" Sasha finally asks, pointing at our booth. She gives no excuses as to why she wants to share our table, and I like how straightforward she is.

"Of course, please do." I scoot over and there's an awkward moment in which Sasha practically pushes Reina down next to me before she turns to Juliette.

"I think I'll get drinks at the bar instead so I can micromanage the assembly of my much deserved first cocktail of the night. Want to join me?" Sasha asks.

Juliette nods and follows Sasha to the bar like a puppy on her heel and then just like that, we're alone. "If I didn't know better, I'd almost think our bumping into each other had been orchestrated," I say, turning to Reina.

"Yeah, me too. It's not, though, I promise."

"I know." I shift in my seat, the energy between us flaring like never before. I expected it to fade but it hasn't. Not one bit. "Are you angry with me?" It's a heavy first question but one I have to ask.

"Yes," she says, looking at my lips. "I'm angry and hurt. You just disappeared."

"I'm sorry."

"No, you're not." Reina picks up my beer bottle, takes a sip and turns to me, handing it back. "You don't have to apologize, though. You didn't want it to be anything more than it was and I've accepted that. I understand, I really do. But my feelings haven't changed, so it's hard for me to see you again." She glances at the bar, where Sasha and Juliette are talking animatedly, laughing like old friends while they toast. "Sasha is not one to argue with; if it wasn't for her, I'd be out of here. Anyway, I'm sorry if I freaked you out."

I shake my head, suddenly not so sure of anything anymore. The effect she has on me is astounding. I want her, I crave her, and I adore her. "You didn't freak me out. I just had to…"

"Protect yourself?" she says, finishing my sentence. "I understand that. And you have different priorities. Suki is still young."

"Yes, and you're…" I pause, letting out a long sigh. "Never mind, we've already had that conversation." I put a hand on her arm and watch the hairs rise on her skin. "How's Nicole? Are you speaking?"

"Nicole's fine. We're fine; she just thinks I'm a little deranged. Maybe I am." She doesn't sound convinced as she says it.

Relief floods my system and I feel like a heavy weight has been lifted off my shoulders. "So I haven't ruined your relationship with her?"

"No, of course not, this was never your fault. Nicole and I are good. If anything, we're talking more than we used to." Reina looks down at my hand that is still resting on her forearm. "It's better if you don't touch me, though. It makes me…"

"Sorry." I retract my hand and move away slightly. "What did you tell her?"

"That it's nothing serious but that I'm crazy about you." Her words linger between us and as much as I try to, I can't keep my eyes off her. She's got me, wholly, fully… "Are you sure about that?"

"Yes, but it will pass. I also told her I think I'm gay, that this is not a phase." She doesn't sound one bit like the nervous Reina from before. She's sure of herself, more confident.

"That's very brave of you."

"It's the truth."

I swallow hard and bite my lip as I let her words sink in, and then this weird statement just rolls off my tongue. "Life was simple until I met you."

Something flashes across Reina's gaze and I know she realizes how loaded that simple sentence really is. "Same here." She squares her shoulders and straightens her back, her beautiful silhouette radiating from the spotlights of the bar behind her. Her lips are shimmering with a subtle coat of gloss and her lashes long and dark as she bats them at me. "Don't you think that means something?"

REINA - THURSDAY

*T*he night has turned out unexpectantly pleasant after the shock of seeing Belle again. It was difficult at first, so uncomfortable that I considered leaving, but with Sasha and Belle's friend Juliette here it's taking some of the pressure off. I'm staying out way later than I normally would, mainly because I don't want this precious time with Belle to end, and I suspect she feels the same. The chemistry is still there, and the way my body reacts to her has only grown stronger.

Sasha and Juliette are getting on like a house on fire; the two of them have been challenging each other with shots all night. I've had a couple myself, and I feel a little light-headed. Belle seems more relaxed too; she's smiling and has an arm draped over the armrest, her fingers playing with my hair like she did that first night at my house. It's making me dizzy with desire for her and even though we're in public, I feel an urge to kiss her so strong I can barely contain myself.

We've mainly talked about our friends. How we met, our history, and our friends have told embarrassing stories about us in return. I've learned that Belle and Juliette go way back.

That they grew up here together and lost touch for a while when Belle was in New York. They reconnected when Belle lost her sister and became Suki's adoptive mother, and Juliette helped her as she had a child of her own. I now also know that Juliette is a booker at Hamptons' Escorts, and I suspect she was the one I hung up on, but I haven't told her that.

Sasha and I told them how we met through our husbands —hers a real estate mogul and mine a big-name architect— who worked on a project together years ago. Sasha and Igor were the ones who suggested we buy a house in the Hamptons and it's because of them that I now live here. Juliette has been very curious about our lives and I think she envies us a little. If only she knew life is not always great just because you're wealthy. I like her; she's funny and warm, she has a wonderful carefree side to her, and I sense that she and Belle are very close.

Belle has talked about her first upcoming job for her new company and I'm impressed with both the brilliant idea and her drive to be independent. I've told her about my new volunteering job that I've signed up for, and about an online photography course I'm doing. It's made me realize how different my life is now. I feel happier and more fulfilled, even though the one thing I really want and can't have is sitting right next to me.

"You claimed our worlds could never work together," I say, lowering my voice when Sasha and Juliette are engaged in yet another animated conversation while they're checking out men. "But what about them?" I gesture to our friends.

Belle opens her mouth to speak but stops herself. She probably wants to argue that Sasha and Juliette are not family, that they're just two people out of many, but instead, she shoots me a flirty smile and tightens her grip in my hair, setting my libido on fire. I finally allow myself to lean into her and cherish the wonderful sensations that rage through my body, and she shifts even closer when I place a hand on her thigh.

I'm sitting intimately with a woman in a public place and maybe it's the alcohol or maybe it's the way she makes me feel drunk with lust, but I really don't care. I've imagined this many times, wondering if I'd feel uncomfortable or self-conscious, but the opposite is true. Belle is seriously sexy and charming, and I feel proud to be here with her, even if it's just within a close circle of people who I now trust to keep my secret. Sasha casts me a curious glance and smiles at seeing how close we're sitting. She whispers something to Juliette and they burst out in laughter and clink their glasses together.

"They're so alike, it's almost creepy," Belle finally says. "Maybe we should leave them to it; I have a feeling they'd have more fun without us."

My breath hitches and my heart starts pounding hard and fast. "Are you saying you want to get out of here?"

"My apartment is only a fifteen-minute cab ride away and Suki and Cameron are having a sleepover at Jackie's." Belle wets her lips and stares at me. "Do you want to come home with me?"

"That depends," I say, ignoring my raging hormones that want me to shout: *Yes! Yes, of course I'll come home with you! Take me. Please, just take me.* "Are you going to disappear on me again?"

"No." Belle hesitates. "But I can't make you any promises of anything serious either. I'm worried we'll both get hurt."

"I don't need promises. I just want you to be open-minded."

"Says the closeted woman," she jokes, leaning in to kiss my cheek. Her mouth moves to my ear and her warm breath sends a shiver down my spine when she adds:

"Although admittedly, you don't look very closeted right now."

"Will you two just get a room already?" Sasha grins at us. "I know you both want to, you're all over each other."

"She's right," Juliette chimes in. "Go fuck. You need to get it out of your system."

"Jules!" Belle widens her eyes at her friend. "A little more subtlety wouldn't hurt."

"Subtlety never got anyone anywhere." Juliette brushes a hand through her long, red hair. "And on that note, I'm going to talk to those guys over there." She points at a booth next to the bar and turns to Sasha. "Are you coming? I'd be delighted to have a wingwoman who doesn't look like she could be my girlfriend."

Sasha welcomes the idea with a roaring laugh and within seconds, we're alone. The tension rising, Belle gets up and holds out her hand for me. "Shall we go?"

I FOLLOW Belle up the narrow staircase. "I hope you're not claustrophobic," she says, glancing at me over her shoulder. "My whole apartment is smaller than your kitchen."

"It's lovely," I say, walking into the small, cozy living room. Kicking off my heels, I step onto the thick, cream colored rug. There's a large navy blue corner couch with a TV and an oak coffee table and behind it is a small dining table with four seats. A bar in the open kitchen looks over the living room and I can picture her cooking here while Suki is playing on the floor. Long, navy linen curtains frame French doors that open up to a balcony and there's a reading nook with a bookcase and a contemporary reading lamp that bends over a Victorian-style chair. It's strange to be in her home with her things and Suki's toys in an open chest by the door. It makes her a real person, not just a fantasy.

"Apologies for the mess. I wasn't expecting company."

"It's inviting," I say. "It's not really a mess, the apartment just looks lived in and I like that. Sometimes I feel like I live in a museum."

"You *do* live in a museum," she jokes. "A very minimalist one. Where do you keep all you stuff? There's never any crap lying around. Nothing unnecessary anyway."

"Nola is very efficient."

Belle chuckles and takes off her shoes. "I'd love a Nola in my life."

I study the pictures on the wall while she turns on the lights. They're mainly pictures of her and Suki, but there are also some of Belle in her younger years with what I assume are her father and late sister. There's one of a woman and a baby too, and she has Belle's dark eyes.

"That's my mom," she says, following my gaze.

"You look like her." I shift my attention to the picture next to it. "Is that your sister? You look like her too."

"Yeah, that's Linda. Apart from our looks, we were very different."

I find a hint of sadness in Belle's eyes, but it fades as quickly as it came, and she inches closer, hinting that she's done talking about her family. "I don't doubt you were a troublemaker."

"If anyone's a troublemaker, it's you," she retorts playfully, brushing my hair behind my ears. "Other than Jackie and Juliette, I've never had a woman up here. You're messing with my house rules."

"You invited me."

"True. Can I get you a drink?"

"No thank you, I've had enough to drink." I smile and

now that we're alone, I allow myself to drown in her eyes. "Is it true? That you never have women over?"

"Yes. I haven't had dates or girlfriends since Suki came into my life. You're the first." Her hand moves to the back of my neck and she slowly pulls me closer, bringing her lips to mine. It's true what they say about absence making the heart grow fonder. Our first kiss is electric; a careful brush of lips as if we're both bracing ourselves for the physical explosion we know will follow. Parting my lips, I let her in and moan quietly as I give in to the sensation of her tongue meeting mine. Everything around me fades and all I can taste, feel and hear is Belle. Dizziness and heat silence all my thoughts as I melt into her and she melts into me. My knees feel like they're about to give in and I think she knows it as she curls her arm around my waist, holding me up. She holds me tight, possessively, and when her hand lowers to my behind to squeeze it firmly, I moan louder and press my mouth harder to hers, deepening the kiss.

Gasping for air, we take a moment, both breathing fast as we lock eyes and smile. The insane attraction between us lingers as I start undoing the buttons on her shirt, slowly, one by one. The smell of her is hypnotic and her eyes are so dark that it almost frightens me. I brush the garment off her shoulders until it falls to the ground, and I trace her strong shoulders and her arms down to her hands. She takes them and laces our fingers together.

"Come, let me take you to my room."

I follow her into the bedroom, my limbs weak and uncontrolled. It's different this time, I can tell by the way she looks at me and I can feel it in the tremble of her hand. There's the undeniable desire of course, but there's also a hint of nervousness and caution in her gaze. This means a lot to her and she's afraid.

Belle opens the curtains, letting in dim streetlight then turns to me, suddenly hesitant.

"Don't be scared," I whisper, using the very same words she uttered on our first encounter. "I'm not." Feeling brave, I walk her toward the bed and nudge her to lie down. It's our time now. I won't let her tie me up; I want to be together, and I want all of her. Belle steadies herself on her elbows and watches me unbutton her jeans, clearly surprised by my assertiveness. Then I move to her sports bra and her boxers until she's lying naked before me. She looks vulnerable and so beautiful, her subtle curves and small breasts calling me. I let my eyes roam over her freely, taking in every inch of her body. Her thick, dark hair, her piercing eyes that set me on fire, her strong jawline and her curled mouth, lips wet and parted. The delicate line of her collarbone, her lean frame and strong arms—the arms of someone who does physical labor—and her small breasts that fit so perfectly into my hands. The beauty mark under her left breast, her hard stomach and her hips, a little rounded. Her strong thighs and her shapely calves and ankles, the small scar on her foot and her cute toes; nails damaged from the beach and being outdoors. I love everything about her.

Slowly, I pull my dress over my head, leaving me only in a pair of white, lace panties. I feel beautiful tonight; Belle makes me feel that way.

"Fuck," she murmurs, staring up at me.

I remove my panties and get on the bed, never taking my eyes off Belle as I straddle her. Leaning in to kiss her, I grind my center into hers and moan at her wetness. I didn't mean to do this, but it feels so good that I continue, taking in Belle's aroused stare and the way she reacts to my movements. She likes it, and I grind harder, feeling myself swell and throb at the contact. I sit up straight, take her hands and bring them to my breasts, holding them there as I arch my back and move back and forth, stimulating her until she's beyond control, jerking underneath me.

"Is that good?" I ask, almost on the edge already, my clit so sensitive that I moan loudly each time I thrust forward.

"Yes, don't stop," she begs, throwing her head back into the pillows before she looks up at me. "That feels incredible, please don't stop." She pinches my nipples hard just as I'm climaxing and I cover her hands with mine, needing more of the stinging pain to elevate me.

"Yes!" she cries and bucks her hips, bringing her hands down to my thighs to pull me in.

I crash hard and so does she, both of us shaking in ecstasy as we ride out our orgasms. A sound forms in the back of her throat, and she groans loudly, then softer, the sound escaping her as if I'm stealing the life out of her. Exhausted, I fall forward covering her with my upper body.

Belle wraps her arms around me and presses her mouth against the hollow of my temple while we breathe heavily.

BELLE - FRIDAY

$\mathcal{T}$he sound of birdsong wakes me and the clock on my nightstand tells me it's only five-thirty. I sigh deeply at the heavenly warmth pressed against my skin. We're lying on top of the covers and Reina is draped along my side, her face resting on my chest and her arm draped over my stomach. She's still in a deep sleep, unaware of me watching her. I take the opportunity to indulge while I swim in raw bliss, my body aching for her all over again.

The upcoming sun I always take for granted brings her face into sharper focus and I'm consciously grateful for the morning rays that bathe the room in yellow hues. She's a sculpted goddess and in this light, only vaguely human. Her long lashes flutter as if she's dreaming and the corners of her mouth are curled up, just a little. She looks happy and content and the sound of her steady breathing soothes me like nothing else ever has.

What we did last night, for hours on end, wasn't just sex. We made love. The panic I feel at that realization makes me tense but I also know that it was worth it, even if she breaks my heart. I gave myself to her. I gave her all of me and she gave me all of her in return. If I lose her, which I probably will, I'll live, and I'll always have last night to remember her by.

She stirs and licks her lips before she wakes, blinking against the light. For a moment, she seems disoriented but then she looks down at her hand on my stomach and smiles, letting out a content moan as she strokes my skin. "You're so warm and soft," she murmurs, bringing her lips to my neck to kiss it before nestling her face there, inhaling deeply against my skin. "And you smell so good."

I pull her closer and kiss the crown of her head, emotions swirling inside me at the intimacy. "I smell of you."

"Mmm… I like that." Reina inches away to look at me and there's no regret in her eyes. "This is amazing." She strokes my cheek and studies me as if she's seeing me for the first time.

"What's amazing?"

"Just…" She hesitates. "Waking up like this. With you."

"So you're okay?" I ask, closing my eyes at her warm touch.

Reina kisses me softly. "Yeah, I'm great. Are you?"

I nod, turn on my side to face her and wedge my thigh between her legs. At this, she moans again, parts her legs farther and pulls me on top of her. We fit so well together, and our movements are natural and instinctive, almost like we're one mind thinking the same. The kiss that follows is long and slow, deep and sensual as our limbs entangle and our bodies melt into one another. Her heat is burning against my thigh and her breath is quickening with every stroke of my tongue against hers. It *is* amazing. A deep-rooted sensation in my core reminds me how much I'm feeling right now. Not just arousal but so, so much more. I bring my hand between her legs and gasp at her reaction. She's so sensitive and knowing how much she wants me makes me ache to pleasure her.

Reina moans and brings her hand to my center in return, stroking me while we drown in a long, exhilarating make out session. I slide inside her and she does the same and we move in a slow, sleepy pace, making love until we're so spent that we're ready to fall asleep again.

When I'm about to pull out of her, she stops me, covering my hand with her own. "Not yet. Can we just stay like this for a little while? It feels so… intimate. I love it."

I pull her closer instead and kiss her again. I'll never get enough of kissing her, of holding her in bed. She's right. It does feel intimate but the good kind, even though it scares me a little.

"If I promised you this is not a phase," she says when she's lying in my arms an hour later. "Would you have any reason not to want to do this again?"

I'm silent for a beat, reluctant to repeat all the excuses I've given her before. Truth be told, I'm so happy she's back in my life that everything seems unimportant right now. I've missed her more than I'd anticipated and now that she's here, in my bed, I don't want her to leave because it feels right and natural, and I need her. Finally, I give her the only honest answer I can without overthinking things. "I don't want to lose you."

Reina smiles and weaves her fingers through my hair. "Good," she says. "Then you won't. Because I don't want to lose you either. Not again."

My heart starts beating in relief but I'm also terrified. We've said it out loud, we've taken the next step and I'm heading into dangerous territory. She could quite possibly shatter me, but I don't have the energy to fight this anymore. Surrendering feels good; I can stop overthinking things now and simply put my future into the slippery, unreliable hands of fate.

I smile and kiss her forehead. "I have to get up soon."

"Of course. I'll leave."

"Wait…" Pulling the covers over us, I bury myself in her warmth. "Just ten more minutes."

REINA - FRIDAY

"Sorry I didn't make you breakfast." Belle shoots me a wink. "You didn't give me time." She slips into a T-shirt and finger-combs her wet hair back.

"Trust me, those extra ten minutes in bed were worth it." I shiver, thinking back to Belle's mouth between my thighs, devouring me until I couldn't breathe. I'm still in a daze, and I don't want to leave because last night and this morning have made me realize just how much I want this. How much I want to be with her all the time. Even during our quick joint shower we weren't able to keep our hands off each other and now Belle is late. It's not really a problem she assured me. Suki is with Jackie and Jackie is flexible, but I don't want to take time away from her daughter. Wearing last night's dress, and my long hair wild and uncombed, it's obvious what I've been up to.

"Yeah, it was worth it, all right." Belle spanks my behind as I slip into my heels. "God, you look hot."

"And you look sexy as hell." I straighten myself and lean into her, fingering the collar of her blue shirt. "So, where do we go from here?"

243

"We could start by exchanging numbers." Belle grins and hands me her phone to enter my details.

"Yes, that would probably be a good start." I chuckle and give her my phone to do the same. "Will you call me?"

Belle's expression turns more serious as she cups my chin. "How about you call me? This is new to you so I think we should take it slow, on your time and on your terms. I'm not going anywhere; I'll be right here."

I nod and swallow hard. "I won't keep you a secret forever."

She doesn't look too convinced, but she smiles and pulls me in for a kiss. "For now, I can come to your house, or you can come here."

Lingering by the door with our lips pressed together, I close my eyes and can't think of a single reason why I should take this slow. If anything, she's the one who needs time, not me. After last night and this morning, I know what I want. Waking up with her, seeing her sweet smile first thing and being able to kiss her whenever I want is something I could get used to. "Will you go out on a date with me? I know I asked you before but I think we're in a better place now."

"Really?" Belle inches back and arches a brow. "Are you sure?"

"Yeah. We were out in public last night, weren't we? It's not that much different from a date." I smile. "I don't think I'm ready to go to any of my local places, but I'd like to take you somewhere."

"Okay." Belle seems shocked by my proposal. Perhaps she'd expected me to freak out after waking up with her, or maybe she still thinks this is just a bit of fun to me, even though it's blatantly obvious that it's not. "How about I take *you* out instead? Next week? We could go for dinner around here?"

"Yeah, I'd like that." Aware of my blush, I feel like a teenager who's just been asked out for the first time. We've done this the wrong way around. We've slept together before we even got to know each other and now there's so much to explore. "I normally go out with Sasha on Thursday, but I can cancel if Thursdays are easier for Jackie."

"Jackie is usually fine, but I'll check with her first and let you know." Belle opens the door but as soon as I walk through, she takes my wrist, pulls me back and pushes me against the door. "You're so damn cute, I have trouble saying goodbye." Again, she kisses me hard, then lifts me and pushes me against the hallway wall. Her strong hands under my behind hold me up and wrapping my legs around her waist, I embrace her and reciprocate as arousal stirs us both.

"I'll never get home like this," I say through quick breaths when she finally puts me down. I grab my purse and straighten my dress, then shoot her a flirty smile over my shoulder as I descend the stairs.

Hailing a cab from the other side of the street, I jump in and roll down the window when it drives off. Leaning out, I let my hair dance in the wind, enjoying this strange but beautiful morning-after feeling that has me on top of the world. Everything looks enchanting and full of possibility today, the world around me happier and lighter. Sag Harbor is waking up at a leisurely pace, and we pass mothers with strollers, runners and dog walkers while cafés are setting up for the day, their staff bringing out tables and chairs and opening parasols. I smile at a happy couple walking hand in hand. The woman's head is resting on the man's shoulder while he whispers something in her ear that makes her laugh. They look like they're having trouble controlling themselves and I can finally relate to people like them.

My energy levels are buzzing even though my body feels

a good kind of tired, the satisfying ache between my thighs and my sensitive nipples reminding me of Belle's touch. I hope she feels it too, and that she'll think of me today. I suspect I'll do little else than think of her, daydreaming and replaying the past twelve hours over and over in my mind.

The sea breeze welcomes me as we turn into my drive and I take off my heels that are killing my feet to continue into the house barefoot. I flinch when I find Nola in the kitchen; I forgot she'd be here, and I hadn't anticipated staying out all night.

"Hey, Reina." She looks me over and raises a brow, wiping her hands on her apron. "That's a lovely dress. Did you have a good night?"

"Thanks." I chuckle as I walk over to the stairs and place my heels on the bottom step, then continue to the fridge to grab a bottle of sparkling water. "I did, actually." I take a long drink, feeling seriously thirsty after last night's cocktails.

"Great." Nola pauses. "So, there was a man after all..."

"Not quite, but something like that," I say in a mysterious tone, not wanting to give myself away. Although I trust Nola, I want to keep Belle to myself for now, and be alone for a while so I can fantasize about her in peace without having to answer a million questions. "I'm going for a walk. I'll be back in an hour if you want to have a coffee with me." I grab an apple from the fruit bowl on the counter, cross the poolside in my black dress and head down to the beach.

Wading in, the sea water feels so nice that I hike up my dress and walk farther out. My apple tastes sweeter, the sun feels warmer, the water calmer and the sand between my toes finer and softer than normal. If it wasn't for the few people on the beach, I'd take off my dress and swim naked, but I can feel their eyes on me, curiously wondering why I'm wading in wearing an evening dress. Three months ago, I wouldn't even have gone into the ocean spontaneously but now, I can't think of anything better than a swim, simply because I feel like it. I lower myself and drift onto my back, my dark hair and the black fabric floating around me as I look up at the sky. I don't care what anyone thinks; I just want to drift and think of Belle.

*J*ackie might actually be psychic. The look on her face says it all but she can't resist voicing her thoughts as she lets me in: "You're late and you're never late." She winks. "I think I know what you've been up to."

"Sorry," I say with a sheepish grin, scooping Suki into my arms when she runs up to me. "It was a late night, thanks for having her." Planting a wet kiss on Suki's cheek, I laugh as she grimaces and wipes it with the sleeve of her sweater. "Have you had fun?"

"Yes! We went to the playground and we had ice cream and pancakes and Cameron and I made a tent to sleep in."

"Wow. That's a very cool tent," I say, carrying her into the living room where a mattress is placed on the floor under a canopy of sheets attached to the four chairs standing on each corner. A string of multicolored lights is placed over the chairs, and it's filled with cushions and blankets.

"Thank you," I say, smiling at Jackie. "Has Jules picked up Cameron yet?" It's more of a rhetorical question as Cameron is loud and active and hard to miss.

"Yes, she came about an hour ago. They've had so much fun."

"I can see. You're so sweet." I put Suki down and follow Jackie into the kitchen where a pot of coffee is waiting on the table. "Yes please," I say when she holds it up. "Unless you're busy?"

"Me?" Jackie laughs. "Never." She pours two cups, opens the back door to let the sun in and sits down with me. "So, are you going to tell me all about it or should I guess?"

A blush creeps onto my cheeks and I hide behind my cup, almost burning my lips on the hot brim. "I bumped into Reina at that bar opening Jules and I went to last night."

"You did? How did that go?"

"I was shocked to see her, after two weeks. I hadn't exactly left it in a good place, but she gave me the opportunity to apologize. She joined us with her friend, and we all had drinks together. It was really nice." I hesitate and chuckle. "Actually, it wasn't just 'really nice'. I didn't know what to do with myself when I saw her, and I think she was pretty shaken too. Whatever is going on between us is much stronger than I anticipated." I hesitate. "But she wasn't uncomfortable to be in my company with her friend there."

"Is that what you were afraid of?"

"Yeah, of course. Reina's straight—at least to the outside world—and sitting next to me with the chemistry we have, it's pretty obvious that we like each other. She seemed totally cool with it, though."

"So I imagine it wasn't just drinks?" When I shake my head slowly, Jackie glances into the living room and lowers her voice. "Lucky you had the apartment to yourself then. Or did you go to her place?"

"No, we went to my place." My grin widens. "We're actually going on a date next week, if you wouldn't mind having Suki for another night."

"Are you now?" Jackie looks delighted to hear this. "Of course I'll look after her. I miss her now that you don't work nights anymore, it's a bit boring on my own." She sips her coffee, sits back and crosses her legs in front of her. "Where are you taking her?"

"I don't know. I was thinking maybe that little place by the harbor? The Italian?" I sigh and rub my temple as insecurity suddenly takes over. "God, it's so difficult with her. She's used to fine dining and fancy places. I'll never be able to keep up with the lifestyle she's used to."

"Will you just stop the overthinking before you've even given this a chance," Jackie interrupts me, slapping my wrist like I'm some disobedient child. "The excuses…"

"They're not excuses. I have to be realistic because I have Suki to think of."

"Come on, this is not about Suki," she says. This is about you. You haven't ever allowed yourself to be close to anyone."

"That's not true. In New York, I didn't want to fall in love or be in a monogamous and committed relationship. I happily slept my way through town and when I came back here, a relationship was the last thing on my mind. I've just been distracted."

"Exactly." Jackie pauses. "Belle, sweetheart, you're scared because it's the first time you're in this situation. One where there's mutual attraction strong enough to be lasting and serious. You're scared because you're in love for the first time, don't you see that? I've never seen you talk about someone the way you talk about her. And yes, I agree that Reina may not be the safest bet, but if you don't go all in, you'll never know. You might get hurt, and then I'll be here to take care of you. Or it might work out, and you'll have a beautiful life together." She looks at me the way I imagine my mother would if she were still alive. The older and wiser woman who knows better because she's lived through it all.

Has she, though? I don't remember Jackie ever dating anyone.

"Maybe you're right," I say. "But what about you? Why have you never dated?"

"Who says I haven't?" Jackie bites her nails, staring down at the table; a sign that she's uncomfortable.

"You've never mentioned anyone."

"It wasn't something I could discuss."

"Oh." I pause and regard her. "I'm sorry, we don't have to talk about this."

She finally looks up at me, her eyes welling up and her bottom lip trembling. She's in distress, and I curse myself for ever bringing it up as this is clearly a very sensitive topic. "I just always assumed you and dad were secretly in love with each other and I didn't want you to think I would have a problem with that." Then I remember Rose, and how she and Jackie looked at each other. I've been meaning to ask her about it but it was never a good time and going on her emotional state, now isn't a good time either.

"No." Jackie shakes her head and has magically managed to compose herself within seconds. "Your father and I are very close but there's nothing but friendship between us." She stands abruptly and glances around the kitchen as if she's looking for distraction. "I forgot; I have an appointment with the dentist this afternoon, so I'd better get ready."

I flinch at this because I know she's lying and Jackie has never tried to get rid of me, ever. "I'm really sorry," I say again, wishing I hadn't touched upon the subject of Jackie's love life.

"For what, honey? You didn't do anything, I just forgot about the dentist, that's all." Jackie manages a smile. "Will I see you for lunch on Sunday at your father's house?"

"Yeah." I get up, too, and start gathering Suki's things. "I'll see you there. Good luck at the dentist."

REINA - SUNDAY

I'm wearing my yellow Camp Rubin T-shirt and my hair is still wet and smelling of chlorine from being in the pool, supervising during the swimming activities. Normally I wouldn't leave the house without drying my hair but here, I don't feel judged. No one cares what I look like as long as I help out with a smile on my face. And I've been smiling a lot. The kids are wonderful and seeing them having such a good time makes my day. We played a pirate game where the kids had to cross the pool on an inflatable raft and find treasure hidden on a fake beach. Jonathan, a twelve-year-old boy with Down syndrome who I looked after in the pool has latched onto me and wants to hold my hand everywhere we go. In his other hand, he's carrying a pirate flag that he waves with each step.

"We're going this way, that way, backward, forward. Up and down, up and down, over the deep blue sea," we sing together as we walk in a line toward the picnic tables. Some kids can't sing, but yell randomly along, inspired by the good vibe.

"Okay, Jonathan. I'm going to let go of your hand now, I have to go and help in the kitchen. Are you okay with that?"

He looks at me, deciding if he's fine with me leaving. The answer can only be 'yes' or 'no' as those are the only words he's used so far. A 'no' means a tantrum will follow; I've had to calm him down numerous times already. "Yes," he says, and I let out the breath I've been holding.

"Are you hungry?"

"Yes!" he yells, waving the flag. "Yes, yes, yes, yes, yes!"

I help Jonathan up on the bench and get him settled, then make sure all other kids have a glass, a placemat and a napkin. One of the counsellors comes over so I can leave, and I make my way to the main building where the kitchen is situated. It's my first full day volunteering. After I came here with Nola, she was surprised that I signed up for three days a week. There are only a few counsellors and volunteers here; the camp has to make sure they're covered before the season starts, but they take on extra volunteers like Nola and myself, who can rotate and lend an extra hand as tending to these children is full-time and non-stop.

"Hi, I'm Reina," I say, introducing myself to the kitchen staff as I don't recognize anyone from the first day. Just like on campus, the kitchen staff rotates too and today, a big, bearded man is running the kitchen. "What can I do?"

"Hey there, perfect timing. I'm Andy." He slides two trays my way. "Here are a couple of gluten free lunches. The kids' names are printed on the stickers in the corner. These are the only tailored lunches; all the others are standard so you can hand them out randomly." Andy starts placing more trays with pasta, fruit cups, yoghurt and water bottles onto the counter and someone comes in to help me bring them all out. There's immense excitement when we put the food down in front of them and discussions about favorite foods are loud and passionate.

253

Three children need help eating, the others are generally fine on their own. When everything is served and under control, I go back to the kitchen to check if there's anything else I can do.

"If you don't mind, we need someone to help wash the dishes." Andy points to the big sink and industrial dishwasher in the back.

"Sure," I say, and gasp when I see the carnage on every surface and the volume of chaos up-close. Pots and pans, roasting trays, a blender, cutting boards, cutlery and the coffee cups the volunteers have been using are piled up high. I don't know where to start and it's insanely hot in this part of the kitchen. Studying the dishwasher, I manage to figure out how to work it and start rinsing everything before I put it into the chunky square trays.

"Sorry. We're prepping for dinner too, so we can leave at five," Andy yells over the noise of the extractor fan. "There will be more dishes after this."

"No problem," I yell back and shoot him a smile. Sweat is dripping down my back as I scrape the leftovers out of the heavy pans and into the trash. My mother would be shocked to see me working as a kitchen porter in shorts and a T-shirt, with my unwashed hair tied into a messy topknot and no makeup on. Nicole would be amused, I think. I don't think she's seen me do anything like this before as we've always had a housekeeper. I cook sometimes, and I used to make the kids breakfast in the morning, but this kind of work is alien to me and it's physically hard. Batches come and go yet clearing the mess is cathartic and I don't mind it at all. Reflecting on how privileged I've always been, I tell myself that now is the time to pay it forward and seeing how I've been enjoying myself today, I know I'm even going to have fun along the way.

I'M clammy and exhausted but in a great mood when I come home. Glancing at the pool, the water has never looked so inviting. I hardly ever used it, not wanting to mess up my hair after drying it in the morning, but right now I can't think of anything better than a swim. Opening the sliding doors, I strip off my clothes, leaving them in a pile by the doorway. Sunlight plays upon the surface as the soft wind causes subtle ripples over the water. Behind it, the Atlantic is wilder than usual and I can hear the waves rolling, crashing against the shore. I love the ocean and the view, the beach and the seclusion, and I don't feel lonely here anymore as today made me feel like I was part of something meaningful, of something bigger. The wind blows against my skin as I cross the terrace naked. I've never been naked in my own backyard and although it feels strange and even a little naughty, it's also very liberating.

Diving in at the deep end, I surrender to weightlessness. The water hugs and soothes me as I cross the full length of the pool, swimming with even strokes as I glide above the floor. After a hectic day, the silence below the surface feels like heaven. Peaceful, calming and wonderfully surreal. Coming up for air, I brush my hair away from my face and turn onto my back to drift, soaking up the evening sun. Enjoying a new sense of accomplishment and the memories I made today, being tired has never felt so good.

BELLE - SUNDAY

"That was a very nice afternoon." My father lights a cigar and adjusts his outdoor recliner, leaning back a little. "You're a much better cook than you claim, Belle. That pot roast was delicious." He takes a drag and puffs out the smoke in circles. "Your mother was always a good cook. You've got that from her."

"I couldn't go wrong with your wonderful fresh ingredients," I say, smiling at him as I refill his whiskey glass and sit next to him with my chamomile tea. Jackie's gone home and Suki fell asleep on the couch a while ago but I'm in no rush to leave. The backyard is peaceful and quiet, the only sound coming from the few lambs still awake in the barn and the chickens that roam around freely. "Dad, can I ask you something?" I say, seizing this private moment.

"What is it, honey?"

"I was wondering about Jackie… why she's always been single. I always thought you two would make a good couple but I'm starting to realize that I might have been wrong about that." I glance at him to gauge his reaction but he's looking away and I can't see his face. "Do you remember her ever dating anyone? A man or a woman?"

My father flinches as he turns back to me. "Jackie and I have only ever been friends. Well, not always, she was…" He stops himself and takes another drag from his cigar.

"She was what, Dad?" If Jackie is gay, I have no idea why she would confide in my father instead of in me. After all, I would understand like no one else. But this isn't just about sexuality because he looks just as emotional as Jackie did when I brought up the subject.

My father's shoulders drop and he leans forward, looking down at his feet. We don't normally have deep conversations but after Friday with Jackie and his reaction today, I know they're both keeping something from me. "It's not just up to me to tell you, honey."

"Then who is it up to?" I shoot him a puzzled look. "Dad, I want to know." A long silence lingers between us, as he continues to stare at his feet.

"Your mother and I were very happy for many years," he finally says, then pauses.

"But?" I ask.

"But…" He lets out a long sigh. "She fell in love with someone else."

"What?" I need a moment as his words hit me hard. I always had this idyllic idea of their relationship; they look genuinely happy in the photo albums I've browsed through so many times. And then I feel for my father, who clearly finds it difficult talking about this. "I'm so sorry, Dad. I didn't mean to drag up painful memories." I scoot my chair closer to him and place a hand on his arm.

"It's fine, honey, it's all part of life." He shoots me a small smile. "We were good together. Very compatible, but there was always something missing. I spent a decade trying to be enough for her, even though I never could be."

"Why? Who did she fall in love with?"

He shifts his attention to his cigar now, tapping off the ash with great care so he doesn't have to look at me. "Jackie."

"Jesus, Dad." I pause as if I haven't heard him correctly. "Mom and Jackie?" It seems too outrageous to be true and I can hardly begin to grasp what he's just told me. My mother was gay? Although I wish it wasn't the case, I don't recall much about her. I remember flashes of the last summer she was with us, when we all used to go to the beach together as a family, but that's it, apart from a fragment of her cooking in the kitchen. Suddenly, it all clicks. Jackie's reaction yesterday, why she never talks about her love life… How understanding and supportive she was when I came out to her. "But I don't get it. You and Jackie are friends."

"We are now. Back then, she was your mother's friend. They talked about girlie stuff and went shopping together, at least before it turned into something more. I was never really a part of it." He clears his throat. "I promised Jackie I'd never tell you but I can't lie to you either."

"Then tell me," I say, gently squeezing his hand.

"She was very sick, your mother." Dad sighs. "Jackie was at her bedside night and day, caring for her, and I was happy for her to be there because sometimes…" He pauses. "Well, sometimes two young kids and a dying wife was too much to handle for me. She helped me a lot too, in the house and she cooked for us. I couldn't see it back then, perhaps it was just too hard to comprehend."

I nod, meeting the sadness in his expression. "How did you find out?"

"Your mother told me just before she died," he says. "She'd been in love with Jackie for two years and they'd been seeing each other intimately several times a week."

I stare at him incredulously. "I don't understand why she told you. Mom was dying and she could have taken that secret with her to the grave. Why hurt you by admitting she'd been having an affair?"

Dad sighs. "Your mother told me it was possible to love two people at the same time. She loved us both equally, just in different ways, she said. And she wanted us to be there for each other after she was gone." He reaches for his whiskey glass and twirls the golden liquid around in the tumbler. "I was hurt, of course. Angry, upset, and I felt betrayed. But she was dying." A single tear rolls down his cheek. "And I still loved her very much, so I promised her I would look after Jackie, and Jackie promised she would look after me."

"And you did…"

"Not at first. I hated Jackie after I found out. A couple of days after the funeral, I was really struggling and decided to go next door and tell her exactly what I thought of her. But when I saw her, she was so upset…" My father swallows hard. "She was just as broken as me and I just couldn't."

"So eventually you did end up finding comfort in each other."

"Yes. She was the only person I could talk to about your mother and vice versa. And we struck up a friendship that made no sense but at the same time it was so natural that we've been close ever since."

Steadying my elbows on my knees, I lean forward and stare at him, only now feeling like I'm starting to understand him a little as a person. "I had no idea."

"You were young. I'm sorry to bulldoze your idea of a perfect marriage. It was far from perfect, but I loved her very much. And so did Jackie." Dad downs his whiskey and finally looks at me. "Are you okay?"

"Yeah. It's just… Jackie and Mom…" I shake my head incredulously. "And why did Jackie never meet anyone after Mom? Are you the only person who knows she's gay?"

"As far as I'm aware. She went on dates sometimes, but

she always compared other women to your mother and her few short-term relationships never worked out." My father shrugs. "I suppose I did the same."

"Mom must have been special," I say, wishing I could picture her better.

"She was." Dad groans as he gets up, shakes out his stiff legs and gives me a sad smile. "You remind us so much of her."

REINA - THURSDAY

"**I**s it too busy for you here?" Belle asks. "We can go somewhere else if you're not comfortable. Honestly, I won't mind."

"No, it's perfect." I smile at her and sit back, enjoying the gorgeous views over the water from all angles. The restaurant's big, private dock is fully booked, and waiters are rushing from the main building and back with drinks and steaming plates of seafood on huge, round trays. There are votive candles on each table and we're surrounded by white hydrangeas growing from the planters on the railing. "Have you been here before?"

"Only for drinks during the day. At night it's a little too romantic for me and Jackie," Belle jokes. She's looking sexy as always in a light-blue shirt and jeans and I'm wearing a casual, off-the-shoulder white dress with simple leather sandals. Although I planned on driving, Belle insisted on picking me up—she even brought me flowers—and we walked here from the street where she parked.

I never thought I'd be wined and dined like this at thirty-nine; not by someone I'm head over heels with and certainly not by a woman. "I don't think it could get more romantic than this." Meeting her intense stare, I blush. When we're together, Belle looks at me like nothing else matters and that makes me feel desired in a way I've never known. Anyone can see we're on a date but once again, I find myself not really caring about the few looks cast our way. In fact, I'm proud to be here with her.

"You look irresistible in that dress," she says, glancing at my bare shoulders as she lowers her voice to a whisper. "I can't wait to take it off."

Licking my lips, I shoot her a flirty look, heat flaring between my thighs. "I've thought of little else than being naked with you. This week seemed never-ending."

"Good, because I have plans for later."

"Ooh…" I say in a dramatic singing tone. "What kind of plans?"

"I just thought you might want to try something new. Since you're discovering your sexuality and all…" Belle grins. She loves teasing me, making me wait.

"Tell me."

She looks around to make sure no one is paying attention to us and leans in closer. "I want to use a strap-on."

"What's a…" I swallow hard when it hits me what she means, at least I have a vague idea. "Oh." It's suddenly feeling way warmer than it was a minute ago and I brush my hair away from my shoulders, letting the breeze hit my clammy skin. "Jesus, Belle."

"Sorry. Too much? We can forget I ever mentioned it."

"No, it's not that." Anticipation flares inside of me and I shift in my chair in an attempt to sooth the ache in my center. "I can't talk about it here," I whisper. "It turns me on too much."

Belle chuckles, her hooded eyes holding the promise of a long and steamy night. "Okay, let's change the subject."

"Thank you. At least until we're alone." I try to wipe the image of Belle wearing a strap-on from my mind and note that I'm probably the most clueless and innocent woman she's ever slept with.

"So… when was the last time you went on a date?" Belle picks up the bottle from the cooler next to her and refills our glasses.

"Hmm…" Raising my eyes to the string light covered canopy above us, I try to remember. "It must have been at least four years since Sandeep last took me out on a date. There wasn't much dating in general after the kids were born and even our anniversaries were skipped sometimes when he was away for business. I guess the last time I can think of was a dinner at a restaurant on Madison Avenue. I dressed up and we had nice food. One of his clients was there, dining with his wife and they ended up sharing dessert with us. It's funny, I don't remember that much about it, but I think it was an anniversary dinner." I shrug. "What about you? When was the last time you went on a date?"

Belle frowns, digging through her memory, then laughs. "Never?" She shrugs. "I took a girl out for lobster rolls in Montauk when I was sixteen. Does that count?"

Laughing along with her, my core flutters at her smile that makes every nerve in my body zing. "Sure, that counts. So it's been…" I pause, mentally doing the math. "Seventeen years."

"That's right." She shoots me an amused look. "So forgive me if I'm a little out of practice."

"You couldn't be more charming," I say with a playful smile, then ask the question that's been on my mind for a while. "Does it bother you that I'm almost forty?"

"No," Belle says resolutely. "Age is the last thing I'm worried about." She winces. "Sorry, I shouldn't have said that. It's a total mood killer."

"It's okay. I know you're worried."

She reaches for my hand over the table. "Look, it's not just Suki," she admits. "This is new to me and I just need to get used to… to feeling vulnerable, I suppose."

"I make you feel vulnerable?" Her words don't come as a surprise. I've seen her put a guard up a couple of times.

"Yes, because I adore you and I'm falling in love with you." She swallows hard and bites her lip nervously, as if she's already regretting saying it.

My breath hitches, and I stare at her, my heart singing with joy. "I'm falling in love with you too. And I'm just as scared as you are. Not because of what people will think of me, but because this is the most intense thing I've ever felt. But this is not a phase, Belle. I won't hurt you."

Belle lets out the breath she's been holding, and the corners of her mouth pull up into a smile. Our mutual confessions hang thick in the air as the waiter puts a plate of oysters between us. "I won't hurt you either. I promise."

BELLE - THURSDAY

*R*eina has been outgoing, flirting with me all night, and I'm seeing a whole different side to her, now that she's completely at ease with me. She's been talking animatedly for hours, telling me about her volunteer work at Camp Rubin. I didn't expect her to get her hands dirty like that and I think she's surprised herself too as she's clearly positively affected by it.

She took my hand as we walked back to my apartment and didn't flinch as we went down the busy street. Perhaps I've underestimated her.

"So, that thing you mentioned earlier," she says, pressing herself against me as I close the door. "I've been thinking about that…"

"I know you have." I smile and run a hand up her thigh, hiking up her dress. "Only if you want to."

Reina nods, arousal flashing through her eyes as she looks up at me, her lips meeting mine for a kiss. I run my tongue over her upper lip, drawing a quiet moan from her mouth, and feel the subtle tremble of anticipation in her body.

"Show me." Her soft voice sounds heavenly as she whispers in my ear.

I lead her to my bedroom and unlock the drawer of my nightstand, where I keep my private toys—the ones I've never used in my escorting career—and pull out the strap-on I bought especially with tonight in mind. "Are you okay with this?" I ask, holding it up for her to see.

Reina's gaze darkens and she takes in a quick breath, staring at it. "Yes," she says, licking her lips. "I want to try everything with you. Everything." She's got her back against the door and doesn't move as she continues to stare at the object in my hand.

"Everything, huh?" Taking charge, I throw the harness onto the bed and pull her dress over her head, sighing deeply at the sight of her. Every time still feels like the first, her naked body startling me to the point that I can barely breathe. She's my dream, my fantasy, and she's here because she wants me and no one else. Kissing her hard, I trace her thighs upward until I find her wet and ready, pushing her center against my hand. She's so aroused and sensitive but it's not enough. I want her to beg me to fuck her, to be so on edge that she'll be delirious with need.

Getting on my knees, I pull her white thong down and when she steps out of the delicate garment, I bring my mouth between her legs. My fingers dig into the soft flesh of her behind and I lick her teasingly before I part my lips and suck at her clit until her knees buckle.

"God, that feels so good," she mutters, steadying herself against the door. Her response turns me on even more and pulling her tightly against my mouth, I bring her to the brink of an orgasm before I move away from her with a teasing look.

"Hey, that's not fair," Reina says through ragged breaths, her shoulders and chest heaving and her eyelashes fluttering.

"It will only make it better in the end, I promise." I watch her press her thighs together in aching agony and straightening myself, I kiss her, letting her taste herself while I push my hips into hers.

"I... want... you." Her words are drawn out slowly between kisses and she chuckles when I lift her up and walk her to the bed. Her legs are still wrapped around my hips when I lay her down and I smile when she won't let go of me. "Patience, Reina." I kiss the hollow of her neck and free myself, then reach for a tube in my nightstand.

"I don't think I'm going to need that," Reina says shyly, chuckling at her own words as she stares at the lube.

"Maybe not, but it feels great." Squirting some onto my fingertips, I kiss her while I bring my hand between her legs, and start massaging her center, slowly, deliberately, mixing the lube with her own arousal.

"Jesus, I had no idea this would—" Reina moans and throws her head back, crying out at the slippery sensation of my hand, once again balancing on the edge. The lube turns warm and liquid making her tingle and so, so ready for me. When I get up to strap on the harness, her hips are still jerking as she stares at the shaft. "Please fuck me," she pleads, taking my hand and pulling me on top of her. "I need you right now." Her expression tells me she's not joking, and her body language is screaming out for me to take her.

Wedging myself between her legs, I kiss my way down her neck and linger on her breasts as I move the shaft between her legs and push inside, slowly. I feel her entire body tense up; her shoulders, her abdomen against my stomach, her thighs against mine, and she's holding her breath while she bites her bottom lip and groans.

"Are you okay?"

"Yes... I want more," Reina says through moans and spreads her legs farther to let me in. "Fuck, Belle…"

Fueled by her pleas and aroused beyond imagination, I penetrate her deeper and take her hands, lacing my fingers through hers. The friction on the harness against my center feels amazing and my core tightens as we kiss and sink into each other. Reina cries out and squeezes my hands, holding me tight as we fall into a slow rhythm, moving together, deeper, becoming one.

"Come with me," I whisper, lifting my head to look at her when she moans loudly against my lips, and she smiles at me and nods, unable to speak as she's about to crash. Thrusting into her harder, we fall into release together, our hips meeting as we cry out in unison. When I finally collapse on top of her, I'm trembling all over, and she takes me into her arms and showers my temple and forehead with featherlight kisses. Reina looks tired and satisfied, licking her lips when I pull out of her and turn on my side.

"This is crazy," she whispers, stroking my face.

"It is." I smile, taking in her face that I could get lost in forever. "And I'm crazy for *you*."

"*H*ow are you and Tyrell now?" I ask when Nicole and I are walking through Montauk County Park. I've spent the morning taking pictures of her until she begged me to stop and now we're looking for birds to test my new wildlife lens.

"We're okay," Nicole says. "It was just a stupid fight."

"That's good." I stop to take a picture of a woodpecker I've spotted in a tree ahead, and I'm pleased with the result. It's actually staring right into the lens, like it's posing for me. "You know you could have stayed in New York for the weekend, right?"

"I know, stop repeating yourself, Mom. I wanted to see you."

"I'm sorry, I'll stop saying it." I snap another picture of the woodpecker and raise my camera higher to catch the sunbeams through the leaves of the tree. "And as I said before, if you want to bring him here, that's fine too. I'd love to meet him."

Nicole blushes and shrugs. "I'll think about it."

"So, a rapper, huh? Does he write his own lyrics?" I ask,

once again pushing away the thought that a rapper is not what I had in mind for my smart, amazing daughter who I'm hoping will be a doctor one day. After all, if my mother said anything negative about Belle, I'd be furious with her.

"Of course. All rappers write their own stuff." She grins and blushes even more now. "He produces too. Stuff for movies and TV."

"Okay, that's interesting, tell me more."

"I'll tell you about Tyrell if you tell me about your love life," she retorts with a smug smile.

Now it's my turn to blush. Nicole hasn't mentioned Belle once after our talk on the beach, but I can tell she genuinely wants to know. "We went on our first date," I say. "She took me to a lovely restaurant in Sag Harbor."

Nicole's eyes widen. "Really? You went out with her in public?" She stops herself and holds up a hand. "Sorry, that came out wrong. I just didn't think you'd actually have the courage to openly go out on a date with a woman."

"Well, I did. I hadn't seen her in weeks. Not since you walked in on us, but then I bumped into her when I was out with Sasha one night and…" I blush even harder now. "And then I went home with her."

"Why had you not seen her? Was it because of me?"

"No, honey, it had nothing to do with you. Our lives are just very different and although that doesn't bother me one bit, it bothered her a lot. She also thought I might be going through a phase."

"You can't blame her for that, they're valid points." Nicole squeezes my arm. "But it's not a phase, is it?"

"No, it's not. I'm sure about that now." I feel completely calm saying it out loud and it even gives me a sense of relief. "I've asked myself if I could date another man, but the truth is, I can't see myself with anyone else but Belle and on a physical level I way prefer women."

"I gathered as much," Nicole jokes, then laughs when I turn crimson. "Sorry, too soon," she says with a chuckle.

"Please don't mention that incident ever again," I beg, shooting her a warning look. "There is no 'too soon', just stick to never, okay?"

"Sure, Mom." She shoots me a teasing look. "Now I know why you wanted to go to that gay bar in New York. How long has this been going on? Between you and Belle?"

"Not long." *At least the unpaid sex part.* I refrain from giving her anymore timeline information and she doesn't pry.

"Well, now that we've established that you're gay..." Nicole pulls me toward a footpath that leads to the beach. "Let's say this works out and you two get serious. Would you come out to the world? Would you introduce her to all your friends? And how do you feel about the fact that she has a young daughter?"

"You sound like Belle," I say, her name causing a tug of longing in my core. "I've thought about it and in theory, I can handle people knowing about us. Now that we've been out on a date together, I'm much more open to the idea." I shrug. "But then again, I can't be sure. I know being gay isn't a big deal in this day and age, but I don't have any gay friends, and it's the last thing people would expect from me."

"If your friends don't accept it, you don't need them in your life." Nicole smiles at me. "And I'll always be on your side, Mom."

"Thank you, honey." I lean in and kiss her cheek. The wind grows stronger as we conquer the last dune, and my hair starts blowing wildly around me. The noise of the ocean forces me to raise my voice. "Sasha knows too."

Nicole gasps. "You told Sasha about Belle?"

"Yes. She was very cool about it and I'm not worried

271

about her gossiping." I don't mention that Sasha and I have a silent understanding. That *her* secret is just as safe with me.

"Are you going to tell Eddie?" she asks.

"If Belle and I are still together when he visits, yes, I suppose I'll have to tell your brother."

"He's not going to care either," Nicole says. "To be honest, I don't think anyone will, apart from Grandma Amari."

"That's true," I say. "My mother won't be impressed but at least she's predictable, so I know exactly how she'll react; she'll just pretend I never told her."

"Yeah. She's still in denial about you and Dad getting a divorce." Nicole rolls her eyes. "Last time I spoke to Grandma she asked me if we were all celebrating the Fourth of July together."

"I'm not surprised. She asked me if we were all coming to Beirut together." Reaching the shore, we take off our shoes, roll up our jeans and continue our walk wading through the water. "But enough about me now. It's your turn," I say. "Tell me about Tyrell."

BELLE - SUNDAY

"They had such a good time. Thank you, it was truly spectacular."

I smile at Mrs. Green, the mother of the birthday girl who joins us in their huge backyard where my team is helping me break down the setup of last night's party. A gardener is picking up trash that has ended up in the flowerbeds and inside, a team of cleaners is rushing to get the house back to its usual pristine state in record time. "Glad they enjoyed it. No trouble?" I ask.

"Absolutely nothing. Even the boys behaved themselves. As far as I know anyway," she adds with a wink, then points to the company logo on my polo shirt. "Do you happen to have business cards on you? Some of the parents have asked about that amazing fountain and the lights you provided."

"Of course." I pull a handful of business cards from my back pocket and hand them to her. "I'm just starting out, so any recommendations are welcome." The woman who was stressed and on edge, bordering on grumpy while we set up, is now all smiles and sunshine. Her daughter's sweet sixteenth went well, and she's managed to impress the other parents. Because that's what it's all about in the Hamptons; showing that she can pull off the best of the best for her kids. Here, being a parent is about as competitive as Olympic level sports. Mrs. Green has hit a home run and therefore, her recommendation is invaluable.

"Great. I'll make sure to pass them on." She slips them into her purse and pulls the strap over her shoulder, jingling her car keys in her other hand. "You have a good day now. I'm out of here so I don't have to look at the mess."

I give her a wave and turn back to help Randy who's loading my big light cube stools into the van. By placing these together, we've created snug seating areas in which the color of the lights can be changed with a remote.

"Is she happy?" he asks.

"Yeah. Very." I smile at Randy. He's been great and genuinely seems to have enjoyed helping me. "Two more bookings came in this week; I'll forward you the details in case you're available."

"Sure thing. The way it's going you might get busier than you anticipated."

"Let's hope so." I pick up the last cube and Randy hops in the van to take it from me. I'm so relieved that it went well, and I'm starting to feel cautiously optimistic. My phone rings, and I see it's Rose, Jackie's staging friend from book club. "Just a minute, Randy, I have to take this."

"Is that Belle Rodgers?" Rose asks in a friendly tone.

"Hi, Rose. How are you?" Although my meeting with her was pleasant and she said she might have work for me, I never expected her to call so soon, and I feel a flicker of excitement.

"I'm great. It was lovely to meet you the other day." Rose pauses and I can hear her flipping through paperwork. "Listen, I have five jobs between the eighth and the sixteenth of July, if you're interested?"

"Five?" My eyebrows shoot up and I give Randy a thumbs-up. "Absolutely." Not wanting her to know that my schedule is practically free, I add: "Just send me the dates and I'll check my calendar."

"Perfect. I'll email you the details. Two of the stagings will be fairly low-key as they're family homes, the other three need to be spectacular."

"I can do that. I'll give you a call to set up a meeting as soon as I've gone through it."

"Excellent." Rose chuckles. "This is certainly making my life easier."

After I hang up, I walk up to Randy and give him a fist bump. "Five more," I say, and he's so excited for me that it's endearing. Best of all, he has enthusiasm and endless energy, and because of his sales background, he's presentable and polite.

"I told you that you had gold on your hands," he says, giving me a pat on my shoulder. "You'll be able to quit that pool job soon. Just mark my words; in a year from now, everyone here will know your company." He hops out and I close the doors.

"I don't know about that, but it's a great start." Climbing behind the wheel, I'm glowing with happiness as life right now couldn't be any better. "How's your wife?" I ask as I drive off. "Is she suffering from morning sickness?"

"Yup." Randy chuckles. "She's sick in the mornings and gets these impossible cravings at night. Yesterday I had to drive all the way to Montauk to get her a fried fish sandwich." He turns to me and glances at me curiously. "What about you? Are you married or seeing someone?"

I'm so used to answering 'no' to that question that I automatically shake my head. "No. I mean, yes." Laughing, I shake my head again. "I've met someone. We've just started dating." Saying it out loud makes it real, and I like how it sounds.

"Who's the lucky guy?" Randy asks.

"Lucky woman," I retort with a wink.

"Oh, sorry." He blushes profusely and settles his gaze back on the road ahead. "I didn't know you were..."

"That's okay." I'm bemused by Randy's cluelessness as very few people have assumed I'm straight in the past. "Her name is Reina."

"Nice name. Sounds classy."

"She is. And she's beautiful." Suddenly I feel an overwhelming urge to see Reina, and I can't get back to the storage unit to unload fast enough. Having been busy with work and Suki, I haven't seen her in two days, and although we've called and messaged, I miss her so much. So this is what it's like, I think to myself as I turn onto the main road. To want to be with someone all the time, to have this constant yearning and smile each time you're with your favorite person. This is what it's like to be in love.

REINA - SUNDAY

"Here's to your first job being a huge success," I say, raising my glass to Belle's.

"Thank you, I'm so relieved and happy." Belle is beaming, her smile so wide that it's infectious. She came straight here after she finished unloading, stealing a moment with me as Jackie is looking after Suki until five. We've taken a bottle of champagne down to the beach and are sitting on the shore, the tide washing over our bare toes. I feel so complete when she's with me that I wish I could see her all the time. "I have another couple of jobs booked in and Jackie put me in touch with a stager who has five jobs in July. Hopefully some more events will come from this one too, so I can quit my job at Pool Masters and focus my energy."

"That's great news." I wrap an arm around her waist and kiss her cheek. "I'm proud of you."

Belle blushes as she stares ahead. "Really?"

"Yeah. You've done an amazing job at building a life and setting up a business while being a single mom. I admire you."

"Well, I'm proud of you too."

I shoot her a puzzled look as I feel like I've literally accomplished nothing in my thirty-nine years. "For what?"

"For being you. For having the courage to be true to yourself. For discovering who you are." She chuckles. "You're awfully wholesome for a Lebanese princess."

"Hey, I'm not a princess," I say, nudging her bare arm. "But thank you for saying that." The sleeves of Belle's polo shirt are rolled up, showing a subtle tan line as she hugs her knees and turns to me. I'm rewarded with another flirtatious smile that makes me want to kiss her again and again. Everything about her is insanely attractive and I wish we had more time today. "You know you can bring Suki here, right? I don't want you to miss out on time with her just because you're meeting up with me." When she doesn't reply, I quickly add: "Sorry, it's probably too soon, I shouldn't have mentioned it."

Belle "Yes, it's soon," she says softly. "But I'd like her to get to know you better. I mean, I don't think we should sleep in the same bed when she's around just yet, but we could just hang out and have fun."

"I'd like that." I'm overcome by emotion, knowing I mean enough to her to bring me into her daughter's life. "And I'd love to get to know Suki better too. She seems like a very sweet and clever girl."

"She is. I don't know what I'd do without her." Belle pauses and locks her eyes with mine. "But honestly, I don't know what I'd do without you either." She puts her champagne flute to the side, takes mine and lowers me into the sand, then lies down beside me and strokes my cheek. "It's strange... I haven't even known you for that long. And I've tried to fight it—trust me, I have—but the attraction was just too strong to ignore."

I nod and brush my lips against hers. "I feel like I was meant to meet you. Does that sound silly?"

"No, not at all. I think I was meant to meet you too. I was

drawn to you from the minute we met and knowing now that it was mutual, well, it's just too beautiful to be a coincidence. I thought this would be difficult, between you and me, but so far, it's not."

"It's blatantly simple," I whisper, pulling her closer. The sand tickles my cheek, the sun caresses my skin and Belle's electric touch and soft lips send a sizzling sensation through my body when she kisses me. Parting my lips, I let her in and as always, it evokes arousal beyond belief, years of pent-up repression released each time we make out. Belle shifts on top of me, and I sigh as I roam my hands under her polo shirt, finding her warm skin. Her weight and the pressure of her thigh against my center causes fireworks in my core and I lower my hands to her behind to draw her tighter against me.

We hear voices in the distance and Belle pulls away before it gets too heated. "I want you all the time," she says in a husky voice. "All the time."

"You have no idea how you make me feel." I bring my fingertips to my lips that are swollen from the heated kiss, our eyes meeting in an unspoken promise of much, much more to come. "When can I see you again?"

"I can come over Wednesday morning, or with Suki on Saturday. Unless you're volunteering?"

"No, I have Monday, Tuesday and Friday on my schedule for next week, so both would be perfect." I raise myself back into a sitting position and brush the sand out of my hair. "What's her favorite food? Any games I should get? Anything for the pool, or the beach?"

"If you want to get her on your good side, she loves ice cream," Belle says with a chuckle. "I'll bring some pool toys for her so we can chill, and I should probably talk to her before we come. Prepare her, you know?"

"Are you going to tell her we're together?"

"I'm not sure yet, but she's very intuitive. Suki will sense something is going on between us so it's best if I ease her into it. She's always had me to herself; I don't know how she'll react, knowing there's another significant person in my life."

"I hope she'll be okay with it." I suddenly feel nervous, as if I'm going to be put through a test of some sorts.

"Hey, it will be fine," Belle says, taking my hand. "You're lovely and Suki will see that too."

BELLE - MONDAY

"You know how some kids have a mommy and a daddy?" I say to Suki, handing her another bucket full of sand. It's just her and me here on the beach. Monday mornings are always quiet and because the weather was beautiful, I cancelled her preschool for this morning so we could hang out together. I've brought sandwiches, a thermos with coffee and a bottle of juice, towels and everything we need to build the perfect sandcastles.

"Yes." Suki looks up at me with a frown, scrunching her nose that has sand stuck to the tip. She takes the bucket and clumsily turns it upside down, adding to the pile of wet sand we've gathered.

"Well, the mommies and daddies are together because they're in love. They're like best friends and they sleep in the same bed. And sometimes kids have two mommies, or two daddies." I'm not sure if she's old enough for this conversation, but I want her to be prepared for another woman in our life.

"Ryan in my class has two daddies. One wears funny

clothes," she says. "And sometimes he has funny shoes. Like lady shoes."

"Right. Yes, Ryan has two very nice daddies, and it's okay for daddies and mommies to wear whatever they like. And Melika in your class, she has two mommies. Did you know that?"

Suki shakes her head and starts shaping a tower, adding water to the sand to firm it up.

"It's true," I continue. "You've only met one of them because Melika's other mommy works, so she can't take her to school."

"Why does she have two mommies?"

Buying time to answer that question, I help her shape the tower, then hand her some shells that I picked up on the way to decorate with. "Because some women fall in love with men, some women fall in love with women, and some fall in love with both. Melika's mommies fell in love with each other, and they're married."

"Oh." Suki contemplates this, then looks at me as if she wants me to get to the point.

"Well, I'm the same as Malika's mommies. I fall in love with women." There's a long silence and I'm not sure if she's taken aback by this information or simply immersed in her task, so I add: "And I would like to fall in love too." Again, she's silent, and I know she's processing by the way she's biting her bottom lip. It must be terribly confusing to her. The four main people in her life—me, my father, Jackie and Juliette—are all single, it's the only lifestyle she knows. "Would you mind if I was in love?"

"No," she finally says. "But you have to stay my mommy forever."

"Of course, sweetie." I kiss her forehead, then help her pat down the base and dig out more sand to go in the bucket. "I'm your only mommy and that's never going to change.

You'll always be the most important person in my life. But I wanted to tell you that I've made a new friend. Her name is Reina. Do you remember Reina? We saw her in town a while back, after we went to the bank."

Suki furrows her brow, digging through her memory. "She has pretty hair."

"Yes, she does. Would you mind if Reina came over to our house sometimes? Or if we visited her?"

"No."

"You mean no, you don't mind?" When I get no answer because she's too fixated on placing shells around the base of the tower, I add: "Reina has a very nice pool, and she lives by the beach."

At this, Suki looks up at me and grins and although I feel a flood of relief, I also regret saying it. Bribing her to accept Reina just because she has a pool is cheating for one, but I also forgot that look in her eyes. The one she got when she saw 'the lammies' for the first time and since we've been to the community pool, 'the pool' has become the new main focus in her life, now that my father's lambs have grown and become a little intimidating to her.

"Can we go to the pool after we finish the sandcastle?" she asks.

"You mean Reina's pool?" I ask.

"Yes. I want to go to Reina's pool." Her enthusiasm is through the roof now, and she waves her hands, bouncing up and down as she crouches.

"Not today, honey," I say, placing a hand on her shoulder to calm her down. "Reina is busy and Mommy has to work. But we could go on Saturday after we've been to the market?" Seeing the timeline confusion on her face, I take her hand and count out the days on her fingers. "Monday, Tuesday, Wednesday, Thursday…" I take her other hand, pinching her little thumb. "…Friday. Five sleeps."

Suki looks down at her hands and juts out her bottom lip. I wonder if she's about to burst into tears at the shear enormity of so many sleeps, but she simply lets out a sigh of frustration and nods. "Five," she repeats quietly, making sure she'll keep track of time.

"Yes," I say with a smile. "We can stay the whole day if you want, and you know what else? I'll bring you one of those pink flamingo pool toys."

REINA - WEDNESDAY

I can't believe I've been coming here all these years and never been for a morning swim. Belle and I are wading out of the ocean, laughing and kissing as we cross the beach to the house. Now having three mornings a week to herself, she came here after dropping Suki off at preschool. She looks incredible in her bikini and board shorts and I find it impossible to keep my hands off her.

"Do you want to go for a walk?" I suggest, thinking I need the sun to warm me as I'm shivering from the cold water.

Belle shakes her head with a wicked grin. "Now that you're wide awake, how about we enjoy our three precious hours left with a little more privacy?" She glances at my body, clearly liking my skimpy, black triangle bikini. Shaking out her wet hair, she takes my hand and pulls me along over the bridge. "Let's go back to the house; I'll warm you up, baby."

I laugh and run after her and as soon as we've walked through the gate, I fall into Belle's arms, moaning as our wet bodies come together. I can feel her need in her tensing muscles and it's warming me up all right. Falling into a delicious kiss, I taste the salt water on her lips and weave my fingers through her wet hair. We stand by the poolside, making out for minutes on end, losing all track of time.

"Wait, let me just close the gate before you take all my sense of logic away," I mumble against her mouth, fighting to tear myself away from her lips. As I look up, I see a figure standing by the gate and wincing against the sun, I gasp when my ex-husband comes into sharper focus. "Sandeep! What are you doing here?"

Sandeep's eyes are wide, his jaw hangs open and he clutches onto the gate like he's a sailor in a storm. "I'm sorry, I shouldn't have walked in but the beach gate was open and…" His voice trails off as he stares at us. "Wait… Is this what I think it is?" he says in a strangled voice.

I grab a towel from one of the lounge chairs, secure it around my waist and cross my arms in front of my chest. Glancing at Belle, I don't know what to say, but she simply raises her brows, not wanting to step in. "Yes, it is," I answer after a moment's hesitation. I'm caught, once again, and there's no point denying anything.

"Oh." Sandeep clears his throat. "I didn't know you were… I didn't—"

"I didn't know either," I say, helping him out. "And you can't just let yourself in like that. This is my home now; you don't live here anymore."

"Yes, sorry." The baffled stare is still plastered all over his face and he doesn't seem to get the words out, so I decide to do the talking. I'm still shaken by Sandeep seeing me kissing Belle, but I'm not ashamed. It's just strange to have both him and my new lover here, and I don't want him to tell people before I'm ready.

"This is Belle," I say, taking Belle's hand. "She's my…" God, what is she to me? My partner? My lover? "We're dating," I finally settle on.

"Dating?" As Sandeep drags the word out, he sounds like a toddler who is just learning to speak. Even Belle seems surprised that I'm being so open and honest about us; she's glancing at me sideways, squeezing my hand.

"Yes." I pause and wait for him to reply but he remains silent. "I'd appreciate it if you could keep this to yourself. For now, at least."

He nods. "Do the kids know?"

"Nicole knows, and Sasha knows. But I'm not ready to tell anyone else yet so please don't mention it to Igor or even to Bree. People gossip way too much around here."

"Of course."

"So, what brought you here?" I ask. "I assume you didn't just drop in for a coffee?"

"No, there was actually something I wanted to talk to you about." He looks at Belle, and she lets go of my hand.

"I'll go have a shower, so you guys have some privacy," she says, and shoots Sandeep an uncomfortable smile. "It was nice to meet you."

"Likewise." Sandeep follows me into the house and sits when I gesture to the stools along the bar, following Belle with his eyes as she heads up the staircase.

"Espresso? Two sugars?"

"No sugar," he says, and that amuses me. Of course Bree has put a stop to his sugar intake. That woman is all lean and green; she once told me that sugar and carbs are the devil.

I make a cappuccino for myself and an espresso for Sandeep and take a seat opposite him. He's glancing around the kitchen and I wonder what he's thinking. This house is his creation; he practically bulldozed most of the previous building because he can't stand gimmicky constructions or features, and he did really love this house. I suppose he still does; nothing has changed.

"So, what did you want to talk about?"

"Ehm, yes. I ehm… I came to tell you that…" He downs his espresso, ready for me to chase him out in case of an angry outburst. Perhaps he's more at ease, now that he's seen that I've moved on too, but the familiar red nervous blotches are still spreading over his neck and cheeks. "Bree and I are having a baby."

"A baby?" I exclaim, managing a surprised look. "She's pregnant?"

"Yes. Five months."

"Wow. I thought you didn't want to have any more kids." *Not with me at least.*

"I didn't, it wasn't planned. But we're happy, of course," he hastily adds. "Anyway, I thought it would be better if you heard it from me rather than from someone else."

"Thank you for telling me." I look him over; his chiseled chin, his chest hair visible above his half-unbuttoned shirt, and I find it hard to believe that we used to have sex. I just don't find him attractive anymore. *I don't find men attractive anymore.* I take a sip of my coffee and remain silent, making him sweat a little while he waits for my reply. "But this is your life now, Sandeep. You don't need my permission or blessing."

He nods again. "But I'd like your blessing. I hope we can get on some day, for the kids' sake." This is nonsense, of course. As long as we can be civilized and we're both happy, our grown-up kids won't care about our personal relationship. But we do have a lot of friends in common and we will be seeing each other this summer. Friction between us will make socializing highly awkward and besides, he lives close by so we might even meet on the beach.

"If this is what you want, then I'm happy for you," I say, then watch his shoulders drop in relief. "No hard feelings."

"Thank you." Sandeep smiles and glances toward the

staircase. "What about you and…" He frowns. "Belle, was it? Are you two serious?"

"I'm in love with her. I have been for a while, but things were complicated. This whole situation is complicated as I'm sure you'll understand."

"Because she's a woman."

"Yes. I'm not uncomfortable about it—quite the opposite actually—but I just need to get used to the idea myself before I tell others." Despite what he did to me, I'm willing to give Sandeep the benefit of the doubt and I think I can trust him. He's been my best friend for over twenty years and perhaps it's good that he's here now so that we can finally be honest with each other.

"Did you always know you preferred women?" he asks, and I know the answer is important to him.

"No." I pause. "Looking back, maybe. There were signs, but it never clicked, and I mean it when I say that I was happy with you. At least until…" I stop myself, not wanting to get into an argument. "Sorry, that's in the past now."

"It's okay, you can say it. I know I hurt you."

We fall silent, both processing the conversation and I suddenly have a moment of clarity. This isn't all his fault. He's not the only one to blame. "It can't have been easy for you either," I say. "I was never very sexual with you. We didn't have that sexual compatibility people talk about."

"I think I wanted you more than you wanted me. Physically speaking at least," he admits.

"Yes." I pause, choosing my words carefully. "Well, I have that physical chemistry with Belle, and I've realized how important that is. Passion was something I couldn't give you —I see that now—and I'm sorry."

"I still should have made better choices but thank you for saying that." He reaches over the bar to squeeze my hand and I think that for the first time, he feels like I understand him.

That I can begin to grasp why he strayed, even if it was wrong. "You with a woman was the last thing I expected. To be honest with you, I'm still recovering from seeing you kissing her. You looked so…" He frowns and looks down at his hands. "So… I don't know, into it, I suppose. Does she make you happy?"

"Very." I smile as I hear the shower running upstairs, and imagining Belle naked in there, I can't wait for him to leave so I can join her. "I never saw this coming but I'm grateful it happened to me. It all worked out better in the end, don't you think? For both of us."

Sandeep closes his eyes and breathes a sigh of relief, the wall of guilt visibly crumbling a little. I've heard guilt can feel worse than pain, that it's a terrible burden to bear, and I don't want him to dwell on the past anymore. "Do you regret marrying me?"

"No," I say resolutely. "We have two beautiful children, and we had a good life together. But now I'm looking forward to my next life, the one that will be about me and what I want." I angle my head and study him. "Do you regret marrying me?"

"No. God, no. I still miss you every day. You were my best friend." He hesitates. "But you're right. Something was missing." He gets up and stands there with his hands in his pockets. "I really hope we can be friends again, Reina." Then he turns and leaves through the back door.

BELLE - WEDNESDAY

I'm flustered from the recent events as I stand under the shower way longer than necessary to give Reina and Sandeep more time to talk. He's a handsome man and I can imagine what she saw in him. This is getting real now. Although he was never meant to see us together like that, he did, and now he's the third person to know. Sandeep looked shocked, and if I wasn't mistaken, there was also a hint of jealousy there. Reina, on the other hand, seemed pretty chilled considering the circumstances but perhaps that's just a front she puts on; I haven't known her long enough to be sure. A shadow moves across the wall and Reina appears.

"Can I join you?"

"Please." I swipe the condensation off the glass so I can see her better. "Are you finished already?"

"Yeah. We've said everything we had to say." Standing before the glass door, Reina wiggles her hips seductively and pulls at her bikini strings. There's not a hint of distress on her face and knowing all she wants is to be here with me, settles my anxiety. I wasn't worried they would reconcile—

she's made it more than clear that this is not a phase—but twenty plus years of marriage is a lot and there must still be something there.

"Then get your cute ass in here." I watch her as she tugs at the ties of both her bottom and her top, causing the tiny garments to fall to the floor. "Damn, woman."

Reina giggles and steps in, aligning her naked body with mine. When she looks up to stare into my eyes, I take her face into my hands. "Are you okay? You don't have to pretend if you're not."

"Yes," she says without hesitation. "I was talking to him and all I could think of was that I wanted him to leave so that you and I could finish what we started." Her hands move into my hair, then down to my behind, and she squeezes my cheeks, pulling me against her. The water cascades down her hair and I feel the rhythmic thud of our combined hearts as I kiss her softly, the light caress soon turning into hunger. Reina kisses me back with such eagerness that my legs start shaking. Never taking her mouth off mine, she pumps some shower gel into the palm of her hands and starts scrubbing my back and my shoulders, her arms embracing me. She pulls away, but only for a moment, to get more soap—a generous amount this time—and she applies it over her breasts and her belly, then takes hold of me again and rubs her body against mine while we kiss. Sexy, hard, slow, her back arching and her hips moving so sensually it sets every part of me aflame. The slipperiness between us, the droplets traveling down her shoulders and her breasts, settling in a puddle between us like we're sealed together. I'm astoundingly moved and aroused, filled with so much longing that my inner dominatrix switches into gear.

"Turn around and face the wall," I say breathlessly, taking her by the shoulders.

Reina shoots me a sexy smile as she turns her back to me. "What are you going to do?"

I don't answer and gently guide her to stand against the wall. Reina gasps at the cold tiles against her skin but she arches her back, begging me to take her. Applying soap all over my torso, I move into her, wedging her between myself and the wall. I moan as I thrust into her cute behind, the friction causing a delicious tightness in my core.

"That feels so good." She pushes back against me, our rhythm quicker now and more urgent.

I take her hands and place them on the wall just above her shoulder height. "Keep them there and you'll feel even better in a minute." Her reaction to my voice when we make love always amazes me, and I can feel the frisson of excitement coursing through her as I whisper in her ear. Switching the lever to the hand-held showerhead, I turn up the pressure and bring it around her, then part her legs with my hand. I aim it at her throbbing center, and she jerks at the hard spray, clawing at the wall in need of something to hold onto.

"Fuck!"

Keeping the showerhead there, I enter her from behind and start fucking her slowly until her uncontrolled movements tell me to go faster. Being inside her is what turns me on the most; it makes me feel connected to her on all levels. I love how she feels, how much she wants me. How much she needs this. Her walls are contracting, her body shaking and her hands are balled into fists while her cheek is pressed against the wall.

"Yes, Belle…" Reina comes so hard that her cry bounces off the bathroom walls and I have to push into her to keep her upright. After long moments, I drop the showerhead and we sink onto the floor together where she falls into my arms so I can hold her. "Fuck." She closes her eyes as she catches her breath.

I stroke her wet hair and kiss her forehead, and we stay there for a while before she sits up and reaches for the showerhead. With a wicked grin, she holds it up, her eyes caressing my naked body before they settle between my thighs.

"Your turn," she says, biting her lip. The floor feels hard when she nudges me to lie down on my back, but I don't care because she leans over me and kisses me hard while she lowers the showerhead between us. Reina is not the shy woman from before. She's not uncomfortable with her nakedness, she's not intimidated by me and she's not afraid to explore. When the water hits my clit, my hips shoot up and she spreads my legs, torturing me by removing it when my orgasm builds. Smiling against my lips, she repeats the action, making me beg the way I've made her beg so many times before.

"Please," I mutter.

"Please what?" She pulls away to look at me, then finally releases me, her eyes locking with mine, totally in awe as she watches the ecstatic expression crash over my face. It's a look of wonder, of curiosity, of joy and there's also something very soft and warm in her gaze, something tender. She opens her mouth to say something, then shakes her head and smiles instead. Leaning in, her sweet voice rings in my ear. "We should have showers together more often."

REINA - SATURDAY

"*H*i guys!" I give Belle a hug and tousle Suki's hair. She's already wearing her bathing costume; a cute yellow suit with ruffles and a duck printed on the front. "It's so nice to see you again," I say, going to my knees so I'm at eye-level with her. "Do you remember me?"

Suki grins at me and nods while she leans against Belle's leg, her arm wrapped around her thigh. "Mommy says you have a pool."

"I do. But it's quite deep so you'll have to wear your floaters."

"I have floaters." She holds them up; a yellow pair matching her suit. The shyness is already fading from her expression and I have a feeling she'll warm to me soon.

"Those are very cool floaters. Do you want a glass of lemonade to take outside?"

"Yes please." Suki follows me and Belle to the kitchen, her face lighting up when she spots the pool through the open sliding doors. "Mommy, it's a big pool! And she has a sea!"

Belle laughs and puts an arm around my waist. "Yes, that's

the ocean behind the yard, but the beach and the ocean belong to everyone."

"We can go down there later," I say, handing Suki a glittery pink plastic pool cup with lemonade and a matching straw that I bought for today. "Cappuccino?" I ask, meeting Belle's eyes. It felt strange not to kiss her when she arrived, and the flirty look she's giving me is not helping.

"Yeah, I'd love one," she says. As Suki heads outside, Belle squeezes by behind and I chuckle as I slap her hand away. "Behave, Belle."

"Sorry." She laughs too and shoots me a wink before following Suki outside. "She's learning to swim. Aren't you, honey?"

"I can swim without floaters, but I still have to practice."

"Wow. That's amazing for a four-year-old," I say, lowering my voice while Belle puts her floaters on and blows them up.

"She's not there yet, but you can't start early enough if you're surrounded by water, right? We'll practice a bit more today; I'm trying to do an hour a week with her." Belle gives Suki a kiss on her cheek and the little girl bravely jumps in at the deep end. When we applaud her, she grins widely and starts showing off her stroke.

"She's so sweet. I miss having younger kids," I say, clapping again when Suki reaches the other end of the pool. "Not that I'd want any more, but you just get so excited through them, don't you think?"

"Yeah. She makes me laugh all the time." Belle keeps her eyes fixed on Suki while we sit down at the edge of the pool and lower our legs into the water. It's sunny and warm and I feel immensely happy and content today. "I was going to ask you…" she says. "You mentioned it's your birthday soon. When is it?"

"It's the thirtieth of July, but I'm not celebrating. Nicole said something about taking me to a spa and going out to dinner together. She wanted to organize a party which is so sweet of her, but... I don't know. I wasn't feeling it back then."

"And you are now?"

"I don't like being the center of attention," I say with a shrug. "And Nicole will be staying in New York for most of July because of an internship, so I'm actually delighted to spend my birthday with her."

Belle nods. "And what about the Fourth of July? Is she not going to be here?"

"No, she's going to a party with her boyfriend. But I've got a couple of party invites, so I'll have fun either way." I look at Belle and smile. "What are you guys doing for the Fourth?"

"We're celebrating at my dad's house. Me, Suki, Juliette, her son Cameron, Dad and Jackie. Just a small group but it will be fun. It always is." Belle hesitates and glances at me for a brief moment, then fixes her gaze back on Suki. "You're welcome to come along but I'm sure you have much more exciting parties to attend."

"Oh..." Her invite startles me and I fall silent, aware of my goofy grin. "I'd love that."

"Really?" Belle returns my smile, surprise written all over her face. I want to kiss her dimples and her delicious mouth, and from the way she shifts her gaze to mine, I know she desperately wants to kiss me too.

"Yeah. Only if the others don't mind. I don't want to intrude."

"No way, they'd love to meet you." Belle puts an arm around me and pulls me in. "It's nothing big, just some steaks on the grill and drinks around the bonfire. We usually walk down to the beach later, to watch the fireworks."

"That sounds perfect," I say, happily remembering the times we used to celebrate as a family. Since the kids started going to their friends' parties, it hasn't been that much fun.

The Fourth of July parties Sandeep and I attended together were busy and full of people who were there to network, rather than to have a good time and last year, I didn't celebrate at all. Spending the day with Belle sure beats going to some hyped-up party by myself and I'm curious about her father and Jackie as she's told me a lot about them.

Suki is now on her third length, practicing her stroke with determination, so I get up and strip off my kaftan.

"Are you trying to kill me?" Belle whispers, looking up at me standing at the edge of the pool in my new yellow halter bikini.

I chuckle and help her up. "Are you coming in?"

Belle takes off her T-shirt and shorts and jumps in, causing a huge splash that makes me scream as the cold water hits my skin. Suki finds this hugely amusing as she swims over to Belle and clings onto her.

"You too!" she says, pointing at me. "Make a cannonball."

"Reina won't make cannonballs," Belle says in a teasing tone. "She doesn't want her hair to get wet."

"Oh, really?" I shoot her a daring look, take a couple of steps back, then run toward the pool and jump in, hugging my knees.

t first, I can't quite place the dark-haired girl sitting on the terrace of The Oyster Bar. There's a familiarity about her and she's sitting by herself, seemingly waiting for someone. I pick up Suki and quickly make my way to the door, juggling the bag of groceries and my keys in the process.

"Belle?"

I realize then that it's Reina's daughter. The girl who walked in on me and her mother in the kitchen. "Hi," I say hesitantly, putting Suki down again. "Nicole, right?" When she gets up and comes my way, my mind scrambles for something to say. "What brings you here?"

"I came to see you, actually. I rang your door, but you weren't home, so I figured I'd just try my luck and wait for a bit." She gives me an awkward smile. "Do you remember me?"

"Yes, of course." I suddenly feel worried because I can only think of two reasons why she's here. Either something happened to Reina, or she's going to tell me to back off and leave her alone. "Is your mother okay?"

Nicole smiles and nods. "Yes, she's fine. She doesn't know I'm here." She gets on her knees in front of Suki to greet her in a cute voice. "Hey there. You're Suki, right?"

Suki giggles when she gives her a high five. Nicole's smile is so much like her mother's and she's clearly just as good with kids.

"She doesn't know you're here, huh?" I repeat, pointing to my door. "Do you want to come up?"

Nicole shakes her head and points to her table. "I don't want to bug you for too long. But can I buy you a drink?" She turns her attention to Suki again. "And maybe a juice for this little princess?"

"Can I have ice cream?" Suki asks, putting on her cutest squeaky voice.

"I think they have ice cream, but you'll have to ask you mom."

Despite the uncertainty and discomfort I feel at Nicole's impromptu visit, I can't help but laugh when Suki jumps up and down in excitement and throws her little arms around me.

"Please, Mommy?"

"Sure. You can have an ice cream," I say, and give Nicole a smile. She seems like a nice girl and I can hardly believe she's only seventeen. Her manners are impeccable as she kindly asks the waiter for an extra chair and a dessert menu. I order a coffee, Nicole a ginger ale and Suki chooses an ice cream sundae. There's some small talk between us about the village and Suki and the weather, while Suki munches on a strawberry-vanilla dessert covered in an assortment of sprinkles and toppings, and I'm getting more nervous by the minute, wishing she would just get to the point.

"So, about my mom..." Nicole begins when Suki's distracted by a couple with a poodle arriving at the table next to us. "God, I don't know where to start." She pauses, searching for words. "My dad left my mom for our interior designer. You may or may not know that."

"I know. She told me." I brace myself for the moment she's going to tell me I've confused her mother to the point that she believes she's gay, then urges me to stay away from Reina in a civilized yet pressing manner.

"Okay. Good," Nicole continues. "Anyway, she's only ever been with my dad and naturally, she was very upset by the divorce. She moved here permanently after they sold their New York apartment and I think she underestimated how quiet this part of the Hamptons is off-season, so it's been hard for her."

"Yes, that's understandable. But she seemed to be doing well."

"Not really. You've only seen her that way because..." She takes a deep breath and pauses. "Because you're the reason she's smiling again."

"I don't think that's true," I say with a frown.

"It is true." Nicole takes a sip of her drink. "I drove all the way to the Hamptons every weekend because I knew that was the only thing that cheered her up, but then one Friday, I came home and there was a shift in her. She had this glow about her, and she just seemed so much better. It was the week you started working for her."

"But that's not just down to me," I say, relieved that at least so far the conversation is heading in a positive direction.

"No, seriously, Belle. It's like your presence has rejuvenated her. Anyway, I just wanted to thank you, for helping her find herself. I don't know what you did but she's a different person and you need to know that she's totally into you."

"Thank you. I appreciate you saying that, and if you hadn't already gathered, I'm totally into your mom too. I wouldn't be dating her if I wasn't serious." I sit back and study her. "I thought you came here to tell me to stay away from her. I imagine it must have been quite a shock when you walked in on us."

Nicole throws her head back and laughs. "I won't deny it was a shock but I'm long over that. I was just having a bad day to begin with and when I needed my mother and found her like that it... I don't know, it was just very, very unexpected and it seemed so out of character. But I've come to realize that she's her own person too, not just my mother and I'm super happy for her. Anyway, I came here to tell you how much I appreciate you being there for Mom. And because I'm throwing her a surprise birthday party and I want you to come. I don't have your number, hence the surprise visit."

"Oh... That's very sweet of you but I'm not sure she'd be comfortable with me being there."

Nicole shakes her head. "Nah-ah. If she knew I was organizing this, she'd insist that I invite you. Besides, it's not like you guys have to make an announcement or anything like that. You can just be there for her as a friend."

"That's true." I suddenly have an idea, so I open my website on my phone and hand it to her. "If you need anything for the party, feel free to pick whatever you like, and I'll bring it over and set it up for you."

Nicole gasps and eagerly scrolls through my site. "Belle, this is incredible. Are you sure?"

"Of course. Anything I can do to help."

"Thank you so much, I'll let you know." Nicole puts a twenty-dollar bill on the table and gets up. She takes a pen out of her purse and scribbles something on Suki's napkin. "Here's my number. Text me yours and I'll be in touch."

REINA - 4TH JULY

"*H*ey, girl!" Juliette greets me with a hug when Belle, Suki and I arrive at Belle's father's farm.

"Hi, it's so nice to see you again." I hug her back and turn to the boy at her side. "And you must be Cameron."

Cameron nods and stares up at me while he sucks on his Popsicle, then spots Suki going into the kitchen and follows her.

"Sorry, he's a bit shy sometimes. He'll be talking your head off in an hour, just warning you." Juliette looks me over and shakes her head with a smile, as if she can't quite believe I'm here. "I'm so glad you could come today. And so are Jackie and Frank."

"Did I hear my name?" An older woman comes out of the kitchen with a tray of marinated steaks that she places next to the grill. She's dressed casually in a T-shirt and shorts, and her gray hair is pulled into a messy topknot. When she spots me, her face breaks into a huge smile and she rushes toward me. "Here she is," she says, pulling me into a hug. "Reina. Finally, I get to meet you." She rubs my arm and looks me up and down. "I'm Jackie."

"It's so nice to meet you too, and thank you so much for having me over."

"The pleasure is all ours," she says, then yells over her shoulder: "Hey, Frank! Come on out here, Belle and Reina have arrived."

"I know, give me a moment I've got a little devil back here hampering my vision." Belle's father laughs as he comes out. He's got Suki on his shoulders and she's covering his eyes with her hands. "Reina?" He says, trying to see through the gaps. "Let me put this troublemaker down, so I can say hi properly." He lifts Suki off his shoulders and tickles her until she screeches and runs off. Still laughing, he shakes my hand. "Frank. Belle's father. Welcome to my humble abode."

"Thank you, I'm so glad to be here." We take each other in; Frank undoubtedly trying to work out what kind of person I am and whether he deems me good enough for his daughter, and me slightly nervous as he's one of the most important people in her life. I don't see a resemblance; he's much more rugged in his features and his eyes are gray. Then he smiles widely, and I know we're going to get along.

"You must be in need of a drink," he says, gesturing to the table. "Why don't you sit down and let Jackie pour you a glass of punch? I'm just finishing something in the kitchen."

"Are you seriously cooking, Dad?" Belle asks, hugging him.

"I'm trying. Under the strict tutelage of Jackie," he adds with a grin. "What?" Frank raises a brow when Belle shoots him a confused look. "It's not just a special occasion, it's a monumental one. Not only are we celebrating the Fourth of July but this is also the first time you've brought a girlfriend home."

"Okay…" Belle blushes, which makes him laugh out loud before he disappears back into the kitchen.

"Never mind your father. He's just a tease," Jackie says,

pouring us both a glass of rum punch. She tops up her own and Juliette's glass, then joins us at the table.

"Should I go help him?" I ask.

Jackie shakes her head. "No, honey. You just relax and enjoy yourself. He genuinely wanted to do everything himself and he wasn't joking when he said he was under strict orders. I wrote everything down for him word for word and helped him chop, but other than that, it's all him."

We sit and chat and enjoy the weather while we get to know each other, and after a while Frank joins us with a whiskey and a cigar. He's a lovely man; funny and warm for someone who has not had an easy life, but then so is Belle. His home is genuinely one of the sweetest farms I've seen in the Hamptons. Although the house is old and small and needs a lot of work, it's got a lot of charm and the yard is simply idyllic, with sheep and chickens roaming around freely, grazing from the field that is awash with wildflowers. The wooden barn in the back is painted yellow, the color matching the windowsills and the door of the white house that has ivy growing up the walls. Behind the stone wall that surrounds the land is another field and, in the distance, I can see the dunes. We're sitting at a long, wooden table that is laid out in the backyard, just in front of the kitchen door and the grill is lit, the fumes of grilled corn filling the air with the scent of the Fourth.

"Are you okay? Is everyone being nice to you?" Belle asks when we get a moment to ourselves. Jackie and Juliette have taken the kids to the barn while her father focuses on the steaks behind the grill further down the terrace. She's relaxed a little herself now and has draped an arm over the backrest of my chair.

"Yes, they're lovely. I feel really at ease with them."

"Good." She winks at me and I go all gooey inside. "They clearly like you too. I've rarely seen my father so excited."

I glance at her father who is whistling a tune while he throws more charcoal onto the grill. "And your father and Jackie are not together, you said? They seem like a couple to me."

"No, they're just best friends, but having them both in my life meant that we were almost like a normal family when I grew up and that was nice."

"I can see how that must have made all the difference after your mom passed away. My parents weren't around very much when I was younger. My father desperately wanted a son as an heir but after complications during my birth, my mother couldn't have any more kids and he was simply never that interested in me." I let out a sarcastic chuckle. "My mother was sweet and even a little maternal, but I was raised by nannies and even now, she's more invested in her cats than in me."

"Ouch. Was it hard, growing up like that?"

"Not really," I say after a moment's hesitation. "I didn't have a bad childhood; I was just very independent and when I had a family of my own, I poured all my energy into my children and husband because I wanted my children to have what I never had. A loving, wholesome home, you know? But in the process, I failed to acknowledge what it was that *I* needed."

"There's plenty of time to make up for that now." Belle strokes my shoulder and plays with a lock of my hair. "Do you miss your father?"

"Sometimes. But as I said, he was never a big part of my life. I was actually surprised he left me so much money in his will. It was split fifty-fifty with my mother." I smile and steal a quick kiss, then move my chair closer and lean into her. "If you'd asked me a year ago, this is far from what I thought my Fourth of July would look like." The sun is lowering behind the barn and the fields look so peaceful, the golden light giving our surroundings a vintage sepia glow. "Thank you. This is really nice."

"I agree. Best Fourth of July ever, and all because you're here." Belle locks her eyes with mine. "Suki just asked me if she could stay with Jackie tonight. Do you want to come home with me?"

BELLE - 4TH JULY

"We're heading back, guys," Jackie says when most of the fireworks are over. We've had a lovely, fun night, with great food, sing-along music and lots of laughter. The fireworks were beautiful and the beach that was busy an hour ago, is quiet again, with only a few people staying behind to finish the drinks they brought.

"We'll be right behind you," I say, still enjoying the sea breeze.

"I'm going with Grandpa." Suki wriggles herself out of my grip and runs after Jackie, Juliette, Cameron and my father.

"Okay, honey, we won't be long." When they're out of sight, Reina and I sit in the sand and I put an arm around her. She's beaming when she looks at me.

"I had such a great time. They're all really lovely."

"I'm glad you think so." I smile back at her. "And you're welcome to join us for anything, anytime. In fact, my father and Jackie insisted I bring you over again soon."

"That's sweet." Reina turns back to the ocean and inhales deeply, then rests her head on my shoulder. "I think it's time that I introduce you to my kids." She chuckles. "Well, I suppose you've already met Nicole, but maybe we should try it again, fully dressed this time. And Eddie... I'm not sure when he'll be back from his travels but I want to call him and tell him about you."

"Are you sure?" I ask, pulling her closer. Her body feels amazing against mine and I realize that tonight, I feel perfectly and entirely content and happy, as if everything is exactly the way it's supposed to be. Just like Reina, I never imagined my Fourth of July to be like this either. The best things happen when you least expect it.

"Yeah. Nicole is taking me to a spa hotel for my birthday, it's in Montauk, I think. Maybe we could have lunch together the next day?"

"Sure. If Nicole can look me in the eyes after she saw me—"

"Please, don't remind me." Reina laughs. "She'll be fine, I promise."

"Okay, in that case, I'd love to." It amuses me that she has absolutely no idea Nicole is planning a party for her, and that I'm having fun helping her, but it's also a little worrying. Not everyone likes surprises and Reina's made it clear that she didn't want a big celebration. That was weeks ago, though, and things have changed. She's started going out more, meeting up with friends she hasn't seen in a while, and she's busy with her volunteer work.

"Great, I'll book a table." Reina's phone pings, and she smiles when she opens a message from her son with the caption 'Happy 4th, love you', and a picture attached.

"Here, this is Eddie," she says, handing me the phone.

"I see Eddie's enjoying himself." I zoom in on him, then back out, studying the selfie of him and a girl lying in a hammock with a tropical beach in the background. "He looks like you too."

"Yeah, he does. And that's his girlfriend, Maddie. She's

lovely." Reina sighs. "God, I miss him, and I worry all the time. I know I shouldn't—he's a grown man now—but still, he's so far away and they both tend to think they're invincible."

"I'm sure you'll see him soon." What Reina also doesn't know, is that Nicole's arranged for him to fly back to surprise her for her birthday. I can only imagine how happy she'll be when she sees him again. "Does he work?"

"Yes, he runs an online business, together with Maddie. They buy beautiful, handcrafted items from all over the world and sell them on their website. Their clients are mainly interior designers, and they sell anything from antique tapestries, paintings and sculptures down to Venetian glass and big vases. He dropped out of college last year, said he didn't need a degree to do what he wanted to do, and I could hardly argue with him, not having been to college myself. Sandeep wasn't happy about it, but he came around when it became apparent that Eddie knew what he was doing. They bought through online channels at first, but then they decided to travel so they could source more unique items."

"That must be a nice way to live and work."

"Yeah, that's Gen Z for you. They're just so free and inventive in their thinking and refuse to conform."

"Suki wants to be a princess when she grows up," I say in a humorous tone. "A pool cleaning princess who swims with sharks."

Reina laughs. "That's cute. Basically like you, minus the sharks and the princess part. I had fun when you brought her over."

"Suki had fun too, she won't stop talking about it."

"Then we should do it more often, and you can always leave her with me while you're working, if Jackie wants some time off. I'm happy to look after her if she's comfortable around me," Reina says.

"Thank you, that's very sweet of you." Her eyes hold so much sincerity that it chokes me up. This woman who I am smitten with is great with my daughter and best of all, Suki loves spending time with her too. Just as I'm about to kiss her, a trail of golden sparkles fan out above us, an elaborate display of last-minute fireworks filling the midnight sky with white and red bundles of light that cascade down into beautiful streaks above the ocean. The few people around us start clapping and cheering, and we lie down to look up at the show, our hands clasped together on my belly while she rests her head on my shoulder. It feels like a significant moment in time, and I kiss the top of her head, inhaling her scent before turning back to the display. Cherishing her closeness and the spectacular fireworks that just go on and on, I realize how special this day has been for me.

"This feels like a new start," Reina whispers as if reading my mind. "The start of my next life."

"Our next life," I say, and when she looks up at me and smiles, tears of joy are clouding her eyes.

*F*orty isn't so bad, I think to myself as I'm lying in a warm mud bath with an algae mask covering my face. Nicole is in the tub next to me; she's booked a mother-and-daughter pampering day at the spa and we're on our last treatment before we'll have our hair done. My feet and hands feel amazing from the mani-pedi and my muscles are entirely relaxed after a long, Swedish massage. The small room with exposed brick walls in the hotel's basement is dimly lit and scented candles are burning to either side of us. Meditation music is playing softly through the speakers, sending me into a tranquil state.

"You couldn't have given me a better present," I mumble, careful not to crack the mask. "Thank you so much."

"It's not over yet." Nicole reaches for the glass of champagne on the side table next to her and takes a small sip. "We're going out tonight."

"I know, I'm excited." I sigh in delight as I shift down and immerse myself farther in the thick, warm goo. "But I don't want you to spend so much on me, so please let me pick up the check." Nicole has never been spoiled with money or extravagant gifts like so many of my friends' kids, and with the little I give her for food and gas a week, I don't understand how she can afford this.

"Don't worry; I asked grandma for money," Nicole confesses. She laughs, touches her face when her mask cracks, then laughs even harder. "If I knew it would be so easy, I'd have tried it a long time ago."

This makes me laugh too, and a green fleck falls off my cheek. "Smart girl, I hope you got a little extra for yourself," I joke.

"Nah. I thought about it but she told me to send her the receipts," she continues with a giggle. "Anyway, she was very generous with your birthday budget, and I hope you brought that red cocktail dress I told you to wear tonight."

"I did. Along with my red heels." I smile at her. "You two kept this very quiet. Mom didn't mention anything when she called me earlier."

"Of course not. That would have ruined the surprise now, wouldn't it? It's—" Nicole stops herself when our beautician lets herself in and walks over to her tub.

"Sorry," I say to her. "I think we might have ruined the facial. My daughter made me laugh."

"Not at all. I'm happy to hear you've been laughing." The friendly lady sets a tray with steaming wet towels next to Nicole and layers them over her face.

"Oh God. That feels so good." Nicole sighs deeply as the beautician slowly starts cleaning the mask off her face, then brings out more warm towels. "Mom, this is incredible."

"You can go and have your shower now," the beautician says after cleaning her face, and Nicole steps out of the tub and heads over to the rain shower at the opposite end of the room to wash off the mud. "Use anything you like from the pumps, but I recommend the macadamia shower oil." Then she turns her attention to me and starts cleaning my face.

"She's right, this is incredible," I say, enjoying the warm sensation against my skin and the liberating feeling of being able to move my facial muscles again.

"Just wait; you'll feel ten years younger once you've washed that mud off too." She steps aside so I can get out of the tub and join Nicole under the huge showerhead. My phone on the side table flashes an incoming message and I smile when I see it's from Belle.

'Happy birthday, baby. Can't wait to see you tomorrow.'

"What are you grinning about?" Nicole asks, running her hands through her hair.

"Just a sweet message from Belle." I try to wipe the smirk off my face as I pump some of the macadamia oil into the palm of my hand. "You're still up for lunch with her, right?"

"Of course. I want to get to know her. She clearly makes you happy and that's all I want for you." Grabbing a towel, Nicole continues: "Is she bringing that cute girl of hers?"

"Suki? Yes, she's coming too."

"So, are you a stepmom now?" she asks, drying herself off. Our bodies are identical, I realize as I look at her. Nicole's a bit fuller than me due to her student diet of pizza and Coke but other than that, her breasts and build are the same as mine.

"No..." I'm just Belle's special friend with a pool; she loves the pool." In the past weeks, I've had them over regularly, and Belle even stayed over last weekend. Suki was delighted to sleep in Nicole's spacious room that has a free-standing tub, a huge TV and a star projector facing the ceiling. A 'big-girl's room', she called it. Although Nicole has grown out of her teenage gadgets, she still uses the projector when she stays over; she told me it's the perfect scene to fall asleep to.

"So it's the pool that did it..." Nicole says with a wink. "Just kidding, Mom. You're the best, so there's no reason why she wouldn't take an instant liking to you. And I'm kind of looking forward to having a little stepsister." She chuckles. "I bet you bribe her with ice cream too."

"Yes, she loves ice cream," I admit, rinsing the last bit of mud from under my breasts. "Just like you when you were younger."

"Hey, I still love ice cream," Nicole retorts playfully. "In fact, I'm getting a craving for chocolate-macadamia just thinking about it." She puts on a robe and hands me a towel. "But first we've got lunch. It's casual, so you don't need to dress up. In fact, we can wear our robes if you want."

"Here we are, sweating away while Little Miss Party Organizer is getting pampered in the Montauk Spa Hotel," Sasha jokes when we sit down for a break. Randy, who had a break earlier, is helping too, and we've done a lot in the past two hours. I'm impressed with Sasha, who is a lot stronger than her skinny frame led me to believe. It must be all the yoga as she hasn't sat down once, carrying tables and seating units, then rearranging them until she was happy with the result.

"She's definitely got the better end of the deal," I agree, downing a bottle of water.

"Yeah. But this is very satisfying. It's looking great already, and we haven't even started on the finishing touches." Sasha looks pleased with herself as she checks her watch. "We have another two hours left before the caterers and bartenders arrive. After that, we can go home and get changed. Nola will be here to oversee them until the party starts."

"Seventy people," I mumble, more to myself as I glance over the seating areas arranged around three firepits on the lawn behind the pool. Along with the standing tables, there will be more than enough space for Reina's guests to be comfortable. "Are you sure Reina will be okay with this? She said she didn't want a party..." I'm especially worried about the enormous white '40' inflatable I ordered at Nicole's request. It's floating in the pool, adorned with a string of solar lights. Perhaps that was just a little step too far, but even I got carried away, wanting Reina to have a spectacular night. Now I'm not so sure anymore.

"Oh, Reina's just very modest. She doesn't want people to go to any trouble for her but trust me, once she arrives, she'll be delighted," Sasha assures me. "Nicole and I put together the guest list and we didn't want to miss anyone because she'd feel bad about that. So, we've got everyone from our yoga class, myself and Igor, of course, ten of our mutual friends and their spouses, Sandeep and his new girlfriend—Nicole insisted that it would be fine so let's see—Nola and her husband, the Johnsons, the Metcalfes, the Harper-Collins family, the neighbors on both sides, a couple of Nicole's friends and their parents, and five of Reina's friends from New York who have rented a house nearby so they can stay the night. Oh, and the Phifers, the Wetherbys, the Rubins and her fellow volunteers from Camp Rubin. Some of them are on duty tonight but the ones that can make it will come. I think that about covers it."

"Nice that you invited the volunteers. She'll love that."

"Yes, they've been a great influence on her. The volunteering makes her happy." Sasha turns to me and smiles. "And so do you."

"I'm not sure how happy she'll be when I turn up tonight, with everyone she knows present." I shrug. "I'm not going to walk up to her and kiss her of course, but even if I'm just here as a friend..."

"Stop worrying." Sasha puts a hand on my shoulder. "Let's

just get this set up beautifully first. How about we clear a space for the musicians next to the sliding doors? That way, we won't have extension cables lying around that people can trip over." She gets up and walks into the kitchen to inspect the sockets. "So many things to think of. I don't understand how people do this by themselves."

"You've never organized a party?"

Sasha looks embarrassed as she shakes her head. "I married Igor when I was young. He was already fairly wealthy, so I've always had others do everything for me. Apart from raising the kids," she says. "My mother was never around when I grew up, she was always working because she had to. I wanted them to be raised by me, not by a nanny, but my mother looks after them when we're away and she's a great help."

"Is your mother retired now? What did she do?"

Sasha laughs. "Nothing fancy, I come from nothing. My mother was a housekeeper and we lived in an annex on the land of the family she worked for full-time. And now, she still lives in an annex, only this one is very, very nice and it's on our land. We had it built for her after we got married. She's quite happily retired now and spends most of her time baking cakes or fussing over her grandkids who are adolescents now and don't really need fussing over."

I'm surprised to hear this as I imagined Sasha growing up rich, and as if she can read the next question on my mind, she says: "I didn't marry Igor for his money."

"I didn't think—"

"Of course you did, and I don't blame you. I was eighteen and he was thirty when we met. Igor was working his way up the property ladder and I was working as a waitress in a restaurant in East Hampton where he came for lunch on a regular basis. There weren't many Russians here back then, and I liked that I could speak my mother tongue with him.

He was handsome and chivalrous and although he grew up wealthy and I didn't, we shared the same values because of our cultural background." Sasha chuckles. "Imagine my mother's delight when I told her he'd proposed."

"And you're still happy?"

Sasha takes a moment to think about that, then nods. "Yes," she says. "We're still happy together. We've had our problems of course. Every marriage has its problems. A while back, I really wanted a change. The kids were becoming independent, and I didn't really know what to do with myself, so I signed up for a reality TV show when the producers asked me. I only did one season as the constant cameras were driving me crazy and I had to watch everything I said at all times." She takes a long drink of her water and wipes the sweat off her brow. "Anyway, that was my moment of fame and it didn't make me happier. Neither did the one-off fling I had with another man, so I've come to realize that what I have is pretty damn good and I'm going to work hard on our relationship. I'm content, you know?"

"That's nice and thank you for being so candid." I smile at her and hold up my bottle. "Cheers to contentment."

"Nah-ah!" She waves a finger in front of me and shakes her head. "You can't cheer with water, it's bad luck. Come to our house and we'll do it properly with vodka. I'd love to have you over."

"Thank you, that's a deal," I say, deciding I really like Reina's best friend.

"*N*o, not that one. Put on the red dress." Nicole shakes her head while I'm standing in front of the mirror, inspecting my navy pantsuit.

"But it's a bit much, don't you think?"

"No." She grabs it from the pile of dresses I've laid out on the bed and holds it up in front of me. "I love this dress. The satin fabric, the thigh high slit... It's your birthday, you're supposed to shine."

"I'm forty now. I'm wilting, not shining," I joke.

"That's total bull. You're a kick-ass yummy mummy and you should show off that amazing body of yours," Nicole insists. "I'll be wearing red too, so we can match."

I laugh at that because Nicole has never been one for matching outfits. In fact, I haven't seen her in much other than her trademark jeans, hoodies and T-shirts lately. "You want to match?"

"Yeah, it will be fun."

"Okay, then." I take the dress from her that is still in the dry-cleaner's bag and rip off the plastic cover. I haven't worn it since the charity ball I bought it for two years ago.

"And don't forget the red lipstick. You always look amazing with red lipstick," Nicole adds.

"You still haven't told me where we're going," I say. "How will I know if it's even appropriate?"

"You're just going to have to trust me on that. Don't you want to show the world how awesome you're doing and how amazing you look?" Nicole winks. "What if we bump into Dad and Bree?"

"We won't, will we?" I frown. "Seriously, Nicole, just tell me where we're going."

"Honestly, we might see them there. But you told me you'd talked to him and that you both hoped you could be friends again someday." She looks a little nervous now, and I regret my sharp tone.

"You're right. I did say that." I smile and playfully mess up her freshly styled hair, just to get back at her for whatever is coming. I have no idea what she's up to but I'm not entirely at ease and can only hope that she hasn't organized an intimate dinner with her father and his new girlfriend in the spirit of family harmony. "But there's no competition between myself and Bree and as you very well know, I have no interest in your father anymore, so I don't need to impress either of them," I say. "I'm happy and I finally feel like I'm growing into myself."

"I know." Nicole helps me strip off the navy suit and helps me into the red dress. "You're growing into the very best lesbian you can be but there's no need for suits just yet," she teases, then zips the dress up. She looks in the mirror over my shoulder and smiles. "Perfect."

The red dress fits me very well and I actually feel good and confident wearing it. Suddenly a thought hits me, and I turn around to stare at her. "You didn't invite my mother over, did you? Since you so desperately want to dress me up?"

Nicole laughs. "No, I didn't. I thought about inviting Grandma, but I figured if I did, she would stay for at least a week and I know how stressful it is to have her over. Anyway, even if I had invited her, I'm not sure if she'd have come since she'd have had to be parted from the cats..."

"Thank goodness, good call." I put an arm around Nicole and place a kiss on her cheek. "How about we visit her instead? I'll look at flights to Lebanon next week. Want to come along in your summer break?"

"Sure. Why not? As long as you make her promise not to play matchmaker for me. I hate it when she does that."

"She won't; your grandmother promised never to invite eligible men ever again while you're there."

"Good. Then I'll come." Nicole fusses with my hair, re-arranging some of the long locks to fall over my bare shoulders. There's a knock on the door, and she jumps to attention. "That will be your birthday present. Wait here, I'll be right back."

"Another birthday present?" I frown as I follow her to the door. "But you've already spoilt me so—" I fall silent when I see Eddie and his girlfriend, Maddie, in the doorway.

"Surprise!" they yell in unison.

"No!" I say, my eyes widening before they fill with tears. I fall around Eddie's neck and hug him so tight that he grunts in discomfort. "You're here! I can't believe you're here!" Then I turn to Maddie. "And you too. Come here, sweetheart."

"Of course we came." Eddie pulls his girlfriend into a three-way hug. "It's your fortieth and I've missed you, Mom." The emotional tremble in his voice is real and it makes me break out in floods of tears. "Don't cry," he says, wiping my tears. "You'll smudge your makeup and you look fantastic."

"I don't care about my makeup." I sniff. "I'm just so happy you're here."

"We're staying for a week, if that's okay," Maddie says.

"Then we'll go visit my parents before finding a place to settle down in New York. We both desperately need to start selling; we've worked our way through our travel savings, but we've shipped three containers of goods over so at least we're good to go."

"I was wondering when you'd run out of money with all the fun stuff you've been doing." I smile at Eddie. "So you've had a good time?" I ask, ushering them into our hotel room.

"We had an amazing time," he says. "And fifteen dollars a day goes a long way in India. We've slept in huts and hammocks and spent all our time outdoors."

"I can tell. You both look so radiant and healthy. And what a nice shirt." Eddie is wearing a white and light blue checked shirt and white chinos that match Maddie's light-blue peplum dress. It's hard to stop touching Eddie as I still can't believe he's here, and Nicole laughs when I hug him once more.

"I'm glad you're happy with your present," she says, kissing me on the cheek. "Help yourselves to a drink from the minibar, guys. I'll get changed and then we can have an early dinner together before we go out."

THE MONTAUK SPA Hotel is situated at the very tip of the peninsula, and we're dining on the beautiful terrace that is built into the cliffs. Looking out over the ocean, our table is shaded by a white lace canopy that lets a sliver of light through, creating sweet floral shapes on the wooden table and the concrete floor. It seems that we're on a schedule today, but Nicole has worked in plenty of time for our early dinner so that we can catch up and hear all about Eddie and Maddie's adventures.

"It's a good thing you didn't fill me in on everything

you've been getting up to while you were away," I say after he's finished telling the story of them being attacked and mugged by monkeys when they decided to sleep on the beach. "I'd have been worried sick."

"We got back just fine," Eddie says cheerfully. "Just a couple of small scratches to remember our time in India by." He attacks his seafood pasta like he hasn't eaten in weeks. "Mmm... I've missed pasta so much. I'm going to eat it all day, every day this week."

"Me too." Maddie is equally delighted with the food, sharing a big plate of lobster ravioli with Nicole. "I had a slice of pizza as soon as we landed. Carbs was all I could think of."

"I'll make sure I'll have plenty of everything in the house then." Topping up the wine, I feel a surge of happiness at sitting here in this beautiful spot with both my children, and my birthday could not get any better. Well, apart from maybe having Belle here, but Eddie still has no idea. "So, what else?" I ask, taking a bite from my pan-fried seabass with asparagus that pairs perfectly with the oaked chardonnay we ordered. "Did you make any friends on the way?"

"Friends for life," he says. "We met so many nice people but enough about us now. I want to know how you've been. You look great, Mom. Happy even, dare I say it."

"Thank you. I'm doing great, actually."

"She is doing great." Nicole looks up from her food and shoots me a wink. "Is there anything you'd like to share, Mom?"

I stare at Nicole and swallow hard, knowing exactly what she's hinting at. "I'm not sure if now is a good time, honey." This seemed easy when I planned it. In my mind, I've told Eddie I'm gay a thousand times but now that Nicole's put me on the spot, I'm nervous.

Eddie and Maddie stare at me too, and Eddie arches a

brow. "What? Does Nicole know something we don't?" He grins when color suffuses my cheeks. "Why are you blushing? Did you meet a man?"

"Not exactly," I say, taking a long drink of my wine for courage.

"Then what?"

"I ehm…" I focus on my food, buying time, but Eddie taps his fingers impatiently on the table, staring at me and I have no choice. "I met a woman." My heart is racing while I await his reaction. In the silence that follows, I expect him to either burst out laughing or storm up and leave, but instead he drops his cutlery and leans in on his elbows, his expression turning serious.

"You're not joking, are you?"

"No, I'm not. Her name is Belle and I'm in love with her. We're dating."

"Wow, Reina. That's so cool," Maddie finally says, regarding me with a weird kind of interest. I'm relieved to see that she's not faking it; she looks genuinely happy for me. Surprised perhaps, but happy nevertheless. "Good for you." She nudges Eddie. "Well, aren't you going to say something?"

Eddie chuckles. "Sorry, but you're my mom and I didn't expect this, so please give me at least a minute to process."

"Of course. Are you upset?" I ask in a trembling voice.

"No, not at all." Eddie shakes his head. "So, you're with a woman?"

"Yes."

He sits back and regards me. "Well, I'm so happy that you've moved on and met someone. I've been hoping you would, I just didn't ever think it would be with a woman."

"Yeah, that was me two months ago," Nicole says to him. "I was shocked, probably way more than you are right now because I walked in on Mom and—"

"Hey, enough," I say, shooting her a warning look.

"Sorry." She laughs it off and I know I'll never hear the end of this. "Anyway, Belle's really nice and she's got a super cute four-year-old daughter."

"You've met her?" Eddie asks.

"Yeah, we—" Nicole stops herself and shakes her head as if she was about to say something she shouldn't. "Mom and I ran into her in Sag Harbor."

"Okay." Eddie still looks puzzled, but he reaches for my hand over the table and squeezes it. "Does anyone else know?"

"Just Nicole, your father and Sasha. I wanted you to know before I told anyone else."

"Dad knows? Jesus, I can only imagine his reaction."

"Yes, I won't deny that he was surprised."

Eddie regards me again for long moments. "Can I meet her?"

"I want to meet her too. I'm beyond curious about this mysterious woman who stole my mother-in-law's heart," Maddie says in a teasing tone.

"You want to meet her?" I exhale deeply, relieved that Eddie hasn't ran off like Nicole did. Although the circumstances are entirely different, it still must be highly confusing for him. "Nicole and I were actually going to have lunch with her tomorrow. Would you like to join us?" I pause. "Or is that too soon?"

"I don't see why we should wait," Eddie says. "In fact, I'm dying with curiosity too."

"Okay. I'll let the restaurant know we're five instead of three." I smile and find myself more at ease now. "I'm sure you'll have lots of questions, so just ask me anything. I want to be honest with you."

"Sure." He lets out a long sigh and shakes his head again. "I still need to let this sink in but I'm happy for you, Mom. I really am."

Maddie, who doesn't seem daunted at all, raises her glass. "I think it's time for a toast," she says cheerfully through a mouthful of pasta. "Here's to Reina and a fabulous year ahead. Happy birthday, dearest mother-in-law!"

"*I* don't know what to wear."

My complaint is met with a giggle from Jackie as I take off the blue shirt I tried on. "I've never heard you utter those words. Just wear what you normally would when you go out."

"But this is a big deal." I sigh and root through my closet, regretting not organizing it properly as I can't seem to find anything.

"Reina won't expect you to rock up in a dress, or even a tux. Not that you have one," she adds, only adding to my nerves.

"She won't expect me to rock up at all," I retort. "*Should* I have a tux?"

"No. Chill out, sweetheart. She knows you well enough by now and she likes you just the way you are." Jackie takes out one of my white shirts and a pair of black slacks. "Here, wear this. It looks great on you."

"I always wear that." I'm aware that I sound sulky and would have laughed at myself if I wasn't so terrified of meeting Reina's friends and family.

"Exactly. You'll feel more comfortable in it." Jackie heads to the kitchen and comes back with a cold beer. "And you'll need this. Just one, though."

"Thank you. I do need a drink." I take a sip, then put on the white shirt and swap my jeans for the black slacks. Wearing this does make me feel better, I have to admit. "I'm not sure if I should go."

Jackie rolls her eyes and chuckles. "No one will know you're together apart from a couple of people. Just go, have a good time and give her a big birthday hug from me. I saw the way she was with you. She's crazy about you and trust me; she'll want you there."

Looking myself over in the mirror once again, I nod, mentally repeating Jackie's words. So far, it's been easy and incredibly good with Reina. Once I let go of my fears it made sense and I was able to open myself up. But things will undoubtedly get more complicated after tonight. Although I doubt Reina will come out, people will see the chemistry between us, and they'll start asking questions. Will she panic? Will she start having doubts?

I've seen it before with friends. They were ready to come out and accept their sexuality, then backed out at the last minute. A woman I used to meet for casual sex is now engaged to a man as her family's approval was more important to her than her own happiness. This party could be a curse or a blessing, I'm yet to find out.

"Want some good news to distract you?" Jackie asks. "You look like you're about to pass out."

"Please." I laugh and roll my eyes. "Anything."

Jackie beckons me to follow her out to the balcony where we sit down in the evening sun. "Your father just called while you were on your way home. He's finally got a date for his hip replacement."

This indeed is good news, and it perks me up a little. "Fantastic. When?"

"A few weeks from now," she says with a smile. "Apparently the recovery isn't that intense, but I've suggested he stay with me in the weeks following. Better to be in a ground floor apartment than in that farmhouse. He'll never take it easy if he stays there."

"That's very kind of you. It wouldn't work here either, with the stairs." I pause. "What are we going to do with the animals?"

Jackie shrugs. "We'll make it work between us." She's never been one to worry and clearly, she's not going to start now. "It's only chickens and sheep. How hard can it be?"

"You're right, we'll make it work." I finish my beer and look out over the street where people are heading for the restaurants and bars. Since moving here, I've been able to categorize them. The locals, the seasonals, the tourists and the ones with the flashy yachts. They're all dressed smart casual, yet the slight nuances in footwear and the way they move around sets them apart. "He really needs to sell that farm," I say absentmindedly, my thoughts still half-lingering on Reina.

"Yes, but I've given up on trying to talk to him about that, he's having none of it."

"I know. And I can't move there either. With all the land it's too much work for me alone and it's in need of some serious renovation which I can't afford."

"It's a unique property, though," Jackie says. "One of the last farms on the peninsula. Give it ten more years and the land value will have doubled. Your mother loved it so, so much, and so did her parents who owned it before her," she adds with a faraway look in her eyes.

"Are you trying to emotionally blackmail me?" I joke. I know exactly why she's so reluctant for the farm to be sold;

just like my father, she has memories there. Now that I know she loved my mother, everything she says and does makes so much more sense. "Because that's not going to work. Even if Dad gives it to me for free—which he's offered a handful of times—I can't afford it. It's not just a fixer upper, it's an out and out money pit. The farmhouse needs gutting and then there's the outbuildings, not to mention the fencing. If he sells it now, he'll be able to buy a nice seniors apartment and then I won't have to worry about him as much."

"But then it will be bought up by developers and raised to the ground. Your heritage will be gone."

"Then so be it. I don't see any other way."

Jackie nods, but although she's putting it to rest for now, she has no intention of giving up the fight for Dad's farm. I've thought long and hard about whether I should tell her that I know what she's been hiding from me all these years, and this seems to be the perfect time to bring it up. "You and my mother…" I start carefully.

A subtle expression of sorrow passes over Jackie's face, but she looks away, pretending to be interested in something going on down the street. "What about your mother?" she asks casually. She's had so many years of practice deflecting her past that I'd have fallen for it again if not for the recent conversation with my father.

"You were in love." I smile at her, letting her know there are no hard feelings, but Jackie's reaction is still one of utter shock. She goes pale and shifts uncomfortably in her chair, her hands trembling in her lap.

"How do you…"

"It doesn't matter how I found out," I say, hoping this won't get back to my father. "But I know."

"Oh…" Jackie swallows hard, fighting her emotions. "You weren't supposed to find out. Ever. Your parents, they were happy together. They really were, but it just happened and neither of us could fight it."

I place a hand on her arm and feel her pulse race. "Jackie, it's fine. And we don't need to talk about this now, but maybe one day, when you're up for it, I'd love to know your story." I hesitate. "I'd love to get to know my mother through your eyes." Sensing it's time to leave her to it, I get up. "I have to go. If you don't want to talk, we don't have to. Maybe another day."

Jackie doesn't answer as I head for the door. She'll need time, but I hope that eventually she'll come around and open up to me.

"*W*here are we going that's so close to home?" I ask when we're all in a cab together. My first thought is that Sasha may have organized something at her place, but then we turn into my street and stop in front of the big gates while we wait for them to open, and I'm starting to get worried. "Oh God, you didn't organize a party for me, did you?" I already know the answer to that question when I hear music and lots of people talking and laughing. "Nicole, this is way too much, it's only a birthday." Deep down, I'm flooded by love and it's so sweet of her that I can't be mad.

"It's not just a birthday." Nicole squeezes my thigh, then gets out and holds the door open for me. "Don't they say 'life begins at 40'. Come on, let's celebrate the start of your forties with a bang." She leads me around the house into the backyard, where a large group of guests greet me and spontaneously break into song as they start singing *Happy Birthday* to me.

Slamming my hands in front of my mouth, I gasp at the amazing setup and decorations. My backyard has been transformed into what looks like a beach club; low, white furniture is placed around roaring firepits, a long bar is set up in the open pool house, standing tables with fresh flowers are dotted around the terrace and a musician is playing acoustic guitar and singing behind a microphone. A team of impeccably dressed caterers is pouring drinks, mixing cocktails and serving finger food on big platters. Cozy spotlights are dotted in and around the pool, an abundance of chunky candles wafts a heady scent through the air and a huge '40' inflatable covered in string lights dominates the premises, making for a spectacular sight and I couldn't have done it better if I'd organized it myself. The sound of voices singing and Nicole and Eddie's hands in mine make my eyes well up for the second time today, and I swallow down the lump in my throat as I greet everyone. I recognize all faces; some I haven't seen in a long time and there are some new friends too.

"Thank you, honey, this is incredible," I say, kissing Nicole on her cheek. There's only one person missing tonight, and I wish she was here. "Did you invite Belle?" I ask.

"Of course I invited Belle. She provided the whole set up and helped put it all together with Sasha and Nola." Nicole winces. "Is that okay with you? Maybe I should have asked but it was a surprise so I couldn't really. She just texted me to say she's going to arrive a little later, in case you weren't comfortable with her coming."

"No, I'm glad she's coming." I smile at her. "So this is all her stuff?" I'm amazed they've managed to keep this from me as I didn't have the faintest idea. Belle even went along with the whole 'meet my daughter over lunch' proposal while all along they've been colluding with each other.

"Yeah, she offered, so I could hardly say no." Nicole smirks. "We've been meeting up in secret. I really like her, Mom, and I'm sure Eddie will like her too."

"This is so sweet. So, you, Belle, Sasha and Nola…" My bottom lip starts trembling and I fight back my tears once more. The four favorite women in my life have gone through great lengths to surprise me. "I don't know what to say."

"You don't have to say anything. Just have a good time." Nicole pushes a margarita into my hand. "Dad and Bree are also coming later. I thought it would be nice since Eddie just came home. Is that okay?"

"Yes, of course. He'll be so happy to see Eddie." I smile and hug Nola and her husband and make a mental note to organize a surprise party for *her* next year, when she's turning fifty. Making my way through the crowd of guests, I throw myself into a frenzy of hugging and kissing, delighted to have everyone I love right here in my backyard. The party must have been going on for a while already because the drinks are flowing and everyone's in good spirits, mingling and laughing, some even dancing to the flamenco rhythm.

"Happy birthday, babe," Sasha yells, grabbing me around my waist from behind a little later. The silver sequins of her dress poke into my skin as she squeezes me.

"There you are. Were you hiding from me?"

"I was afraid you might want to kill us after taking over your home while you were away."

"I'd never." I turn around and hug her tightly. "Thank you. I'm completely overwhelmed but this is incredible."

"Thank God," she exclaims, letting out a dramatic sigh. "It was a hit and miss decision; we weren't sure if you'd be furious or not." She notes my glass is half-empty and replaces it with a fresh cocktail. "I've been hanging out with your girl-friend today," she whispers, leading me to the poolside where Igor is waiting. "She's so cool. I feel like we bonded, you know? And I invited her over to our house for vodka shots, so we'd better set a date."

"Yes, I would love that. So you didn't scare her?"

"You know me; I'm a pussycat." Sasha blinks innocently. "Oh, and you look stunning by the way. That dress is seriously smoking on you."

"Thank you. You look great too." I hook my arm through Sasha's and laugh at her enthusiasm. "I can't believe you managed to get all these people here at such short notice, I don't think you've missed anyone. And having Eddie here…"

"Now that's a big, fat cherry on top of the cake, isn't it? He told me they're staying with you for a week, how wonderful."

"Yes, I'm so, so happy." Narrowing my eyes, I glance at a woman talking to Igor. "Oh look, it's Cindy Ashworth; I haven't seen her in ages. Don't you think she looks good?"

"Cindy Ashworth…" Sasha digs through her memory. "I don't think I know her."

"It's Danielle's mom. Nicole's friend, Danielle," I clarify. "She's a little strange but very nice. Nicole used to tag along when they went out on their yacht. Let's go and say hi."

BELLE - 30TH JULY

I'm starting to feel nauseous as I turn the corner and take in the birthday vibe. The poolside looks stunning, just as I imagined it would in the dark, and a guitarist is playing sweet background music. The guests are dressed beautifully, the women in cocktail dresses and swanky pantsuits and the men in smart casual attire. They have no idea I'm here, watching them in the dark, working up the courage to join them. Clutching the bottle of champagne, I hope Nicole was right. I hope Reina won't mind me being here.

My stomach drops when I spot a woman in a gaudy purple dress. *Fuck... it's Mrs. Ashworth.* Out of all the ex-clients who could possibly be here, it could literally not get any worse. She's standing very close to what I assume is her husband, as her hand is covering his while they're talking at one of the standing tables. I don't think her husband knows I've been visiting his wife once a month over the course of a year but I'm glad to see they're still together. *So, they're friends of Reina's...* I should have anticipated that I might know someone here. It's a small world after all but I can't possibly join the party now. Just as I'm about to turn to go, Nicole spots me and rushes toward me. I've only seen her in hoodies, T-shirts and jeans, and it's remarkable how much she looks like her mother in a dress, with her hair down and a little makeup on.

"There you are!" She takes my hand and pulls me along. "I was worried you wouldn't show up. Let me get you a drink."

"Actually, I'm not sure if I can—"

"Nonsense, it will be fine," Nicole says, shooting me a huge smile, then continues animatedly, waving her hands as she speaks. "Oh my God, it looks so amazing here, it literally exceeded all my expectations. Mom nearly fainted when she walked into the backyard. I'm pretty sure it's the best day of her life. She's loving the party and she asked me when you were coming."

"I'm so glad she likes it." I stall, terrified now, but Nicole pulls me along again, and I have no choice but to follow her.

She takes the bottle of champagne from me and hands me a glass of chilled white wine "Sorry, do you prefer champagne? Or a cocktail? The bar staff can make you anything you like."

"No, this is great, thank you." I keep my head down, hoping Mrs. Ashworth won't see me and my hand trembles as I bring the glass to my lips. Without looking, I know she's spotted me, even though I'm half hiding behind another guest. It's the same feeling I had before I knew she'd followed us to the café; like her poisonous eyes are burning holes into me. "You know what? I'm really sorry but I can't stay. Will you please tell your mom I'm sorry and that I'll call her tomorrow?"

Nicole frowns and shakes her head. "No, absolutely not. She wants you here, and you should at least go and say hi."

"I'm sorry," I say again. "I have to go." Unable to explain my weird behavior to Nicole, I simply hand her back the glass and turn to leave. I don't want her to think I'm rude but it's better than Mrs. Ashworth causing a scene in front of Reina and all her friends and family. Not tonight, not ever. Just as I'm about to leave, someone approaches me from behind and grabs my wrist.

"B."

Turning abruptly, I pull my hand back. "Please don't do this," I beg when I'm face to face with Mrs. Ashworth. "Please just let me leave quietly. And please don't touch me," I add, when she reaches for my hand again.

Nicole is looking from Mrs. Ashworth to me and back, highly confused as to what's been going on. "You two know each other?" she asks when she sees me wrangle myself out of Mrs. Ashworth's grip.

"We do." Mrs. Ashworth seems to have forgotten all about her husband, who is staring in our direction now. "Did you follow me here? You could have just told me you wanted to be my date."

"I didn't follow you. If I'd have known you were going to be here I wouldn't have come." I immediately regret saying that as her face turns to thunder in a heartbeat, her expression both hurt and furious. Bloodshot eyes pierce through me, telling me she's more than a little tipsy and therefore highly unpredictable. "Don't cause a scene," I beg. "You'll ruin Reina's birthday. I just want to leave." A thousand doom scenarios run through my head, each one worse than the other, as I slowly take a step back, retreating from my predator. Her husband is still staring at us, and I hope to God he won't come over.

"Can someone please tell me what the fuck is going on?" Nicole asks irritably. She puts the glasses down and crosses her arms in front of her chest.

"Is she really a friend of your mom's?" Mrs. Ashworth glances in the direction of Reina.

"Yes. Why?"

"A good friend?"

"Yes, they're very close," Nicole says, careful not to give her too much information.

"Right." Mrs. Ashworth points a finger at me. "Does your mom know she's an escort?"

REINA - 30TH JULY

*T*urning forty isn't so terrible after all. I have a glass of champagne in my hand, the poolside looks spectacular, I feel good about how I look, and I'm actually really enjoying catching up with friends and acquaintances. Last year, I couldn't have imagined feeling so happy turning forty, but I do now. The flamenco music is upbeat, my guests are having a good time, I have my beloved children here and Belle will arrive soon. I can't think of a single reason why I would still hide my feelings for her from the outside world, because with the support of my kids, I can handle anything.

I feel like a new person and that the future is full of possibilities, that I'll grab whatever it holds. Before I met Belle, I was a depressed, divorced mother without any direction in life. Now, I'm Reina Amari, a confident and happy woman whose glass is half-full instead of half-empty. I'm on good terms with my ex-husband and we have two wonderful kids who genuinely care about us. Three days a week, I volunteer at Camp Rubin. I'm a hobby photographer and I'm not bad if I say so myself. I feel incredibly close to my housekeeper who is the most kind and loyal woman in the world, and to Sasha, my friend who confides only in me and vice versa. I like yoga, long walks on the beach, a glass of wine during sunset and my mother thankfully lives on another continent because she may or may not accept what I've recently learned: I'm gay and in love with Belle.

"You look like you're having a good night," Sandeep says when we get a moment alone. He was quiet when he first arrived, but the champagne has loosened him up. I suppose the fact that I've been so chilled has helped too; we've caught up with Eddie and Maddie and even had some laughs together. "I'm sorry Bree couldn't come." He chuckles. "I mean, not that you would care if she's here or not, but I really appreciate the fact that she's welcome. Thank you."

"That's okay. I hope that maybe some time in the future, we can occasionally get together with all of us, including Bree," I'm surprised to hear myself say. "I don't want there to be any awkwardness between us."

Sandeep's eyes almost pop out of his sockets at hearing this. "Are you serious, Reina?"

"Yeah. Don't you think it would be nice? You, me, Belle, Suki, Bree, Nicole, Eddie, your future baby… I don't mean we should be one, big happy family. But perhaps just for our kids' birthdays and maybe Thanksgiving."

"Of course, that would be fantastic," he says, swallowing hard. He's always been sentimental, and I know this past year has taken a toll on him too. To leave your wife, to abandon the woman you promised to be loyal to for the rest of your life, must have had a pretty hefty impact in the guilt department. Now that there's redemption at the end of a long, dark tunnel, he looks five years younger.

As I lift my glass to take a drink, something in my line of vision alerts me. Someone who makes my pulse race. I think I sensed her presence before I saw her. She's wearing black slacks and a white shirt; simple but elegant and sexy in an understated way and her hair is styled playfully, one dark lock falling over her eyebrow. Suddenly, two days without her seems like a lifetime and I can't wait to hold her. I'm as ready as I'll ever be.

"Wow. She's here," Sandeep says, following my gaze.

"Of course. She's my girlfriend." I don't even bother to keep my voice down and excuse myself before I cross the terrace to greet her. She's talking to Nicole and Cindy Ashworth and I frown, sensing the tension between them.

"I will tell everyone," I hear Cindy hiss when I approach them, and she looks like an entirely different person to the sweet woman I talked to only twenty minutes ago. Belle looks shocked, rather than happy to see me and Nicole equally so. This worries me as Nicole rarely looks at me like that; the last time was when she found me on the kitchen counter with Belle between my legs.

"Hey," I say to Belle. I contemplate hugging her, but she doesn't seem in the mood. "I'm so glad you're here." Hesitantly, I turn my attention to Nicole and then to Cindy. "Is everything okay, you guys look upset?"

"I think it's time we head home." Cindy's husband steps in and puts an arm around her. I see him recoil when he looks at Belle, as if he recognizes her from somewhere. "Come on, honey, you've had too much to drink."

"Let go of me, I'm not drunk." She shakes him off but gives in when he tries again, more persistent this time.

"Cindy, come on. You're acting crazy again and causing a scene."

"Fine. But only because it's Reina's birthday." Cindy casts another furious glance at Belle over her shoulder before he escorts her away. "Mark my words, I will tell everyone," she murmurs.

"Tell everyone what?" A tight knot forms in my stomach at seeing Belle in distress, shaky and pale.

"I'm so sorry," she says. "I didn't know she'd be here; I'll go now."

"No, wait. Please don't go. Whatever it is, we can deal with it. I can deal with it, I promise."

"I'm not sure you can.'

"Did you know, Mom?" Nicole asks, gesturing to Belle. "Did you know she's an escort?"

My breath hitches as I turn to Nicole. There it is. My worst nightmare, the moment I've dreaded, and it's come a lot sooner than I anticipated. I know what Cindy was referring to now, and I have no doubt everyone in my circle will know within a matter of days. "Yes," I say, and Nicole seems surprised to hear this as her eyebrows shoot up.

"You knew." She pauses. "Did you..."

I nod slowly, letting all the contradicting emotions settle one by one. I feel frightened but also a little relieved that my secret is out. I feel furious with Cindy and terrible for Belle as she looks like she wants to dissolve into thin air. "But she's not an escort anymore and whatever she does or used to do is nobody's business but hers. It's certainly not Cindy's story to tell."

"Fuck. I'm so sorry, I've ruined your birthday," Belle says. "I think it's best if I stay out of your way for a while."

"No!" I yell, way louder than I meant to, taking her hand. "Don't you dare disappear on me again. Cindy can talk all she wants. I'm not ashamed of what I did, and neither should you be. If anyone should apologize it's me because it's my friend who's crossed the line and I know how badly you wanted to keep this private. So please don't go, Belle. I need you." I swallow hard, fighting back my tears. It's all so very clear to me now. Tomorrow, Cindy will do her rounds, people will talk, and I will have to explain this to Eddie and Nicole, but I'd rather be the topic of extensive gossip for a hundred years than not have Belle in my life. "I love you." As I say it, I realize everyone in close proximity is staring at us, including Nicole. It's true. I do love her, and reaching out, I take her hand. "I love you so much and I can handle this. I can handle anything as long as you're by my side."

Belle's eyes focus on mine, her gaze so intense that I'd give anything to know what she's thinking. But then her expression softens, and her shoulders drop. She pulls me into an embrace, and I sigh deeply at the contact as I bury my face in her neck. "I love you too," she whispers, stroking my hair. "I love you, Reina."

*R*eina inches away and cups my face. We smile at each other, the stress fading away. After we've uttered the words, nothing matters all that much because as long as she's okay, I'll be fine too. I run a hand over her soft cheek in return and smile as I watch her shiver. "You know we're being watched, right?"

"I know. And I really, really want you to kiss me."

"Are you sure?" I ask, moving my hand to the back of her neck to pull her in.

Reina doesn't answer but meets me half-way, and when our lips touch in a gossamer, feathery kiss, the atmosphere around us changes. The musician is still playing but the party has fallen silent. *An escort and her client, a queen and her servant.* I don't care what anyone thinks and neither does she because nothing has ever felt more real. Love is a beautiful new sensation. It's precious and fragile, yet united, it's unbreakable and from now on, we're one, facing the world together.

When we break apart, conversation picks up again, and we chuckle uncomfortably, knowing we have a lot to explain.

Hushed whispers ring through the air but in the end, all people really need to know is that we love each other. All the rest is just white noise. Reina is stronger than I thought. With her background, what she's just done would seem unthinkable three months ago. Someone is clapping and I see that it's Sasha.

"Finally!" she yells, whistling through her teeth. "Now go get a room!"

Reina chuckles, rolling her eyes at Sasha. She's completely calm when she turns to Nicole and puts a hand on her shoulder. "Honey, I'm so sorry you had to find out like this. Can we please talk about it tomorrow? I just want to enjoy tonight."

"We don't need to talk about anything," Nicole says, and seeing tears roll down her cheeks, I'm worried she might run off again. But she wipes her eyes, composes herself and then does something that leaves us both baffled. She falls around Reina's neck and hugs her tight for long moments. "I love you, Mom."

"I love you too, honey. So, so much." Reina sighs in relief and mouths, "Thank you."

Then Nicole turns to me and does the same, wrapping her arms tightly around my neck. "Fuck everyone, it's not important. Nothing is important, as long as Mom is happy. I like you, Belle."

Her approval chokes me up, and I know this isn't a show. This isn't Nicole making a statement in front of everyone, showing them that we have her blessing. This is heartfelt and real, and I squeeze her back, desperately wanting her to know how much I love her mother. "I promise I'll take care of her," I say. "Forever."

Conversation continues in a whisper and heads swiftly turn away from me when I look up. It must be a strange scenario to witness, and I imagine highly confusing for the other guests who have no idea why Cindy Ashworth left under a cloud and why Reina is suddenly kissing a woman. They'll find out soon enough, perhaps even tonight.

A surreal moment follows, in which none of us know how to behave or what to say, but a young man walks up to me and holds out his hand, saving us. "Hi, I'm Eddie, and from what I just witnessed, I can only assume you're Belle?"

I smile and take in the handsome boy who, just like Nicole, is the spitting image of his mother. "Yeah, that's me. It's so lovely to meet you."

"Likewise." He beckons over a girl who joins him. "This is my girlfriend, Maddie. She's been dying to meet you. So have I, to be honest."

Maddie looks me up and down like I'm some rare species, then grins as she shakes my hand. "I can see why my mother-in-law is so smitten with you. It's so sweet to see her in love." She leans in closer and says, "Never mind the stares. Trust me, I know these people and they might be shocked for a while, but they also seriously envy your connection with Reina. It's rare, isn't it, honey?" She shoots Eddie a loving look and he puts an arm around her.

"You're right; I think everyone will get used to it soon enough," I say, taking Reina's hand. "Nicole told me you flew in from India this morning. You must be exhausted."

"We're fine, actually," Maddie says cheerfully. "Nicole arranged the journey back for us because the last-minute flights were above our budget. Courtesy of their grand-mother, apparently. Anyway, we had a twelve-hour stop-over in London, where we slept, and then we fell into a food coma on the plane after all the pizza and pasta we ate to make up for lost carbs, so we've actually had more rest than we've had in weeks. Don't get me wrong, I love, love, love Indian food, but I've really missed melted cheese."

I laugh and point to a caterer serving fancy looking

cheesy garlic bread. "Well, it looks like there's more than enough to go around tonight, so you can continue to eat your heart out."

"You're all welcome. I put my favorite foods on the menu," Nicole admits with a smirk. "The yoga crew is panicking because there's no celery in sight."

"Why am I not surprised..." Reina helps herself to a snack, holds it out for me to take a bite, then eats the rest, shooting me a sweet look. She's leaning into me, and it dawns on me then that we're totally fine and comfortable together around her kids.

"So that's what's been going on." Nola comes over and grins at us. "I should have known you two had been sneaking around but it just didn't click. Looking back now, though, I don't see how I couldn't have missed it."

"Sorry I couldn't tell you," Reina says.

"Honey, that's your and only your business." She glances at our entwined hands, and shakes her head incredulously, still getting used to the idea. "Huh... you actually look very good together. Happy."

"You seem surprised," I say, shooting her a wink.

"Hell yes, I'm surprised." Nola lets out a roaring laugh. "Pleasantly surprised but my God... you two..."

We laugh along with her and once more, I tell myself that everything will be fine. My secret is out, and Reina's secret is out, but maybe that's not the end of the world. I've had enough of looking over my shoulder and I suspect Reina feels the same. The love in her eyes is pure and intense as I take her hand. "May I have the next dance?"

*E*veryone has left, Nicole, Eddie and Maddie have gone to bed and Belle and I are left in silence on the terrace. The caterers have cleared up and if it weren't for the furniture and the props scattered around, it would almost feel as if tonight had never happened. In the background we can hear the hypnotic swell of the ocean and we're lying on one of the loungers together, listening to the sound of the waves, both coming down from an intense night that neither of us will ever forget. As we mingled with my guests, we found ourselves overwhelmed with positive vibes and smiles, and even though some had no idea what to say, they still wanted to show their support. Sandeep, Sasha and Igor kept us entertained for most of the evening, and when I introduced Belle to my friends and acquaintances, she was charming, funny and sweet and I was so proud to have her by my side. It's strange to be out and it hasn't quite sunk in yet. I turned forty, I was reunited with my son, I told Belle I loved her, and I came out to the world. It's a lot in one day.

"I don't regret anything," I say, wanting Belle to know that whatever I said or did tonight was not on a whim. "I love you and I want everyone to know." We've turned off all the lights, apart from ones on the enormous '40' inflatable, that is gently bobbing in the pool.

"I love you too, baby." Belle wraps her arms tighter around me. "Are you not worried about the gossip?" She hesitates. "Concerning me, I mean."

"No. I'm more worried for you. Will you be okay?"

"Yeah, I'll be fine. It was bound to come out at some point anyway, it might as well be now. By the time Suki is old enough to understand she'll be oblivious to what I used to do for a living, it will be long forgotten."

I nod and lift my head to kiss her. I love that I can kiss her all the time now, that we don't have to sneak around and be careful. She returns the kiss, parting her lips to welcome my tongue and I moan as she weaves her fingers through my hair. Soon, we find ourselves entangled, making out hungrily. My breaths are quick when I pull away and smile at her. "Do you want to go for a swim?"

"From that mischievous look on your face, I take it you don't mean you want to swim lengths with me. Won't they wake up?"

I shake my head and lick my lips. "Eddie and Maddie will be jet lagged, and Nicole always sleeps like a log, so I think we're safe if we're quiet."

"I can be quiet," Belle promises.

"Can you?" I get up, kick off my heels and strip off my red dress. Belle's eyes darken when she sees me in my red lingerie set, and I want her so much that I can hardly wait. "I think I'll keep this on," I say in a teasing tone, glancing up at Nicole's bedroom window. "Just in case."

Belle gets up too and strips off to her underwear. Her body looks amazing in the dim twinkling lights surrounding the '40' inflatable and I push myself against her and kiss her again, sighing at the sensation of her warm skin. "You feel so good," she murmurs, running her hands over my behind. When she squeezes me and kisses me so deeply that my legs almost give way, I wiggle myself out of her grip and cast her a flirty look over my shoulder as I head to the pool. Slowly lowering myself quietly, the water feels amazing, and as I turn on my back, the big glowing '40' looms over me against the dark sky. The number doesn't scare me. Growing older doesn't scare me because I know I will grow old with Belle and I'm excited for the future.

She joins me in the pool, and I wrap my legs around her waist and my arms around her neck, basking in the blissful weightlessness of the cool water. The moon is full and bright, radiating in the dark as our lips meet in a passionate kiss.

"Have you ever made love in a pool?" Belle asks through ragged breaths.

Her husky voice causes a flash of arousal between my thighs and I push my hips into her, the ache for release almost agonizing. "No. Have you?"

Belle shakes her head and smiles, then paddles over to the shallow end of the pool where she wedges me between herself and the wall. "There's a first time for everything." Her mouth moves to my neck and she kisses me softly, then harder, sucking at my flesh while her hands slip into my bra to caress my nipples. I stifle my moans by pressing my mouth against her head.

"I've missed you," Belle whispers, sliding a hand inside my panties. She rubs me gently and I push myself into her, gasping at her touch. Staring deep into my eyes, she smiles as she puts more pressure on my center, and I reach between us, mimicking her actions that are slow and deliberate. Our energy has changed tonight. The same all-consuming lust is still there but there's so much more. There's love, and it's apparent in the way we look at each other, hold each other, more tenderly now. The deep connection I'm feeling is unlike anything I ever thought I'd feel and as my climax builds, the bedazzled '40' inflatable shines proudly behind her, reminding me it's the end of an era, and the beginning of a new one.

"Come with me," I say when I feel her tensing in my arms, and she kisses me to stifle our moans. Being quiet is strange but beautifully intimate, a secret moment shared, yet so still, yet so intense, the energy flowing between us as I pour all my pleasure into her and she pours all her pleasure into me.

"I love you, Reina, happy birthday, my love." She holds me, resting her forehead against mine.

"*H*ey, beautiful," I say when Reina wakes up. I've only just woken up too and can see that she was sleeping with a smile on her face. It warms my heart to know that she's happy, that the drama from last night hasn't affected her. It's light in the room; we forgot to close the curtains before we fell asleep, and her skin is glowing from the sun that pours in through the sliding balcony doors.

"Good morning." She nestles herself in the crook of my arm with a sleepy groan. "Mmm…" Her smile widens, and she kisses me. "Last night was amazing."

"It was." I stroke her hair and marvel at her beautiful face. "Still no regrets?"

"No. No regrets." Reina leans into my touch, suppressing a yawn. She's so cute when she wakes up, so adoringly vulnerable. "What time is it? I can hear Eddie and Maddie downstairs."

"Only eight. But I need to get up soon; Randy is coming with the truck."

"Oh no… not now we both happen to be naked." Reina pulls a dramatic face and traces a fingertip over my breasts, teasingly circling my nipples until I moan. "How long do you have?" The look in her eyes tells me she's aroused and so am I, even after all our lovemaking last night. The pool, the shower, the bedroom... I feel a twitch when I remember fucking her from behind over her dressing table, watching us in the mirror.

"Ten minutes."

"That works for me," she says in a flirtatious tone, and rolls over to search for something in her nightstand drawer.

I shoot her a surprised look when she pulls out a vibrator. "I didn't know you had toys."

"It's ancient but it works fine." Reina chuckles as she turns it on. "Luckily the walls are thick; it's a bit noisy." Lowering the device under the covers, she chuckles when I gasp, jerking my hips as the vibrator skims my clit. "See? Told you it works fine. It was very expensive back in the day." Her mouth melds into mine then, and I lace my fingers through her long locks and surrender to her. She massages me with it until I have no idea what to do with myself; my only thought that I need her to release me from the throbbing ache between my legs. Putting more pressure on my sensitive flesh, she deepens the kiss and moans when she hears the cry of my pleasure, stifled against her lips. She turns off the vibrator and replaces it with her fingers, entering me as I'm about to climax. It feels incredible and the tightness in my lower abdomen builds, her fingers inside me and her weight on top of me sending me higher.

"I love you," I whisper when she starts moving into me in a slow rhythm. Her eyes are dark and seductive, her intense gaze spectacularly sensual when she lifts her head and licks her lips to see me drown in ecstasy.

"I love you too," she whispers back, and I shatter underneath her.

~

"Do you want to stay for breakfast?" Reina tightens the tie on her robe before she picks up Randy's empty coffee mug.

"I'd love to, but I have to get back to Suki after we unload this stuff," I say, glancing at her cleavage. "It's too heavy for Randy to do on his own and besides, I think you need some time alone with your family. I imagine you have a lot to talk about." I close the door to the truck and give Randy a thumbs-up. "Thanks, buddy. I'll take my own car and meet you at the storage unit."

"Sure." Randy waves at Reina and gets in the truck. "Have a great day, Miss Amari!"

"Thank you, you too." Reina waits for Randy to disappear before she leans in and kisses me. "Sorry, of course you have to get back. I'm not thinking clearly today," she mumbles against my lips. "Are you still up for a late lunch at the beach? I know the lunch plans were just a decoy so I wouldn't find out about the party, but I'd still like to get together."

"Yeah. I'd love to spend time with you and your family. I'll bring Suki." I kiss her again just because her delicious mouth is too tempting to resist. I'm on top of the world today. Reina loves me and I love her. This is real and knowing that makes me feel safe and warm.

"Oh God, not again…"

We quickly break apart to find Nicole standing in the front door. She grimaces, then bursts out in laughter at seeing our flustered faces. "Never mind me," she jokes. "I was going to get something from my car, but I think I'll wait."

"If it's so traumatizing you shouldn't keep sneaking up on us," Reina says goofily, letting go of me and moving into the shade of a tree to hide her blush.

"Right. I think it's time to go." I feel a little embarrassed too, but I laugh it off as I get into my car. "I'll see you guys later."

REINA - SUNDAY

"So… that's everything." Three enthralled faces stare at me as if disappointed I am about to conclude my story. The only thing I left out was Sasha giving me the Hamptons' Escorts business card but other than that, I've told them the truth about my sexual exploration, my feelings, my struggles, and how Belle and I fell in love. We came here a little earlier so I would have time to fill them in before Belle and Suki arrived as I didn't want to talk about Belle's escort job while she was here.

"Wow." Eddie looks at me pensively. "I had no idea you'd been so sad and lonely. If I'd known, I wouldn't have left."

"That's sweet, but I had to go through this on my own," I say, smiling at him. "It wasn't loneliness that drew me to her, though. If I hadn't met her, I'm pretty sure I'd still be single because I wouldn't have known I liked women."

He nods. "She seems nice."

"She does," Maddie agrees. "And she's kind of…" She hesitates. "Well, I'm not into women but there's something very sexy about her. Do you think she's the one?"

"Yes," I say without hesitation. "I've never felt such an

attraction or connection before and I wanted to be entirely honest with you because the truth about her past may come out and there's a chance you might hear something from your friends, if they hear their parents talking about me. I want you to understand."

"I do understand," Nicole says, rubbing my arm. "Seeing you two together made total sense last night."

"I kind of understand too." Eddie chuckles. "It just takes time to get used to the idea, that's all."

"Well, I for one think it's cool that I have a lesbian mother-in-law." Maddie slides her plate aside and leans in, crossing her arms over the table. "It makes you more interesting somehow."

I laugh at that and shake my head. "Was I really that boring?"

"Not boring, perhaps just a little uptight," Nicole teases. She helps herself to more sparkling water from the bottle, then bites her lip as she looks at me with a grin. "Hey, Mom, can Tyrell come over this week, while Eddie and Maddie are here?"

"Of course, honey." I clap my hands in excitement and kiss her on the cheek. "I can't wait to meet him."

"Does my little sister have a boyfriend?" Eddie asks.

"He's not my boyfriend." Nicole rolls her eyes at him. "We're just hanging out."

"They're just hanging out," I repeat with a chuckle.

"Right. Just like Mom and Belle were 'just hanging out', he says, making quote marks in the air.

Lowering my voice, I say: "He's a rapper. Quite accomplished from what I've heard."

Nicole nudges me. "Where did you hear his music?"

"YouTube," I say, innocently batting my lashes. "I found him on your Instagram feed, then looked him up. It wasn't hard, you should really consider changing your privacy settings."

"I did it this morning in case Eddie started snooping, so please keep it to yourself until he meets him."

"Woooow… Nicole is dating a rapper!" Eddie regards her curiously. "Is he famous?"

Nicole blushes but I know she's secretly enjoying the fact that her new love interest has given her an air of mystery. Having done a little research myself, I've learned that he is, in fact, quite well-known, and that he has a huge fan base. "I'm not going to tell you anything," Nicole says cheekily, then waves at Belle who is walking up to our table with Suki.

"Hey, guys." She smiles at everyone and gives me a kiss. "This is Suki, my daughter."

Suki comes up to me and hugs me. She's delighted to see Nicole too and climbs onto her lap, then shyly shakes Eddie and Maddie's hand over the table.

"She'll be talking your head off in no time," Belle says, shooting Suki a wink. "How are you all feeling today? Hungover?"

"A little rough," Eddie admits. "Too many cocktails perhaps but nothing a good lunch can't fix. How about you?"

"I'm great." Belle drapes her arm over the backrest of my chair and I lean into her. She looks great too, I think to myself, the white shirt a beautiful contrast with her tanned skin. Her eyes are sparkling and she certainly doesn't look like she's been up all night, but I noticed I had a glow about me too this morning. It must be all the endorphins raging through our system. "Hungry though," she continues. "I heard the food here is fantastic." She doesn't seem uncomfortable here with us and I'm glad she feels she can be herself around my kids.

"Yes, it's very good and they have triple cooked fries." Maddie pours a glass of water for Belle and hands her a menu. "Reina was just telling us about how the two of you met."

"Did you tell them everything?" Belle asks me, a hint of worry flashing through her gaze. She knew Eddie and Maddie would find out one way or another—either from Nicole or from one of their friends—but perhaps she hadn't expected me to open up so soon.

"Yes. Everything. At least now we can start with a clean slate." I give her thigh a reassuring squeeze and smile.

"And you guys don't have a problem with it?" Belle asks, fixing her attention on Maddie and Eddie. She checks if Suki is still distracted with Nicole and lowers her voice. "With what I used to do for a living?"

"No. I find it rather an intriguing story and besides, that's your business." Maddie nudges Eddie to speak up too.

"I don't have a problem with it either," he says. "As long as Mom is happy."

"Thank you. That means a lot to me." Belle pulls me closer and my eyes well up at all the love surrounding me. Resting my head on her shoulder, I hope they know how much I love them in return. *As long as Mom is happy.*

BELLE - ONE WEEK LATER

*E*ddie and Maddie are lovely and just like Nicole, they've already stolen Suki's heart. Now that we've met up a couple of times, we're comfortable around each other and Eddie is having fun teasing Nicole as we wait for her strictly non-boyfriend-just hanging-out-friend to arrive. Maddie is in the pool with Suki, while Eddie, Nicole, Reina and I are sitting around the coffee table in the lounge area on the terrace. Reina is snuggled up against me with her feet propped up on the rattan couch, Eddie is perched on the coffee table and Nicole has made herself comfortable sideways in one of the big rattan chairs, her legs dangling over the armrest. We're drinking sangria in the shade of the linen canopy that covers the seating area, and a delicious smell is coming from the kitchen where a traditional Lebanese rice dish is crisping up in the oven. Reina doesn't cook very often but when she does, she cooks up a feast, and I've been impressed by the selection of salads and dips I helped her prepare earlier.

"I've never seen you this nervous before, sis. Are you dating Snoop Dogg or something?"

"No, gross, he's old. Stop making such a big deal out of it," she says, slapping Eddie on his arm after another comment about her nervous state. "He's just coming here to chill around the pool with me, that's all."

"And for romantic walks on the beach," Eddie shoots back, only adding to Nicole's anxiety. "And to meet his awesome brother-in-law, and for lots of se—"

"Stop making fun of your sister, Eddie," Reina cuts him off, shooting her son a warning look.

Nicole is about to give him a mouthful but her phone pings, and she turns a deeper shade of crimson as she gets up and heads for the kitchen to buzz open the gates. "If you say anything to embarrass me, I will kill you," she hisses at Eddie over her shoulder.

Last week, I was the outsider, anxious to meet Reina's nearest and dearest but now that someone new is arriving, we shoot each other knowing looks and I feel like I'm part of the family. We give Tyrell a welcoming smile when he follows Nicole out onto the terrace and despite his unconventional looks, he's sweet and polite as he greets Reina.

"It's nice to meet you, Miss Amari." He hands Reina a bottle of Barolo and I can see his hand trembling ever so slightly. "Nicole told me you like this one. I hope I got it right." I vaguely recognize him, mainly due to the neon-colored elastic bands that hold his afro hair in a dozen or so knots, and the snake tattoo that coils around his neck.

"Fuck me, you're *Bear Cub*," Eddie says incredulously, then turns crimson himself. His cheeky demeanor is gone, replaced by a sense of admiration and if I'm not mistaken, he even looks a bit intimidated.

"Yup. That's me." Tyrell shakes Eddie's hand. "Nice to meet you, bro."

"That's Maddie there in the pool," Nicole says, and Maddie waves at him and yells that she'll be out in a minute.

363

"And that's Suki, Belle's daughter. And this is Belle, Mom's..." She hesitates. "Girlfriend? Can I say that?"

I laugh as I get up to greet him. "You can say that."

"Cool." Tyrell looks at me, then at Reina. "You didn't tell me your mom had a girlfriend."

"Yeah well..." Nicole shrugs and smiles at me. "It's a fairly recent development." She looks adorable in her shy state, but she grabs the jug of sangria and pours him a glass. "Here. Do you want me to show you around?"

"Yeah, this is an amazing place you've got here," he says to Reina. "I've never been to the Hamptons, it's so quiet and beautiful and it smells so good."

"That's partly mom's cooking." Nicole pushes the glass into his hand and grabs her own. "Come on, I'll show you the beach."

We watch them disappear through the gates but not before we've caught a glimpse of Tyrell putting an arm around her waist.

"I can't believe it," Eddie says, staring after them. "My little sister is dating a famous rapper."

"Is he really that famous?" Reina asks.

"Hello, ehm yes." Eddie looks at her incredulously. "Don't you recognize him?"

"Only from the YouTube videos I watched. I did figure he was popular, but I didn't know he was such a big deal. Anyway, he seems sweet and this bottle he brought is very good," she says, studying the label. "How thoughtful."

"Maybe I should grab a bottle of champagne from the fridge." Eddie gets up and it's clear that he now is the one out of sorts, worrying about what Tyrell will think of us.

"Yes, why don't you bring two? It's your and Maddie's last day here and as you've made it more than clear, we have a special guest." Reina shoots him an amused grin. "And check on the rice while you're in there, will you?"

"*H*ow is your father?" I ask, kissing Belle on her cheek before I greet Suki.

"He's a little nervous but otherwise in good spirits," she says, handing me Suki's overnight bag. "Thank you so much for looking after her."

"No problem. We'll have a good time, won't we, Suki?"

Suki grins and wraps her arms around my legs, and when I pick her up, she hugs me. We've grown close, and she likes staying with me on the rare occasions Jackie isn't available to look after her. "We'll meet you at the hospital tomorrow morning to check in on Grandpa."

"Is Grandpa sick?" Suki asks.

"Not really, honey," Belle says. "But his hip is old, so he needs a new one." She pats her hip to demonstrate what part of the body she's referring to. "But after the operation, once he's recovered, he'll be able to walk again just fine."

Suki nods, seemingly content with that answer, then points to her bag. "Can I take my toys to my room?"

"Of course. But let me go with you, the stairs are a little dangerous." I put her down and carry the bag for her, walking behind her up the stairs. By the time we built this house, our kids were old enough for us not to worry as much about someone falling down the staircase, but I realized a while ago that it's anything but child friendly. I love that Suki is referring to Nicole's room as 'her room' now, as she's only slept there a couple of times. We tried to sell one of the other three bedrooms to her, but she insisted, and even asked if she and Nicole could have a sleepover together. I slip down the stairs while she's busy organizing her toys and yell for her to call us when she wants to come back down.

"Don't worry; I won't let her go up and down by herself and she's generally careful."

"I know. You're so good with her." Belle suddenly looks emotional, and I reach for her hand, wrapping my other arm around her waist. "Hey, what's wrong? Are you worried about the operation?"

"No." Belle shakes her head. "I mean yes, of course I'm a little worried, but just seeing you with her, it's…" She swallows hard and cups my face. "It's so wonderful and I still find it hard to believe that everything is so easy with you and so damn perfect."

"Yeah, it really is perfect, isn't it? I haven't felt so happy in…" I shrug. "Well, never, actually, not counting the birth of my children." The love in Belle's eyes as I say this warms me and I contemplate telling her what's been on my mind for the past week. We've been over at her father's farm a couple of times to check what needs to be done while he's away and I've fallen in love with the place. "Do you have time for a coffee? There's something I want to talk to you about."

"Sure, I don't have to leave yet." Belle makes two cappuccinos and we sit down at the kitchen island. "You sounded serious."

"Don't worry," I say, putting her at ease. "I've been

thinking about your father's farm. You had it valued last week, right?"

"Yes, but that doesn't necessarily mean anything. He doesn't want to sell it yet."

"And you don't want to live there?"

Belle frowns. "I love the farm and Dad wants me to have it but it's totally unrealistic. I don't have the money or the time to do it up and besides, he'll have to sell it eventually so he can buy a ground-floor apartment."

"But what if none of that was an issue?" I ask. "Would you want the farm?"

"Of course. It's a special place to me and I'll be sad to see it go. But I made peace with that a long time ago; some things aren't forever." Belle smiles but it doesn't reach her eyes.

"What if I fixed it up?" I say, deciding to just get it out. "What if I arranged for it to be renovated and extended so that your father could live there too? Or we could build a small place on the land for him to live. There's plenty of space."

Belle stares at me for long moments but as expected, she shakes her head. "I could never let you do that. I don't want your money, you know that."

"But what if you just thought of it as rent? I'll live there for free, so I'll pay for the work."

"You'd want to live there? With us? And my father?" She hesitates. "Is that what you're saying?"

"Yes..." I swallow hard. "I'm sorry, I understand if it's way too soon, I just wanted to discuss it with you now before it goes on the market. Not that I'd want to buy it," I hastily add. That's not my intention, the house should be yours and Suki's one day."

Belle stares around the living room and the kitchen then

out to the pool and the yard. "I don't understand. Why would you want to move away from here?"

"This was never really my house," I say softly. "I like it here, at least I do now, but Sandeep designed it and Bree did all of the ground floor interior. I love old buildings, places with character. Glass boxes aren't my thing, but I was charmed by your father's farm the first time I saw it. It's such a beautiful location and it has genuine character." Belle remains silent and taking her hand, I smile to let her know it's no big deal. "I'm sorry, I shouldn't have brought it up. Forget I ever said anything."

"No... I just didn't think you'd ever consider living on a farm, especially not with my father on the premises."

"Hey, I have Lebanese roots," I joke. "Where I come from, it's totally normal to take your parents in when they're old. Not that my mother would ever want to live with me. Anywhere would be too small for her and her cats, which trust me, is a blessing."

Belle laughs, and this time it's genuine. She gets up and embraces me from behind, nuzzling her face in my neck. "Are you serious about this?"

"I am." I turn around on my stool and pull her between my legs. "I love you and I want to be with you every day. And I've thought about asking you and Suki to move in here, but I don't think this is the right house to start a life together. It has too much baggage and as I said, it's just not me but I could rent it out during the summer season, or maybe even sell it back to Sandeep, if he's interested."

"You have no idea how happy you've made me by saying that," Belle whispers. "I want to be with you every day too. And if the farm is genuinely somewhere you could see your-self, then I could think of nothing better."

"Another game?" I ask when Jackie places her last tile down having just beaten me at Scrabble for the third time.

"Nah. I'm so much better than you it's getting boring," she jokes, pushing the board aside. We're sitting in a café close to the hospital, waiting for the surgeon to call us once they've finished operating on my father. "How about a glass of wine? I've had enough coffee for today." She beckons the waiter over, brags about her Scrabble skills when he asks who won and orders a bottle of red.

"We should have ordered wine hours ago," I say when I take the first sip. "Would have helped with the nerves."

"Then we would also be two sheets to the wind by the time he came to." Jackie chuckles. "Well, no news so far is good news, I suppose. Isn't that how it works with operations?"

I shrug because I have no idea and stretch my legs out, stiff from sitting in the same position for hours. "Thank you for taking him in while he recovers."

"It's my pleasure. I just worry about what's going to

happen long-term. What did the estate agent say about the value of the farm?"

"One point four million."

"What?" Jackie gasps. "Are you serious?"

"Yes. It's the land, mainly. It's worth a lot, especially because it's so close to the beach. I didn't know this but that wide strip of land between the farmland and the beach—the section where all the poppies grow— it's protected so the view is guaranteed to be unobstructed."

Jackie stares into the distance, and I'm waiting for her to tell me she thinks he should sell it after all, but she doesn't. I don't want to tell her about my conversation with Reina yet as we have to discuss this in depth first. Although the idea seems fantastic, I don't want her to make any hasty decisions and have regrets later. Moving in together is a big step, especially if Suki and my father are involved.

"Jackie, are you okay?" I notice Jackie is suddenly deep in thought, her eyes glazy as if transfixed.

"It all started there," she says with a sad look in her eyes. "In the poppy field. I haven't been there in decades."

"What started there?"

"Your mother and I." Her eyes meet mine and she gives me a nervous smile. "It's where we first kissed."

"Oh…" Wanting her to continue, I remain silent. I hadn't expected her to bring up my mother. Not here, not today.

"I'd been in love with her for a long time and I think she knew it. I never told her how I felt until that day, and I never made a move on her; she was married after all, but she must have known how I felt. Besides, she was straight, as far as I knew, and I didn't want to ruin our friendship. We'd grown so close and loved to spend time together." Jackie pauses. "We decided to take the long route down to the beach, through the fields, instead of following the path. The poppies were in full bloom, and she was wearing a red dress in the same color. I couldn't help myself; I told her she looked beautiful." Jackie takes a long drink from her wine and swallows hard. "And then she kissed me." A single tear rolls down her cheek. "She kissed *me*. And with that, she changed our lives forever. We lay down and made love in the field and then we became inseparable. She didn't want to divorce your father; she loved him, and I never asked her to. When she was dying, I begged her not to tell him, but she was adamant that it was for the best. Looking back, I suppose she was right. I had your father after all, and you, and Linda."

"You loved her," I say, swallowing down the lump in my throat.

"Yes, I loved her with all my heart, and I still miss her every single day."

"Is that why you never dated?" I ask.

"Yes. No one compared to her. She just had this special aura about her, this radiant glow that made people around her smile." Jackie takes a deep breath. "I have many pictures of us together. They've been hidden away in a box as I couldn't bear looking at them. But you can see them if you want."

"Thank you, I'd like that." I reach for Jackie's hand over the table. "You should have told me."

Jackie shakes her head. "No, I couldn't. What we did was wrong, and it hurt your father. I wasn't proud of it, but I've never regretted it either because it was the most precious time in my life. Perhaps I should have told you my story when you grew up and came out to me, but you were so secure in yourself and so at ease with your sexuality that I didn't think you needed help in that sense. Besides, you were like a daughter to me and I was so afraid you'd be angry and that I'd lose you." She sighs. "But now you know."

"You'll never lose me, Jackie." I squeeze her hand. "Can I ask about Rose?"

Jackie smiles in relief. "Rose and I are dating. It's still very new, but when I met her, I felt that genuine spark, like I did with your mother. The Hamptons hasn't exactly been inundated with eligible lesbians, especially not back in the day, so I never met anyone I felt attracted to until now. Rose is wonderful."

"Thank you for telling me. I like Rose very much and I'm happy for you. You deserve love." I pause. "And I'd really, really like to see those pictures."

"Okay, honey. Come over one night and I'll tell you all about her. With Rose in my life I think I can handle it now."

My phone rings, and we both snap to attention, my hand trembling as I take the call and hear the surgeon's voice.

"Miss Rodgers? Your father is just waking up following his surgery, but the operation went well, he's back in his room and we expect to have him up and walking in a day or two."

I thank him and give Jackie a thumbs-up and we get up to give each other a long hug. "He's fine."

"Thank God." Jackie holds me tight. "Come on, let's go and see him."

EPILOGUE

Reina - 1 year later

"Happy Fourth of July!" I raise my glass and smile at the full table. Belle is sitting next to me and Juliette, Suki, Cameron, Eddie, Maddie, Nicole, Tyrell, Jackie, Rose, Belle's father, Sasha and Igor and their two kids, and Sandeep and Bree are gathered around the feast that Belle and I put together. Sandeep and Bree's baby is sleeping in a stroller next to the table. She's an adorable girl with thick, dark hair and big eyes, called Harmony—Harmie for short—and she's stolen our hearts with her happy and curious nature.

"Happy Fourth!" My family and friends yell back, and we drink to a year of change.

This day feels like a milestone, the first day that we're all socializing as a family—both genetically and chosen—and I couldn't be happier to have everyone here. The grill is smoking with the extra corn I just put on, and salads, breads, dips and steaks are passed around while laughter and animated chatter blend in with the background music.

Sasha is stroking her huge baby bump. It wasn't planned, and it was a bit of a shock after raising two teenagers, but she's delighted to have another daughter soon and Igor's been fussing over her all night, making sure she doesn't eat anything rare and stays hydrated.

A lot has happened in a year. After recovering from his hip replacement, Belle's father moved back to the farm to take care of the animals during the renovation. We built the annex first, so he wouldn't have to live on a building site. It's a sweet bungalow in the far corner of the yard and although he's never been one for change, he's delighted with all the modern comforts and looking forward to us moving into the farmhouse at the end of the year so he'll have his grand-daughter close by. We want to restore the house and the barn to its former glory with some modern additions and it's starting to look really beautiful. I'm looking forward to tending to the animals and I've suggested organizing 'farming day trips' for the Camp Rubin kids.

This will be my last year celebrating the Fourth of July in Villa Reina and that feels fitting as it belongs to a different life. Sandeep had no desire to move back here, so I've decided to sell it and it will go on the market soon. From the sale, I could buy something extravagant, but I know I'll never be happier than in the sweet farmhouse that will soon have an extension with a new kitchen and a pool in the backyard. Belle belongs there and I belong with Belle. One day, it will be Suki's.

"Babe, this is so nice," Belle whispers, kissing me on the cheek. "I love having everyone together and next year, we'll be celebrating in—" Belle stops herself as she catches Suki slipping food under the table. "Suki, please don't feed Rascal until we've finished eating, will you? I'm trying to teach him not to beg and it's not helping," she says, but Suki has already thrown him her last piece of steak.

Suki finally got her dog and they're inseparable. We figured a Labrador was a safe choice as they're generally well behaved but despite weeks of intense training, Rascal has a mind of his own. He's not bribable with treats, he's totally unsensitive to praise and does exactly what he wants so after a while, we changed his name from Beanie to something more fitting. The white couch is permanently decorated with muddy footprints, the floors are constantly wet as he jumps in the pool and likes to shake himself dry inside the house, his ever-wagging tail has swept many glasses off the coffee table and he steals food from the counter whenever he sees an opportunity. He's also a sweetheart, though, and always by Suki's side.

"But I've finished eating," Suki retorts. "Look, my plate is empty."

"That's because you gave everything to Rascal."

"My plate is empty too," Cameron announces, and I suppress a chuckle when I see him lowering a fistful of food under the table. "Can Suki and I go swimming with Rascal now?"

Belle and Juliette exchange knowing looks but decide to let them off the hook, just for tonight. "Sure, go on. But no cannonballing," Belle warns, then turns to me. "I shouldn't have moved the table to the poolside."

"I know, I told you it was a bad idea." I roll my eyes and laugh, then shoot her a loving smile. "But it's really warm today, it might be refreshing."

A few seconds later, we're showered, as Suki and Cameron—who can both swim now—jump in at our end, followed by Rascal, who causes the biggest splash of all. There's screaming and howls of happy laughter.

"Nicole, come in!" Suki yells. She looks up to Nicole like a big sister and has been counting down the days for her arrival.

"Nicole is eating, honey." I brush the pool water from my shoulder and laugh even harder when Nicole gets up and spontaneously jumps in still wearing her denim onesie.

"Oh boy, so much for a civilized dinner," Belle jokes, shielding her face from another splash.

Tyrell follows Nicole's impromptu action, jumping in the water wearing his baggy jeans and T-shirt, and we all laugh and clap when they reappear above the surface, Nicole with her arms around his neck. I love the chaos, the smiles on the faces of my favorite people but most of all, I love having Belle by my side. Her business is doing well and I'm so proud of her. She inspires me to do better, to embrace every single day as if it were my last, and to enjoy the little things in life. I don't care about my standing in society, or what my mother thinks of me. I've told her about Belle last time I visited and as expected, she's in denial. A butterfly captured through my lens, waking up with Belle, the sun on my face and moments like this is what I live for now. It's simple and blatantly clear. Love is the only thing that matters. The only thing.

AFTERWORD

I hope you've loved reading *The Next Life* as much as we've loved writing it. If you've enjoyed this book, would you consider rating it and reviewing it on www.amazon.com? Reviews are very important to authors and we'd be really grateful!

ACKNOWLEDGMENTS

A big hug to everyone who has supported us throughout the process of writing The Next Life.

Camilla, thanks for being our friend, our sounding board, and for giving us a wonderful and inspirational space to write.

Claire Jarrett, thank you for being supportive, patient and always honest about our writing. This one went super smoothly, so onwards and upwards! We really value our working relationship as well as our friendship.

We also want to thank our proof/beta reading team. Laure Dherbécourt and DJ - you guys are amazing!

ABOUT THE AUTHOR

Lise Gold is an author of lesbian romance. Her romantic attitude, enthusiasm for travel and love for feel good stories form the heartland of her writing. Born in London to a Norwegian mother and English father, and growing up between the UK, Norway, Zambia and the Netherlands, she feels at home pretty much everywhere and has an unending curiosity for new destinations. She goes by 'write what you know' and is often found in exotic locations doing research or getting inspired for her next novel.

Working as a designer for fifteen years and singing semi-professionally, Lise has always been a creative at heart. Her novels are the result of a quest for a new passion after resigning from her design job in 2018. Since the launch of Lily's Fire in 2017, she has written several romantic novels and also writes erotica under the pen name Madeleine Taylor.

When not writing from her kitchen table, Lise can be found cooking, at the gym or singing her heart out somewhere, preferably country or blues. She lives in London with her dogs El Comandante and Bubba.

Made in United States
North Haven, CT
06 October 2021